THE SCORPION JAR

Jonah throttled forward, taking the *Stinger* downhill at a lumbering stride, deliberately holding back the 'Mech's speed so as not to outpace the soldiers of his company running along with him. Trees and underbrush splintered and crunched around him; then the ground opened up and he knew he had reached the antivehicle minefield. If he didn't cripple himself with an unlucky step, he was through.

He saw Ma-Tzu Kai troops to the right, left, ahead . . . a wash of red light dazzled in his 'Mech's ferroglass viewscreen . . . enemy laser? A flamer? He couldn't be sure with his instrumentation so messed up. But it didn't matter. Whatever it was had scored a crippling hit on the *Stinger*'s light armor. Only the safety webbing that kept him strapped into the 'Mech's command couch kept him from being tossed about the cockpit as the *Stinger* swayed, toppled and fell.

The impact when the 'Mech hit the ground was bone-jarring, and his body slammed against the safety webbing with bruising force. His head rang and his vision blurred, but he knew that he had to get out of the 'Mech and keep on going.

MECHWARRIOR®
DARK AGE

THE SCORPION JAR

A BATTLETECH® NOVEL

Jason M. Hardy

A ROC BOOK

ROC

Published by New American Library, a division of
Penguin Group (USA) Inc., 375 Hudson Street,
New York, New York 10014, USA
Penguin Group (Canada), 10 Alcorn Avenue, Toronto,
Ontario M4V 3B2, Canada (a division of Pearson Penguin Canada Inc.)
Penguin Books Ltd., 80 Strand, London WC2R 0RL, England
Penguin Ireland, 25 St. Stephen's Green, Dublin 2,
Ireland (a division of Penguin Books Ltd.)
Penguin Group (Australia), 250 Camberwell Road, Camberwell, Victoria 3124,
Australia (a division of Pearson Australia Group Pty. Ltd.)
Penguin Books India Pvt. Ltd., 11 Community Centre, Panchsheel Park,
New Delhi - 110 017, India
Penguin Group (NZ), Cnr Airborne and Rosedale Roads, Albany,
Auckland 1310, New Zealand (a division of Pearson New Zealand Ltd.)
Penguin Books (South Africa) (Pty.) Ltd., 24 Sturdee Avenue,
Rosebank, Johannesburg 2196, South Africa

Penguin Books Ltd., Registered Offices:
80 Strand, London WC2R 0RL, England

First published by Roc, an imprint of New American Library,
a division of Penguin Group (USA) Inc.

First Printing, December 2004
10 9 8 7 6 5 4 3 2 1

Acknowledgments

The process of writing this novel was not normal, which means the acknowledgments are a little strange, too. But still, there are some people who need to be thanked:

- Sharon Turner Mulvihill, for giving me a shot and being supportive and helpful throughout the whole odd process;
- Randall N. Bills, for being the exact right person for me to leech on over a number of years;
- Loren L. Coleman, for being encouraging as I gradually stuck my toes into the ocean of the BattleTech universe;
- Past editors—notably Donna Ippolito and Janna Silverstein—who were encouraging and positive even when projects didn't work out as planned;
- My wife, Kathy, for being . . . well, for being my wife, Kathy;
- My son, Finn, for similar reasons;
- Everyone who ever wrote a book I loved. You know who you are.
- And though they'll likely never see this, thanks to Ethan Cannon and Sam Cannon (distant cousins, not brothers) for first introducing me to RPGs. The adjustable-length ten-foot pole will never be forgotten.

$$=== 1 ===$$

Paladin Steiner-Davion's Residence, Santa Fe
Terra, Prefecture X
1 October 3134

The final glimmer of a purple-and-orange sunset had disappeared into the chill of a late-autumn night. Even here, away from downtown, the sky-glow from greater Santa Fe overwhelmed all but the brightest stars, while the background noise of city traffic, machinery and, above all, people, underlay everything like a heartbeat, or like breath.

At well past midnight, the sprawling headquarters of the Knights of the Sphere was, for the most part, dark and silent. Even in its residential wings, quiet ruled. The majority of Knights with quarters in the complex worked hard and valued their rest, and those who were of a mind to relax or work off tension usually wandered to other parts of the city to play.

The suite of rooms belonging to Paladin Victor Steiner-Davion appeared, from the outside, to be no different from the rest. Only in the office was there light—and that merely the glow from a single data screen. All the curtains were tightly drawn; no one outside would know that the Paladin was awake and at his desk.

You'd think that at my age I wouldn't need to hide in the dark and work in secret, Victor thought to himself. He gave a tired, quiet laugh. At my age, I shouldn't have to do this kind of work any longer, period.

We believed we'd taken care of all these problems, he thought. We told ourselves that we'd left them behind along with everything else from the bad old days—the family ties and alliances that we set aside, the BattleMechs that we gave up and turned in for scrap—because Devlin Stone's vision of a new order was going to make all of our fears and precautions obsolete. Maybe we should have known better. The darker aspects of human nature do not simply disappear because some of the tools are taken away. Power will always be contested. In so much you were wrong, Kattie, dear sister, but about this aspect of human nature you may just have been right.

Yet the dream had become real; for a few brief decades it had worked. Until the day Devlin Stone made the mistake of thinking that he could step away from his creation and let it run without him.

Was the dream flawed, then, from its very inception? Surely The Republic of the Sphere ought to be able to continue without the charismatic presence of its founder. What did it say—about Devlin Stone, about The Republic, and about those who had given their lives and their loyalty to both—that it might not?

I have to believe, Victor thought, that we did not choose wrongly, and did not fight in vain.

His data screen pinged, distracting him from his reverie to announce a file arriving. He checked the address from which the file had been sent, and smiled. The sender's true name—which appeared nowhere in the document—would have shocked respectable people and would have shocked The Republic's intelligence services even more had they known that Victor Steiner-Davion was in correspondence with its owner.

But Victor had lived for a long time. He had been a MechWarrior during the turbulent, bloody years before the founding of The Republic. In his youth, and even in his middle age, he'd associated with any number of people whose names and dossiers would have made law enforcement and intelligence services distinctly nervous. And quite a few of those people still owed him favors.

The information contained in this particular file had been bought with the price of several of those favors. But Victor considered the favors well spent. At his age, he wasn't likely to find another reason to need them, and the information was good to have. The work he was doing now was like building a mosaic. He had in his possession a great number of small pieces, each one individually nothing—but when put together in precisely the right fashion, they would make the picture plain.

Collecting all the tiles for the mosaic was the easy part, he reflected, at least if you happened to be him. You only needed sufficient money—or a sufficient number of favors owed—and sufficient patience, combined with decades of practice at standing back and taking the long view. Anyone could have done it, given those qualities.

The next part, though, would be much harder. He had to present his mosaic in such a way that even the dimmest Senators and Knights and—especially—Paladins could see and understand the picture he created. Not to single out any individuals, but if the truth were told, some of his comrades-in-arms had always been more notable for courage and fighting skill than for brains.

So he couldn't just lay out the evidence and let the facts speak for themselves. He had to lead his audience step by obvious step to the right conclusion. This would be his legacy to The Republic of the Sphere, one last act performed for the sake of the dream of Devlin Stone, and it had to be done just right. The forthcoming election could hinge on how well he did his job, on how many of the Paladins understood what he now knew.

It was more than simply arranging the facts and ideas; he had to find the exact right words and tone, and put everything in the right order. He'd never been much of a man for talk, and not much of a diplomat either, although the newsreaders now called him a statesman—a reward, he supposed, for having lived so long. He was a MechWarrior first and always, and the task of moving others to his way of thinking through convincing argument was a far different task than piloting a 'Mech.

It was late. Eventually the words and the sentences blurred together, and Victor dozed, sitting upright in his chair. Then he slept more deeply, as the chair—a marvel of modern design and medical engineering—adjusted its contours to his slumbering form.

Morning came, bringing with it daylight streaming past cracks in the closed curtains, and he woke with a start to a cheerful voice saying, "Good morning!"

Both the voice and the good cheer belonged to Elena Ruiz, the housekeeper (though he and she both knew quite well that she was more nurse than housekeeper) who looked after his suite of rooms. She was a pleasant sight for an old man's eyes, even in her plain white uniform—dark hair, olive skin, and a face always open and ready to smile. Her greeting was followed by a blaze of light as she drew the curtains mercilessly open, letting in the bright desert sun.

Victor responded with a good-natured grumble. "Woman, they pay you to keep me healthy, not to kill me."

"Hah," she said. "You'll outlive all of us. And if you slept in your bedroom like most people, you wouldn't have to worry about me opening the curtains in the morning."

"I was working," he said. The display on his data screen was on and glowing, bearing out his words. He frowned briefly. The display should have followed his lead and gone into sleep mode sometime last night. It must have been brought back to life by some vibration or bump to the desk.

Victor shut down the file. He would work on it again later, after the coming of night once more brought privacy. Then he turned to Elena Ruiz.

"Now—what's for breakfast?"

2

Sheratan, Prefecture IV
20 October 3134

Knight-Errant Robert Goldberg saw his first political advertisement on Sheratan within minutes of his arrival at the main planetary DropPort. The display on the wall outside the DropPort's vehicle rental office said FOUNDER'S MOVEMENT—KEEPING THE DREAM ALIVE! in glowing orange letters that practically jumped off the poster.

After that, elections and electioneering were everywhere he looked. The streets of the city were gaudy with neon-and-laser billboards, and tri-vid ads flashed and rotated atop newsstands and information kiosks. The displays said things like PEACE AND SECURITY in bright green, superimposed on images of a bucolic, tranquil countryside and bustling, unworried cities. The images were accompanied by voice-overs between the musical numbers that played over the audio system in the vehicle Robert had rented at the DropPort: "In these troubled times, mutual trust and fellowship are more important than ever. When you vote, reach out—"

The music eventually segued into the midday newscast. Still listening, Robert left the city, heading for the country estate where Paladin Otto Mandela was staying during his sojourn here. The estate belonged to one of the local bigwigs—a veteran of Stone's Revenants from the old days, now turned prosperous gentleman farmer—who had graciously made it available for Mandela's use.

Robert's journey took him out into the open countryside, where a lightly traveled winding road took him through acres of rolling green pastureland dotted with sheep and dairy cattle. He spared some attention for the newsreader of the hour, a woman with a pleasant voice. The title "Knight of the Sphere" sounded glamorous, but the reality was sometimes less impressive. Functioning as part of the Exarch's private courier service was only one of the not-so-exciting tasks involved.

The newsreader said, "And it's time for the top planetary news of the hour. With election day close at hand, voter unrest continues in urban areas. In Pittston, supporters of local Founder's Movement candidate Ella Geraldo broke up a rally for Prosperous Unity opponent Dan Harwicke with taunts and heckling. When Harwicke attempted to address the crowd, estimated at some three hundred, he was drowned out by shouts of "Appeaser!" and "Clan-Lover!" and "No More Sellouts!"

"Interviewed later on this station, Harwicke said only that he was disappointed that some of his fellow Sheratanites could not tell the difference between independent traders like Clan Sea Fox, with whom he freely admits to having done mutually profitable—and legal—business in the past, and violent and territorially ambitious groups such as the Jade Falcons and the Steel Wolves. Meanwhile, in—"

The news went on, a depressing tally of political meetings disrupted by one local faction and election headquarters vandalized by another and riots instigated in the streets of depressed neighborhoods by a third. The first planetwide elections since the dramatic collapse of the HPG network had signaled the end of what people were already referring to as The Republic of the Sphere's golden age, and the electorate on Sheratan was bitterly divided. People were not taking the ongoing crisis well.

Under the circumstances, Robert thought, it was not surprising that there had been a mostly bipartisan call for an official observer to be sent from the government of The Republic—preferably, an observer who also had the authority to settle any arguments that might arise. Paladin Otto Mandela was an ideal choice. He had worked on disputed elections before, and had made a name for himself previously in investigations of brutality and corruption on various worlds.

Nor was anybody likely to call either his honesty or his devotion to The Republic into question. Mandela, for all his fidelity to fairness and the rule of law, was still willing to demand that his accuser meet him in single combat, 'Mech to 'Mech, and repeat the accusation there.

Robert turned off the main road, following the directions he had picked up at the DropPort. The narrow farm road he traversed provided him, not surprisingly, with views of more sheep and more cows, as well as an occasional field planted with crops Ortega didn't recognize. He wondered if the tall grain was meant for human consumption or for livestock fodder, and realized that he might never know.

He could always ask, he supposed—if he didn't mind looking ignorant in front of the locals, which he was willing to do when the situation demanded it, but not out of mere curiosity. He was still getting used to the confidence others placed in him as a Knight of the Sphere, and he had no intention of jeopardizing it.

At the end of the road, he came to a low, sprawling farmhouse—an estate, really—built of the buff-colored local stone and roofed in slate. He parked the rented vehicle out front. The man who came out from the building's capacious attached garage to meet him looked not so much like his expectation of a chauffeur/mechanic as a farm worker with an occasional sideline into taking care of things with engines.

"You the man from Terra, supposed to come see Paladin Mandela?"

"Yes." Robert felt relieved that he was expected. He'd sent a radio message as soon as the DropShip came within communications range of Sheratan, but one never could tell these days. "Robert Goldberg."

"He'll be inside. You go on in—I'll put the car in the garage for you."

"Thanks." He handed over the keys and entered the house.

The rooms within were shadowed and cool, making a pleasant contrast to the bright day outside. A short entrance hall led to a large, open-plan room, its floor of dark, polished wood scattered with wool rugs in muted natural colors. One wall held an enormous fieldstone hearth, cold now in the summer; another was made up entirely of windows. The floor-to-ceiling glass panes afforded a view of lush green hills and the inevitable livestock.

Paladin Otto Mandela, an imposing man with skin the color of dark coffee and grizzled hair cropped close to his well-shaped skull, rose from a chair by the window. He held a tumbler of amber liquid in his hand. At the sight of Robert, he set the drink down on the nearest end table and strode briskly forward.

"Lord Robert." Mandela's eyes were bright and eager. "What word do you bring for us from Terra? Does Damien Redburn have something for me to do besides watching the Sheratanites vote and making certain that everybody is too scared to cheat?"

"You could say that," Robert replied. He reached into his inside jacket pocket and pulled out a stiff rectangular envelope with a holographic seal. He proffered it to Mandela. "He's set the date for the election."

The Paladin took the envelope and slit it open with a thumbnail. He perused the contents, and his eyebrows went up. "December twentieth? Why the rush?"

Mandela had a point, Robert thought. By law, Damien Redburn was required to step down as Exarch no later than the end of calendar year 3135. Holding the election on the date Redburn had chosen would mean inaugurating his successor on the fifth of January of that year. It didn't count as stepping down early, under the strict interpretation of the law, but it came near enough. Robert shrugged.

"I'm just a Knight," he said. "The Exarch doesn't tell me stuff like that. All I officially know is that I'm supposed to deliver the formal announcement and tell you that the Exarch requires your presence in Geneva."

Mandela raised an eyebrow. "How about what you know unofficially?"

"Not much more. If I had to guess, I'd say that the Exarch was hoping to take all the assorted factions by surprise. He means to hold the election before they have a chance to get their political machines running in high gear."

"Hmph," said Mandela. "It's a good thought. Damien isn't stupid, and the damned factions are going to kill everyone if something isn't done about them first. Here, so far it's only rioting and dirty tricks—it could be worse. But on Terra—" he shook his head "—on Terra, the factions mean business. They have dozens of different ways to follow Devlin Stone's vision, and each of them thinks they're the only ones who have it right. Believe me, if I wasn't here, the situation would be far worse. Don't let the fact that there aren't any armies involved yet fool you."

"I heard the news stories while I was driving out from the port. The situation sounds . . . complicated."

Mandela snorted. "That's an understatement. Anywhere you've got two people on Sheratan you've got at least three political factions, and the locals can't even vote for town dogcatcher without having two protest marches and a riot about it first."

"Is the situation safe enough for you to leave it without an observer?" Robert asked.

"Not really," Mandela said. "But a Paladin isn't necessary for a simple matter like overseeing the local planetary elections." He looked at Robert. "A Knight of the Sphere should be more than sufficient, now that we have one on hand."

3

Bernhard Island
Kervil, Prefecture II
22 October 3134

The morning of Operation Aftershock dawned fair and bright. The tropical sky arcing overhead was a clear matte blue, the ocean below it was scarcely ruffled by the gentle breeze, and the sunlight glittered over the surface of the water like a layer of golden spangles. Bernhard Island was a dormant volcanic cone, its seaward approach dominated by rugged cliffs above vivid green slopes falling down to a long arc of black-sand beach. From the ocean, Bernhard looked like an unspoiled paradise, the stuff of a hundred tourist brochures.

And all of it was lies.

Bernhard Island was in fact a pirates' haven, and under ordinary circumstances it would have been cleaned out long ago. Kervil Marine Law Enforcement was a well-armed and thoroughly professional combat force, quite capable of rounding up the typical piracy ring as soon as its criminal activities came to light.

These pirates, however, were not merely local criminals. When KMLE agents tracking half a dozen apparently unrelated cases compared notes, they saw similarities in methods and structure that pointed to the existence of a larger organization. Nor, upon investigation, did all of the stolen cargoes and prisoners' ransoms stay on-planet; KMLE's detective work found links to off-world buyers of goods and suppliers of weapons, as well as ties to smuggling rings on Terra and elsewhere. The criminal enterprises that preyed on Kervil's shipping lanes, they discovered to their dismay, were only the planetary branch of a multiworld organization almost as large in its scope as the pirates of Sadalbari had been in their heyday.

Even worse, after several months of careful investigation and infiltration it became clear to Kervilian intelligence that the nerve center of the greater criminal organization was not located somewhere safely off-world in somebody else's jurisdiction. The interplanetary pirates had hidden their main administrative-and-support base in the depths of the lava caves of Kervil's own Bernhard Island.

Today, a task force assembled for the occasion waited just over the horizon from the island. In their current position, the ships of the task force could not be seen by human observers, even on the island's high ground, and they had maintained radio silence for the past thirty-six hours. Kervil Marine Law Enforcement stood poised to hit Bernhard without warning in overwhelming strength.

The interplanetary scope of the pirates' endeavors was responsible for the presence among KMLE's current assets of an *Atlas* BattleMech piloted by a Paladin of the Sphere. The *Atlas* took up most of the well deck of Kervil Marine Law Enforcement's Amphibious Assault Ship *Waverley*. Operation Aftershock's other landing craft had been dispersed to her sister ships *Ellis* and *Cuthbert*, also taking part in the assault.

The goal of Operation Aftershock was to smash the pirate organization's nerve center before its members could escape. There would be no advance warning, no chance for the high-level bosses to flee, no time for the incriminating documents to be wiped or shredded. Nothing but the hammer of justice, smashing down—and Paladin Jonah Levin and his *Atlas* had come to swing it.

The landing ships waiting offshore were specialized craft, their hulls painted pale blue to blend in with the ocean mists of Kervil, each of them carrying many smaller boats. The largest of the ships could ballast down, flooding the vessels' well decks so that small cargo craft loaded with heavy tracked and wheeled units could float out. The smaller landing ships carried boats hung from davits, each boat large enough to hold a squad of regular or armored infantry.

At the moment, a rainsquall obscured the distant horizon. Just beyond that horizon, on the shores of Bernhard Island, the pirates waited. Jonah Levin was sure that they weren't asleep; even with radio silence in effect, the approach of the landing force would be putting out too much noise on the electromagnetic spectrum for them to rest easy. No one had accused these freebooters of being anything other than ruthless and effective. That was why an army with both regular and armored infantry, and with wheeled, tracked and hover armor, lay just over their horizon—and that was why Jonah's *Atlas* squatted in a specially constructed hold in the *Waverley*'s belly.

The *Atlas* was still attached to the ship's service power lines, but was otherwise ready to move as soon as Jonah climbed into the cockpit and strapped himself into the pilot's seat. The *Atlas* had no jump jets, which meant that Jonah, little as he relished the prospect, would have to wade his 'Mech ashore while every artillery piece on the island poured energy and projectile fire onto him.

The ships drove forward, toward the horizon. Jonah ascended from his 'Mech's resting place to meet the *Waverley*'s captain on the ship's bridge for a final conference before the assault.

"They have to know we're coming now," the captain said, "if they aren't blind rather than just dumb."

Jonah nodded. "So they must."

"You wanted the charts?"

"Yes."

"Here you go, then."

Jonah looked at the display the captain brought up on his data terminal. "Can you give me a picture of the subsea contours?"

"No problem." The captain touched a sequence of keys, and the false-color display melted and changed, now showing the water off the coast in gradations of blue and green where it had previously been a solid-colored area.

"How recent is this data?" Jonah asked.

"Some years old. This has been a poorly charted area."

Jonah pointed at a bar of lighter color that thrust outward from the southern promontory of the shoreline. "Do you see this spit matching data from the task force today?"

"Nothing to contradict it," the captain said.

"Then put me over the top of it . . . here," Jonah said, pointing again. "Kick out your boats; I'm going for a stroll."

"We're getting illuminated with fire control," a sensor tech on watch said. "G and H band, ranging and identification."

"Countermeasures," the captain said. "Active and passive. Keep them guessing."

"They have to have figured out by now that something big's coming," Jonah said. "They're going to be hitting us with everything they've got."

"So they will," the captain said. "At the same time as we're hitting them with everything that we've got. Thanks to you, we have something more."

"Start line," the navigator said.

"Very well. Commence launching boats, form up wave circles, guide on me."

"Commence launching," the radio talker said. Jonah left *Waverley*'s bridge crew to their work and headed back to where his 'Mech waited in the dark of the lowest hold, power cables snaking over it. The 'Mech's support crew— which, in these cramped quarters, was only two men—was standing by.

"Armed and hot," the head rigger said. "Awaiting your orders."

"Secure from ship's power," Jonah ordered. "I'm mounting up."

"Secure from ship's power, aye."

While the two crewmen labored to disconnect the *Atlas* from *Waverley*'s power, Jonah stripped down to his shorts and a thin mesh shirt. As chilly as the humid morning was against his bare skin, he knew the atmosphere inside his 'Mech's cockpit would be full of the literal heat of battle, where sweat running into a warrior's eyes could be as deadly as inbound missiles. Without the concealment of his uniform shirt and trousers, the tanned skin of Jonah's limbs and torso showed the silvery, knotted tracks of myriad old scars.

He climbed the ladder to the cockpit of the *Atlas*, reviewing the weapons systems as he went. Then he entered the hatch to the cockpit, closed the hatch behind him, strapped himself into the 'Mech's command couch, and convinced the 'Mech to recognize him as its commander. He brought the 'Mech up to its full standing height, stretched all its limbs to confirm response and agility, and cycled its weapons and communications console. Then he keyed on the intraship communications link.

"All right. I'm ready."

4

Hotel Egremont
Woodstock, Prefecture V
22 October 3134

When the DropShip *Amphitrite* touched down at the DropPort on Woodstock, Gareth Sinclair was the first passenger to disembark. His luggage, which would otherwise have been subject to customs inspection, received its entry stamp without needing to be opened, and Gareth himself was waved to the head of the passenger line.

As a Knight of the Sphere, he was often extended such privileges whether he asked for them or not. He refused them when he could—he already felt guilty enough about the doors opened by his family's wealth and position, and having more deference shown him did not make him more comfortable.

Today, however, he was willing to accept the advantage. He was on business for The Republic of the Sphere, he had a message to deliver, and the sender would not want him to dawdle.

The information desk in Woodstock's DropPort concourse had an actual person on duty behind the counter, in addition to the usual data screens, input terminals and racks of brightly colored folding brochures. Gareth approved. He had wrestled with enough planetary communications directories and computerized mapping services to know that what seemed intuitively obvious to the locals often appeared far less so to off-worlders. Interrogating a live human being was not as fast and efficient as implementing a properly functioning data search, but Gareth had found people to be a lot easier to work with when things went wrong.

The woman at the desk looked up at his approach, and her eyes brightened. He wasn't surprised. The working uniform of a Knight of the Sphere wasn't as dazzling as the full-dress regalia, but the rank it proclaimed was nevertheless capable of impressing spectators. He knew the attendant wasn't glowing because of his face; it was too thin, too long, too raw-boned to make pleasant young ladies smile at his approach.

"May I help you?" the desk clerk asked.

"Yes," he said. "I need to know where the mercenary contract talks are being held."

The clerk's expression cooled markedly. The topic of mercenaries, it seemed, was not a popular one on Woodstock at the moment.

Gareth was not surprised. Some years earlier, when the Steel Wolves under Kal Radick had first begun to exhibit signs of military adventurism, the citizens of Woodstock had grown nervous. Their uneasiness prompted them to hire elements of the Eridani Light Horse mercenary unit as a planetary garrison. As matters fell out afterward, the Steel Wolves—first under Radick himself and later under Anastasia Kerensky—turned their attention elsewhere, and the contract between the government of Woodstock and the Eridani Light Horse expired without any combat having taken place on-planet.

The good people of Woodstock, far from being relieved, felt that they had promised to spend a great deal of money to no purpose. They attempted to renegotiate the terms of the contract to a lower payoff, on the grounds that the mercenaries hadn't done any actual work. When the mercenaries objected and brought the matter before the Mercenary Review and Bonding Commission for adjudication, the local government countered by accusing the Commission of institutional bias and denying that its decisions were binding without the consent of both parties.

The mercenaries had objected again, vehemently this

time, and with what the government of Woodstock chose to regard as threats of violence. It had taken direct intervention on the part of Exarch Damien Redburn, and the promise of a Paladin, no less, to handle negotiations, before the mercenaries' tempers would cool.

The clerk said, "The talks are at the Hotel Egremont."

"Neutral ground?"

"I really couldn't tell you," the clerk said distantly. "Do you need a map?"

"Yes, please." Attempting to pinpoint the location of the hotel by wandering about and asking possibly hostile strangers for directions would not be good, Gareth thought, for the dignity of a Knight of the Sphere.

"One moment." A light flashed within the depths of the info-booth console, and a moment later a sheet of printout flimsy emerged. The clerk picked up the sheet and handed it to him. It was a map of the city, showing the Hotel Egremont marked with a star and the route from the Drop-Port picked out in red. "Here you go."

"Thank you."

After a pause, the clerk added, almost reluctantly, "It's a long walk. If I were you, I'd take a taxi."

Gareth followed the clerk's advice. The last thing he wanted, considering the gravity of the message that he bore, was to show up at the talks looking sweaty and rumpled.

The Hotel Egremont, when he arrived, was full of mercs in uniform. Gareth suspected they had scared away all of the other customers within the first day or so of negotiations. He asked the desk clerk where the contract talks were being held.

"In the Rose Room," the desk clerk replied. "Off the mezzanine."

"Thanks," Gareth said, and headed toward the staircase.

"Hey!" the desk clerk protested. "Those are private negotiations. You can't just—"

Gareth paused long enough to speak over his shoulder— "I have a personal message for Paladin Heather GioAvanti from Exarch Damien Redburn. I believe that gives me authorization."—and continued up the stairs.

The mercenaries had a guard posted outside the Rose Room. The man came from relaxed parade rest to a posture of readiness as Sinclair approached.

"I'm sorry, sir. These are private negotiations."

"So I've been told. And I'm a Knight of the Sphere with an urgent message for the Paladin."

There was a thoughtful pause. Then the mercenary stepped away from the door. "Proceed."

The Rose Room, Gareth thought when he entered, must have been named after something besides the flower. The décor inside involved no roses whatsoever, only curtains and carpet and bland, nonrepresentational art in shades of ivory and dusty green.

The tension in the room hit him even before the door closed. The mercenary officers on one side of the long central table glared at the representatives of Woodstock's planetary government, who, though they were bureaucrats and their opponents were battle-tested warriors, attempted to glare back in turn. All of the porcelain cups waiting in neat rows beside the silver coffee urn on the sideboard remained untouched, as did the trays of breakfast pastries. From the look of things, nobody involved in the conference was willing to break even symbolic bread with the opposition.

Paladin Heather GioAvanti, seated at the head of the table, wore an expression of long-suffering patience. Gareth paused for a moment to look at her. Until now, he had only seen her from a distance, or in pictures. Close up and in person, the Paladin looked much younger than her media image—barely old enough to possess her rank or resume.

Heather GioAvanti had been a mercenary commander herself, and a successful one, before her acts of self-sacrificing heroism during an incursion of the Marik-Stewart Commonwealth into Prefecture VII had prompted the Exarch to make her a Paladin. She was a tall woman, with fair skin, strong bone structure, and a face saved from washed-out pallor by the trick of heredity that had made her brows and lashes several shades darker than her yellow-white hair.

When she turned to look at Gareth as he entered, he saw that she had gray eyes. Their gaze was sharp and penetrating, and he knew that she had probably guessed his errand already. There were not many messages that required a Knight of the Sphere to deliver them in person.

The other men and women at the table weren't making the same connection, but they were smart enough to know that Gareth's arrival was important. With all eyes fixed upon him, Gareth strode to the head of the conference table.

"Paladin GioAvanti?"

"Yes, Sir Knight?"

"I am Gareth Sinclair." Having named himself, he withdrew a sealed envelope from the inner pocket of his uniform tunic and gave it to the Paladin. "I have an urgent message from the Exarch of The Republic of the Sphere, to be hand-delivered to you personally."

"Thank you, Lord Gareth." Heather GioAvanti opened the flap of the envelope and slid out a thick sheet of monogrammed paper. After reading the letter's few lines of script, she put the paper back inside the envelope and laid it on the tabletop in front of her. Then she looked again at the forces arrayed along either side of the long table.

"All right," the Paladin said, and her voice had a note in it that—judging from her auditors' reaction—had not been there before. "I've heard both sides of the story now—several times each, at length—and I don't want to hear them any more. Up until now I've been patient, because I was hoping that, given the chance, you'd come around to seeing reason on your own. But I have a letter here calling me to Terra, and so I can't wait any longer. So listen up, because this is how it's going to be.

"You people of Woodstock—you're going to stop trying to weasel out of a perfectly legal and standard contract just because the mercenaries you hired did too good a job of convincing trouble to go somewhere else instead of coming here. Pay them what's owed to them, and shut up.

"And you"—she glared at the mercenary leaders—"where do you get off even *thinking* about threatening your employers? I'm assessing you a fine of two hundred thousand stones for actions committed against the civic order, and you're going to pay it with no grumbling.

"Do you all hear me?"

The question came like the snap of a whip. The silence that followed was broken by mumbled assents from both sides of the table.

"Good," said Heather GioAvanti. "See that you do what I've said. And next time, think twice before you ask for a Paladin to come and render judgment."

5

Jonah Levin wished he could pace, but the cramped space of the *Waverley*'s deep hold left him no room. He sat tight, waiting completely out of the pirates' sight. He hoped to be a very unpleasant surprise when the time came, but until then he could do nothing but wait.

If he had his way, battles would begin the moment they became inevitable. There would be no waiting, no buildup, no time-consuming travel. The two sides would appear instantly on the battlefield and open fire.

He checked his chronometer. The time was getting closer, though seconds ticked like minutes. So far, the operation was on schedule.

The comm crackled. "Time to see if anyone's home," said Lieutenant Smith of Kervil Marine Law Enforcement. "Circles to lines on my command."

Jonah waited for the command, his 'Mech echoing the forward lean of his body.

"Execute," Smith said.

Jonah exhaled. There wasn't anything for him to do yet, but at least something was happening.

The boat group, which had been circling near the island shore, straightened into lines running parallel to the beach. Unless the pirates were blind or lax, they knew what was coming and were preparing their response. Jonah glanced at his secondary screen, displaying a feed from a boat-top camera. The coast was silent and looked empty, but offered plenty of dense foliage to hide the hostile guard.

"Turn course zero-one-seven, again, zero-one-seven," Smith said over the comm. "Speed at five knots."

The boats turned, three lines starting a curve toward the shore. Infantry would land first, then artillery, then missile tanks. If Jonah did his job, most of them would make it onto the shore alive.

Flashes like fireworks sparked across the coastline, followed brief seconds later by dim reports. Missiles arced into the sky, closing on their targets.

"Hold fire. Don't let them startle you," Smith cautioned, but it wasn't necessary. The pirates had fired early and their missiles fell short, vanishing in white sprays and exploding columns of water.

"Gentlemen, let's get wet," Smith said, and the first wave dove into the water churned up by the pirate missiles. More missiles fired, most still missing their marks, but a few denting hulls in the first line of boats.

"They're starting to feel cocky," warned Brigham, captain of one of the forward boats.

"All right, let 'em know we see 'em. Area fire!"

Jonah reached for his trigger reflexively, but it was still too early.

Greenery along the shore exploded into black-and-brown clouds. Tree trunks shredded, their broad tops falling onto the rocky shore.

The pirates weren't deterred, and sent a more intense wave of fire. Jonah watched columns rise around him like geysers, strangely beautiful in their way.

Finally, Smith came through with a message meant only for him.

"One minute to position, Paladin. Flood the hold."

"Copy that," Jonah said, trying to hide the relief in his

voice. The crewman disconnected his 'Mech and scurried out of the hold, sealing the watertight doors. Water flooded in as Jonah waited for sixty seconds to pass.

"In position now. Release."

The door beneath Jonah opened, and he fell quickly into the dark sea. He flicked on beams to help him navigate to shore.

Soon the feet of his *Atlas* touched sand. Walking underwater was only slightly faster than moving through quicksand, but at least he was pushing ahead. Above him, the incoming attack waves would continue their arc toward land while he made a beeline for the shore. If the timing was right, they'd arrive on the beach at the same time.

He checked his secondary screen to follow the progress of the battle above, but between the poor signal and the sprays of water above, he couldn't make out anything. He flicked it off and waited for Smith's commands to tell him what he needed to know about the fight.

"First wave, report. Looks like you lost one."

"Yes, sir," Brigham crackled back. "One ship hit and entirely lost. Others proceeding apace."

"Second?"

"We've had a breakdown, one boat out and heading away. No hits from the hostiles."

Smith didn't bother asking about the third, which was still out of range.

"All right, fill the gaps. Keep the pressure on."

"Yes, sir," came the replies, and Jonah added his own assent as he slogged through the water. The pirates could have no idea what kind of pressure they were about to feel.

The surface of the water drew closer to his 'Mech's head. He could see waves passing, though not yet breaking. Missiles and shells skipped overhead, some from in front of him, some from behind, echoing through the sea like a sounding dolphin. Jonah slowed his 'Mech further, making his machine squat as it practically walked on its knees. It wouldn't do for his head to stick out too soon—it would just make an inviting target, and it would ruin the surprise.

Smith spoke again. "Wave one, prepare to launch; wave two, hold your fire. Launch on my mark . . . execute! Nail it down!"

Jonah thought he could hear the jump jets of the armored

infantry firing, though that might have been his imagination or the blood in his ears. Either way, his time had come.

He came out of the water and stood outlined against the churning sea, the saltwater streaming off the carapace of the 'Mech.

Off to his right, he could see the power discharges of lasers and pulse cannon. In a moment the defenders would notice him—which was the plan. Moving into their gut, he'd draw and return fire, allowing the landing wave to get into position and, hopefully, maneuver around the sides of the pirates' forces. He pushed forward hard and the 'Mech surged ahead.

A scout vehicle with a rear-mounted heavy machine gun burst through the vegetation ahead of the *Atlas* BattleMech. Jonah didn't recognize its markings. The vehicle turned and its gunner opened fire, hosing down Jonah's *Atlas* with fifty-caliber armor-piercing rounds. They had no effect on the 'Mech.

"No, you don't," Jonah said. He leaned on the throttle, kicking the speed of the *Atlas* up a step, closing on the scout vehicle. A quick push on the left pedal while easing on the right sent the 'Mech's leg into a kick, pummeling the scout vehicle. It flipped over on its side, one wheel hanging at an angle that told Jonah the axle had broken. He then brought the 'Mech's foot down heavily on the machine gun.

The wrecked vehicle, and its scattering troopers, weren't worth any expense of ammunition. Jonah headed straight in from the beach, turning his *Atlas* toward the area marked on his heads-up display as the location of the pirates' headquarters.

Someone in that area was broadcasting at high power over multiple frequencies. Jonah couldn't make out what was being said—the broadcasters had good crypto, whoever they were—but he figured that taking out command and control would be a fine way to start the morning. He vectored in on the transmission site and pushed the *Atlas* into an earth-shaking run.

The beach continued to explode with fire from both directions, rocks and dirt pattered across his side, and his footing kept slipping as the impact of the artillery altered the landscape beneath him.

He felt calmer than he had all day.

6

Red Barn Cafeteria, Geneva
Terra, Prefecture X
22 October 3134

The greater Geneva metropolitan area contained twenty-four Red Barn restaurants, and each of those restaurants had a table six. It was in the middle of the restaurant's floor, away from the windows and far from the restrooms. Table six, in each of these locations, would be the first choice of exactly no one.

Cullen Roi liked it that way. No matter which Red Barn outlet he chose for his meetings, he knew table six would be open. He also knew that, as long as he kept rotating between the two dozen locations, he would never be remembered. The staff at each restaurant seemed to turn over every six months or so, and no one ever treated Roi or his companions as regulars, since they went to each restaurant only once or twice a year.

The other customers were almost as transitory as the staff. Red Barn restaurants thrived in areas filled with cheap apartment buildings, pawnshops and all-night convenience stores. People in these neighborhoods generally didn't get to know their neighbors, knowing that within a year, either one or the other of them was likely to have moved on. In the middle of this sea of shifting faces, Cullen felt at home.

Plus, truth be told, the food at the Red Barn really wasn't that bad.

Today's meeting was southeast of downtown, and Cullen had arrived early, munching on sausage rolls and sipping watery coffee while he waited for the others to arrive.

He was short and wiry, with intense brown eyes, and he wore his hair cut short after the fashion of the MechWarrior he had once been. The leather jacket that he wore over his drab work clothes bore a dark spot where a Stone's Revenants patch had once been.

He heard Hansel approach long before he saw him. By now he could recognize Hansel by the way he opened a door—forcefully, a whoosh of air followed by the crack of the door against the outside wall. Thudding footsteps, seemingly loud enough to drown out conversation, paced to Roi's table.

"Captain," Hansel said as he slid behind the table. It was an old habit from their days in the Revenants, and it died hard. Cullen just nodded. Hansel squirmed to fit into the too-small wooden chair, dwarfing the table that fit Cullen just fine.

They sat wordlessly, Hansel only speaking to order roasted chicken. Cullen continued to eat, watching Hansel's eyes to see when Norah entered. Then it came—the flinch, the slight squint that flickered across Hansel's brow whenever Norah came in.

She was seated to Cullen's right before he heard anything. Her distaste for small talk extended even to greetings, so neither Cullen nor Hansel spoke. They waited for her vegetable stir-fry to arrive, which customarily signified the meeting's commencement.

The plate arrived, the weary waitress strolled away, and Cullen began the meeting of the Kittery Renaissance.

"It will only be the three of us tonight," he said, "but we're going to need to bring in more people soon. The pace will be rapid, starting now."

Hunger for something other than food showed in Norah's face. "You have word?" she asked.

Something in her voice suggested that she might have been originally from Liao, but Cullen knew not to broach the subject of Norah's past. She had made it quite clear that the subject was off limits, though her intense hatred for the Capellan Confederation and its rulers in House Liao—an intensity unmatched throughout the whole of Cullen's organization—kept Cullen curious.

"Yes," Cullen answered her. "My source tells me the elections will be held shortly."

"Already?" Hansel asked.

"You're sure the information is reliable?" Norah asked at the same time.

"Yes. My source saw copies of documents summoning the Paladins back to Terra for the meetings preliminary to the election."

" 'Meetings preliminary to the election'?" Hansel echoed. "That doesn't sound too definite."

"It is," Cullen said. "Remember, this is the government—it does not move quickly. This is the start of the process, and everything points to it ending before the year is done."

"This is going to throw our timing way off," Norah said.

Cullen shook his head. "Not really. We'll just need to step up the pace a bit."

Norah, protesting, said, "The people won't—"

"Our people will," said Cullen. "And they'll make sure that the rest of the crowd follows where they're needed."

He looked from Norah to Hansel. "Most of the hard work is going to fall on the two of you—sounding out potential crowd leaders, training them so that they can train. their groups, keeping everything undercover until the day. If you don't think that you're up to the job, say it now so that I can bring in somebody else."

Hansel said only, "I'm all right with it."

Norah shook her head peevishly. "If it were anyone but you, Cullen Roi, I'd be bowing out right now. But if you say that it can be done, then I suppose I'm in."

The shadow of a thought passed across her face. "How about our man on horseback? How is this going to affect him?"

"It shouldn't affect him at all," Cullen Roi said. "The beauty of all this is that our man doesn't even know he's involved in our plan."

He smiled. "Genuine sincerity. It's the hardest thing in the world to fake—so we aren't even going to try."

7

Bernhard Island
Kervil, Prefecture II
22 October 3134

Jonah had lost track of the beach a few times, so he couldn't be sure, but he thought the attackers were about to put down the third wave of the assault. If he wanted this done smoothly, that meant he didn't have much longer to keep the defenders away from the beach.

Tradition dictated that the fifth wave was when the attackers would come under the heaviest fire. The defenders, confused, disoriented, and unsure what they were facing during the first waves, would rally for a push against the landing defenders. The casualties of the fifth wave could be far heavier than the first. Unless Jonah made sure the defenders didn't get organized.

Two SM1 tank destroyers appeared around the corner of a building, off to Jonah's left. They had him locked in and tracking. He sent out a beam from the *Atlas'* extended-range large laser, just to let the Smileys know that he saw them and—with luck—to ruin their firing solutions. Then he swiveled the 'Mech, bringing its torso-mounted and right-arm-mounted weapons to bear. The tanks were worth expending some missiles on; Smileys were dangerous.

He pushed left hard, firing, letting the weight of the *Atlas* pull him sideways as it leaned. Leaves and woods exploded, and a secondary explosion followed closely. He'd gotten something.

He sent his 'Mech forward in a lumbering trot toward the Smileys. One tank was a heap of burning, twisted metal now, its fuel and ammunition cooking away. The other, intact, fired.

A stream of metal slugs mostly passed wide of the *Atlas*, but a few connected, catching the 'Mech in the left shoulder. They packed enough of a wallop to push the 'Mech's torso back a little, and Jonah let it move. As it swiveled, Jonah pushed his joystick out, let the 'Mech's right arm fly up a little. His aim stayed on the Smiley.

Pulling the trigger, Jonah sent a volley of missiles into the Smiley's teeth. It soon became an exact twin to the other smoldering tank.

Turning from the light popping of exploding ammunition, Jonah started to wonder what the tanks were guarding.

He had barely taken two steps when a trapdoor in the earth opened and flames shot out. Jonah throttled back, but the hundred tons of steel surrounding him did not reverse quickly enough, and flames scorched his 'Mech's skin. Angrily, he briefly pulled up then stomped on his right pedal, and the *Atlas'* foot came down, shattering the trapdoor, the man beneath it, and the portable flamethrower he carried.

Checking his readouts, Jonah saw that the flamer had hit the *Atlas* directly enough to raise its temperature into the red zone. He slowed, allowing heat to dissipate.

Jonah took the opportunity to consider the surrounding terrain. Buildings of concrete and steel lay on every hand. The transmitter was off to his right, still a little bit out of range. He detected more infantry in motion, not coming from the proper direction and lacking an IFF signal marking them as friendlies. He lobbed a short-range missile volley in their direction to keep them from planning anything unpleasant and kept on thinking.

This particular spot hadn't been a good place for an ambush by SM1 tanks—as demonstrated by the fact that the ambush hadn't worked—which suggested that either his opponents were incompetent, or they'd had some other reason to guard this area. Jonah Levin hadn't reached the rank of Paladin of the Sphere by assuming that his opponents were incompetent.

He turned toward the closest building, pushed the joystick to move out the *Atlas*' powerful right arm, and reached for the building's outside wall.

That brought the last line of defenders to life, three of them springing from the opposite side of the building, pointing a shoulder-mounted rocket launcher at Jonah's chest.

Jonah swore. The bastards had done a good job digging themselves into the ground, out of reach of his sensors. But they couldn't fire a rocket as fast as he could pull the trigger of his laser. Blue light shot out, incinerating the man holding the launcher along with his weapon. His comrades fell back with the heat of the blast from the exploded rocket.

Jonah surged forward and lifted his 'Mech's right foot high in the air. The burned and bleeding pirates looked at the black spot that used to be their companion and at the huge metal foot over their heads. They made the easy choice and ran.

Jonah lowered his foot and watched them go. With their burns, they wouldn't make it far.

He quickly scanned the area for any other late-emerging defenders and found it clear. His 'Mech's hands once again extended to the tan wall near him, pulling it down into a pile of dust and rubble.

"Well, what do you know?" he said—without amplification, so that nobody outside the 'Mech's cockpit could hear.

Inside the wrecked building, a group of civilians with blindfolds on their faces were handcuffed and chained to the inner wall on the top floor. Jonah keyed up his 'Mech's external speakers.

"Friends," he said. The amplification in the speakers sent his voice booming over the noise of battle. "Stand fast, friends are here."

Then he keyed the internal communications circuit to the command channel. "I need a squad of infantry over here as fast as possible," he said quietly. "With medics. I'm dropping a marker-transponder. Get me some people. I've found the hostages."

Below him, by the beach, the defenders scattered as they heard their prize possession had been lost. The fifth wave landed on a beach free of gunfire.

Late in the afternoon, a VSTOL aircraft with Republic markings flew low over the beach, turned and came in for a landing. The beach was littered with broken machines; the ocean had not yet smoothed away the explosion craters. The medics and the Graves Registration unit had already cleared away the bodies and parts of bodies.

The door of the VSTOL opened and a lone man emerged, resplendent in the uniform of a Knight of the Sphere. He walked down onto the sand.

"Paladin Jonah Levin," he said, taking the arm of the nearest trooper.

"Over there," the soldier said, pointing, and continued on his way.

The Knight turned toward the Shandra scout vehicle that the trooper had pointed to, and walked over. The man sitting beside the Shandra was wearing only the shorts and light singlet of a dismounted MechWarrior, with no identification or rank insignia visible, but the Knight recognized Paladin Jonah Levin from his pictures on the tri-vids. Levin's current uniform, or rather the lack of it, also showed what the tri-vid news interviews generally didn't: a truly impressive collection of battle scars.

"Sir," the Knight said. "I have a message for you."

"Wouldn't radio do?"

"Hard copy, to be delivered in person," the Knight said. He looked again at the Paladin—who appeared tired but satisfied, like a workman contemplating a tough job well finished—and asked, "How was the fight?"

"No real problem. They didn't have any 'Mechs. We rescued the hostages. Got some prisoners; they're being interrogated."

"That's good to hear. May I deliver the message I bear?"

"You came a long way. I might as well take a look at it. Walk with me."

Jonah Levin stood and walked down to the packed sand of the lower beach. Wavelets rolled up the beach, then retreated, smoothing the sand and making it easier to walk on. The tide was going out, leaving bits of wreckage behind: broken weapons, packing material, the shattered hull of the boat wave commander's vessel.

"What's your message?" Jonah asked.

"Here," the Knight said, and pulled an envelope from the inside pocket of his tunic. It bore seals from the very highest levels of government in Geneva.

Jonah took it. He felt reluctant, suddenly, to open the letter. It would be so much simpler to merely throw the envelope into the surf, to send the Knight on his way, to return to his 'Mech and live out his life as a warrior, nothing more.

But he'd never chosen any option simply because it was easy. He slit the envelope open. The paper inside was embossed with the symbols of Devlin Stone and of The Republic of the Sphere. The message was short.

"Sir?" the Knight asked. "Do you have a reply?"

"Yes. Tell them, 'yes.' "

The Knight saluted, turned, and trotted back to his VSTOL.

Jonah stood on the beach. There was a lot to do, including readying his 'Mech and arranging transportation. And he would have to explain things to Anna.

"I've been summoned," he said aloud. The words sounded strange in his ears, and he couldn't imagine them sounding any less strange to his wife, whom he would have to leave behind on Kervil. "To Terra, in order to participate in the election of the next Exarch."

A changing breeze brought the acrid smell of fire and corpses across the sand. This morning, Jonah realized, had been the easy part. What awaited him on Terra—that would be the challenge.

8

Office of the Exarch, Geneva
Terra, Prefecture X
24 October 3134

Exarch Damien Redburn preferred to hold most conferences in his private office, rather than in the ceremonial one reserved for formal meetings and official photos. The ceremonial office occupied most of an entire floor in the Hall of Government; it was long on elegance and impressive decor but short on security and convenience.

His private office, on the other hand, featured a combination of conservative decor and plain working furniture that could have belonged to an executive in any of a hundred Terran corporations, and it was located in a building whose directory did not mention the Exarch's name at all. For all that the world outside knew, this was the office of The Republic's Deputy Undersecretary for Economic Redevelopment.

Soon he'd leave both offices behind for good. He had already bought a retirement home in Terra's Pacific Northwest and he was looking forward to spending some time doing nothing but fishing. He'd also be happy to leave behind the more unpleasant parts of politics—the endless meetings, the stultifying ceremonies, the blizzard of bureaucracy.

But then there was the rest of the job, the things that had gotten him involved in the first place . . . the plans, the goals, the continued hope to build something lasting, something better than had been in place before. Redburn had never known anyone to leave that part of political life for good. Except for Devlin Stone, and even he promised to come back. There were many things to be done; many ways, large and small, that he could peddle his influence from his distant northwoods outpost. He had some idea what was coming, and it would be impossible for him to sit on the sidelines and let it all go on without him. He sometimes pretended otherwise, but that was just for show, to let those who wanted to believe that he was going to shrink away keep their mistaken opinions for a little longer.

For now, though, he was focused on getting through the meetings that separated him from his fishing pole. And in truth, his current appointment was one of the more pleasant items on his agenda.

The Paladin who sat composedly at one end of the office couch was not officially in the room, any more than the room itself officially existed. Until Redburn took office, in fact, he had sometimes thought that this particular Paladin—the Ghost Paladin, the eighteenth of the seventeen Paladins, the Paladin whose identity was never revealed save to the reigning Exarch—was a legend, a tale made up to frighten those who were tempted to swerve from The Republic's straight and narrow.

The Ghost Paladin's very existence was the subject of much rumor and speculation among the people at large. But by this point during his term in office, Damien Redburn had come to know the Ghost Paladin very well—enough so that their meetings were often as much social as business. What better friend could there be, after all, for a ruler who could not afford to play favorites, than a Paladin whose identity was unknown?

Redburn took a decanter and a pair of tumblers from the cabinet in the corner. He poured two fingers of amber liquid into each tumbler.

"Of the two of us," he said, as he handed one of the tumblers to his guest, "I'm the lucky one."

The Ghost Paladin took an appreciative sip. "Why do you say that?"

"I get to quit my job. So far as I can tell, you're going to be doing yours up to the day you die in harness."

"True." The Ghost Paladin took another sip of the drink, visibly savoring it. "On the other hand, I don't have to do politics. That's what ages a man, you know."

"You won't get any argument from me," Redburn said. He leaned his head back and contemplated the ceiling. "I nearly didn't recognize myself in the mirror the other day. I said to myself, 'Who *is* that tired old man?'—and then I realized it was me."

"You'll be done soon." The Ghost Paladin chuckled. "Everyone is convinced that you have some kind of devious power play going, holding the election this early."

"It's just the call of the redwoods."

The Ghost Paladin slowly shook his head. "Other people may buy that. I don't."

"It's the story I'm giving," Redburn said with a shrug.

"Even though you know you'll be back in politics, somehow, before the year is out."

"I know no such thing," Redburn said placidly. Then he cracked a small smile. "But I have my suspicions."

"You may not even get to leave Geneva. You know that whoever succeeds you will want to cling to you for advice."

Redburn's face grew sober. "I won't be here. Whatever else I may or may not be planning, I'm going to give the next Exarch plenty of breathing room. Their term will be their own."

"A fresh start?"

"Something like that."

"And the turmoil that will follow the election? You think you'll be able to see all that on the streets and just watch it go past?"

The Ghost Paladin had hit a nerve. As bad as things were now between Terra's political factions, the election could make it worse. Now, at least, each faction had at least a slim hope that its candidate—whoever that might be—had a chance to be Exarch. After the election, most of them would be disappointed, knowing they'd lost a chance to gain power, to advance their agenda, for at least four years. Disappointment would make some hopeless, hopelessness would lead to desperation, and desperation could make the streets of Geneva run red.

"I'll have to. I can only hope our investigations will subdue some of the more dangerous groups before things get out of hand."

"You have someone on it?"

Redburn nodded. "GioAvanti. But I'm afraid the insurgents may be multiplying too fast even for her."

"She's a good choice," the Ghost Paladin affirmed. "I'll make sure any information I get makes its way to her somehow."

Redburn ran his finger around the lip of his glass. "She might make a good Exarch," he said.

The Ghost Paladin's expression didn't waver.

"No response, eh? Don't tell me you have no feelings on who should succeed me."

"Devlin Stone did a wise thing when he set up the office of Ghost Paladin to be apart from politics. There would be too much temptation to play kingmaker, otherwise."

Redburn nodded agreement. He was not one of those faithful who believed Devlin Stone never had a bad idea. In fact, he had a long list of "what in God's name were you *thinking*?" questions that he was planning to ask The Republic's vanished founder if the man ever turned up again. This time, however, Stone had been right.

"That being the case," Redburn said, "I won't bother asking who would get your vote if you could cast one. On the other hand, I can certainly ask you if there's any Paladin out of the current lot whom you think *shouldn't* be made Exarch."

The Ghost Paladin took another thoughtful sip of the amber drink. "I think it's fair to say that either Tyrina Drummond or Thaddeus Marik would be a howling disaster in the role. Even if Drummond weren't a Clan warrior—which would alienate all of those worlds where the Clans have lately taken to causing trouble—she's also one of those 'Devlin Stone can do no wrong!' people. And Marik . . . well, you know what he's like."

Redburn nodded. He knew Marik: a self-exiled scion of the deposed ruling family of the defunct Free Worlds League, prominent in the Founder's Movement . . . and tainted, inescapably, by his family's rumored involvement in the Word of Blake Jihad. Marik could be as honest and capable as any other Paladin, yet he would never have the people's wholehearted trust.

"Unless we have a run of spectacularly bad luck, however," the Ghost Paladin continued, "neither Tyrina Drummond nor Thaddeus Marik is likely to get elected. Their fellow Paladins are not stupid, after all."

"Leaving aside the obvious ones, then," Redburn said, "have we got any Paladins who *could* get elected, but who really shouldn't be?"

The Ghost Paladin's answer was prompt. "Anders Kessel wants it too much, for either himself or Sorenson. And David McKinnon—he's honest and brave and loyal, but he's not flexible enough to deal with the world as we must live in it now."

"I see your point," Redburn said. "He's one of the old guard, though—Devlin Stone's man since the Kittery Prefecture days—and that's bound to carry weight with archloyalists like Drummond. Add in his reputation as a MechWarrior and his personal charisma . . . nine votes out of seventeen is all it takes, remember. If the mood of the electors were to swing in the right direction, he could do it."

The Ghost Paladin smiled grimly over the rim of the glass of whisky. "Then we'll have to make certain that the mood doesn't swing. It looks like choosing the right replacement for Ezekiel Crow is going to be fairly vital."

"We've got a number of up-and-coming young Knights to consider, even eliminating the obvious nonstarters." Redburn paused a moment to contemplate with regret the fact that Tara Campbell, Countess of Northwind, had turned down his offer of Crow's position. The Countess would have made a triple-threat Paladin, as courageous as Drummond and as loyal as McKinnon, but considerably more intelligent than either.

There was no use in mourning what would not be. The thought of Tara Campbell, however, brought up the image of yet another young Knight who had also proven herself both loyal and intelligent.

"What do you say to Lady Janella Lakewood?" Redburn asked.

"Lakewood?" There was a long pause, during which Redburn imagined Lady Janella's dossier unfolding in the Ghost Paladin's mind, from her first day in preschool up through her present rank as a Knight of the Sphere. At last the Paladin's gaze returned from the middle distance and focused again on Redburn. "Yes. Lady Janella is an excellent choice."

9

Everyone agreed that Henrik Morten was an up-and-coming young man. He was a diplomat on the rise, a man whose problem-solving abilities had made him valuable to more than one politician. He came from a noble family; the Mortens had been among the original settlers on Mallory's World, and had grown and maintained the family fortune over the intervening centuries. At one point or another, members of the Morten family had held most of their world's important planetary offices. They had also thrown in their lot with Devlin Stone early enough that they retained most of their political and economic clout even after Stone established The Republic of the Sphere.

Henrik's only shortcoming, as an inheritor of the family's political power, was that while he had been abundantly gifted with golden hair, azure eyes and a pair of cheekbones that could draw attention a full city block away, he had failed to receive from his illustrious ancestors the physical stamina and aptitude necessary to become a MechWarrior. And while being a MechWarrior was not absolutely required by law in order to become a Knight or, subsequently, a Paladin of the Sphere, the hard truth was that custom decreed otherwise. No one was going to ascend to the second-highest rank in The Republic of the Sphere who had not first climbed into the cockpit of a 'Mech and made ready to do battle.

But if the path to the Exarch's throne was closed to him—since the Exarch was elected by the Paladins from among their own number, and the Paladins were, with rare exceptions, elevated from the ranks of the Knights—Henrik could still aspire to a position of influence. Diplomatic and ambassadorial posts did not require MechWarriors to fill them, and neither did the ranks of the Senate. A capable man, with the right backing and blood, could go far in The Republic of the Sphere, even in these troubled times.

Henrik Morten had that backing, and he was grateful for it. He also had a strong sense of what was owed to his patron. He considered it part of his duty—as well as in his plain self-interest—to keep his ears open for anything that might be of use. Scraps and tidbits of information from odd sources, properly organized, often proved to be of value if they were given to the right person at the right time.

Tonight he was dining at the Restarante Del Sol in Santa Fe with his local girlfriend, Elena Ruiz. The restaurant was furnished and decorated in the old Southwestern style, all stucco, dark wood and hand-painted tile. His companion's delighted reaction to being there told him that this was the first time she had ever been to so elegant—and understatedly expensive—a place.

Elena worked as a nurse in the residential wing of the Knights' Santa Fe headquarters complex, though she often complained that she functioned more as a housekeeper. Her complaints held an element of truth, though Henrik was not so foolish as to tell her so. She was, in his private assessment, essentially an overeducated maid, and certainly not nobility. She could fish all she wanted for a proposal of marriage and the chance to be, someday, Mrs. Ambassador (and, subsequently, Mrs. Senator) Henrik Morten, but it wasn't going to happen.

Henrik didn't try to dissuade her from her illusions, however, at least not yet. She was too good in bed to lose for no reason; and she was a talker, too, at the dining table as much as between the sheets. Henrik, ever on the alert for news and information that might have escaped the general notice, was good at listening.

". . . haven't gotten enough sleep the past few days, I'm yawning on my feet, and it's all Paladin Steiner-Davion's fault."

He looked at Elena over the beeswax candles and the floral arrangement and the basket of napkin-wrapped breads. "I can understand how you could make a man stay awake just so he could keep on watching you, but surely Victor is too old to actually *do* anything along that line."

"I wouldn't know." She giggled. "But it wasn't anything like that. He's been working late every night, and falling asleep at his desk."

"That must be hard on you," Henrik said sympathetically.

She sighed. "Yes, it is—I can't go to bed for the night myself until I'm sure he's sleeping. I have to monitor his vital signs on the room security monitors, and make at least one in-person check after he's out."

"Inconsiderate of him to keep you awake that way."

"None of the long-term senior residents know how close a watch we keep on their good health," she said.

"Somebody has to do it," Henrik said. "A man of Victor Steiner-Davion's age shouldn't be burning his candle at both ends, staying up until all hours working on . . . what? Do you know?"

She made a moue of discontent. "He's hardly going to talk about it to me. I'm just the person who annoys him by coming in and tidying things up when he doesn't believe they need it. You'd think at his age he'd realize clutter is hazardous and unhygienic."

Henrik thought that a veteran MechWarrior and politician who'd survived as many years of battle and intrigue as Victor Steiner-Davion was not likely to care too much about the dangers of an untidy room. Aloud, however, he only echoed, "You'd think."

She said, "But he's taken it into his head that he has to present whatever he's working on to the Paladins when they meet for the election, and he isn't going to stop before he makes his speech."

Henrik felt the tingle in the back of his neck that meant

he was in the presence of potentially useful information. He chose his next words carefully. If Elena thought that she was being pumped for information, the flow of chatter would dry up, and he would learn nothing more.

"Did he say it has to be the Paladins?" he asked. "Telling the Senate won't work? They're in Geneva all the time; he wouldn't have to push himself so hard to get everything done before the end of the year."

"I told him so, the one time he mentioned it. He just mumbled something about needing to put the problem in front of the right people, and ignored me after that."

"His loss." Henrik's mind was engaging with the problem, seeing the potential in it, and the interest to his patron. Carefully casual, he went on, "It might be something my department could help him with. If you could get a look at some of his work sometime, just enough to give me an idea . . ."

She gave him a shrewd look. "And then you could be all helpful, and he'd be grateful, and you'd add Victor Steiner-Davion to your legion of supporters."

Well, he thought, not exactly. "Clever girl. What do you say? Can you do it?"

"He sometimes leaves his data terminal running when he falls asleep at his desk," she said. "I couldn't do anything with his files—that would be wrong, and besides, he'd know it if I touched anything—but there's nothing to stop me from remembering something that I accidentally happen to see, is there?"

"No," he said. "There isn't. You could even take notes."

10

The small residential hotel known as the Pension Flambard had been Jonah Levin's customary place to stay in Geneva ever since his initial visit as a newly elevated Knight of the Sphere. That first time, he had picked the Pension randomly from the hotel listings provided at the DropPort because he couldn't afford to stay at an expensive place like the Hotel Duquesne, and it wasn't his type of place anyway. At the Pension Flambard, he had found lodgings that were not only within his budget, but soothing to his nerves.

At the time he had just finished a long and difficult convalescence, a fact which caused him to feel simultaneously old before his time and—when confronted with the glittering activity of diplomatic Geneva—painfully young and provincial. The Pension's small size and unfashionable appearance reassured him that his new life still had room in it for things that were neither pretentious nor intimidating.

For that reason, even after Jonah had more money, and after he had learned that the Hotel Duquesne traditionally provided complimentary accommodations for Knights and

Paladins of The Republic, he continued to stay at the Pension on his visits to Terra. The old building and the cozy decor suited his tastes, and Madame Flambard—in addition to being the soul of discretion and offering a profound respect for his privacy—knew his requirements without being told. He had no reason to change his quarters.

Today Madame herself was waiting for him at the front desk. In keeping with the rest of the pension's decor, the desk's outward appearance was carefully antique, with a brass bell resting on the polished wood of the counter next to a handwritten registry book and an arrangement of dried flowers in a porcelain vase. Appearances could, and in this case did, deceive; as Jonah had good reason to know, the Pension Flambard maintained sophisticated voice communications and a powerful data connection. But Madame preferred to keep such things tucked away, and Jonah—who enjoyed having at least the illusion of being hard to find by the curious and by the general public—considered her taste in these matters to be part of the Pension's charm.

"It's good to see you again, Monsieur Levin," Madame said. "Will you want your usual room?"

"If it isn't occupied," Jonah said. The situation with the still-patchy HPG network made getting an advance reservation difficult. One could never be certain that a message had reached its recipient intact and in a timely fashion.

Madame smiled. "When I heard on the news that Exarch Redburn had called for the election, I said to myself, 'Monsieur Levin will be returning to us for this,' and I put down your name for your customary accommodations."

"Thank you," said Jonah. "Believe me, I appreciate your consideration."

She gave an expressive shrug that said more with silence than most people say in a handful of sentences. "You are a quiet man, Monsieur, and you do not leave your rooms in wreckage. I would be a fool to lose you to the likes of the Hotel Duquesne." She produced a plastic card from one of the many pigeonholes behind the desk and handed it to Jonah. "Your key. Will you be staying with us for very long this time?"

"Longer than last time, I'm afraid," said Jonah regretfully. "These things take a great deal of preparation. Not even Damien Redburn can hold an election on almost no notice."

"Very true, Monsieur."

Jonah looked at Madame's courteous but noncommittal face and wondered which of the candidates for Exarch she might favor. Not that Devlin Stone had trusted such a decision to the masses; he had chosen instead to put it into the hands of the Paladins.

Still, Jonah thought, a wise man should consider the wishes of those who would be living with his choice. He thought about asking Madame about her preference directly, then abandoned the idea. Madame Flambard never discussed politics or personal matters with her guests. It would not be right to ask her to abandon her business principles purely to gratify his curiosity.

He accepted his key and went up the stairs to his usual room. He had carried a single bag from the DropPort; the rest of his luggage would arrive by taxi later today.

After locking the door behind him, he allowed himself to relax into the room's comforting familiarity. Madame Flambard replaced items as they broke or showed signs of wear, but she had not changed the pension's decor during all the time Jonah had known her. The room's crisply ironed floral print curtains, its varnished floor scattered with rugs, its antique wooden bedstead, desk, chair—all of these were the same as when he had checked into the Pension for the first time.

Jonah liked that. Too many things changed too fast in life; it was good to have a few things remain the same.

He went to the room's data terminal, which was concealed within the rolltop desk. After a moment's thought, he began composing a letter to his wife Anna, back home on Kervil:

> *Dear Anna,*
> *I have arrived safely in Geneva. The journey was uneventful, which made for a dull time of it, but some things don't improve by being made more interesting. Space travel, in my opinion, is one of them.*
> *All of the Paladins have been recalled, although*

one or two have yet to arrive. It is clear from what I read on the journey here, and from what I have seen myself, that our presence here is causing a great deal of political uneasiness. Demonstrators fill the streets, and everyone I meet seems to have a platform to stand on and a candidate for Exarch to favor, even though this election is one in which none of them can vote. All that means is that they need to find other ways to exert their influence. Some opt for marching through the streets with placards, others for creating disturbances damaging or violent enough to get them on the news vids, while still others—mostly rumors, at this point—seem to be set on getting what they want by intimidating the Paladins.

They don't know my fellow Paladins very well.

There are splinter groups of all varieties. Some of them believe that The Republic should not only defend its current boundaries in the present crisis, but should expand them. Others believe that The Republic should pull back from the areas where it's been hurt the most and is spread too thin; save the core in exchange for losing some of the worlds on the edge.

And those are the relatively sane ones. I don't even want to think about the people who believe that Devlin Stone is asleep under a mountain someplace along with Charlemagne, King Arthur, Frederick Barbarossa, and the Hidden Imam, waiting to come back and save us in his people's hour of greatest need. Or even sillier things.

This is going to be a long election. I wish that it could be quickly over and done with so that I could return home to you . . . but I don't think I'm going to get my wish.

11

Hotel Duquesne, Geneva
Terra, Prefecture X
26 November 3134

Night was drawing on toward morning when Gareth Sinclair exited his taxi at the main entrance to the Hotel Duquesne. To be honest, he preferred the Clermont, where his family customarily stayed, or any number of other hotels that were not the target of the glaring light of Geneva's politics. But his DropShip had made planetfall later than scheduled, it was a wet, foggy two a.m., and Gareth lacked the energy to trek all over Geneva in search of a bed. If ever there was a time to take advantage of The Republic's standing arrangement with the Hotel Duquesne to hold a block of rooms on a permanent basis for Knights and Paladins traveling to Geneva on business, this was it.

The rain that had been falling when Gareth arrived in Geneva was still falling as he stood at the door of the taxi and paid the fare. Warm golden light, made hazy by the falling rain, spilled out through the open doors of the hotel lobby and onto the pavement, and onto Gareth's suitcases—standing in the puddle where the taxi driver had dumped them.

Gareth wondered if dumping the suitcases just there had been a political statement, or if the driver had merely been moved to unpleasantness by the combination of foul weather and the late hour. He suspected the latter but tipped the driver properly all the same. The taxi departed in a spray of water, soaking both Gareth and his luggage.

Definitely a political statement, Gareth concluded. There goes a man who blames The Republic of the Sphere for something, and who will take it out on The Republic's visible representatives whenever he gets the chance.

The phenomenon, unfortunately, was not an uncommon one in these unsettled times. With a faint sigh, Gareth picked up his suitcases and, squelching only a little, entered the hotel lobby.

Somewhat to his surprise, even the working uniform of a Knight of the Sphere turned out to be enough to bring the hotel's concierge out from his office behind the main desk. Gareth suspected that the man must have hidden surveillance cameras monitoring the hotel entrance; there certainly wasn't a direct line of sight between his office and the front door.

"Welcome to Geneva, Sir Knight!" The concierge was a short man whose crimson jacket was ornamented with enough gold braid and gold buttons to cast even a Paladin's full-dress uniform into the shade. The lack of hair atop his rounded skull was made up for by the luxuriant abundance of his impeccably groomed and waxed mustache. "Will you be requiring accommodation just for this evening, or for a longer stay?"

"I'll be staying in Geneva through the election, at least," Gareth said.

The concierge smiled broadly. "Yes, sir. Simply present this to the clerk at the desk, and all the proper arrangements will be made."

Gareth knew of The Republic's arrangement with the hotel, but that never stopped him from attempting to pay his own way. "I have an account at the Bank du Nord. I can draw on that to cover—"

The concierge waved his hand. "No, no. The Duquesne is always honored to serve The Republic, and what favors we extend to one of The Republic's servants, policy requires us to extend to all."

"Yes, yes," said Gareth, sighing. Maybe if he carried his own luggage that would make him feel less uncomfortable at the accommodations being thrust upon him. "Thank you. I'll just—"

"Emil!"

The word blew in on an exhalation of cold air from the closing doors of the front entrance, followed by light, sharp footsteps crossing the lobby at a quick stride. Before Gareth could turn, Heather GioAvanti swept past him to envelope the concierge in a quick hug before stepping back and looking the man up and down.

"Good lord, Emil, it's past midnight. Doesn't this hotel ever let you sleep?"

The concierge's answering smile was one of friendly recognition and genuine personal regard. "Not when all the Sphere is coming to Geneva for the election, Paladin GioAvanti."

Heather GioAvanti noticed Gareth for the first time and turned to include him in the conversation. "Lord Gareth. I should have realized you'd be staying here as well; we could have shared a taxi from the DropPort. Has Emil—"

"Provided me with a room?" He knew that he sounded a bit stiff and awkward, but he couldn't help it. "Yes."

She gave him a smile warmer than the concierge's. Gareth had trouble believing she was the same woman he'd last seen putting the government of Woodstock and the Eridani Light Horse in their place. Her loosened hair and friendly smile made her seem much younger, and he wondered which face belonged to the real Heather GioAvanti.

"I would have been completely lost my first time in Geneva if it hadn't been for Emil," Heather was saying. "Before that, I'd never even been to Terra."

Gareth recalled what he knew of Heather GioAvanti's personal history, specifically, the rumor that she had broken with her family after her elevation to Paladin, so that no one could reproach her for conflict of interest. He wondered if the change had come as shock to her, moving in one leap from a life spent among mercenaries to a position as one of the seventeen most powerful men and women in The Republic of the Sphere.

"It must have been quite an experience," he said aloud. "I remember how impressed I was by everything, the first time I came here." He didn't add that he had been scarcely an adolescent at the time.

"Oh, it was," she said. "But Emil took good care of me, and I've stayed at the Duquesne on my visits ever since."

She bade a polite farewell to the concierge, then headed for the front desk. Gareth followed. They both registered and were given room numbers: she on the fifteenth floor, he on the twenty-second.

In the elevator, Gareth asked, "Do most of the Paladins stay here at the Duquesne?"

"Some," she said. "Most? I don't think so. Tyrina Drummond stays here, I know, and so does Otto Mandela. I don't know about the others. One or two have places they keep year-round—flats in the city, chalets up near the mountains, that sort of thing. Anders Kessel has rooms practically on top of the Paladins' meeting chamber; I believe he'd sleep in the chamber itself if that was a possibility."

"Have you ever thought of buying a place of your own?" He might, he thought, if he were ever made a Paladin. The family's money would certainly extend to it.

"Not really. For a long time I couldn't have afforded it, and now that I can, it still seems like a waste. A room is a room. Besides—" she smiled again "—the Duquesne is optimally suited for people watching and rumormongering. If I stay here, I can see everyone else in Geneva come and go."

12

***Grand Ballroom of the Hotel Duquesne, Geneva
Terra, Prefecture X
26 November 3134***

The Exarch's reception took place in the grand ballroom
of the Hotel Duquesne, on the eve of the opening of the
Electoral Conclave. Tri-vid reporters and videographers
prowled the streets outside, capturing images of the
Sphere's most important men and women for the benefit
of the masses. Emil the concierge was in his element, greeting each new arrival by name as he or she passed through
the Duquesne's lobby on the way to the reception.

Everyone, from reporters to hotel workers to government staffers, complained about the timing of the elections.
Wasn't the last week of November supposed to be a long
holiday? But this was the timing the Exarch had chosen,
for reasons he wasn't explaining. And since the Exarch said
people must work, they would work.

The Republic's Hall of Government most assuredly had
spaces in it big enough to hold the reception, but Jonah
wondered if its catering resources matched the Duquesne's
five-star kitchen. The tables in the hotel's grand ballroom
were spread with exotic foodstuffs from a score of different

worlds, accompanied by drinks of all kinds, from throat-clawing Northwind whiskies to pure water from springs deep in Terra's own granite mountain ranges. Presumably, the Exarch believed that an abundance of food and drink would work toward easing the inevitable tension.

Jonah hoped that Damien Redburn was right. It was difficult to get the seventeen Paladins—along with their aides, support staff, and the inevitable hangers-on—to agree on anything, including what appetizers to serve, and the high stakes of the upcoming election only heightened the tension. If drink were going to ease this tension, it would have to be plenty strong.

Jonah, as usual, had brought no staff members with him. He maintained an office and employed several staffers back on Kervil, but he had left them all behind to keep an eye on local affairs in his absence. He didn't want the Knight who'd taken over for him pro tempore to make too big a hash of things before he could return. Any support personnel that Jonah required on Terra he would engage on a temporary basis, per his long-standing habit.

"Paladin Levin?"

The speaker was a youngish man in the dress uniform of a Knight of the Sphere. There were a fair number of those uniforms scattered throughout the ballroom; Jonah supposed that all of the Knights currently on Terra had received courtesy invitations to the reception. This particular Knight was tall for a MechWarrior, with light brown hair and a pleasant if rather long and angular face. Jonah found the man's appearance vaguely familiar—another moment, and his memory supplied him with a matching name and context.

"Gareth Sinclair, isn't it? We worked together on Ryde a few years ago, after the meteor strike."

"That's right." Sinclair smiled, as if happy to be recognized. "I'm surprised that you remember me. I was mostly running errands and directing traffic."

That was, Jonah reflected, a massive understatement. When the meteor had hit the continent of Kale, one of the few habitable places on Ryde, the resulting social and ecological breakdown, combined with spilled chemicals from Ryde's many plants, had required the full-time attention of a Paladin and half a dozen Knights of the Sphere. The seven of them, along with a support team the size of a small army, had labored for more than six months just to get things back to where long-term aid and reconstruction might actually have a chance to work.

Jonah said, "You also had to deal with that enterprising gentleman who believed that losing comms with the planetary capital meant that he could set up his own little kingdom out in the backwoods. I believe there was some fighting involved—you were piloting a *Black Hawk* 'Mech at the time, if I recall correctly."

Sinclair nodded. "I still do, whenever I get the chance. I like *Black Hawks*. I did my initial training in one, and they're what I know best."

"They're good 'Mechs," Jonah agreed, although he himself preferred a heavier 'Mech such as his own *Atlas*, now safe in a hangar at the DropPort. He didn't like resolving disputes by force, but when only force remained, he felt happiest with a 'Mech that could deliver a blow strong enough to settle the issue. He'd seen the principle stated most clearly in an inscription cast into the iron barrel of a cannon on display outside one of Terra's many museums: *ultima ratio regum*, the final argument of kings.

Sinclair, meanwhile, was looking around the crowded ballroom. "I don't think I've ever seen this many Knights and Paladins in one place before."

Jonah nodded agreement. "It's only a few of the Knights, relatively speaking, but you're right about the Paladins. All but three of us are here this evening."

"Three?" Sinclair's gaze flickered around the room again. "I know that Victor Steiner-Davion isn't here—he doesn't travel these days, so he's going to be addressing the convocation tomorrow by tri-vid hookup—and David McKinnon is still on Skye, but who else is missing?"

"You're forgetting the Ghost Paladin."

Sinclair reddened a little—the curse, Jonah supposed, of a fair complexion. "Oh. Yes. I'd forgotten about him."

"Or her," Jonah said.

"Yes. He or she isn't here tonight either. So far as we know."

"So far as we know," agreed Jonah.

Silence fell for a minute. Then Sinclair's expression brightened. "I see Paladin GioAvanti over there, by the potted palms. We traveled from Woodstock on the same DropShip; I should go and wish her a good evening."

He faded away into the crowd, wearing the expression—had he but known it—of a young man determined to speak with a pretty girl.

Jonah suppressed a smile. Paladin GioAvanti was strong, forceful and opinionated, characteristics that occasionally alienated her more old-fashioned potential suitors. But she was a handsome woman, and she possessed an undeniable charisma. Most Paladins did. Jonah wondered, not for the first time, what an essentially unremarkable man like him was doing in such dazzling company.

He abandoned that line of thought—his Anna, if she knew of it, would have already scolded him for giving in to imposter syndrome. He moved around the ballroom instead, taking in the groupings and constellations of the guests.

Thaddeus Marik and Otto Mandela held court with a group of Knights, describing a battle they had fought together before either were even Knights. It was a safer topic than politics, and their relaxed listeners laughed easily at their account.

Tyrina Drummond and Meraj Jorgensson were talking together earnestly in one corner, next to a table serving smoked salmon on flat crackers and some kind of transparent liquor in frosted glasses. Jonah made the mistake of reaching for an hors d'oeuvre, putting him in their conversational orbit.

"Victor will try to control us," Drummond said in dire tones. "He thinks he can play at kingmaker."

Jorgensson shrugged. "That is okay. Victor has shown that he is on the right side of things often enough. If he wants to use his influence to make sure someone qualified ascends to Exarch, what harm is there in that?"

"Steiner-Davion did not form The Republic. He had his chance; he was far more powerful than Devlin Stone early in his life. But he failed where Stone succeeded—he could never unite the Sphere. He could not do it then, and I do not see why we should trust him to do it now." Her eyes caught Jonah's. "Paladin Levin. Surely you will not be subject to Steiner-Davion's manipulations."

"Nobody, not even Steiner-Davion, has attempted to manipulate me yet," Jonah said through a mouthful of fish. Until you, Tyrina, he silently added as he ducked away.

He was buried in a mass of staffers for a time, finally emerging in front of Kaffyd Op Owens and Maya Avellar.

"We are here to preserve Devlin Stone's vision," Owens

said in insistent tones. "Our borders are being eroded, our weakness is being exposed. We need to restore our strength and restore our borders." Staffers around Owens murmured their agreement.

"I agree that we must defend against further invasions, but escalating the war is asking for trouble," Avellar returned. "The more we encourage the Clans to hate us, the stronger their future assaults against us will be. We have to find a way to deal with them besides incessant warfare."

"We didn't choose that method! They did! They brought the war to us, we are only responding!"

"The vision of The Republic is one of peace! We are supposed to rise above petty provocation!"

Jonah could see where this discussion was headed, and he wanted no part of it. He stepped backward, bumping squarely into Anders Kessel.

"Neither of them is going to convince the other," Kessel said with a sad shake of his head, "especially with Owens spouting the lines David McKinnon would use if he were here. Their eloquence is best saved for Paladins who might be swayed."

Jonah glanced at the sparring partners over his shoulder. "I don't think they're considering politics right now," he said.

Kessel smiled, an expression that always seemed more genuine on him in the vids than it did in real life. "They have that in common with you," he said.

"I suppose."

"You know you can't avoid it, though," Kessel said, crinkling his gray eyes. "By yourself, you represent nearly six percent of the vote. Did you know that? Have you thought about the power a single vote has in our council?"

Jonah looked Kessel square in the face. "Yes. Honestly, I've given it a lot of thought."

"I knew you would have. While the rest of them are playing games, you're doing the real spadework."

Jonah sighed, hoping Kessel noticed. Flattery was the inevitable first step of a political courtship.

"You and Victor, that is," Kessel added.

"Victor?"

"Rumor is he's putting in long hours on a secret project. The smart money says whatever it is could determine the outcome of the election. Though I'm sure you've heard similar rumors already."

"I don't hear many rumors," Jonah said, applying a light veneer of scorn to the final word.

Kessel ignored it. "Then start listening. I know you think I'm just playing silly games, but the future of The Republic is at stake. There's nothing silly about getting the right person in place."

Jonah noticed that Kessel was not yet ready to commit to who that "right person" might be. Just then, a loud burst from Owens and the crowd surrounding him drew Kessel's attention, and Jonah took advantage of the moment to slip away.

He found a corner free of any other Paladins. He looked over the room, thinking of how all these people were going to be penned up together in Geneva until they agreed upon the next Exarch. The Paladins had originally been a close-knit group, bound together by loyalty to Devlin Stone and to The Republic; but like any small group that needed to work together for a long time, familiarity had produced its own tensions and disagreements. The troubles of recent years, and the void left by Stone's resignation and disappearance, and the fact that The Republic was large enough to keep the Paladins apart at most times, had only made things worse. Damien Redburn was a good man and Devlin Stone's chosen successor, but he wasn't able to inspire an equivalent level of profound emotional commitment. And now the Paladins were expected to choose one of their own number to take over his position.

The situation reminded Jonah Levin of the story he'd once heard about an old hermit in the North American desert who would amuse himself by capturing scorpions and throwing them into a jar, then sealing the lid. He would leave the jar sealed overnight, and by morning all of the creatures inside it would be dead—stung to death by their comrades in misfortune.

A shiver passed down Jonah's back. The story was not really that amusing . . . but it was an explanation, perhaps, for why Damien Redburn had chosen to call for elections at the earliest legal moment. The man had been living inside that jar for years.

$\equiv$ **13** $\equiv$

***Residence of Paladin Victor Steiner-Davion,
Santa Fe
Terra, Prefecture X
26 November 3134***

Darkness had fallen once again in Santa Fe and Victor Steiner-Davion was back in his office, leaning back in his desk chair, a glass of whisky in his hand. The whisky wasn't good for him, but he didn't care. No matter what the medical staff here thought, he'd reached an age when a man was entitled to a few moderate vices. After all, it wasn't as if he had to worry much about the long-term effects of anything.

Tonight, moreover, was an occasion for at least modest celebration. His report to the Paladins was finished—both the extended version for publication, fully annotated and with transcripts of all the evidence, and the short summary version that he would present tomorrow in his live speech to the assembled Paladins. He would put on his full-dress uniform for the first time in years, he would go down to the tri-vid studio in the headquarters complex, and he would tell the other Paladins in his own voice exactly how bad the problem was.

He would have preferred to make the physical journey to Geneva and deliver his speech in person, but he had known from the start that such an appearance, personally satisfying though it might be, was unlikely to be possible. His energy failed him too easily these days, and the mere mention of so much travel would set his nurses and physicians to shaking their heads and making grave pronouncements.

A real-time hookup, then, would have to do. He had labored over the speech for long enough; anything he did tonight would be mere nervous tinkering. He would finish his whisky, then go to bed and rest for tomorrow and an old Paladin's last hurrah.

Victor lifted his glass. "Here's to The Republic and to the dream of Devlin Stone."

He drained the last of the whisky and set the glass down on his desktop.

All of the lights in the room went out.

In the silence that followed, he realized that all of the electronics in the room had gone quiet as well. Their mostly unheard and forgotten sixty-cycle hum, that on a normal day droned on steadily beneath everything, was dead.

The outer door to his apartment clicked open. No light followed the sound; the hall outside was also dark. No power there either, Victor thought. Whoever had entered would have had to use the emergency key—and yet, no alarm had sounded.

Somebody was in the outer room, moving with deliberate quiet.

This, thought Victor, was not good. He pushed his chair away from the table so that he could stand unimpeded. He marked where faint beams of light from outside penetrated the windows, making the shadows of the room even deeper by contrast. He knew where the intruder would have to walk to reach him. The intruder would have night-vision goggles, while Victor would have his knowledge of the room's furnishings to guide him.

All the instincts honed by a lifetime spent in war and politics were sounding an alarm even louder than the one that should have been shrilling throughout the entire headquarters complex. Victor had understood as soon as the door had opened that they wanted him dead.

He didn't have much doubt as to who "they" were. He'd outlived or made peace with all of his old enemies—except, of course, his sister, but if she came after him she wouldn't strike in the dark. She'd want to be sure to see his face.

Anybody else left from his youth or his middle age who might harbor a lingering grievance against him had stopped trying to act on it years before. This was a new quarrel, and he'd only done one thing lately that might account for it.

In the dark, he smiled a little. If he'd wanted a final proof that the structure of ideas he'd built up so laboriously was solid, he had it now. Somebody intended to kill him over it.

They would succeed. He had no illusions about that. He was an old man, older than he'd ever expected to be, older perhaps than he'd ever had a right to expect, and the person moving quietly through the darkened outer room would be without doubt a professional in the prime of life. That person would kill him, and would destroy his work.

Moving in silence, he reached out and grasped the empty whisky glass. His other hand found the decanter. He stood, the glass in his left hand, the bottle in his right, and stepped away from the desk. He backed to the wall and allowed the bottle to hang from his fingertips. Then he swung it backward, so that the bottom rim struck the wall. The glass shattered away from the point of impact, leaving him with a jagged dagger below the bottle's neck. The noise of its shattering was as loud as blasphemy in the deadly silence. The scent of alcohol surrounded him.

He had a weapon now. Not enough to save his life, or even to take his assailant down with him. But enough, even in the hand of an old man, to mark the other, and mark the scene.

One of the beams of outside light flickered as a black-clad shape passed through it and stepped closer. Victor realized that the plan must be to make the agency of his death look like some natural cause or accident of fate—a heart attack, a pulmonary embolism, something that his doctors could shake their heads sadly about and say, "Well, he was an old man." That would explain why the killer hadn't already used a laser pistol or other projectile weapon. They must have expected him to be asleep, allowing them to slip in, do the job, and leave with as few traces as possible. They wouldn't expect him to be awake, and they hopefully wouldn't expect him to put up a fight. It was a small advantage, but at least it was something.

Considered in that light, Victor thought, his course of action was clear. If he could make it plain enough that his death had been not accident but murder, then all the rest would come out in time.

No point in waiting any longer. Victor threw the heavy crystal tumbler with a sidearm toss he'd learned nearly a century before on the grenade range, aiming for the intruder's head. The man would duck, or, if luck ran wild, might even lose his goggles. And the low coffee table barely a foot away would hamper him, maybe even trip him, if he tried to sidestep.

Victor was no longer as quick on his feet as he had been even twenty years ago, but when fighting for his life, a man can do wonders. He was moving fast, forward, around his desk, toward the spot where his would-be assassin had yelled with surprise and fallen.

Victor shouted out a hoarse and wordless war cry of his own. A warrior dies bloody, he thought, and am I not a Paladin still? In the next breath he was on his opponent, clawing for the night-vision goggles with his left hand, stabbing downward with the broken bottle in his right.

Then strong arms seized him from behind, pressing a cloth over his face, and his heart sank. There had been two assassins, and not just one.

He kicked backward and felt his heel strike a shin. The second man's grip loosened. He tried to twist, tried an elbow strike, but a pain bloomed in his chest, running up to his jaw and down his left arm. A pinched nerve, he thought. Cold sweat started on his forehead. He couldn't breathe.

The cloth over his mouth and nose pressed harder. He felt like a 'Mech was standing on his chest. He stabbed backward with the neck of the broken decanter and felt a slight resistance. Then the pain overwhelmed him and he dropped the bottle. He heard nothing more. The pain grew, becoming worse than any he had ever felt, and he fell into blackness darker even than a lightless room in Santa Fe.

*   *   *

Elena Ruiz came to work in the morning with a cheerful heart. She'd had a good night last night; dinner with Henrik was always nice, but this had been one of their better evenings. The old Paladin had gone to sleep early, and her periodic remote checks on his health and welfare showed nothing on her pager but a darkened apartment, with all security and biometric systems reading green. She'd enjoyed a pleasant meal, for once free from concern about Victor Steiner-Davion's habit of burning the midnight oil, and had slept soundly afterward.

Today was a clear, sunny morning, and the November air was dry and cold. Inside the building, Elena took a moment to hang up her jacket in the staff coatroom—the heat in the retirement wing was always kept higher than in the main part of building. From the coatroom, she made her way to Victor Steiner-Davion's suite.

The door was locked—not surprising, since the old man was careful enough about such things to qualify as paranoid—so she had to open the outer door with her passkey. She put on her professional smile and cheerful voice. "Paladin Steiner-Davion?" she said as she opened the door.

Elena wasn't surprised when she failed to get an answer. She expected that the Paladin had fallen asleep at his desk again, as he so often did these days. She let the outer door swing shut behind her and moved on into the apartment, purposefully making no effort to be silent. The noise of her voice and her footsteps usually proved sufficient to wake him, if he happened to still be asleep after sunrise. This time, however, there was no response.

"Paladin Steiner-Davion?" she asked again. And then she found him.

14

Jonah Levin, wearing the full-dress uniform of a Paladin of the Sphere, presented himself at the Hall of Government in the early afternoon.

For this trip, Jonah had taken a taxi from the Pension Flambard, rather than traveling on foot or by public transport as was his more usual habit. The streets of Geneva, today and for the next month, were going to be crawling with tri-vid photographers and with news reporters of all stripes. A taxi could deliver him straight to the main entrance of the Hall and into the arms of the security cordon stationed there, while giving the predatory newshounds only a minimal chance to attack.

Jonah was a firm believer in the public's right to know, but he was an even firmer believer in his own privacy. As far as he was concerned, his opinion of the Exarch's decision to call for an early election, and his thoughts on which of his fellow Paladins might be suitable for the job, all fell into the category clearly marked as "personal information; nobody else's business."

Once past the security barrier, he ignored the shouted questions, the clicking and whirring of tri-vid cameras as operators jostled one another for position, and strode quickly into the Hall. Answering just one question would be worse than answering none. He could look earnest and in a hurry and preoccupied with important Paladin-level thoughts, and get away with saying nothing—but if he said anything at all, he would either have to throw the floor open to questions from all sides, or risk an accusation of playing favorites.

Inside the Hall's rotunda, a couple of the Exarch's aides were deftly moving the arriving Paladins off to a small waiting room at one side. The room was crowded, and rapidly growing overheated as well; it wasn't really meant to hold so many people at once. Tempers were already starting to fray.

The first thing Jonah saw and heard as the door to the rotunda closed behind him was Tyrina Drummond, impressive in the combination of a full Paladin's uniform and Clan Nova Cat ritual tattoos, complaining sharply to Maya Avellar, "What are we being kept in here for?"

"They want us to cross the rotunda and enter the Chamber of Paladins together, I think," Paladin Avellar replied in calming tones. "It will look better, this first day, than having us straggle in one at a time."

Drummond remained unmollified. "Better to whom?"

Jonah felt moved to rescue Avellar, who had never, to his knowledge, meshed well with the Nova Cat Paladin. "For our friends outside with the tri-vid cameras, I suspect."

"Scavengers," said Drummond, tight-lipped, and Jonah reflected that none of the Clans had ever dealt easily with or truly understood The Republic's press. "Voyeurs."

"Mouthpiece of the people," Kessel countered. His steel gray hair looked as perfect in person as it did on camera, the location of each strand carefully chosen. "Remember the people? The ones we're supposed to serve?"

Drummond only glared in return.

"They're the eyes and ears of all those who can't be here today," Jonah said, not entirely comfortable to be agreeing with Kessel. "If they see us do this right, their support will come more easily."

"We shouldn't have to keep winning their support," Drummond grumbled.

"Being seen entering the chamber together in good order will reassure people," Heather GioAvanti chimed in. "Right now we have their future in our hands; they'll want to believe we're not treating it as a casual matter."

"You trust them too much," Thaddeus Marik said in a quiet voice that somehow carried across the room. "The people—the media—they thrive on innuendo, on rumor, more than on truth. They will tear us apart sooner than encourage support for us. We're letting vipers into our home."

Drummond, GioAvanti and Kessel all started to reply, and Jonah rolled his eyes. They weren't even going to get into their chambers without an argument.

"Either we take this election seriously, or we do not," Drummond was saying heatedly. "Feigning for the tri-vids will not change what is within."

"There's no harm in showing our dedication," said Heather GioAvanti, "so long as we're not simply posing. But if we feel contempt for our people instead of respect"—here her glance flicked to Marik—"that will show."

Marik opened his mouth, but the opening of the doors behind him stole away his retort. The Exarch's senior aide stuck her head in through the gap. "Everybody here? Good. We're all set up for you to enter the chamber now."

The Paladins fell silent. The door swung all the way open, and they proceeded across the rotunda to the massive double doors of the chamber. Somebody had thoughtfully laid down a strip of deep red carpet to mark the path—nobody wants to risk the Paladins getting lost on the way, Jonah thought; it would look bad for The Republic—and had put up gold barrier cords on either side. Looks like they don't want us escaping, either.

He knew he was doing the Exarch and his staff at least a partial injustice, out of a dislike for being forced into so much show. The cords would have primarily been set up to keep the spectators and reporters from getting underfoot.

One after another, the Paladins filed into the chamber and took the half circle of seats nearest the Exarch's podium. Unlike the rest of the tiered rows of seats that filled the Chamber of Paladins and the balcony above, these seventeen places were more like booths. Each one contained a fully equipped desk and two chairs, one for the seat's official occupant plus another for conversations and conferences.

The rest of the chamber filled up quickly. The rows closest to the Paladins were filled by those Knights of the Sphere who were in attendance, and the aides and staff members of the seventeen Paladins. Beyond that, the seats were packed with commentators and tri-vid reporters and sound and camera operators. As many as there were in attendance, they still didn't fill the giant, echoing hall.

The Exarch's place remained empty; Redburn would enter the chamber last, through a different door. More theater, Jonah thought, to emphasize the Exarch's separation from the Paladins, despite having been elected from among their number. At least half of Devlin Stone's genius—the underappreciated half, in Jonah's opinion—had been for public relations and the language of dramatic symbolism.

Three of the Paladins' seats were empty today as well. One of them had been largely unoccupied for as long as Levin had been a Paladin, since Victor Steiner-Davion seldom left his semiretirement at the Knights' headquarters complex in Santa Fe. The second was a more recent emptiness. Until last year, that seat had belonged to the traitor and fallen Paladin Ezekiel Crow. The third was David McKinnon's; he was involved in the fighting on Skye.

Today the tri-vid cameras—on booms, or on wands, or in the hands of nimble operators standing on chairs or balanced in window embrasures—were focusing on Crow's empty seat. One of Damien Redburn's last important decisions as Exarch would be the appointment of a new Paladin to fill it. Speculation about likely candidates had been rife in the newssheets and on the live media, and on the street as well, ever since Jonah's arrival on Terra.

The small door next to the Exarch's podium opened. A hush fell over the chamber as Damien Redburn entered and moved to stand behind the podium. Light flashed off a hundred lenses as the myriad cameras changed position to record the Exarch's words and actions for posterity. Even from his seat among the Paladins, Jonah could see that Redburn looked more tired than usual, as though he had either stayed up all night or had been awakened rudely from sleep.

"Greetings," said Redburn into the quiet, "and welcome to the Paladins of the Sphere gathered here. I also welcome the members of the media gathered here, and the vast throngs watching our deliberations today. On this solemn occasion . . ."

It had taken years, but Jonah had finally mastered the art of sitting completely still and looking attentive when the Exarch made a speech. He'd also mastered the other skill crucial to surviving Paladin meetings: reading and typing messages on the desk's data screen while seeming to pay rapt attention to the Exarch's words.

> What's the over/under on the time of the intro remarks?—Jorgensson
> I had five minutes in the pool.—GioAvanti
> If our Exarch can speak for only five minutes, he's truly tiring of political life.—Mandela
> DISRESPECTFUL.—Drummond

Most of Drummond's contributions to their side conversations were along that line. Jonah thought they would be better served by not including her in the off-topic messages in the first place, but some of the others enjoyed provoking her.

> Sooner he ends, sooner we get to the real business: replacement for Crow. Any thoughts?—Kessel

There was a pause before Heather finally responded.

> We never got around to taking bets on that.—GioAvanti

Everyone, of course, had some ideas—or at least hopes—of who might be appointed. But no one was willing to share them, especially with Kessel. The sooner Kessel had a name in his head, the more time he'd have to plan how to win them to his side.

". . . meets the high standards for Paladins set by Devlin

Stone. It is my honor to present Lady Janella Lakewood, Knight of the Sphere, as the next Paladin of the Republic."

Applause swept the chamber, and all fifteen Paladins in attendance rose to their feet to welcome their new colleague. Lakewood was both competent and well liked, and people in the chamber, including some of the Paladins, were still clapping and whistling as she rose from her place with the Knights and came down to take her seat among the Paladins. Lakewood herself appeared nervous but determined, and at the same time happy—not an unexpected combination of emotions, Jonah thought.

As soon as the Paladins were seated, most of them reached for their keyboards to send congratulations to Lakewood and exchange reactions with each other. But a note in Redburn's voice stopped them.

"I had planned, at this point, to officially commence deliberations on the choice of my successor. I would give anything to be able to follow that course.

"Unfortunately, I must make an unanticipated announcement. This morning . . ."

To the astonishment of everyone in the room, Redburn's voice broke. He looked down, picked up a piece of paper, and read directly from it.

"At seven-fifteen local time this morning, Paladin Victor Steiner-Davion was found in his office in Santa Fe, dead of an apparent heart attack."

The collective audience in the chamber gasped as one. At least one reporter dropped his noteputer to the floor, while others dashed out of the room to get the news out as quickly as possible. Others stayed, waiting for any further information Redburn might supply.

"The Republic of the Sphere knew no greater friend or servant than Victor Steiner-Davion. In the course of his long life . . ."

Long live Victor Steiner-Davion!—Owens

The words stood alone on the screen of each Paladin before anyone else responded.

Several Paladins then followed with tribute messages of their own. It didn't take long, though, for politics to rear its head.

What happens now? Another appointment, or
do we deliberate with only fifteen?—Avellar

Jonah's first impulse was to respond with anger, saying
it was too soon to talk about Victor's successor. Legends
are not simply replaced.

But he knew it wasn't too soon. With the unrest spreading across The Republic and Redburn's call for an election,
the Paladins could not take time to mourn.

He must be replaced. We cannot vote without a
full seventeen.—Drummond
Wasn't Victor scheduled to speak today?—
Jorgensson
Yes. Anybody know his planned topic?—
Mandela
Not as far as I know. He was playing his cards
close to his vest.—GioAvanti

The speech. Jonah hadn't thought about that. He'd been
anxious to hear what Victor had to say, hoping that some
part of the elder Paladin's address would help him clarify
his own thoughts on voting for Exarch. He didn't slavishly
follow Victor's direction—not by a long shot—but Jonah
knew he'd be foolish to disregard the senior Paladin's input.

This timing is nightmarish. Poor Victor.—
GioAvanti
I had counted on him being here to help us.—
Avellar

Something tickled the back of Jonah's mind. The timing
was incredibly bad; suspiciously bad, even. Redburn had
mentioned a heart attack, but the timing of Victor's death
could not help but raise suspicion. His remarks would have
been pivotal; now they were lost. That might prove convenient for someone.

He glanced at his screen again. Kessel surely had some
reaction to the news, but he had sent no comment. Neither
had Sorenson, widely known as no friend of Victor's. Surely
they had something to say, and chances were they were
saying it only to each other. Kessel, in particular, must have

immediately realized that Victor's death threw the election wide open, and would have immediately moved to take advantage of it. In fact, if anyone had something to gain . . .

Jonah squelched that line of thought before it even started. The political debate was going to be bad enough, and it wouldn't help to start casting aspersions on his fellow Paladins.

". . . a decision especially crucial in this time of election," Redburn was saying. "I cannot, I will not promise you that the new Paladin will take the place of Victor Steiner-Davion. No one could. The new Paladin will make his own place, as all Paladins have done. Paladins of The Republic, officers of the Sphere, ladies and gentlemen of the media, I present to you Knight Gareth Sinclair."

Sinclair—looking overwhelmed—left the Knights and walked down to Steiner-Davion's empty desk. The applause this time was more hesitant and muted, not from disapproval of Sinclair, Jonah knew, but because people were still processing the news of his predecessor's death.

Jonah applauded quietly along with the rest of the Paladins as Gareth Sinclair took his seat. Not until the sound had died away did Jonah happen to look back at his desk screen. A new message had appeared.

Levin: Preliminary reports suggest that Victor Steiner-Davion's death was not due to natural causes. I want you to conduct the investigation.—Redburn

15

Chamber of Paladins, Geneva
Terra, Prefecture X
27 November 3134

"In the name of everything, Damien—why me?"

As soon as the brief opening session of the Electoral Conclave had ended, Jonah had cornered Damien Redburn in the small office just off the chamber. The room was little more than a nook for transacting private business, with its interior and exterior doors separated by a desk-and-chairs setup that had plainly come out of the same design box as the Paladins' seats in the larger room. The main purpose of the space was to connect the Exarch's side entrance to the Chamber of Paladins with the rest of the Hall of Government. Only the presence of a single narrow window overlooking the street outside kept it from being a well-lit, carpeted closet.

At the moment, neither Jonah nor the Exarch was sitting down. Redburn stood by the window, looking defensive; Jonah faced him from a point barely inside the closed door.

"It's necessary," Redburn said.

And again, Jonah demanded, "Why me?"

"I need to assign a Paladin to handle the investigation,

and I need to do it immediately." Redburn's expression was grave and sincere. "Anything less, and no one will believe that The Republic is taking Victor's death seriously."

"I have to question your judgment on this," Jonah said. "I'm not a political man, and Victor Steiner-Davion's death, natural or otherwise, can't possibly be anything except political."

"That's exactly why I want you to do it."

"I must be growing stupid in my old age, Damien. Explain."

The Exarch sighed. "It's *because* you're not political; or at any rate, you're about as apolitical as it's possible for someone in your position to get. Which isn't very, so you can stop playing the I'm-not-worthy card. It isn't going to help."

Jonah ignored the Exarch's last comment. There was enough truth in the accusation that replying to it was probably not a good idea. Instead he asked, "What advantage will my supposedly being apolitical bring to the investigation?"

"For one thing," Redburn said, "you don't have any ties or obligations to Victor Steiner-Davion beyond the absolute minimum. Given the man's longevity and his history of involvement in factional struggles, that makes you a rare bird."

"I'm beginning to think it's made me a sitting duck."

Redburn smiled. "No, your personal integrity did that."

"I'm flattered," Jonah said dourly.

"You're also the Exarch's Special Investigator for this death. I need a preliminary report from you no later than the end of December—before the election."

Jonah resigned himself to the inevitable. "What resources do I have?"

"Whatever you want, within reason. You can call upon the office of the Exarch to make good any expenditures, or to handle any research and paperwork. And, of course, to back any action that you need to take."

"Thank you."

"Don't thank me." Now that he had what he wanted, the Exarch favored Jonah with a wry smile. "I'm handing you a hot potato, and it's undoubtedly going to burn your fingers. I don't know who is involved in this and I don't want to guess, but I have my ideas. Follow this however high it may go, even if it leads you to one of your peers."

"One of my peers? You have a reason to think—"

"No." Redburn cut him off. "I don't. But I've seen the path The Republic's been on. I know what we're in for. And I know your investigation could end in some very high places."

Jonah was still thinking about Redburn's words as he went back out into the main chamber. The atmosphere there continued for the most part to be one of restrained mourning, though small knots of people had gathered around the two new Paladins. Both Janella Lakewood and Gareth Sinclair looked a bit shell-shocked; no one could ever fully prepare for the event of becoming Paladin, and Sinclair most likely had known of his promotion only a few minutes before his appointment was announced.

Jonah made a point of seeking out Sinclair. The group of Knights and others clustered around Sinclair parted as Jonah approached. That automatic deference had been one of the hardest things for Jonah to get used to after having been himself raised to Paladin status. Sinclair, though, came from a political family on his own world; maybe his settling-in period wouldn't be as long or as awkward as Jonah's had been.

Don't fool yourself, said the voice of reason in Jonah's head. He's got a long way to go. Look at you—in some ways, you're *still* settling in.

He gave Sinclair a cordial nod. "Gareth. Congratulations."

"Thank you, si—"

"Jonah." He met the younger man's eyes and added, "Paladin Sinclair," the better to get the point across.

Sinclair blushed and corrected himself. "Jonah." The man had never been good at dissembling, Jonah recalled, and his fair complexion was as good as a message board for whatever he was feeling at the moment. "Thank you— though I never wanted to advance like this."

"Victor Steiner-Davion is a hard act for anyone to follow."

"I feel like I'm expected to follow in the steps of a legend."

"You are." Jonah glanced toward Janella Lakewood, and saw that Sinclair followed his gaze. "But it could be worse."

Sinclair grimaced. "Taking a traitor's seat? I suppose you're right. Just the same, I—"

"You'll do fine, Gareth." Jonah looked about the chamber. A few reporters and officials still straggled in the empty hall. Some of them were probably waiting for a chance to interview Sinclair. They tried to look nonchalant, but Jonah knew they were straining to hear every word he and Sinclair said.

Jonah made a courteous good-bye to Sinclair, then returned to his seat. With the shortened meeting, his schedule was suddenly clear. He could get to work on his project immediately.

He called up an address on his data screen and sent a message to an old friend. Well, an acquaintance, really, but a valuable one.

Are you at liberty to take on some work for me? If so, come to the Pension Flambard in the Rue Simon-Durand this evening at seven.—Jonah Levin

16

**Pension Flambard, Geneva
Terra, Prefecture X
27 November 3134**

The early winter darkness pressed against the windows of the sitting room of the pension in the Rue Simon-Durand, and a damp wind blew down the street outside. Jonah Levin sat in front of the burning faux-logs in the fireplace, enjoying the warmth and the yellow-orange glow. The dancing flames were a randomized tri-vid display powered by the fireplace unit's internal computer, but the illusion they provided was as warming to the soul as the heat given off by the formed and textured ceramic logs was to the body. Jonah had fortified himself with an early dinner and a glass of wine at his favorite neighborhood restaurant, and now he waited.

He heard the sound of the street door opening, followed by the sound of the bell at the front desk. A moment later, Madame Flambard came to the sitting room entrance.

"A person to see you, Monsieur Levin. He says he is expected."

"He is," Jonah said. "I'll talk with him in here."

"Very well, Monsieur. If you need anything—"

"I'll ring. Thank you, Madame."

She ushered in the investigator, Burton Horn, then made herself discreetly absent. Levin gestured his guest to the chair on the other side of the fireplace.

Burton Horn was a medium-sized man with bland, forgettable features. He wore the uniform of the Republic-spanning General Delivery messenger service, for whom he worked when he was not involved as a freelance courier and private investigator. Jonah had first hired the man to do legwork for him during the Ezekiel Crow affair of the previous spring, and knew him to be competent, reliable and, above all, discreet.

"I got your note," Horn said. "Do you have something for me?"

"First things first," Jonah told him. "Can you arrange to take some time off from General Delivery?"

"Maybe," Horn said. "For how long?"

"A month, give or take a few days."

Horn gazed for a moment at the artificial yellow-orange flames and red coals of the faux-logs. Whatever he was calculating, it didn't show on his face. Finally he said, "I should be able to swing a leave of absence. Much longer than a month, though, and General Delivery might decide they could do just as well without me. If your project isn't done by the start of the new year, I'll have to hand it over to somebody else."

Jonah thought back to his meeting with the Exarch. Redburn wanted results before the last day of December and the date set for the election. "I think I can safely promise you that, one way or the other, the project will be finished before that."

Horn gave a decisive nod. "We're good, then."

"Good," said Jonah. "Consider yourself hired at the usual rate, plus expenses."

"I'm at your disposal, Paladin. What's the job?"

"I've been appointed by the Exarch to investigate the death of Victor Steiner-Davion."

Horn looked curious. "I hadn't heard that there was anything suspicious about it. He was an old man, after all, even if he was tougher than boot leather."

"He certainly appears to have been tougher than somebody expected," said Jonah. "There are indications—you'll see what I mean when you read the folder from Santa Fe—

that his death needs to be attributed to foul play, rather than to natural causes."

"And I suppose the Exarch wants to know the who and why to go with the how?"

Jonah nodded. "I'll be doing most of the political work here in Geneva, but I'll need you to handle the street-level investigations on-site. And a word of warning—this may become dangerous. It's not impossible for a Paladin of the Sphere to be murdered by a random housebreaker looking to crack his wall safe and steal the family silver, but it's unlikely. Extremely unlikely, in this case. You may find yourself drawing the attention of some very powerful people before you're done. Watch your back."

"I always do. But if there're high-ranking people involved, I'd appreciate it if you kept an eye on it, too."

Red Barn Cafeteria, Petit-Saconnex
Terra, Prefecture X
27 November 3134

The executive core of the Kittery Renaissance Action Committee had met this week at the Red Barn in Petit-Saconnex. The perpetually unpopular table six was waiting for them, and, thankfully, the cook had remembered to wear a hairnet today. Since it was approaching midnight, most of the rest of the tables were empty, and those that were filled contained people in no condition to eavesdrop on nearby conversations.

The meeting tonight had been larger, spilling to a second table, as the pace of planning increased. Now, though, only the core officers remained in what Cullen called "executive session" and Hansel called "dessert."

At the moment, there was only one thing on Cullen Roi's mind.

"Victor Steiner-Davion," he said.

"Dead," Norah said.

"What about him?" Hansel asked.

"What have you heard about his death?"

"Heart attack," said Hansel.

"There's going to be an investigation," Norah said.

"Probably by a Paladin. There's something more there, but no one's saying what yet."

"Anyone linking us to the death?"

Norah looked at him sharply. "Should they?"

"No." Cullen paused. "Probably not. We have some skilled people in Santa Fe, and I can never be sure when someone is going to freelance. But for my part, I had nothing to do with it."

Norah sipped at a daiquiri. "Maybe we should have."

"Not with a Paladin investigating. We don't need extra heat on us at the moment."

"So how do we respond?" Hansel asked.

"We capitalize," Cullen said. "Everyone on Terra already knows about his death. They know we're going into an election with two new Paladins and the most influential of their number dead. If we thought there was uncertainty before . . ."

"Uncertainty's no longer the word," Norah said, pursing her lips in satisfaction.

"Right. Things have just moved closer to the edge. It'll be that much easier to push them over when the time comes. We can't let things settle before the election." Cullen Roi contemplated the dregs of his coffee for a moment, weighing plans and possibilities in his head and balancing one thing against another until something clicked. "We need a riot."

"I thought we were saving that for—"

"No, no," he said impatiently. "Not *the* riot. We're still saving that. Just *a* riot. Small enough that nobody important gets hurt; big enough to keep everyone on edge."

Hansel said, "Do we want it in Geneva, or somewhere else?"

"Geneva," said Norah. "Rioting anywhere else won't even make the evening news in Geneva."

"And getting on the news is the key," Cullen said. "I'm turning this over to you, Norah. This is your specialty—do whatever you like so long as it makes the news."

Norah's expression brightened. "Casualties?"

"Are acceptable." He caught the look in her eye. "Remember, I want people on the edge—but not yet over it."

17

Senator Mallowes' Penthouse, Geneva
Terra, Prefecture X
27 November 3134

On the evening after the first session of the Electoral Conclave, Gareth Sinclair had dinner with Senator Geoffrey Mallowes of Skye. The invitation to the Senator's penthouse apartment in downtown Geneva had not come as a surprise, since Mallowes was an old and close friend of the Sinclair family. Gareth had known the Senator since childhood, and had grown up regarding the man as a sort of honorary uncle.

For that reason, he'd always made a point of visiting the Senator's apartment whenever he happened to pass through Geneva. He would have done so within the next couple of days if Mallowes hadn't invited him to dinner first.

The Senator lived in an elegant set of rooms near the Hall of Government. His home was luxuriously furnished, floored and paneled in dark natural woods, and curtained and carpeted in earthy greens and browns. It was fully staffed as well, with personnel alert and prepared to serve at any time of day. They could make a cheese soufflé at midnight and set a table for four at three in the morning.

At the moment, one member of the staff stood directly

behind Gareth, waiting to serve his every whim. Gareth hated for them to be bored, and tried to come up with a whim that might keep them happily occupied, but creating off-the-cuff orders for servants was not one of his strengths.

By contrast, the servant behind Senator Mallowes had, in the past ten minutes, cracked pepper over the Senator's salad, fetched a fresh napkin because Mallowes detected a faint stain on the corner of the one he had been given, and retrieved an extra ice cube for his scotch. Mallowes knew how to make sure the people in his employ did not stay idle for long.

Apart from a brief congratulations on Gareth's promotion at the outset of the meal, the Senator had focused conversation on mutual acquaintances, pressing Gareth for any and all news about his entire family. His features, which looked stern beneath his flowing gray hair on trivids, had relaxed into grandfatherly lines—though the type of grandfather still capable of taking a switch to you when necessary.

From the consommé to the roast lamb to the meringue torte, Mallowes' posture remained straight, his eyes keen and the crease in his pin-striped wool trousers sharp. When he was younger, Gareth had found Mallowes intimidating, though the Senator had always treated him with nothing but kindness. Nonetheless, the dark suits, silk ties and the crested cuff links still brought him to attention as quickly as the dress uniform of a Paladin.

Mallowes did his best to establish a convivial atmosphere, regaling Gareth with stories of the Sinclair family, often delivered with a dry, understated wit. Gareth knew the Senator had more on his mind than family history, but the important conversation would come later. Mallowes never liked to spoil a good meal with talk of politics.

With the clearing away of the dessert plates and the arrival of after-dinner cordials, the talk changed to business like a sailboat responding to the wind.

"Now, Gareth, I hope you will not perceive me as overly blunt, but I need to ask you a question, and I believe the direct approach to it is most appropriate," Mallowes said.

Gareth simply nodded.

"Good lad. The question is, what is your assessment of your abilities to fill your new position?"

"I have to admit," Gareth said, "I'm still getting used to the idea."

"It may take you longer to accept than anyone else in your family." Mallowes sipped at his cordial. "They will be surprised at the timing of the announcement, but not at its occurrence. You deserved the appointment."

Gareth shrugged. "I can make a case for elevating any of half a dozen Knights who were just as ready as I was. Maybe readier."

"I've seen the lists. The others may have been brave and well trained, but they lacked your background." The Senator frowned, and all traces of the grandfather vanished. "Devlin Stone was not always as careful as he should have been about who he decided to raise to Paladin, and look where that got us—Ezekiel Crow! I'm glad to see that Redburn has started looking at things more sensibly."

Gareth smiled. "Too bad he's ending his term just as he started to be sensible."

Mallowes, thankfully, took the remark in its intended spirit. "Of course I mean no criticism of either Exarch. If I am concerned about any of Stone's later actions, it is only such actions as undermined his own goals. Stone had a clear vision in founding The Republic, and it is a vision to which we must closely hew."

Vision. Founding. Gareth recognized those words—political code words used often by factions making assorted noises across Terra. He realized, uncomfortably, that he was not sure where Mallowes stood on some of the issues tearing at The Republic, and knew he needed to speak carefully until he did.

"And now we need a third Exarch," Mallowes said. "A decision in which you suddenly play a crucial role. I realize, of course, that you have just ascended to your new position, but I also realize that the whole Republic, not merely the Paladins, has opinions to offer on this subject. Have you given much thought to the matter?"

"Only as an abstract question," Gareth said carefully. "And that was based on what I had heard about the Paladins, not on any extensive personal interaction with them. I suppose getting to know the men and women themselves may adjust my thinking."

"You should be sure to speak with Kelson Sorenson," Mallowes said. "He is a man of integrity and vision."

He was also a man with an unpopular family, Gareth thought to himself. The Sorenson name carried a heavy burden dating to Free Rasalhague's struggle for independence, where the Sorensons were seen as too conciliatory to the Draconis Combine. Once Rasalhague finally achieved independence, the Sorenson name had been dragged through the mud, the family painted as traitors to their own people for supporting the Combine. Whether it was fair or not, Kelson Sorenson still carried the burden of his family's past. He would not be a popular choice.

"He's capable, so far as I've seen," Gareth said aloud. "Honest, too, which I used to think would be a given among Knights and Paladins." He paused a moment before continuing. "As for vision . . . I can't say I've ever heard him put forward an original idea."

"Some people might say we've had enough original ideas for a while," Mallowes returned quickly. "They might believe that it's time for The Republic of the Sphere to remember why it was founded and live up to those ideas."

"Perhaps," Gareth said.

Mallowes gave him a sharp glance. "You don't agree?"

Gareth began speaking, and surprised himself by how quickly and passionately his words flowed. "I think speaking of The Republic only in terms of planets—who holds what, when and why—is to treat it as a large collection of rocks instead of a body of humanity. We have factions within our borders, we have enemies without, and we must take into account their actions, their armies and their goals when planning future action. We cannot just choose to focus on one rock or another."

He had said too much. Mallowes' face was suffused with the anger renowned throughout the Senate. Gareth braced himself against the coming fury.

It didn't come. Mallowes managed to push away his wrath with a smile. "You are both thoughtful and compassionate. You have been well trained indeed."

The Senator stood, brushing away loose crumbs with his napkin. "Remember, though, that your education is not yet complete. There will be much to learn, and you do not have the leisure of time. There are many forces at work in this election, and not all respond to reason and kindness as you do. They have other, less attractive methods at their disposal. Be wary."

"I will," Gareth said, clasping Mallowes' hand. He still sees me as a student, a child, Gareth told himself, forgetting the years I have spent as a warrior.

Gareth had seen methods of persuasion that the Senator faced only in nightmares.

18

Pension Flambard, Geneva
Terra, Prefecture X
27 November 3134

At the Pension Flambard, Jonah Levin and the newly hired Burton Horn conferred late into the evening. Madame Flambard, forewarning them of her arrival by a discreet cough, brought in coffee and chocolates on a silver tray.

Once agreement on the terms of Horn's employment had been reached, Jonah laid out his plan for dividing the work.

"To begin," he said, "we're working from the assumption that Victor Steiner-Davion is dead because some person or persons physically intervened and made him so. Law enforcement in Santa Fe is tracing the perpetrators of the physical attack; we don't need to duplicate their efforts."

He shook his head ruefully, and went on, "Whoever did the work was undoubtedly outside talent hired for the occasion, and if they haven't already left Terra then they've gone so far to ground it would take a MiningMech to dig them out."

"I could find them," said Horn. There was no false modesty in the words, only a statement of fact.

"It would be a wasted effort," Jonah replied. "They will

have been hired by somebody anonymous working for somebody unknown. And such people are well paid to be incurious."

"What should I be looking for, then, in Santa Fe?" Horn asked.

"The anonymous," said Jonah. "Or better yet, the unknown. As well as any hints you can pick up concerning what Victor might have been doing that required his death at this particular time."

"As old as he was," Horn said, "he can't have been up to doing very much."

"Victor was scheduled to give the opening address to the conclave, and now that address will never be given. It's hard to not make a connection. So, first—" Jonah counted off on his fingers "—he *was* doing something. *And* somebody found out about it. *And* whatever he was doing scared that person so badly that he or she sent for professional assistance."

"I think I follow," Horn said, nodding gravely. "I'm to leave the job of apprehending the actual perpetrators to the Santa Fe police, while I concentrate on finding out what Steiner-Davion was doing and who might be threatened by it."

"Just so."

Horn looked thoughtful. "The source of the initial security leak is probably the best place to start."

"You know best how to do your work," said Levin. "Meanwhile, I'll be taking the other end. There's a lot of people who stood to benefit from Victor's death, and I'm afraid some of them are my colleagues."

"Anyone particular you'll be looking at first?"

Jonah sighed. "I don't want to suspect any of them. But if I look at who benefited the most, there're Kessel and Sorenson. They were the core of a bloc most likely to oppose whatever it was Victor was going to say. Their bloc just got more powerful. And there's Tyrina Drummond. I don't think she'd ever be involved in something as underhanded as an assassination, but there was no love lost between her and Victor. I'll at least need to speak with her."

Horn nodded. "What about the guy who replaced Victor?"

"Gareth Sinclair?"

"Right. Didn't he benefit the most from Victor's death in the short run?"

Jonah didn't hesitate. "I suppose. But he'd have no way of knowing he'd be Victor's replacement. And besides, I know Sinclair. He's as decent as they come." He shook his head. "Sinclair's the last person I'd suspect."

19

Elena Ruiz's Apartment, Santa Fe
Terra, Prefecture X
29 November 3134

Santa Fe in November was warmer than Geneva, but a chill still held the night. The air was warm and dry, and smelled of desert vegetation.

Upon his arrival, Burton Horn had secured accommodations for himself in a budget-priced hotel. Once settled, he took advantage of his first opportunity for a long, private look at the file on Victor Steiner-Davion's death. The file's contents were detailed: witness statements; an autopsy report; a report on the crime scene by the responding officers of Santa Fe law enforcement; more witness statements and another report on the crime scene, this time from representatives of the Knights of the Sphere. Horn sat in the hotel room's comfortable if somewhat worn armchair, with a tumbler of iced spring water close at hand, and worked his way through the pages while the tri-vid set flickered in the background, its sound turned off.

According to the medical report, Paladin Victor Steiner-Davion had died of a sudden, massive heart attack. The report, Horn conceded, might be telling part of the truth.

All sorts of things could bring on such a fatal attack, including putting up active resistance to a murder attempt.

Local law enforcement officers, in their account of the crime scene, had reported the presence in Steiner-Davion's rooms of a broken crystal liquor decanter and a similarly broken tumbler. Both decanter and tumbler could have shattered by accident when the Paladin collapsed, but the local law wasn't buying that explanation. Not when the decanter had been smashed in a way that turned it into a sharp-edged weapon—and not when the blood that stained those edges belonged to someone other than Victor Steiner-Davion.

Reading between the lines of the account, Horn experienced a wave of new respect for the old man. In spite of his age and ill health, the Paladin hadn't gone down quietly. He had wounded at least one of his assailants. He'd marked a trail.

Santa Fe law enforcement was already involved in the search for the perpetrators of the crime; Horn intended to leave them to it. A DNA analysis of the bloodstains would give them a trail to follow, a trail that would, in the fullness of time, yield the identity of the killer. Once that was known, there would be warrants issued and communiqués sent out and contact made with law enforcement agencies on other worlds, whereupon the object of their search would have to either resign himself to capture or abandon The Republic of the Sphere entirely. Such a search would be remorseless—the death of a public figure like Victor Steiner-Davion was not going to drop off of the law enforcement community's monitor screens anytime soon—but it would be slow.

Furthermore, as Jonah Levin had pointed out to Horn in Geneva, the search would yield only tools. It was unlikely to produce the men or women who had put them to use. For Horn's purposes, the crucial question was how the killers had penetrated the impressive security around the Knights' Santa Fe headquarters. Either they're made of smoke and air, he said to himself, or they had inside help—witting or, perhaps, unwitting.

Horn locked his files away in the hotel room's jewelry safe and ventured out into the chilly, arid Santa Fe night to chat with the person who had seen and spoken with

Victor Steiner-Davion the most often in the weeks just preceding his death; his nurse-housekeeper, Elena Ruiz.

Ruiz lived in a one-bedroom apartment in an unfashionable part of Santa Fe. It wasn't a bad neighborhood—there were no deals in illicit substances being struck on the street corners under the lampposts, no uncollected trash bags or abandoned vehicles left out by the curb, no empty buildings with broken windows—but it was drab and unpromising just the same. After an interval during which she had obviously been checking him out through the security peephole, Ruiz opened the door to his knock.

"I'm Burton Horn," he said, before she could tell him to go away. He unfolded his ID case, with its formidable array of authorizations, and held it up long enough for her to inspect it thoroughly. "I'm investigating the death of the late Paladin Victor Steiner-Davion at the request of Paladin Jonah Levin and of the Exarch. May I come in?"

"Sure."

The woman sounded tired. She opened the door all the way and let Horn into her apartment. He sized it up at a glance. The living and dining areas were sparsely furnished but tidy, and Ruiz herself was a petite, dark-haired woman with a ready smile that was currently weighed down, disappearing almost immediately. Wearing a matted blue bathrobe and no makeup, she looked as if she had gone too long without sleep.

Ruiz gestured him to a place on the couch and took a seat herself in the overstuffed armchair next to it.

"I've already talked with the Santa Fe police," she said. "And with my boss, and my boss' boss, and a couple of Knights of the Sphere. If you're working for one of the Paladins, you already know all this."

"I do," he said. "But if you don't mind, I want to hear the story from you directly."

"Story?"

"About what happened the night Victor Steiner-Davion died."

She looked faintly puzzled, but attempted to answer the question just the same. "I didn't find him—find his body, I mean—until I came in to work the next morning, and saw that he was . . ."

"I know," he said, as soothingly as he could. "I've already been over the scene with the police. You don't need to revisit it. Right now, I'm more interested in what may have happened in the apartment the night before."

"I've already told the Santa Fe police that it wasn't one of my nights on call," she said.

She sounded a bit defensive on the subject, he thought, and wondered whether the police and the Knights between them had been making her feel guilty about having a personal life outside of her work. Aloud, he asked, "You were out, then?"

"Yes. With a friend."

The slight pause and the bit of warmth in her voice suggested that the friendship was more than casual. Horn made a mental note of that and continued.

"I understand from the police report that as Paladin Steiner-Davion's regular caregiver, you were able to monitor his status remotely?"

She nodded. "I can—I mean, I could—access his security status and his biometric telemetry through my personal datapad."

"Which would give you—?"

"A condensed version of whatever the on-call staff would be seeing when they looked at the big monitors," she said.

"And you were in the habit of checking this information nightly, even when you were not officially on call?"

"Yes," she said. "At about ten o'clock every evening. Sometimes I'd do a second check just before going to bed, but not always. He is—he was—an old man, and things can go bad in a hurry without warning sometimes."

"Did you make a second check on the evening that Steiner-Davion was killed?"

"No."

Again, he heard the fractional change in her tone of voice. Whatever she'd been doing the rest of the night, Horn thought, probably involved her "friend."

"But everything was in order at the time of your ten o'clock check."

"Yes. According to the readouts, Paladin Steiner-Davion had turned out all the lights and was sleeping soundly."

"Interesting," said Horn. His opinion of the hired assassin went up a notch; the killer or killers had spoofed both the on-call staff and Elena Ruiz's unofficial long-distance monitoring. They couldn't have found out about the latter by accident; somebody in the know must have tipped them off.

Aloud, he said, "So you had every reason to believe that all would be well until the next morning."

She gave him a weak smile. "That's what I keep telling myself."

He made a brief show of reviewing his notes, then said, "All right. Thanks. You've been very helpful."

"I wish I could see how," she said forlornly.

Without any comfort to offer her, Horn rose and moved toward the door. Just inside the threshold, he paused, counting off the seconds in his head and watching her relax.

Then, as if an afterthought, he said, "Strictly for the record—could I have the name of the friend you had dinner with that evening?"

"Henrik Morten," she said.

"Ah," said Horn. "Thank you."

Interesting, he said to himself as he headed back to his hotel. Henrik Morten.

With a first name like that, the man might be one of the Mallory's World Mortens. If that were true, young Henrik definitely wasn't the sort of person you'd expect to find keeping company with an old man's nurse-housekeeper.

It was a loose end, and Burton Horn liked loose ends. If you pulled on them just right, things began to unravel.

20

Bank du Nord, Plateau de St. Georges Branch,
Geneva
Terra, Prefecture X
30 November 3134

The woman called Norah had come to Geneva in order to start trouble, and she was happy with her assignment. For entirely too long, as far as she was concerned, the Kittery Renaissance had been all about talk, with no action taken. She had almost stopped believing in the one big day that would push their man to the top.

The dream of that day was what had brought her into Cullen Roi's orbit in the first place, and into the ranks of the Kittery Renaissance. She never spoke of her past—she had buried it along with her dead—but she had brought from it into the present a hunger for vengeance against the Capellan Confederation so fierce that nothing less than the might of the entire Republic of the Sphere was sufficient to carry it out. Only an Exarch could command such a vengeance, and only the right Exarch *would* command it, but the structure of Devlin Stone's Republic left her with no voice in the selection of the next Exarch save through the Kittery Renaissance and the activities of Cullen Roi.

This little job by itself wouldn't be enough to make the necessary changes, but it was a start. A promissory note from the Kittery Renaissance, a little taste now of the cup that would be hers to sup from in the fullness of time.

Mindful of Cullen Roi's instructions, she had chosen her location carefully. She had avoided the heart of downtown Geneva, where The Republic of the Sphere had its government buildings, and where those in power had their exclusive hotels and residential apartments. That territory was set aside for later.

Nor had she gone into any of the city's poorest and most dangerous precincts. Trouble happening there was barely noted elsewhere, unless it threatened to spill out and engulf the whole city. No. What she'd wanted—and what she had found—was a middle-class, middling-expensive part of the city, a neighborhood where trouble and conflict were rare enough that even a slight unpleasantness would be enough to make the news.

Trouble in this neighborhood would be taken seriously. The Bank du Nord had a large branch office on one corner, and the Unity Mercantile Corporation had its Genevan establishment on the corner diagonally opposite. The other two corners held a block of business offices, with a law firm taking up most of the bottom floor, and a municipal parking garage. The police station covering this precinct was several crowded blocks away—far enough that their response time would be slower than that of the roving tri-vid team from the local news channel, with a studio only one block over.

Norah derived a certain amount of pleasure from the fact that the place best suited to her goal had also turned out to be on the edge of Geneva's largest Capellan enclave. As far as she was concerned, it didn't matter that most of the Capellans living in Geneva were the sons and daughters of people who had occupied these few blocks for generations before Devlin Stone conceived of The Republic. The Republic should have rooted them out and sent them home years ago, she thought. Ten to one they're only waiting for their chance to sell us out, just like those bastards on Liao. She had trusted the people of the Confederation before, during the past she no longer spoke of, and it had cost her everything she once held dear. I will never, she had vowed, make the mistake of trusting any of these people again.

And now that she had the opportunity to sow chaos on some of their doorsteps—well, so much the better.

At half past noon Norah was in place, along with certain members of the Genevan cell of the Kittery Renaissance noted less for the subtlety of their political thought than for the hardness of their fists and the heaviness of their boots. They might have trouble following a line of philosophical argument, but they could follow orders, and—in matters like this, at any rate—they knew how to improvise.

Norah was wearing Capellan-style clothing for the occasion. Her appearance was not, in fact, particularly Capellan, but cultural identity these days was as much a matter of choice as of genetics. What counted was that anyone catching sight of her would see the clothes and think "Capellan" instead of looking closer.

Thus disguised, she waited.

A well-dressed young man stepped into the vestibule of the Bank du Nord, punched a few keys, scratched his temple idly, then left. He had all the appearances of an ordinary man passing through the neighborhood on an errand. In the light of what was to come, no one would remember him.

Henrik Morten had planned his route and activities carefully, right down to his bored nonchalance in the vestibule. It helped that he had actual business to transact—he'd recently come into possession of funds that were best transferred at a location other than his normal bank. Tomorrow, the funds would be transferred again as they made their tangled way to their final destination.

If his timing was right, he'd be just an innocent bystander to what was going to erupt any minute. He passed through the security barrier at the building's front entrance and paused on the exterior steps to let his eyes adjust to the outside light.

An instant later the sun-dazzle cleared from his eyes, just in time for him to see a Capellan woman stumble and fall away from the crowd, into the path of an oncoming bus. He watched her, and the scene he knew she would cause, out of the corner of his eye.

The woman was lucky. She managed to roll away from the vehicle a fraction of a second before it would have hit her, and scrambled, red-faced and panting, to her feet. Pointing a trembling hand at the man—*not* a Capellan, Henrik saw—who had been standing nearest her in the crowd, she shouted out an accusation that Henrik didn't quite catch.

The argument escalated faster than Henrik could follow, collecting a sympathetic crowd of partisan onlookers. He hesitated, acting as if he was torn between the desire to watch the conflict unfold and the desire to get away fast. As he waited, the knot of shouting, gesticulating people grew larger and took up more and more of the sidewalk.

Somebody shouted a political slogan—"Strength and Dignity!" it sounded like, although what those qualities had to do with a woman nearly being run over by a bus in downtown Geneva, Henrik wasn't sure—and somebody else shouted an insult. One man shoved another into the street, and was himself promptly knocked down by a third. The woman whose stumble into traffic had started the whole altercation was no longer anywhere to be seen.

Henrik turned and walked up the bank's stairs, jumping quickly to his left to avoid a couple of bank guards moving down the stairs. He quickly returned to his right, placing himself back in his chosen path.

Safe enough, at least for the moment, Henrik stood to watch the end result of the work by a woman whom, before today, he'd only heard about.

21

Office of the Exarch, Hall of Government, Geneva
Terra, Prefecture X
1 December 3134

Heather GioAvanti swore not to look at her noteputer the next time it beeped. She needed to have at least two minutes of uninterrupted thought if she was to accomplish anything.

It beeped. She ignored it. It beeped again, then twice in quick succession.

She cursed and let her thoughts be interrupted.

Kerensky's Bastards swear vengeance.

Rumors of "Neo-Blakists" found to be groundless.

Two more groups claim responsibility for death of Steiner-Davion.

Two more groups. That brought it up to eight. If these groups were to be believed, a small army had invaded Victor Steiner-Davion's home on the night of his death.

She quickly scanned the text of the message below the header. She'd never heard of the two groups. But then, she'd never heard of Kerensky's Bastards before yesterday, and today she knew at least one Knight was convinced that they were plotting to bomb the Geneva offices of Prefecture IX within the next week.

She scanned the evidence compiled in the letter. It was all rumor, circumstance and innuendo, but it was piling up to the point of being pretty damn impressive. The Knight wanted a militia squad to root out the threat, and Heather decided he'd earned it.

"Paladin GioAvanti!" Duncan, an intern, stood at the open door to her office as if a force barrier prevented him from going further. Heather waved him forward. He approached her desk like a deacon walking to an altar.

"Stone's Cutters are holding a rally in Founder's Plaza this afternoon," he said in urgent tones.

"I thought that was Stone's Legacy."

"Yes, Paladin. The Cutters are joining them."

That wasn't good. Stone's Legacy was usually content just to demonstrate, but the Cutters preferred more violent confrontation. Still, they were a small group. "Alert the police. They should be able to keep a lid on it on their own. But keep an eye on the situation."

"Yes, Paladin." He hurried away, then stopped at her office door. "Oh, I should mention, a messenger arrived with a summons from Exarch Redburn. He would like to see you in his office as soon as possible."

Heather was out her door almost before Duncan. One of these days, she thought, I'll have an intern who doesn't almost forget to tell me about meetings with the Exarch.

While she waited for Redburn, Heather's noteputer beeped three more times, each with a supposedly urgent message about unrest in the capital. The general public might not be able to vote in this election, but they seemed determined to participate.

When she had a brief moment between messages, she scanned the newssheets for any word of progress into the investigation of Victor Steiner-Davion's death. They reported no progress, and continued to not mention the name of Paladin Jonah Levin. His ability to fly below radar was impressive, as always. At this point, Heather thought, I may be one of three people besides Jonah who knows he's working on this. But that couldn't last—the only way Jonah could continue to maintain complete secrecy is if he didn't do anything.

The Exarch hurried in at last, looking frustrated and a bit out of breath.

"Paladin GioAvanti!" he said, as she rose to greet him. "Allow me to apologize. I was ambushed by a flying squad of tri-vid reporters and cameramen, and I had to give them a statement before they'd let me go."

"The perils of high office," she said.

"It would be worth it if I could believe the people actually listened to anything from the news," he replied. He waved at the chair she had just vacated. "Please. Sit down."

She sat down.

"So," she said. She was a Paladin; and she was near enough in rank to the Exarch that she didn't need to stand on her dignity around him. "What more can I do to serve The Republic today?"

"Have you been keeping up with the newssheets?"

"Some," she said.

"What have your sources told you about the riot in Plateau de St. Georges?"

"It wasn't good. Three dead, and people are blaming Capellan nationalists. It's not doing much to make anyone feel more secure."

"Have you heard anything about who may have planned it?"

"Planned it?" This took Heather aback. "Everything I heard pointed to it being a spontaneous disturbance."

"It may not be. What do you know about the Kittery Renaissance?"

Heather sank into her chair. The dark leather harrumphed. "Oh, God."

"Exactly."

Heather had been receiving updates on the Kittery Renaissance for months. Unlike other insurgent organizations, Kittery wasn't flashy; they didn't act as if they were desperate for attention. Their actions were precise, focused and always aimed at sensitive targets. Though they were known to be associated with the Founder's Movement, their exact goals and reasons for doing what they did were unclear. They would have been on the top of Heather's list of Dangerous Operatives except for an unaccountable silence that had overcome them in recent months.

"They're back?"

"They're back," Redburn said. "At least, that's where the information is pointing. We've gotten a few video feeds from the area and identified a woman there who has been present at some of their previous actions."

"Let me guess—this is the woman we still haven't identified?"

"That's her."

"Why a riot? Why now?"

"We can only guess; we still can't get an operative into their organization. I'd imagine the timing of it was to capitalize on the unrest following Victor's death. As far as why they chose a riot, I can think of two options. One is that their organization has been depleted, and a riot is the only action they can accomplish right now."

"I hope that's the case," Heather said.

"Me, too."

"I don't think it is."

Redburn just shook his head. "The other option is they are ramping up to something bigger. Something that will probably happen before the election."

"How big?"

Redburn frowned. "The atmosphere of this election is taking on an air of desperation. Too many groups seem to feel it's now or never as far as getting what they want. They will do just about anything to end up with the government they want. How big are their plans?" He paused. "Anything up to and including the entire eradication of Geneva."

Heather started. "You don't think . . . ?"

"No, I don't. But I can't be sure."

"Yes, sir."

"There's one more thing." Redburn took a deep breath. "We've never been able to conclusively identify anyone in this group. We have no idea who they are, or who supports them."

Heather nodded. KR's shadowiness was one of the constant frustrations of her work.

"However, the information I received linking KR to this riot also contained a disturbing note. Their support may come from very high up."

"How high?"

"I've sent you a file. Look at it carefully."

"Yes, sir." Heather stood. She didn't need to ask any more questions—her expected course of action was quite clear.

She walked out of the office and turned on her noteputer. It beeped four times. One of the messages was titled: *Past and current political affiliations of Paladins and Senators*.

Her heart chilled. Redburn wanted her to look at her fellow Paladins. Could one of them be supporting the KR? Had their process broken down so far?

Her thoughts were interrupted by a flurry of red hair rushing toward her.

"There you are, Paladin!" Duncan said as he waved a scrap of paper. "I have an urgent message about House Liao . . ."

22

Pension Flambard, Geneva
Terra, Prefecture X
1 December 3134

Rain was falling again in Geneva, a steady daylong drizzle, and a gray mist filled the street outside the Pension Flambard. Jonah Levin had taken advantage of the pension's excellent connections to Geneva's data-and-communications net to spend the day working in his room, putting off until tomorrow those tasks which had to be dealt with in person.

At noon Jonah left the pension long enough to purchase a loaf of fresh bread from the bakery on the corner, then ate the bread at his desk with jam and butter while reading an encrypted report from Burton Horn in Santa Fe, sent to an address Jonah maintained outside of government networks.

Jonah didn't like having to work outside the networks, because it meant he was seriously considering the prospect of corruption and murder at the highest levels of The Republic. Nevertheless, he had to acknowledge that Victor Steiner-Davion was unlikely, at his age, to have made new enemies outside of his regular circle—and that circle included people who possessed some of the most exalted positions in The Republic of the Sphere. Painful as it might be to contemplate, it was better to take unneeded precautions than to suffer the consequences of a betrayal of trust.

Jonah poured himself a cup of black coffee from the room's glass-and-silver brewing set, and returned his attention to the report waiting open on his desktop. So far, according to Burton Horn, a visual inspection of Steiner-Davion's chambers had led the operative to agree with Santa Fe law enforcement: the Paladin had died of a heart attack brought on by overexertion, to wit, self-defense against a murder attempt.

Horn wrote:

> The circumvention of all relevant security systems during the critical time period was professionally done. The tampering was evident—minimally—after the fact, but it would have been undetectable on the night. Santa Fe law enforcement remains confident of their ability to locate the killers, given time and the DNA signature taken from bloodstains left at the site. I have left a standing request with them that I be notified if/when they have any individual(s) in custody.
>
> The electronic data in Victor's office was erased all too easily with an electromagnetic pulse. No muss, no fuss. Whoever was in there didn't even need to touch his machines.
>
> I have decided to conduct a second interview with Elena Ruiz, Victor Steiner-Davion's nurse-housekeeper in the last months of his life. By all reports, the Paladin was closemouthed with friends and colleagues alike about his final project. As you are aware, even the subject of his projected remarks at the opening of the Electoral Conclave remains unknown.
>
> It is possible, however, that Steiner-Davion may not have been so reticent with someone like Ruiz, who was not a part of that world. Also, as someone who had daily contact with him, as well as virtually unrestricted access to his living quarters,

> *she may have known or at any rate suspected*
> *more about his endeavors than he was aware.*
>
> *Furthermore—in our first interview, I discovered*
> *a possible link between Ruiz and people back in*
> *Geneva. She is involved romantically with a gentle-*
> *man named Henrik Morten. This is suggestive;*
> *it would probably repay your efforts to determine*
> *if any of the Mallory's World Mortens by that*
> *name are working in Geneva or on Terra in gen-*
> *eral. The gentleman's connection with Ms. Ruiz*
> *may be only what she says it is. On the other*
> *hand—if you will forgive me for saying so—she*
> *does not strike me as the sort of person likely to*
> *enthrall a young man of Henrik Morten's proba-*
> *ble station by her looks and personality alone.*

Jonah closed the message and poured himself another cup of coffee. Burton Horn was indeed a bit of a snob, he reflected—but the operative was also an acute observer of human nature.

If he thought that the unknown Henrik Morten bore investigating, he was probably right.

Office of Senator Leeson, Geneva
Terra, Prefecture X
4 December 3134

The easy part had been confirming Horn's suspicions. Henrik Morten was indeed of noble blood and seemed to be a promising young man. Jonah found mentions of him connected to trade negotiations in Skye, crafting legislation for military aid to Prefecture IX and organizing humanitarian relief for refugees from attacks by Clan Jade Falcon. Morten, of course, played only a peripheral role in all these activities, but he was prominent enough to get his name mentioned. He was clearly a diplomat on the rise.

The more difficult job was finding out about the man behind the headlines (or, in Morten's case, the man behind the brief mention buried in paragraph eleven). Jonah knew from long experience that only a small part of a politician's life was covered by the newssheets.

Luckily, this was an ideal time to be gathering political information, as most high-ranking government officials had gathered in Geneva, awaiting the election. This included Senator Kay Leeson of Prefecture II, who happened to have spent a few years on Kervil.

"Paladin Levin!" she said enthusiastically when he entered her office. "How unusual that we should both be on the same planet at the same time."

Jonah smiled back. Thin, dark-haired and sharp-featured, Leeson hadn't changed much in the ten years since Jonah had met her. She had more energy and enthusiasm than her twenty-year-old interns, despite being well over twice their age.

"Good to see you, Senator."

"Now, I'd love to get caught up with you on things back home, but something tells me that a Paladin walking into my office at eight p.m. with an election imminent is not here for small talk. How can I help you?"

"Well, Senator, the election's exactly the reason. It's already started—the bargaining, the negotiating, everything. You know how that works. I, on the other hand—" Jonah spread his hands in a display of helplessness "—have never been gifted on that side of my job. Can you believe I arrived on Terra without a single staff person?"

Leeson laughed and shook her head. "The trappings of office were never your interest," she said. "No staff? Do you know what those other Paladins are going to do to you?"

Jonah chuckled ruefully. "I know, I know. But I thought maybe you could help me."

"I'd love to, except I don't have any staff to spare. We may not be voting in this election, but the Senate is still quite busy."

"I understand. Actually, I wasn't going to ask for one of your people. I just wanted you to tell me your impressions of a diplomat I was thinking of bringing in. A young man named Henrik Morten."

Leeson smiled quizzically. "I'm afraid I don't know the gentleman."

"Henrik Morten? Of Mallory's World? Seems to be just about everywhere lately."

"Not here."

Jonah tried to prevent his jaw from clenching visibly. Leeson was lying. A few of his sources told him that Morten, claiming to be on a fact-finding mission from Senator Leeson, had directed a team to explore the ruins of the Yori MechWorks. Whatever "facts" had been found on that mission had never been released to the public.

Jonah trod carefully. "No, no, not here. On Al Na'ir. He gathered some information for you on the Yori MechWorks?"

Leeson grinned. "What information? The place is a wreck. I don't need to send someone floating around an asteroid to tell me that."

"You never sent Morten to Al Na'ir?"

"No."

"I'm sorry, Senator, but some of my sources, people I trust a great deal, say he was working for you, armed with full credentials."

"They are mistaken." Leeson said that with a note in her voice Jonah had never heard from her. The warmth, the sociability, had disappeared. The friendliest politician he had ever known spoke to him with ice in her tone.

"But, Senator . . ."

"Paladin Levin, you may sit there and call me a liar while I, in turn, call your sources liars, but I can think of a thousand more productive ways to spend my night. If that's all . . ."

No, Jonah thought, that's far from all. The rest, though, will have to wait. "Thank you for your time, Senator," he said.

23

Elena Ruiz's Apartment, Santa Fe
Terra, Prefecture X
4 December 3134

If I'm going to be living in a hover vehicle, Burton Horn thought, I should rent a larger one. After all, Levin's paying.

The passenger seat of his rental held a thermos of coffee and two pastries he'd picked up from a diner staffed by tired waitresses and grumpy cooks. In back were his noteputer and several handwritten notes he hadn't gotten around to entering into it yet. On the floor was a blanket he used in the odd moment when he could grab some sleep.

He'd just tossed the noteputer back there after reviewing the latest dispatch from Levin, which confirmed that his instincts about Morten were right—and then some. He'd immediately called Elena Ruiz to ask if he could talk to her again, though he didn't mention Morten's name. She said he could come over right away.

Ruiz's neighborhood didn't look much better in broad daylight than it had at night. Most of the buildings were worn and dusty-looking. So were the people. The streets were clean, though, and he judged that he could park the rental vehicle in an unattended public lot without much fear of theft.

And Levin would cover the cost of a replacement, anyway.

He locked the car and walked the short distance from the lot to Elena Ruiz's apartment. This time she didn't inspect him through the security peephole for quite as long before letting him in. She looked somewhat less tired than before, giving Horn a fleeting glimpse of the attractiveness that—as much as her level of access to Victor Steiner-Davion—might have caught the eye of someone like Henrik Morten.

"Good morning," she said. "I have coffee; would you like a cup?"

"I had some already, thank you." He paused, and allowed a slightly embarrassed expression to cross his features. "In fact, if you could tell me where—"

"Oh. Yes." Ruiz pointed. "It's over there."

"Thanks."

Horn walked to the bathroom, locked the door and quietly slid the medicine cabinet open. He didn't know what, if anything, he'd find that was useful in there, but experience told him more information was always better than less.

Somewhat to his disappointment, the cabinet shelves turned out to hold nothing of a betraying nature. Instead, he found an unexceptional collection of over-the-counter remedies for headache, stomachache and the common cold, a box of adhesive bandages, a bottle of rubbing alcohol, a jar of lip balm and a tube of antibiotic cream. If Ruiz had a darker secret life, the evidence of it wasn't here.

He closed the cabinet door and turned to go back out into the apartment's main room—only to pause, his hand on the doorknob, at a noise from the room outside. The noise came again, a muffled knock, followed by low voices and the sound of the outside door opening.

The chance that he had been betrayed made him unlock the door as quietly as possible. The muffled click of the lock sounded loud in his ears. He swung the door toward him a fraction of an inch, so that the bolt no longer caught in the lock plate.

Then he heard a crash of breaking glass from the living

room. The odds that Elena Ruiz had betrayed him, he thought, had just gone down.

Horn eased forward, slipping his single-shot slug pistol from its hiding place in his ankle holster.

Outside in the living-dining room, Ruiz screamed. The cry was followed by the sound of a slap, and of a body falling.

Horn pulled the door open and stepped through, swinging wide so that he could bring his weapon to bear. Single shot—just one chance. The little holdout pistol wasn't a weapon for long-range shooting. He wished he'd brought his revolver.

He saw a man standing in the middle of the living-dining area, straddling Ruiz's fallen body. The woman lay sprawled on the floor, her legs out of sight behind the broken coffee table. The man turned toward Horn. He had a laser pistol in his hand, he was bringing it up—

Horn fired. At the last moment he adjusted his point of aim from the center of the man's body mass to the man's head. Ruiz's assailant might be wearing an armored vest under his baggy sweatshirt, and the little pistol didn't have the knock-down power that a Gauss or a laser weapon packed.

The change of aiming point caused Horn to miss the greater part of his target. Instead of going down with his head in ruins, the man slapped his hand to the side of his face and howled, "You shot my ear off! You shot my goddamned *ear* off!"

Bright red blood poured out from between the man's fingers. It would be only a moment, though, before he remembered that he had a pistol.

Horn threw the holdout pistol at the stranger's face. Instinctively, the man ducked. In that moment Horn was on him, taking the man on the side of his knee with a reaping side kick and knocking him to the floor on top of Elena Ruiz.

The man began to push himself up on his hands. Horn stamped down heavily on the stranger's back above his right kidney. The man cried out in pain and went down. He hadn't been wearing an armored vest after all.

Horn reached down, grabbed the man's shirt, and pulled

him off Elena Ruiz. He rolled the man over onto his back and stepped down hard on one of his wrists.

"Who are you?" Horn demanded.

The man glared up at him. "I'm nobody."

"You can do better than that." Horn put his weight on the man's wrist, and ground in his heel a bit. "Listen. You're already dead. If you answer my questions I'll make it quick. Otherwise . . ." He stepped down hard on the wrist again. The man moaned. "Now—who are you?"

"Delgado," the man said. "Tony Delgado."

"Good start, Tony," Horn said. "Who hired you?"

"Some guy," Delgado said.

Horn started to press down his heel again.

Delgado gasped. "I swear, he never said his name! He offered me two hundred stones to come mess with this lady, that's all."

"That's all, Tony? I think you know more than that." Horn eased up with his foot. "Let's save some time and trouble. What did this guy look like?"

"An ordinary guy," Tony said. His voice was getting fainter. "Light eyes, pale hair . . . I never saw him before. Please, I was just going to fool with her, nothing big."

"What did this guy say to you? Exactly."

"I was supposed to come here, and tell her that if she knew what was good for her she'd leave town and not talk to anyone."

"And that was it? I don't believe you."

Tony's words tumbled out. "As God is my witness, that's all he said. A hundred up front and a hundred after, to convince her to leave!"

"Are you sure that's all he said for you to do?"

"He said if she got scared enough she'd run for sure."

Horn looked down at his prisoner. The man's face was white, and getting steadily whiter wherever the blood from the bullet crease along the side of his face wasn't caked or running. His skin was getting sweaty.

"What then? If she ran, where were you going to go to collect the other half of your money?"

Delgado's breathing was getting faster and shallower. He was gasping for air. "He said I should just . . . come to the bar . . . he'd . . . find me."

"What bar?"

"The Clover . . . Cloverleaf." Delgado's voice was faint. "I want . . . something to drink. I'm thirsty."

"No," said Horn. "You're dead."

His blow to the man's back had ruptured the renal artery, from the look of things, and Delgado was bleeding out internally. Horn moved away from Delgado's wrist, but Delgado didn't make a move. He was too busy trying to breathe.

24

After a long day's work, Jonah Levin usually ate dinner alone in his favorite small restaurant near the Pension Flambard. The Golden Apple Restaurant had been run by the same family for three generations; it had starched linen tablecloths and sparkling crystal and heavy, solid silverware, and its kitchen staff was devoted to making meals that caused you to forget everything except what was currently in your mouth. Tonight Jonah had enjoyed roasted chicken and herbed rice and a glass of white wine from the Bernkastel vineyards, a good meal that didn't do much to lift his mood of growing dissatisfaction.

He was, abruptly, buried in politics. A diplomat had a connection, however tenuous, to Victor Steiner-Davion's death, and a Senator of The Republic had lied to his face about that diplomat. This wasn't the battlefield, where his enemies were clearly marked. This was a game where even those who lied to him might, in the end, turn out to be on his side, while those he trusted the most might be working to undermine everything he did.

He hated this game.

Leeson's lie convinced him of the need to find out more about Henrik Morten. To get what he really needed, he had to abandon official channels for a time. He had to talk to people that Burton Horn would be better equipped to interrogate, do things that were best left to people who were not Paladins. But Horn was in Santa Fe, and other help, at such short notice during the holidays, was tough to find.

With the help of a name or two supplied by Horn, Jonah had poked and prodded enough to turn up someone who, provided with the proper incentive, might tell Jonah what he needed to know. *This investigation is only a few days old*, Jonah told himself, *and I'm already perfectly willing to pay a bribe. Politics.*

This wasn't what he was built for. This wasn't what had gotten him this far. He could move an army ahead; he could engage in single combat; he could do anything that war demanded. The rest of this—the investigation and all its trappings—seemed like a black hole of inaction, sucking the life out of him.

He did not like thinking of himself as an action addict; he'd known people like that long ago, when he was only a captain in the Hesperus militia, and he had learned first-hand how they got other people killed.

"Don't be silly." He could hear Anna's remembered voice in his head—as always, like reason and conscience in one. "Being good at something isn't the same as being addicted to it."

He had some skills, though, that made him nervous. He recognized his own tendency to use calculated and metered force simply because he was good at it; he knew that sometimes, in a crisis, he could completely set aside emotion and see himself and others only as means to a necessary end.

Yet he despised this same quality in politicians. They saw governance as a game of power, and the vast quantities of cash and people at their disposal as mere means to the end of building and consolidating power. If he was to get through this investigation and the election, he would have to subsume that part of him that begged for simple clarity, for forceful ways to achieve simple goals.

He had finished the last of his meal. The waiter brought the pastry cart to the table, but Jonah shook his head.

"Coffee only," he said.

When it came, dark and aromatic in a porcelain cup, he sipped at it thoughtfully. He had enough self-awareness these days to know that a return of the dark moods of his youth usually signaled an idea trying to work its way out of his subconscious, and running into unpleasant memories on the way. If he didn't want to spiral downward into several days' worth of profound depression—and that would be a bad thing, with Anna so far away—he would have to haul the idea out into full view and look at it straight on.

Well then, he said to himself. Let's see what triggered it this time.

He ran over the past few minutes' train of thought, looking at the memories and images it had evoked, testing them one by one as they came past.

Violence . . . no.

Suppressed urges toward rash behavior . . . closer, but not quite.

The need for action, and the use of others in carrying out that action . . . yes, *that* was the thought that brought a twinge of pain, like pressing on a bruise.

Jonah sighed. "All right," he murmured under his breath, checking his chronograph. "I'll just use myself."

"Hey, hey, hey, that's my spine! What do you think you're . . ."

Jonah shifted his left arm and gave a slight twist with his right.

"AHHHHH! *Stop* it! I don't even know what that *is*, but you're hurting it!"

The bartender, as Jonah had suspected he would, paid no attention to the conflict. He sat back on an unpainted wooden stool and waited for Jonah to exert enough effort that he'd work up a thirst.

The only other customer, who looked like a mouse in a trench coat, had darted away as soon as Jonah leapt off his stool and grabbed the informant. They had the bar to themselves—thirty square meters of worn, stained linoleum was now Jonah's interrogation chamber.

Jonah eased the pressure a little. "You want to renegotiate the deal now?"

"Yeah, yeah," the man gasped. "I've decided, ah, I don't need any more cash."

"Good."

"How about, here's a deal, you stop hurting me, I start talking."

Jonah nodded. "Sounds good." He let the man go, picked up his stool and signaled the bartender for another round. The stool the informant was sitting on had shattered when Jonah knocked him off it, so he pulled over a new one.

The man next to Jonah wiped beads of sweat off his upper lip, grabbed an ice cube from his drink and rubbed it on his now-bulbous nose.

"It's not broken," Jonah said.

"Yeah, yeah, but it hurts, okay?" The man shook his head. "I gotta get out of town. Things are a little out of control right now. And not in the way I like it."

"Henrik Morten," Jonah said.

"I've heard the name. He's a troubleshooter."

"What kind of trouble?"

The man squinted, though his eyes were little more than slits anyway so the change was minimal. "Same kind you seem to be in. Trouble where the cops and the politicians and all the clean channels don't work right. The kind where the trouble goes away, and no one ever hears about how."

"Morten does this himself?"

"Naw. He's what you call a layson."

"Layson?" Jonah paused. "Liaison?"

"Right. You got a problem, he goes and finds the right people to deal with it, they take care of it. He's like, you know, insulation. A layer of protection."

And he had an in to Victor Steiner-Davion, Jonah thought. Morten was looking like a more promising target every minute. The question was, who was he insulating?

25

Elena Ruiz's Apartment, Santa Fe
Terra, Prefecture X
4 December 3134

Burton Horn turned to where Elena Ruiz lay half under the broken coffee table. The woman had curled herself up into a ball, with her face turned away from the violent scene that Horn had just created.

"It's all right," he said. "He won't hurt you now."

Slowly, Ruiz unfolded herself and focused on her surroundings. Her breath was fast and shaky, and the pupils of her eyes were dilated with fear; her voice quavered as she asked, "Are you sure?"

Horn bent over Delgado's motionless form. The man still lay sprawled on the floor where Horn had left him, but his labored breathing had ceased. A quick touch of fingers against the carotid artery told Horn that Delgado's pulse had stopped as well. Horn straightened and turned back to Elena Ruiz.

"I'm sure," he said. "I'll call the police in a moment—they may be able to tell us more about who this man was. But if you feel up to talking, there are a few things I'd like to ask you first."

She blinked, slowly. He could see the shock of the sudden attack giving way to gratitude toward her rescuer. The awkward fact of Delgado's body a few meters away had not yet fully entered her awareness. If she was going to open up to his questioning, it would be now.

"If you think it would do any good—" she said.

"It would be a very great help," he told her.

He assisted her to her feet and cleared a place for her on the couch. When she was settled, he sat down next to her. "But first—is there anything you would like to know?"

She glanced quickly at Delgado, sidelong, and away again. "Him," she said. "Who was he? And why did—?"

"I believe somebody thought you might be in a position to reveal something," Horn said gravely, "and they grew nervous enough to take active measures."

"I don't understand. I'm just a nurse-housekeeper. I don't know anything important enough to tell."

Horn could tell Elena Ruiz desperately wanted to believe her own statement, but couldn't. Her conscience was not entirely clear. She either knew something or feared she knew something.

Horn decided to make giving up the knowledge easier for her by supplying a fig leaf to cover up the possibly unflattering truth. He said, "It's always possible that you may not be aware of what you know."

"What do you mean?"

"Memory is a tricky thing," he said. "You were in and out of the late Paladin's private office almost every day. Not even his friends and allies would have been in his presence as often as you were."

Ruiz nodded thoughtfully. "Yes. That's true."

"You may not be aware of it—if the story made the newsfeeds before his death, it would only have been a line or two at the most—but Victor Steiner-Davion was supposed to have given the opening address to the Electoral Conclave in Geneva."

"Oh, yes." Her expression was brighter now, and her complexion was regaining its normal color. "We all knew about it, here in Santa Fe. He was going to give it from the Knights' headquarters complex over a tri-vid hookup, because of his health."

"You see?" Horn told her. "That's something you know because he lived here, and because you knew him."

"Everybody knew about the speech, though," she said.

"But they didn't know its subject. The Paladin was keeping very quiet about that. Even his closest friends don't know what he was planning to say."

"If they don't know it, what makes you think I do?" She sounded slightly belligerent now.

"You spoke with him every day," Horn said. "You had free entry to his private rooms. Even if the two of you never talked politics, you had plenty of chances for an accidental glimpse of what he was working on—papers on his desktop, pictures on his data monitor, that sort of thing."

He paused for a moment, giving Ruiz time to grasp the full meaning of what he was saying, and then went on. "Even if you know nothing, somebody out there thinks differently. Tell me what you *do* know, and I'll see what I can do to get you away from Santa Fe and out of the line of fire."

"All right." Her tone now was one of grudging gratitude. "I didn't get a chance to look all that often—I'm not a snoop—but a couple of times I did see something."

He made an encouraging noise, careful not to startle her now that the information tap was flowing. She continued.

"He had names," she said. "Lists of names. He'd printed them out from his data terminal, and he had them all marked up in colored pens, connecting them with lines. Sometimes he wrote numbers next to the names, and sometimes not."

"Ah." Horn felt the hairs lift on the back of his neck, and knew that he was on the track of something important. "Do you remember any of the names?"

26

Counterinsurgency Task Force
Temporary Headquarters, Geneva
Terra, Prefecture X
6 December 3134

"**A**nd there's the Fallen Phantoms just south of the city."

"Fallen Phantoms? Are you sure they're not just a street gang?"

Duncan shrugged. "They may be. But they're making a lot of noise, and the citizenry is getting nervous."

Heather rolled her eyes. She'd like to just ignore this group, but she'd already had two other messages today giving her the same information as Duncan. "All right. If the police want militia backup, they can have it. But they're being spread awfully thin."

Duncan nodded. Heather's noteputer beeped, but her finger was already poised to turn it off. The screen faded before she caught even a glimpse of the new message's subject.

No longer confined to her relatively small office, Heather strode down the hallway of her new headquarters. She had six rooms attached to this hallway in addition to her own new command room, and each was filled with staffers trying to keep a lid on Terra until the election. The rooms were windowless and gray, giving her suddenly expanded staff nothing to look at besides their work.

She walked into a large room dominated by a gray oval table. Eight staffers awaited her arrival.

She walked to her chair at the table's head but didn't bother to sit. Pressing a button beneath the table, she made the words "Kittery Renaissance," written in large letters, appear on the wall behind her. She waited for a brief murmur to pass.

"They're back," Heather said. "And whatever it is they've been working toward seems to be coming to a head this time. The rest of my staff, with the help of the Geneva police and the local militia, is working to keep a handle on the hundreds of other groups out there agitating. Our job is to contain this one."

The questions came in a flurry. "How do we know they're back? What do they want? What are they planning? What kind of measures can we take against them?"

Heather raised her hands. "We need to focus. We don't have time for a full-scale investigation, we can't get anyone into their ranks, and we may not even be able to find out why they're doing what they're doing. First we stop them—the rest comes after."

"Here's what we know, or at least suspect. They may not be officially tied to any of the Founder's Movement groups, but they share sympathies. Simply put, they don't want The Republic giving ground to anyone. Ever."

"They sound okay to me," said Estrin Koss, one of the Knights of the Sphere at Heather's disposal.

"As far as maintaining and defending our borders goes, yes. But the more extreme elements—and you can be sure Kittery is among them—aren't content with mere defense. They want to keep us safe by eradicating our enemies, current and potential, once and for all."

"Preemptive strikes against potential enemies?" said Rick Santangelo, the other Knight on Heather's team. "Have they heard about the HPG problems? We don't even know what's going on inside our own borders, much less in the rest of known space. This is not a good time to run out on a preemptive crusade."

"Is there ever a right time for a preemptive crusade?"

asked Duncan, the intern who never seemed to be more than five meters from Heather. She shot him a look reminding him he wasn't supposed to speak, but she couldn't say she entirely disagreed with his sentiment.

"Do you think they're getting any outside support?" Santangelo asked. "One House or Clan secretly pushing for a preemptive strike against another?"

"I don't think so. It would be too much of a gamble for the outsiders—Founder's Movement extremists don't differentiate between groups that aren't part of The Republic, and you can't be sure who they'll want to go against first. Hell, they may lobby for us to charge in every direction at once."

"At least it's just an internal threat," Koss said. "Not a problem with foreign influences."

"I hate to say it," Heather said, "but we may be getting close to a point where internal threats are just as serious as external ones. Let's be honest, the current state of The Republic is giving a lot of people plenty of things to be upset about."

No one replied. Koss opened her mouth, but closed it again without speaking.

"So here's the battle plan. We have a few video feeds from the riot. We need to scan every inch of them, identify who in the crowd is an insurgent and do everything we can to put a name with the face.

"Second, if they're planning something big, they need firepower. We need to watch as many points of entry as we can, see if we can catch them bringing guns, bombs, anything else into the area.

"Finally . . ." Heather took a deep breath. "We need to push anyone we know with strong Founder's Movement connections." She kept talking as Koss tried to break in. "I'm not trying to paint everyone with the same brush here; I know plenty of Founder's Movement people who I consider dedicated Republicans. But if anyone can point us in the right direction—if we can find a link to the extreme elements of the movement—these are the people who can do it."

Everyone in the room, even Koss, nodded.

"Does that mean," Santangelo ventured, "that you'll be speaking to some of your colleagues?"

Heather grimaced. "That's exactly what I mean. On the eve of an election, I'll be asking some other Paladins if they have connections to traitors and insurgents." She grabbed her noteputer and started to leave. "They should be enjoyable conversations."

As she walked out, Duncan trailed her, a small phone held to his ear. She hadn't heard it ring.

"Paladin GioAvanti, I'm getting something about the Armed Brotherhood of Belgium claiming a link to the Stormhammers . . ."

27

"He's discreet," Cray Stansill said. "Nothing illegal about that."

He was on the defensive. Jonah backpedaled.

"No, no, of course not. I'm not looking to get the man in trouble—just information."

Stansill did not look convinced. He leaned forward in his chair, glaring, trying to summon the power of his surroundings to cow Jonah a little—even though Jonah was a Paladin and Stansill a Knight.

It didn't work. Jonah had been in one government office or another all day, and they had all started to look alike. When he only entered one or two a year (including his own), he didn't notice the similar drabness that pervaded the government building. Every office had the lacquered desk, the tall bookshelves, the plush leather chair for the occupant, the hard-backed chair for the visitor. Small details, like pictures of family, changed, but the general impression remained overwhelmingly the same.

In the space of two days of interviews, Jonah had amassed a sizable dossier on the career of Henrik Morten. He was indeed impressively discreet, leaving a long trail of satisfied sponsors but no actual evidence of illegal activities. There was plenty of rumor and hearsay, but no proof.

The thread that had led him to Stansill was a tangled one. He'd spoken with two Knights, four Senatorial aides, and a handful of lower-level politicos, and a few of them had mentioned Stansill as a person who had spoken admiringly of Morten.

That's where I am after two days, Jonah thought to himself. Calling someone who'd said nice things about another person a "lead."

Stansill seemed to be a good sort, a Knight pleased with his position and more concerned with serving The Republic than moving up through the ranks. His salt-and-pepper crew cut made him look like a middle-aged cadet in basic training. But word of Jonah's interviews had been traveling rapidly through the office building, and Stansill had been defensive from the beginning.

"Why do you need information about Morten?" Stansill said, steel ringing in his tone.

"I've been hearing good things about him," Jonah said calmly. "Taking care of a sensitive problem is one thing, but taking care of a sensitive problem without causing a fuss—that's a special ability."

"Exactly. That's all I'm saying," said Stansill, temporarily mollified. "I'd heard you'd been asking around about him, and word is you've been appointed to look into Paladin Steiner-Davion's death. I'd hate to think somehow Henrik was coming under suspicion just because he's an excellent troubleshooter."

Jonah laughed, knowing it was too late to deny what he was working on. "I wish my investigation had progressed far enough that I could put *anyone* under suspicion. No, I'm still in the earliest stages—I'm looking for good help. A troubleshooter. But I need to make sure anyone I hire is capable."

"So this is all just . . . vetting?"

"Exactly."

Stansill visibly relaxed. "All right. Good. That, I can help with."

"Great. So you obviously know Henrik Morten."

"Yes, yes. I could tell you a few stories, in fact."

Jonah smiled congenially. "Go ahead!"

Stansill leaned back, resting his hands behind his head. "I've only met him once, myself, at a reception here in town. I can't even remember who introduced us; those evenings become a blur, you know? We only talked briefly, but he didn't seem too enthusiastic about being there. I got the impression he'd rather be doing something else."

"What else?" Jonah asked.

"*Anything* else. A reception isn't about *doing*, and Morten is a guy who gets things done. He was out of place there, so we didn't say much to each other."

"So he's a doer—but what does he get done?"

"Oh, I've heard a lot of things. But there's one, there was this one time, out on Ryde, during the rebuilding. Do you remember when that meteor hit?"

"Remember? I was there after it hit. Six months on-planet."

"Really? Okay, so you know what it was like. Well, this was after the worst part of the chaos had been quelled, when the long, slow work of reconstruction was under way. There was a dispute that should have been nothing, but, with the tensions of the lengthy assignment, it grew way out of proportion."

"What kind of dispute?"

Stansill shrugged. "It was about a woman. What else? A couple of Knights got into a feud when one ran off with the other one's wife. Only he couldn't exactly run off, because he was assigned to the reconstruction. So he was there, working side by side with the guy whose wife he'd taken.

"Now ordinarily the two would have had to settle it themselves somehow. Fight a duel, or just punch each other out, or something, and it would be over. But the feud just got bigger and bigger as time went by, and everyone assigned to the reconstruction started taking sides. Suddenly, you had two reconstruction teams, each taking every opportunity to find fault with the other, even undermine the other's efforts. The whole process was breaking down."

"I never heard about any of this."

"That's exactly the point I'm getting to. Another Knight who was on planet called in Morten, I guess because he knew his reputation. Morten spent a day with one of the guys in the feud, then a day with the other. Next thing you know, they're best friends. They're in public everywhere together, saying nice things about each other, showing everyone that their feud is over and done with. As quickly as they'd been divided, the workers came back together. The reconstruction was saved."

"And the wife?"

"Stayed with the guy she ran off with. How Morten made that all work, I'll never know. But he did."

Jonah made a few notes, but, impressive as the story was to Stansill, there was little to help him out. Except for one small thing that was nagging in his mind.

"The Knight who brought Morten into the dispute—do you remember who it was? I'd like to hear the story from him."

"Of course I remember! He was just elevated to the conclave!"

Jonah's heart dropped a little as Stansill said the name. "It was Gareth Sinclair."

= **28** =

Cloverleaf Bar, Santa Fe
Terra, Prefecture X
6 December 3134

It was another dry, chilly Santa Fe night. The distant stars were points of cold blue-white, like chips of diamond against the black sky. Burton Horn was where he always thought he should be at this time of night—in a bar. Unfortunately, he was there on business.

The days just past had been strenuous, by anybody's reckoning, but things had worked out well enough in the end. Elena Ruiz had been soothed, supported and sent away to recover in the home of her widowed mother in Albuquerque. The police, for their part, had been satisfied with her story of a home invasion interrupted by the good luck of Horn's timely arrival.

Whatever their suspicions (since Horn doubted they'd missed the fact that Ruiz's alleged assailant had been dealt with professionally), they weren't likely to push further. The Santa Fe law enforcement community already knew that Burton Horn was a Paladin's operative. Furthermore, Horn was willing to bet that the late Delgado was already in their files as a known troublemaker, hoodlum and general bad egg. People who took money from strangers to intimidate young women living alone were seldom upstanding citizens.

The Cloverleaf Bar, when Horn entered it shortly before midnight, was exactly the sort of place that might have attracted someone like Delgado, full of loud music and people who never looked you directly in the eye. The smell of beer and bourbon hung in the air along with tobacco smoke.

Horn had dressed for the occasion. He'd made no effort to look local; he wasn't familiar with the Santa Fe outlaw style, and knew it would be pointless to try. But he knew the interstellar spaceport version of that same style quite well. It wasn't his usual look—give him nondescript invisibility any day—but in black trousers, a muscle-hugging black knit shirt, and a loose black coat obviously cut to conceal weapons, he would be recognized at once as a serious player from out of town.

Horn let the inner door of the Cloverleaf slide shut behind him and moved through the crowd to the bar. He took a seat on a stool near one end, out of the bright lights, and waited for the bartender to finish filling a quartet of frosted beer mugs and putting them onto a tray. The waitress sashayed off to a table on the far side of the room with the beers, and Horn took the opportunity to catch the bartender's eye.

The bartender came over to him. "What's your poison?"

Horn laid a fifty-stone note on the bar. "Bourbon, straight."

"Bourbon it is." The bartender poured a shot of bourbon and set the glass on the bar in front of Horn. He picked up the fifty-stone note and looked at it. "Planning on running a tab?"

Horn didn't touch the shot glass. "No."

"I might have trouble making change for this."

"Not necessarily."

"Uh-huh." There was a long pause. The bartender gave Horn a summing-up glance. "With that sort of cash, are you looking for one of our . . . special services?"

Horn smiled smugly and played dumb. "Special services?"

"Look, I'm not playing games. You know what you want. Ask, and I'll help you if I can."

Horn acted like he was pondering the offer. "What if I want something stronger than bourbon?"

"I've got what you see behind me," the bartender said, waving at two shelves of dusty bottles.

"Come on," Horn scoffed.

"I don't know you. For strangers, what you see is what you get."

Horn peeled off another bill. "How many do I have to put down before we're not strangers?"

The bartender's eyes were drawn to the money like rats to a sewer. Finally he said, "Look, I don't sell anything like that. I run a completely legit business, you understand? But what I can do is make referrals."

"Referrals?"

"Right. There's a guy in the back, wider than he is tall, named Snorky. He might be able to help you out. And there's Pritt."

"What's he got?"

"Nothing. But he knows people. People looking for companionship. He's a kind of . . . matchmaker, right?"

"Right. Sorry, I don't want any of that stuff. Anyway, what if I'm a cop?"

"Then go introduce yourself. Snorky *loves* cops."

"Scary guy, huh?"

"Uh-huh," the bartender said.

He broke the ensuing silence by going off to serve a new arrival at the other end of the bar. Horn watched him go, then picked up his shot glass and drained it. The bourbon was cheap stuff, too sweet for Horn's taste. He was glad that this job didn't require him to pretend to like it for long. He set the empty shot glass down on the bar.

The bartender came back, and Horn said, "Another."

"I thought you weren't running a tab."

"Things change," Horn said. "If I can't get what I came for, I might as well get what I can."

The statement drew a curious look from the bartender. He poured Horn another shot and asked, "What did you come here for?"

"The answer to a question."

"What kind of question?"

Horn took a swallow of the bourbon before answering. The bartender's curiosity was piqued now; a little delay would serve to draw him in further. "A simple one. A question of identity."

"I don't give out names."

"What about Snorky and Pritt? Those names came out pretty easy."

The bartender scowled. "They can take care of themselves. They come in here to do business five or six nights a week; they like it when I point people their way."

"Respected regulars, I can tell," said Horn. "Don't worry, you won't have to name anybody."

"What do you want, then?"

Horn reached into his inside coat pocket and pulled out the picture of Henrik Morten that Levin had sent him earlier from Geneva. He unfolded it and spread it out on the counter. "A simple yes or no—did you see this man talking with Tony Delgado anytime recently?"

The bartender studied it, frowning. "Yes. I don't know who he is, just that he isn't one of our regulars and probably isn't a local, either. But he and Tony were here once or twice. Tony never introduced me. Your boy never seemed too comfortable, always seemed antsy to move on."

Horn refolded the picture and put it away. "Thanks."

"You going to let me know who it is?"

"I don't believe I am," said Horn, rising to leave. "And you can keep the change."

The late-night air outside the Cloverleaf Bar was chill and crisp. Horn breathed deeply, clearing his lungs of the Cloverleaf's smoke-fouled atmosphere. The stars overhead were sharp and there was a ring around the moon: high ice crystals, he thought, and maybe the prospect of snow.

He thought about the photograph of Henrik Morten, now tucked back inside his coat. The bartender had identified the man in that picture as someone who had been seen with Delgado earlier.

He'd read the stream of information Levin had sent him about Morten. And now he had directly connected him to the attempt to intimidate, or harm, Elena Ruiz.

It was time to stop beating around the bush. They had enough to go after the rabbit himself.

29

From time to time, Jonah Levin experienced moments of gratitude that, unlike most of his fellow Paladins, he was not a physically memorable person. He didn't have the striking, Clan-bred looks of a Tyrina Drummond or a Meraj Jorgensson, both of whom were the products of generations of selective breeding for strength and symmetry and commanding appearance. And unlike Gareth Sinclair or Maya Avellar, he lacked the easy assurance that came of being born into wealth and high position.

He was only a man of average height and average weight, with hair and eyes a nondescript shade of average dark brown and a face that could have belonged to a hundred other men of the same general age and ethnicity. In much-laundered street clothes a year or so behind the fashion, he could sit in a workingman's bar drinking beer with a whisky chaser, and none of the observers would recognize him as a Paladin of the Sphere.

The sharper-eyed ones among them might have frowned for a moment, puzzled, before going so far as to remark,

"Say, did anyone ever tell you that you look a lot like that guy What's-his-name—you know, the Paladin from Kervil?"

And Jonah would say, "Yeah . . . lots of times," in tones of bored resignation, and that would be that.

This functional anonymity allowed him to nurse his drink and eat salted peanuts at a back table in the First Stop Bar, undisturbed by the comings and goings of the shift workers and truck drivers who made up the greater portion of the First Stop's boisterous clientele. Left alone at his vantage point, he watched the front door of the bar and waited to see if the man he had contacted would show up.

He didn't have to wait for long. The time was still an hour short of midnight when the door opened to admit a broad, heavy-shouldered man who walked with a distinct limp. The man's long-sleeved shirt and denim jacket couldn't disguise the fact that his right arm was a prosthetic attachment.

The man's worn face lit up at his first sight of Jonah, and his lurching gait became faster. Jonah stood up to greet him, and the two men shared a handshake that turned into a quick hug. They sat down together at the table. The other man spoke first.

"Captain."

"Sergeant," Jonah replied. "You're looking well."

"You're not looking too bad yourself." Wilson Turk's gravelly voice hadn't lost its Hesperus accent after all these years on Terra. "Married life still agreeing with you?"

"I'd sooner be at home on Kervil than working here in Geneva—but you and I both know life doesn't always give us what we want."

"Ain't that the truth."

The waitress came over from the bar. Turk nodded toward Jonah and said, "I'll have one of whatever he's having."

She left and Turk turned back to Jonah, all business now. "I came as soon as I could when I got your call. Whatever you need, Captain, I'll do it. Or try my damnedest, anyhow."

"It shouldn't be difficult."

Jonah finished his drink and contemplated ordering another. He decided against it. He had no fondness for drunkenness for its own sake, and he didn't have either the stamina or the constitution of the young militia captain he'd been when he learned to drink beer with whisky chasers during the campaign on Kurragin.

"I don't know if all of what I'm about to tell you has made it out onto the streets or not," he said, after the waitress had brought Turk his whisky-and-chaser. "It's probably safest to assume that if you haven't yet heard something similar on one of the major news feeds, then you don't officially know about it until you do."

Turk looked unsurprised. "I didn't know you were doing intel work these days."

"You'd be surprised," said Jonah. He moved on to the business at hand. "To begin with—how much do you know about the death of Victor Steiner-Davion?"

"Only what everybody else does," Turk said. "Have to admit, it shook me up a bit. I know he was nine years older than God, but he'd been around for so long it felt like he was going to last forever. Hard to believe that he's dead."

"Not just dead," said Jonah. "Murdered. And the Exarch has put me in charge of the investigation."

Turk whistled. "What did you do to make Damien Redburn hate you that much?"

"I'm still trying to figure that one out myself," Jonah said.

"Cracked the case yet?"

"Yeah. Looks like the butler did it." That earned a weak grin from Turk. "No, it's far too early to know anything. But there's a distinct possibility that Steiner-Davion's murder was planned by persons very high up in the government."

"How high? As high as you?"

Jonah nodded gravely. "Maybe. But I hope not."

Turk shook his head. "They still don't give you the easy jobs, do they? Where do I come in?"

"You and your people come and go in the government buildings at all hours," Jonah said. "You see the stuff that the workers bring in and the stuff that they throw out; you see who's meeting with whom off the record; and nobody ever sees you. The custodial staff in a large building is effectively invisible—you could be plotting the overthrow of the government and no one would even notice."

Understanding crossed the other man's broad face. "Anyone in particular you need me to put the word out on?"

"Henrik Morten."

Turk showed no recognition. "Anything in particular about him?"

"Who he works for. Who's acting as his main sponsor. I've got him doing odd jobs for half a dozen politicians, but I know there must be someone out there giving him a majority of his work, and protection to boot. He's been in more than one sticky situation and come out smelling like a rose. Someone powerful is watching his back."

Turk nodded. "I'll get the word out, and we'll see what people try to tell me."

"Thanks, Sergeant."

"No worries, Captain. I owe you one."

Jonah shook his head strongly. "I thought we'd established a long time ago on Kurragin that *I* owe *you*."

"Not the way I figure it. If you hadn't been with us, we'd never have held down the flank without breaking, and I'd have gotten chopped up just the same."

Jonah looked at the other man. Turk's expression was firm; nothing was going to sway him from his position.

As Jonah drove home, Turk's expression stayed with him. Everyone needed someone they could trust with the important work. He had Horn, Turk and a few others. A few people, it seemed, had Henrik Morten.

Morten certainly seemed loyal enough, but his ethics looked quite malleable. Unfortunately, that's all some people demanded. The people that Jonah valued were the ones who proved themselves beyond Jonah's expectations, the ones who did a better job than he could have thought of ordering.

Turk was one of those. His face hadn't changed much from the days in the Kyrkbacken militia, and it didn't take much to push Jonah's mind back to those days.

30

The headline displayed in the scrolling marquee atop the newsstand read:

> EXPEDITIONARY FORCE LOST. CAPELLANS DENY
> INVOLVEMENT.

Captain Jonah Levin was making his way through the public transit station when he saw the marquee and paused. After a moment's consideration, he went over to feed his personal card into the newsstand's payment reader.

The bored young clerk watching the transaction observed Jonah's militia uniform and said, "Checking to see if you know any of the missing troops?"

"No. Just interested in what people have to say about why we're doing it."

A JumpShip was gone. One day it had been stationed near the Capellan border. The next day it was gone, and Republic military commanders had fallen completely silent about it. If they received any transmissions from it, or knew anything about its fate, they weren't telling the public.

This was bad, Jonah knew. More and more voices were proclaiming that war with the Confederation was inevitable even before this ship disappeared, and those voices were only going to grow louder. But Jonah wasn't sure The Republic was ready for conflict with the Capellans. Not yet.

Jonah took the news printout with him onto the public transit car and read the full story on his way to Militia Headquarters. Units from five planets spread over three Prefectures had been aboard the ship. The force had been touted as a prime example of the cooperative spirit of The Republic. Now it was gone, and Jonah wondered how cooperative those planets were feeling.

He checked the names of the planets. Elnath, Yunnah, Palos, Wei, and Holt. All border planets. All pivotal to The Republic's defenses. We can't afford to lose their support now, Jonah thought.

The newssheets offered a few personal reactions, mostly politicians and family members saluting the troops' bravery. A few, though, questioned the buildup of force on the Capellan border and wondered why people from so many other planets needed to be involved. And this was only the first day of the story—things would get worse as time passed, especially if the missing JumpShip never turned up.

At the HQ transit stop, he exited the train and made his way through the main gate to the building where he had been assigned an office. The Kyrkbacken Militia was mostly a reserve force; the bulk of its personnel drilled one night a week, one weekend a month and two weeks out of the year. A small permanent cadre—of which Jonah was a member—provided administration, training and the framework of a regimental structure. All in all, the militia was a quiet, low-key posting for a young officer who needed to pay his dues before moving to a more interesting assignment.

Based upon the news stories, and upon the apprehensive energy pervading headquarters when he arrived, that peaceful time was about to end. He went to the cell-sized office that he shared with fellow militia captain Rafaella Graves, and found her already at work at her desk.

"Jonah," she said.

"Raffi." He nodded a greeting, then slipped into his chair and called up the desk files for this morning's paperwork. "How did we manage to lose a JumpShip?"

"That's the big question, isn't it? I've squeezed a few bits and pieces from a few contacts I have near the border. They say the JumpShip might have wandered a little off course before it disappeared."

" 'A little off course'? As in, into Capellan space?"

"That's the gist of it, yeah."

"They wandered into Capellan space and disappeared?"

"From what I hear."

"Refresh my memory," Jonah said, though he knew full well the answer to the question he was about to pose. "Do the Capellans like their borders being crossed?"

"Hmmm, I'm pretty sure they don't."

"So when a JumpShip disappears after wandering into their space, we can pretty well assume . . ."

". . . the worst," Raffi finished.

Jonah shook his head. "This is going to get worse. At least we have a pretty good vantage point from which to watch it all unfold."

A month later, Jonah found out he was going to do more than watch.

"Called up? To where?"

"The border," Raffi said. "First and Third Regiments both."

"The *border*? What the hell? We're supposed to be support for the border troops, not border troops ourselves! If we're guarding the border, who's guarding us?"

"I don't think we're guarding the border. We're going to it, where we're supposed to wait further orders."

Jonah didn't like the sound of that at all. "There aren't too many places they can order us to once we're at the border," he said. "Tell me they're at least equipping us decently."

The Kyrkbacken Militia possessed two BattleMechs, a *Mad Cat III* and a *Legionnaire*, and Jonah had trained in both. He leaned toward the *Mad Cat*, preferring its greater strength and mass, but lowly militia captains piloted the 'Mech they were assigned to and learned to like it.

Raffi grimaced. "You're not going to like this. The 'Mechs are staying here."

"What?"

"You said it yourself. Support of the border. If they're going to take away manpower, they want to at least leave firepower. We're supposed to get new equipment out there."

Jonah's hopes raised. "New equipment? Like, fresh-off-the-assembly-line new?"

"No," said Raffi. "Like, stuff-that's-been-sitting-around-because-no-one-else-wants-it new."

"Old equipment, you mean. Ancient."

Raffi flashed a smile brimming with false cheer. "It's new to us!"

"Did they say what we're getting?"

Raffi glanced at the new orders. "Says here they're purchasing a couple of clapped-out, secondhand *Stingers* from a disbanded mercenary unit."

"They're giving us used *Stingers*? To defend the Capellan border?"

Raffi nodded. "Yup."

In the past ten days The Republic, or at least these parts of it, had been enveloped in turmoil. Politicians on Holt were talking secession. Senators were openly questioning the military's ability to protect the brave soldiers assigned to it. Anti-Capellan factions were urging for an immediate, overwhelming display of force—a display that, Jonah knew, could wipe out large portions of The Republic's military and fatally weaken the border with the Confederation.

"I wish I knew what they're going to ask us to do," Jonah said. "But whatever it is, I don't think I'll like it."

Kurragin, Capellan Confederation
June–July 3110

The secondhand *Stinger* BattleMechs were even worse than Jonah had initially feared, and so was the assignment. Both 'Mechs had been stripped of their jump jets—their former merc owners must have been cannibalizing them for parts before putting them up for sale. The fact that the 'Mechs also lacked proper repair-and-replacement schematics and had only a minimal number of critical spare parts was another bad sign.

For the first time, Jonah appreciated the cynical comment that he'd heard on occasion from the older officers at headquarters: Nothing's too good for our men and women in the militia; too bad the government hasn't figured out how to give us less than nothing yet.

He'd have to rely on his people, who, though not regular military, were not without promise. They ranged from weedy pseudointellectuals taking a year off from college, through the usual assortment of troublemakers, slackers and steady, reliable, young men and women, all the way to Sergeant Wilson Turk—who was, in Jonah's considered opinion, something close to a gift from on high.

Unlike most of the Kyrkbacken Militia's enlisted personnel and noncommissioned officers, Turk had actually seen combat. He had served for two years in a front-line mercenary unit before cashing in his bonuses and returning home to semicivilian life on Kyrkbacken. Jonah, whose own battlefield experience to date was purely theoretical, soon found himself leaning heavily—but, he hoped, unobtrusively—on Wilson Turk.

Jonah and his men found themselves near a small town with the unpromising name of Rotten Creek on Kurragin, only a jump away from the Capellan capital of Sian. The fact that he was there, combined with the way he'd arrived, caused him no end of astonishment. He'd been in a JumpShip escorted by Capellan troops, guided into the heart of the Confederation. The missing JumpShip—or what was left of it—had been found. The troops within it had been located, mostly alive, but in deep trouble.

The JumpShip had, in fact, wandered accidentally into Capellan territory. Their mistake had been seized upon by House Ma-Tzu Kai, one of the more extreme elements of the Capellan Confederation. The Republic troops had run, only to dive deeper into Capellan territory. The ship, on its last legs, eventually managed to expel its DropShips near Kurragin, where the troops landed in a wide, desolate mountain range. The JumpShip was destroyed soon after, and House Ma-Tzu Kai had pursued The Republic's troops to the planet.

The Confederation, in a display of generous diplomacy that struck Jonah and many others as quite out of character, announced to The Republic that the lost unit had been found on Kurrigan, and that they would allow a relatively small force into Confederation space to retrieve it. The Confederation reported that it had asked House Ma-Tzu Kai to cease molesting the Republican troops, but, regretfully, Ma-Tzu Kai had not responded well and seemed to be pursuing its own agenda against the troops, and the Confederation was not going to move militarily against one of its own Houses. If The Republic wanted the troops to return safely, it would need to extricate them with its own people.

Jonah, and many of the other soldiers he spoke with, were immediately suspicious of the Confederation's strategy. They already had one unit stranded in Capellan space, and now they were asking The Republic to send more troops in far beyond The Republic's border. Though Capellan diplomats repeatedly promised a safe escort to the Republican troops many considered such promises to be worthless.

The Republic knew it had to send troops in or risk alienating the government of several border planets, but it also knew it could not risk top-of-the-line troops on what could be a fool's errand. So it had scraped together a ragtag group of militias, many similar to Jonah's in composition and experience. This was a group that was supposed to go up against elite Capellan troops and somehow hold them off long enough to get the lost unit safely away from Kurrigan. If they succeeded, the Confederation promised to look the other way on any losses suffered by House Ma-Tzu Kai. If they failed—well, the Capellans would take the position that The Republic had lacked the strength to rescue its own troops.

Once on Kurrigan, most of the Republican troops were busy trying to root out the Ma-Tzu Kai forces and give the wandering army room to escape. Jonah's company had been assigned to a backup role, ordered to hold its post and wait. Even in a desperate situation, Jonah thought bitterly, there's little use for us.

They sat in the middle of hostile territory and waited. After two weeks on Kurrigan, he and Turk had run out of jokes to tell each other about Rotten Creek. By the end of the first month, his unit had its first fistfight, quickly followed by its first arrest and brief confinement. Jonah's plans grew more and more detailed, but no orders came through.

They eventually spent six weeks encamped near Rotten Creek. Somewhere beyond the range of hills that lay to the west, the troopers of House Ma-Tzu Kai and the main Republic force fought and maneuvered and fought again while Rotten Creek remained completely and totally secure.

Then it came.

The order that changed Jonah Levin's life forever arrived with a simple beep. After loading in the day's encryption keys, Jonah watched the message organize itself from gibberish to coherent orders.

FIRST KYRKBACKEN ECHO COMPANY
PROCEED IMMEDIATELY 45'36" REIN-
FORCE REPUBLIC FORCES AGAINST
MAJOR HOUSE MOBILIZATION

House Ma-Tzu Kai was on the move. They must have pooled a large force, making The Republic desperate enough to call in all available personnel. The journey to the given coordinates wouldn't take long, but it would force them to cross mountains and make a steep descent into the wide valley protecting the House troops.

After months of waiting, constantly wondering when they would be asked to *do* something, Jonah's troops were hesitant. When you're being asked to throw yourself at a larger, better-armed, and better-trained force, boredom suddenly doesn't look that bad. The drill to break camp, which they'd gone over at least fifty times, proceeded slowly and clumsily.

Jonah, angry with his whole unit, vented at the first person he found, who happened to be Turk.

"What the hell are they doing out there? When orders say 'immediately,' they don't mean 'immediately, or, if not, as soon as you can get yourself together.' We should be halfway to the blasted meeting point by now!"

Turk let Jonah vent, then met his anger with calm. "Have you walked through camp?"

"Walked through camp? No! I've been doing my part,

prepping the *Stinger*. There's not supposed to *be* a camp any more."

"Just walk through. Don't yell, at least not yet. See how things are going. Just take a quick walk, okay?"

Jonah was about to retort that the last thing his company needed was one more person wasting time, but it was Turk he was talking to. It wouldn't hurt to trust him on this.

The fear in camp was palpable. A drill prepares you for real combat about as much as your first kiss prepares you to be married. The real situation is a whole lot more complicated than the practice.

The soldiers, Jonah saw, were trying to get their work done, trying to focus, but mental pictures of their own looming death kept wiping everything else away. They weren't ready.

Jonah had no idea how to help them. They were right to be scared. He was scared, too, but had managed to bury his fear under the call of duty. He didn't think he could bury the fear of an entire company.

He walked through the camp, and his soldiers watched him pass. His mind may have been whirling, reaching for something, anything to help his soldiers, but his face remained calm. Resolute. And as he passed, his troops found another image they could place in their head, one that finally pushed away the hundred images of death. Their commander was calm, and they followed him.

Within minutes of the completion of his tour of the camp, Echo Company was ready to move.

31

Prospect Hill, Kurragin
17 September 3110

For Jonah Levin, the active part of the campaign on Kurragin ended soon after it began, on a bright autumn day on a wooded hilltop, amid a stand of hardwoods glorious in their red-and-orange autumn foliage. The air, quiet and unmoving before the start of battle, carried the faint sounds of movement from far away. Somewhere downslope, amid the low brush, waited the troopers of House Ma-Tzu Kai.

Back in The Republic, Devlin Stone had made a ringing speech about the efforts to recover the lost troops, saying no world or individual that had sworn to The Republic of the Sphere need fear abandonment, but should trust The Republic and its member worlds to send aid. Transcripts of the speech eventually trickled their way to Kurrigan, and, reading it, Jonah was both stirred and worried. If the situation turned out well, it would be proof that Stone could back up his desire to watch over every single citizen of The Republic. If it failed, it could show that The Republic was overextended and unable to protect those willing to lay down the most for it. It would be a sign of weakness in a time demanding strength.

Echo Company had been cut off on its way to the rendezvous. To the north were the other regiments that had accompanied them to Kurragin. To the south were the tired, bedraggled troops they'd come to rescue. In between, and cutting off Jonah from either group, was House Ma-Tzu Kai. And when House Ma-Tzu Kai decided to move, it sure as hell wasn't going to go against either of the larger groups. It had its eyes set on Prospect Hill, currently occupied by Echo Company.

Their new orders had come through this morning.

> HOUSE MOVING WEST TOWARD HIGH
> GROUND OF PROSPECT HILL. HOLD
> HILL UNTIL BODY OF ARMY MOVES IN.
> HOLD AT ALL COSTS.

Jonah turned his attention from the slope outside to the sensor scan in the cockpit of his secondhand *Stinger*, wishing that his opposition shared his equipment problems. The recon reports, though, showed a well-armed, well-supplied force ahead of them. They had ammunition dumps scattered near Prospect Hill, while Jonah's Echo Company had only what it carried. If House Ma-Tzu Kai figured out how paper-thin was the opposition they faced on the hill, Jonah and his soldiers were done for.

Jonah tried to coax a reading out of his 'Mech's barebones display that might give him some idea of the nearby forces, but the *Stinger* wasn't helping much; the probability curve on known and unknown units looked bad, and the heads-up display in his 'Mech's cockpit windows hadn't been updated recently. Available information on the opposing units was sliding from known green to unknown red all along his section of the line.

"Dammit," he muttered. Even the reports from his own troops were fading to pink, then going red as the time-since-update deteriorated. He glanced away from the heads-up display to check again on the real-world terrain outside.

The view showed him nothing that he hadn't seen a few minutes before. He stood on a gently wooded hillside. He could make out a mortar section to his right, tubes implanted in hastily dug pits. To his left, an armored trooper with a shoulder-mounted flamethrower leaned against a tree while another soldier worked on the man's jump jets.

The spread of the valley below was entirely within Jonah's field of vision. A well-equipped battalion would be able to hold this spot indefinitely, controlling the entire valley below. That was what House Ma-Tzu Kai intended. That was what Jonah was supposed to stop. If he could hold them off long enough, a door might open for the troops to get past the House battalion and finally get off planet.

If he failed, Devlin Stone's promises to The Republic would ring hollow. Tenuous threads holding some prefectures together could snap. If Jonah failed, the dream of The Republic might fail as well.

On the plus side, Jonah thought, if I fail it's because I'm dead, so I won't have to witness the aftermath.

He flicked his comm switch to put something in his mind besides gloom.

"Sergeant Turk. Any sign of the main army?"

"Yes, sir!" Relief flooded over Jonah, but Turk's next words took away that relief. "They're mired at the river. They're trying to catch Ma-Tzu Kai's rear, but they're not going to make it. Ma-Tzu Kai will get here first."

"Roger." Jonah flicked off the switch.

He allowed himself one breath—a single intake of air—to feel sorrow. Then he chased it away. This was his hill, he told himself. He would hold. He would bend, he would dodge, he would scamper all over the hilltop, but he would hold.

His right foot almost started tapping, and Jonah couldn't tell if it was nerves or excitement. He stilled it and waited.

Static hissed over his 'Mech's command circuit, and white fuzz ate at the edge of his position-plotting scopes. Wonderful, he thought. They've set up jammers. It can't be long now.

His cockpit suddenly grew ten degrees warmer, and he told himself it was from a splash of sunlight creeping over his 'Mech. His palms grew slick, but the grips of the 'Mech's controls held them in place. Sweat trickled down his forehead, down his neck, down his chest and legs. He cleared his throat, and it cracked with dryness.

The comm sprang to life again, still mostly static, but his techs were already finding a way around the jam. Buried in the sea of white noise were three distinct words: "Here they come!"

Jonah drew a deep breath and steadied his own voice before activating his 'Mech's external speakers so that all of Echo Company could hear.

"Stand fast," he ordered, his voice firm and clear—an illusion, but a convincing one. "Report enemy force and weapons."

A moment later the trees overhead exploded in a world of flame as a pack of missiles slammed into his position.

"Counterbattery!" Jonah ordered.

The mortar section started sliding rounds down the tubes. Each round left the tube with a *whump!* and a puff of thin smoke. The man with the flamethrower was gone, either dead or moved forward, Jonah didn't know. The soldier who'd been helping the man earlier was still in view and unhurt.

The command comm radio was dead again, rejammed by House Ma-Tzu Kai. Whining white noise filled Jonah's ears, but he left it on in case someone managed to get a message through. Meanwhile, all of the *Stinger*'s position scopes went to solid red, leaving all of the unit symbols in the heads-up display frozen where they'd been at last report. Jonah had no new information coming in, no extrapolation based on current positions, nothing.

A current-generation BattleMech in good repair could have stood up to an electronic assault on this scale, but his used and—at least until the militia took possession of it—badly maintained *Stinger* couldn't, and neither could the equipment of the men under his command. They'd have to fight blind and deaf.

But that's what they'd drilled for. This was a militia unit, after all, and as such they had become accustomed to getting the short end of the stick when it came to equipment. They'd been working on backup measures for some of the most common failures and deficiencies since Jonah had taken command. He knew how to get at least part of their hearing back.

Jonah keyed the 'Mech's exterior speakers. "String wire," he ordered a nearby sergeant. "I want field phones."

The sergeant saluted and trotted off. Echo Company of the First Kyrkbacken Militia might be reduced to communicating via the equivalent of tin cans and string, but at least they would not be silenced.

A trooper on a Shandra scout vehicle slid into the clearing through a whirl of dust and fallen leaves. He dismounted at the foot of the *Stinger* and saluted, then picked up a bullhorn hanging from the Shandra's controls.

"Sir," he said over the hailer. "First and Third squads report combined arms assault, infantry backed by hovers. Holding their own. Request ammo resupply."

"Lead me to them," Jonah replied over the exterior mike.

"Sir."

The trooper remounted his vehicle and turned it in place. Jonah followed.

He could pick up the noise of small-arms fire as they moved ahead, the telltale sound of men using their weapons carefully: a single shot, a group of three, another single shot, no one going full auto and burning up a full box of ammunition in a second or two. Such a deliberate rhythm meant that the troopers doing the shooting were seriously low on ammo; and if Jonah could tell as much just by listening, that meant the House Ma-Tzu Kai troopers knew it too.

Jonah spoke to the scout on his vehicle. "Radio HQ," he ordered. "Message: 'Ammunition resupply and reinforcement urgently required.'"

"Sir," the scout said, and turned away, throttling up as his vehicle sped uphill.

Jonah heard more small-arms fire coming from the edge of a gully ahead. He flipped on his cockpit screen's visual enhancement in order to pull in IR-spectrum light. With its aid, he could see the House Ma-Tzu Kai hovercraft screened by brush on the far side, bringing its missiles to bear on his own dug-in troops.

He sent a beam from the *Stinger*'s medium laser downrange at the hovercraft. The vehicle dipped and slewed sideways as the beam hit; then it withdrew, pulling back out of sight behind a rise.

The hover's retreat didn't give the Kyrkbacken Militia any time to catch their breaths. The Ma-Tzu Kai troopers continued to press the attack, and a tank thrashed forward through the trees to the left of the retreating hover.

Jonah swiveled his joystick to raise his right arm in a sweeping motion, hosing down the advancing line of Ma-Tzu Kai troops with the *Stinger*'s medium laser. The troopers went to ground, taking cover in the tall grass and underbrush wherever they could. The tank ground to a halt, its progress blocked by a larger tree. It jerked back, turned to pass the obstacle, just as a Kyrkbacken Militia missile salvo slammed into its thin side armor. The vehicle froze in place, a large smoke ring puffing upward from the open hatch on its top.

A voice from the ground shouted, "They're falling back!" It was the squad's sergeant, back from his earlier errand.

"Let them go," Jonah said.

He looked at his ammo readouts. One single-shot missile pack—the *Stinger* should have carried two, but the second pack had turned out, upon inspection, to be empty, and none of the militia's repeated requests for replacement ammo had borne fruit—with fifteen missiles onboard. After that, he'd be down to nothing but the medium laser, plus whatever morale effect twenty tons of steel could provide.

A signals team arrived with a field connection. Finally, he thought. The team plugged into the jack at the left heel of Jonah's 'Mech, and a signal reappeared on the position plotting indicator.

The news it gave him wasn't good. Only about a third of the troopers that he'd started with this morning were still on the line. The rest were lost, passed beyond the limits of his effective command. Or dead.

"All units," he said over the external link. "Report!"

One by one the remnants of his company came up.

"First squad, fifty percent effective, down to personal ammo packs."

"Second squad, no heavy weapons left. Ten percent casualties."

"Third squad. In place, on line, and ready."

Then a silence.

Into the quiet, Jonah said, "Fourth squad?"

No reply.

"Fifth squad?"

"Fifth squad, in place, antivehicle minefield . . . here they come again!"

The signals crew unplugged the field connection from the foot of Jonah's 'Mech, setting him free to take the *Stinger* off toward Fifth squad's location at an ungainly lope. The Fifth, with Sergeant Turk in charge, was Jonah's rock. They held down the farthest-left position on the flank, the absolute end of The Republic's extended battle line, and the Ma-Tzu Kai forces would be concentrating on them.

An antitank mine exploded from the open ground to Jonah's front, letting him know that he'd arrived at the Fifth's location. He brought his 'Mech to a halt and let a trooper plug him into the Militia's makeshift field phone net.

"Fifth squad, report."

"We got hit by an SM1 with a couple of squads of infantry for support," came Sergeant Turk's reply. The field phones had a peculiar echoing sound, and the sergeant's voice was whispering and distant in Jonah's ears. "An AT mine screwed up the Smiley's hoverjets, but the gun turret is still in play. We can stop the infantry if we can suppress the turret, or we can suppress the turret if we can stop the infantry. But we can't do both at once with what we've got left."

"Mortars, grid posit 132082," Jonah said. "Anti-infantry."

"We have two salvos left, nothing more," the mortar section commander said.

"Then fire two salvos." To Sergeant Turk, Jonah said, "I'll suppress the infantry. You take out the tank. I'm almost out of ammunition."

The first of the mortar bombs arrived, landing in a flash and a flurry of earth mixed with broken trees. Jonah brought the *Stinger* striding forward, breaking the field phone connection again, and brought his 'Mech's lone remaining missile pack to bear on the target.

Enhanced visual, he thought. There they are.

He launched the missiles.

One missile pack, fifteen missiles—that was all that he had, but he'd made the Ma-Tzu Kai infantry keep their heads down for long enough. Now the SM1 was on fire, its main gun pointing crookedly skyward, and the troopers who had been guarding it were scattered and running back, away from the Republic lines.

"Good job, sir," Sergeant Turk said, plugging Jonah back into the field phone net. The jury-rigged comms were better than nothing, but just barely.

"Better job if we could do it again," Jonah said. "Stick with me. I want you to be my eyes and ears."

"On you."

The scout he'd sent off earlier to main HQ returned. "Sir. HQ responds: Ammo resupply impossible. Hold the line."

Jonah clicked off the exterior communications link, isolating himself for a moment in the 'Mech's cockpit.

"We're dead," he observed to the unresponsive silence, and switched the link back on. "All units. Report!"

"First squad, running on empty, sir. Request permission to fall back."

"Denied. Hold fast."

"Understand hold fast. First squad out."

"Second squad. We took it in the shorts, sir. What can you give us?"

"Encouraging words, sergeant."

"Roger, understand encouragement. Second squad out."

The report from Third squad was just as bleak, Fourth still hadn't reappeared, and Jonah could see for himself how badly Fifth squad was faring. Everywhere in his field of view were medics working on the wounded, sergeants checking fighting positions, supplies being doled out, boxes turning up empty, men scrambling among the fallen to find unused energy packs.

"One more assault and we're going to be overrun," Sergeant Turk said.

"Then we won't give them time to regroup," Jonah replied. The idea had come to him as he watched the Fifth through the cockpit window—not a plan, really, so much as an acknowledgment of the only thing left that could be done. He felt as if he were holding the entire Republic on his line, and he'd be dead or damned if it would break.

Over the field phone net, he said: "All squads, listen up. On my command, on your feet and charge forward. The Ma-Tzu Kai have a supply dump just behind their lines at the foot of this hill. We're going to go get it. Take man-portable weapons only. Go bare-handed if you have to. Acknowledge."

"First squad. Aye."

"Second squad. Aye."

"Third squad. Aye."

Silence again from Fourth squad.

"Fifth squad. Aye."

"On my signal," Jonah said, "forward at the double. Stand by. *Execute.*"

Jonah throttled forward, taking the *Stinger* downhill at a lumbering stride, deliberately holding back the 'Mech's speed so as not to outpace the soldiers of his company running along with him. Trees and underbrush splintered and crunched around him; then the ground opened up and he knew he had reached the antivehicle minefield. If he didn't cripple himself with an unlucky step, he was through.

He saw Ma-Tzu Kai troops to the right, left, ahead . . . a wash of red light dazzled in his 'Mech's ferroglass viewscreen . . . enemy laser? A flamer? He couldn't be sure with his instrumentation so messed up. But it didn't matter. Whatever it was had scored a crippling hit on the *Stinger*'s light armor. Only the safety webbing that kept him strapped into the 'Mech's command couch kept him from being tossed about the cockpit as the *Stinger* swayed, toppled and fell.

The impact when the 'Mech hit the ground was bone-jarring, and his body slammed against the safety webbing with bruising force. His head rang and his vision blurred, but he knew that he had to get out of the 'Mech and keep on going.

He couldn't afford to stay with the 'Mech and wait for field repairs and medical assistance—not now, when all that mattered was keeping the troops moving forward. He had to keep up with them, 'Mech or no 'Mech, and make sure that they didn't lose the advantage of their charge.

Working frantically, he unstrapped himself from the command seat with clumsy fingers and unhooked the neurohelmet and the cooling vest. Then he pulled open the rear hatch of the cockpit and half-climbed, half-fell to the ground. Sergeant Turk came up out of nowhere to drape a field jacket over Jonah's sweating shoulders and hand him a Gauss pistol. The indicator on the pistol showed fewer than a dozen shots remaining.

"Here you go, sir."

"Right," said Jonah. He raised his voice to a shout—he had to remember now that he didn't have the 'Mech's speakers to carry the sound for him. "Forward!"

The militia broke into a downhill run, and Jonah ran forward with them, conscious of Sergeant Turk's presence a few meters away, keeping pace. I wonder if my family will be told what happened here? he wondered. Then a Ma-Tzu Kai trooper popped up in front of him, and he abandoned thought for reflex in time to snap a shot at the man.

The trooper fell; his companion sprang to his feet and turned to run. Jonah watched him go, not wanting to waste a shot on a fleeing soldier. He pushed on downhill.

He could hear shooting from his right and left. It sounded scattered and unguided. Then a sudden pain hit his leg and he collapsed. It felt like he'd been kicked. He looked down. Blood was running from his left thigh in a dark red flood.

Sergeant Turk was beside him, tying on a field dressing.

"Help me up," Jonah said

"You're hurt, sir."

"I'm aware of that, Sergeant. Help me up."

The sergeant grasped Jonah's wrists and pulled. Jonah came to his feet, swayed, tested his leg. "It'll do. Forward!"

The sergeant put his shoulder under Jonah's left arm. "I'll help you, sir."

The sergeant had a knife, Jonah noted. No rifle, no grenades. Just that knife, and his knife hand was red up to the elbow.

This is bad, Jonah thought. This is getting very bad.

"We're going to do this, right?" Sergeant Turk asked. Jonah realized suddenly that for all his prior service, the man was no older than he himself, and possibly younger.

"Right," Jonah replied. "Let's go."

The two of them hobbled forward like contestants in some bizarre three-legged race, stumbling downhill at a clumsy run.

Jonah heard a falling hiss, followed by an explosion from the right. Someone nearby—the sergeant, maybe, he couldn't tell—shouted out, "Incoming!"

"Never mind that," Jonah said. He thought he shouted

it himself, so everyone could hear him, but he couldn't be sure. "We're close now. Keep going!"

The ground underfoot was leveling off. They could run faster now, and not stagger as much. Jonah was surprised he had gotten this far.

"Up ahead!" he shouted. He was certain he shouted, this time. "The ammo dump! Go!"

A voice, he didn't know who, yelled "Republic! Republic troops breaking through!" Someone else yelled, "They're running! The bastards are running!" and the air filled with hoarse and breathless cheers.

Then Jonah heard an explosion, closer than any of the others, and knew nothing more.

══ 32 ══

Republic JumpShip **Unity**
Prefecture VI
26 October 3110

After a period of gray fogginess during which voices came and went, saying things that he didn't understand and couldn't concentrate on long enough to force into meaning, Jonah Levin woke up. The fog hadn't receded completely, but he had an awareness of himself now that he hadn't before, enough to tell that he hurt all over, and that there was something he was supposed to remember. That he was supposed to ask, to know.

He wet his lips and tried to find his voice. ". . . the troops . . . off planet?"

"Shh. You need your rest."

"No." He couldn't rest, not in the middle of a battle. If he'd fallen—he was lying down, so he must have fallen—then he had to get up. He struggled to rise, and collapsed again under the weight of sudden pain. "Sergeant! Sergeant Turk!"

"It's all over now. You need to lie still so you can heal."

He *wanted* to lie down. He was tired, so very tired, and

he hurt all over. But he couldn't rest. Not yet. "Sergeant, we have to—"

The grayness rolled him under again like a giant wave, and he knew nothing.

Much later, he opened his eyes. His mind was awake and clear, and he knew at once that he was lucid for the first time in a long while. The inside of his head felt empty and unused, like a room with its furniture missing. He still hurt all over, and was aware of needles and tubes binding him, holding him down. He couldn't have moved even if he'd been strong enough.

He wasn't on Prospect Hill any longer, but in a windowless, high-ceilinged room. Somewhere outside his range of vision, quiet machinery hummed and beeped.

"Good to see you awake again, Captain."

That was Sergeant Turk's voice, off to his right. With considerable effort, Jonah turned his head in that direction on the pillow. Turk sat in a wheelchair by the bed with one leg out and up, encased in orange casting plastic. His right arm ended in a bandaged stump just above where the elbow had been. He was pale and thin, but smiling broadly despite his injuries.

"It's good to see you, too, Sergeant." Jonah's voice came out faint and thready, but he pushed on anyway. It was important that he know. "The company . . . we pushed Ma-Tzu Kai back? Held the line?"

"We held the line, Captain. They were confused by our rush, and the Republic troops took advantage and smashed through. Ma-Tzu Kai broke when we hit the ammo dump. By the time they pulled themselves back together, everyone was on their way out. We all got off-planet in a hurry. And now we're back in The Republic."

Jonah experienced a tremendous relief, like a lightness running all through him. He felt thin and insubstantial, as if he were scarcely present in his body at all. His eyes watered, so he closed them and waited for the feeling to pass.

"Captain?"

He opened his eyes again with an effort. "It's all right, Sergeant. I'm just . . . tired, is all. What hit us, there at the end?"

"Rocks, Captain. Lots and lots of rocks."

"Rocks?"

"Ma-Tzu Kai long-range laser strike blew up a boulder close to where we were standing. We kind of got in the way of all the pieces."

Jonah pondered that for a moment. Pummeled by a ton of rocks. That meshed pretty well with the way he felt. "Ouch," he said.

"No kidding, Captain."

"Where are we now?"

"Prefecture VI. Not far from Kyrkbacken, actually. You were out of it for quite a while."

"So I gathered." His throat and mouth were dry; he swallowed, trying to ease it. "And the rest of the company? What were our losses?"

"Sixty-two dead, 220 wounded."

Staggering. Eighteen people came out of that battle unhurt. Eighteen. Echo Company no longer existed as a fighting force. It might eventually be brought back up to strength with new recruits, but that would mean re-creating the unit from scratch. With those casualty figures, not even enough able troopers remained to make up a training cadre.

And what of the rest of the militias? Their losses can't have been that severe, Jonah thought—they weren't standing between Ma-Tzu Kai and their goal, like we were. But the losses still had to be heavy. How many more hundreds lay on Kurragin, forever out of the reach of their mourning families?

But still, it was a miracle. More than two hundred of them still lived. Outmanned, outgunned, and ordered into a suicide charge, and most were still alive. He felt the pain of each death, but marveled that it hadn't been more.

He closed his eyes again, feeling moisture well up in them, and letting it flow. "What a troop," he said. "What a bloody good troop."

"Roger that."

"Bunch of rookies. Probably didn't even know they should all be dead."

Footsteps sounded in the hall outside. A medic came in, all brisk efficiency. "Time to change your dressings, Sergeant Turk."

He wheeled Turk away, leaving Jonah alone and empty, staring at the sterile white light above. He wasn't alone for long before he heard more footsteps, two sets this time.

The footsteps turned out to belong to a woman he didn't recognize, in the uniform of a Knight of the Sphere, and a civilian man in a well-cut suit. The civilian had a vaguely familiar face, Jonah thought . . . had he seen it before on the tri-vid news? He didn't know, and trying to remember was too much work.

The Knight was smiling. "Captain Levin! It's good to see you awake at last."

At last? Jonah wondered silently. How long was I—

The civilian spoke before he could say anything. "The Republic owes you a very great debt, Captain."

Even when healthy, Jonah would have been pressed to come up with a good response to that remark. In his current condition, there was no chance.

"If you hadn't held the hill," the Knight said, "House Ma-Tzu Kai would have controlled the whole valley. They would have smashed into us as soon as they could. It would have been a rout."

"It—it was . . ." He ran out of words, uncertain what he was supposed to say to a statement like that. "Orders," he said finally. "We had orders."

The Knight said nothing, but she nodded, and he saw from her face that she understood. "I am Lady Maya Avellar," she said. "And this is Senator Geoffrey Mallowes from Skye. He is here to convey The Republic's thanks in person."

"Indeed," said Mallowes. "We had some quite vigorous debate, you might like to know, on the question of exactly how the Senate should honor your valiant defense of Prospect Hill."

" 'My defense' . . . my company, you mean. I wasn't the only one up there." Jonah pushed the words through cracked lips.

The Senator continued as if Jonah hadn't spoken. "There was considerable discussion as to what decoration might be appropriate—there was even some controversy over whether a member of a planetary militia, even one on loan to The Republic for a specific campaign, would be eligible for any of The Republic's awards—but in the end the

Council of Paladins trumped us." Jonah heard a strange note in Mallowe's voice that, had his mind been sharper, he might have been able to recognize. "They have recognition for you that is likely beyond anything the Senate can offer."

He turned to Lady Avellar, his expression seeming to sour. She spoke. "The Paladins of the Sphere are pleased to offer you thanks for your heroic actions, and to inform you of your appointment as a Knight of the Sphere."

Jonah's face hurt, his throat hurt and his lips hurt, but despite all that he almost laughed. Reward? Becoming a Knight, with the heightened profile and notoriety that came with it, seemed as much curse as reward.

"My company," he said, stifling a laugh in a way that looked like he was choking a sob. "Reward my company first."

Senator Mallowes looked taken aback. Apparently he thought his announcement would be met with deeper gratitude.

Lady Avellar's smile, though, remained steady. "In recognition of your service you are being made a Knight of the Sphere, but you will remain attached to Kyrkbacken for a time. Should you know of any soldiers or companies within your jurisdiction who deserve special recognition, you will have several resources at your disposal with which to reward them."

Jonah relaxed a little, letting his head sink into the pile of pillows behind him. Whether she knew it or not, Avellar had said exactly the right thing. Had she tried to appeal to his pride, or convince him the promotion was something he deserved, the conversation would have headed in a very different direction. But by telling him this promotion gave him the means to help people who deserved it, she gave him only one option.

"Thank you. You can be sure I'll hold you to that promise."

Avellar bobbed her head. "We're here because of your dedication to keeping a promise. We hope you'll recognize that quality in many of your fellow Knights."

Mallowes, still seeming off-balance, tried to reassert himself in the conversation. "You have a bright future in The

Republic, young man. Your actions have already taught us to expect the best of you."

Jonah bowed his head in acknowledgment of the Senator's words, but he thought to himself: if you truly knew anything about me, you'd know that such words have very little effect.

Jonah bore many scars from that battle, some of which still ached when the weather changed. But many members of Echo Company suffered far more.

The upper ranks of the Kyrkbacken Militia were filled with veterans of Echo Company. Some had retired from the military, a few to teaching positions in military academies, a few away from the military altogether. Jonah kept careful track of each and every survivor, never letting a single one fall through society's cracks, helping where he could.

That was why he was willing to become a Knight, and later a Paladin. He hated politics and the trappings of office, but, as he saw it, those things weren't the core of his job. Across the Sphere, there were millions of lines—in battle and in peace—that needed to be held. And he knew how to hold them.

33

Mallowes' face hadn't changed much in the past quarter century. The crags were a little deeper, his earlobes hung slightly lower and his hand occasionally shook when he held it out too long. But the hair was still thick and white, the eyes cold steel, the jaw firmly set in place.

"Paladin Levin," Mallowes said warmly, clasping Jonah's hand in both of his. "I'm always honored when your path intersects mine."

And he still had the same formal way of speech, Jonah thought to himself.

"Good to see you too, Senator," Jonah said. "Though the circumstances could be better."

Mallowes dropped his smile. "Very true. You sit in the center of an uneasy Republic, and recent events have done nothing to bring it peace. Please, sit."

Mallowes' office was clearly distinguishable from the others Jonah had visited recently. It should be—Mallowes had had decades to customize it to his liking. Its décor was a miniature history of politics, with framed replicas of the Declaration of Independence from the ancient United States of America, the Ares Conventions, and the Constitution of The Republic of the Sphere. Surrounding them was a miniature hall of fame of great diplomats featuring nearly twenty portraits, most of them personally inscribed to Mallowes. Jonah noticed with some amusement that Mallowes had pictures of Victor Steiner-Davion and his sister Katherine on the same wall, though placed far from each other.

"Should I be troubled, Paladin, that your investigation has led to me?" The Senator's tone was light, but it held a clear message—Mallowes knew why he was there, and there was no reason for Jonah to play any games.

"No, Senator. I'm currently gathering information on someone you've worked with before, a man named Henrik Morten. You've sent him on a number of tasks over the past few years."

Mallowes nodded. "Yes. A very capable young man. A noble, one of the Mallory's World Mortens, as I'm sure you know. He crafted more than a few successes for me." Mallowes paused. "It makes me regret, to a small degree, the fact that I have not been able to utilize him recently."

"That's what I noticed. It seems he was working for you regularly until about half a year ago, then, from everything I've been able to find out, your connection to him dried up. He's been freelancing for about half a dozen others recently, but not you."

"Yes." Mallowes clasped his hands, index fingers extended, and rested his fingertips on his chin. "I assume you've heard of some of Morten's most valuable qualities? His discretion, his ability to deal with highly sensitive matters with a minimum of detection."

"People have mentioned that, yes."

"I discovered some unfortunate information on how he achieved those ends. I never had enough concrete proof to bring formal charges against him, but suffice it to say he sometimes pays people to keep secrets—" here Mallowes delicately cleared his throat "—and sometimes he makes others pay in advance. If you take my meaning."

"I'm guessing the payment he extracts isn't always monetary."

"You have it precisely."

"Are you pursuing any of this information? Looking to bring charges?"

Mallowes sighed. "I intend to. However, with the election and assorted doings, my mind has been focused elsewhere. Hopefully, when the new Exarch is seated, I will be able to pursue a case with more vigor. I assure you, however, that I have done my best to spread the word about the young man's activities to my colleagues, hoping to dissuade them from employing his services. Possessing noble blood brings with it a responsibility for noble behavior, and this young man seems to have forgotten—or never learned—this principle."

"And how have they responded?"

"Most of them trust me, knowing I do not convey information lightly. A few, though, have noticed the lack of substantial evidence against Morten and choose to ignore my counsel and employ him anyway."

Jonah leaned forward. A list of officials willing to use Morten even after hearing about some of his seamier activities could prove valuable. "Who?"

"Hmmm . . . actually, there are only two I can think of offhand. Governor Newberry of Dieron seems to believe the young man's coalition-building capabilities are second only to Devlin Stone, and continues to employ him. And an old friend of mine, your newest colleague—Gareth Sinclair. He actually remains a firm supporter of Morten, from what he has told me."

That was the fourth time Sinclair's name had come up in the course of Jonah's investigations. He'd already scheduled a meeting with him, and it was shaping up to be an unpleasant conversation.

"I'm sorry if I haven't given you the help you sought," Mallowes said, noticing Jonah's silence.

Jonah forced the corners of his mouth into a warm smile. "You've been plenty helpful, believe me. I appreciate your time."

"And I would appreciate yours, if you're willing to lend me a few more moments of it."

"I'd be happy to. How can I help you?" Jonah asked, even though he knew full well what the Senator wanted to talk about.

Mallowes stood, pushing his shoulders back slightly, looking for all the world like a man about to deliver an important speech. "As you well know, had Devlin Stone intended the Senate to play an active role in the election of an Exarch, he would have given us a vote."

Jonah sighed inaudibly. *Why doesn't he just come out and ask the question he has undoubtedly been thinking about since I first called,* Jonah asked himself.

"But he, in his wisdom, bequeathed sole responsibility in the manner to the Paladins of the Sphere, people who ascended to their lofty position by virtue of their honor, honesty and incorruptibility."

Ask the question! Jonah yelled in his head.

"However, it is abundantly clear that Stone intended his Paladins to be people of wisdom, and it is equally clear that Stone believed a major portion of wisdom to be the ability to hear and receive counsel. And we must not forget that he intentionally allowed only those of noble blood into the Senate, filling that body with individuals whose families have vast experience in matters of government."

Here it comes, Jonah said. *Either the question, or an hour-long lecture on the role of counselors in Devlin Stone's life.*

"While I'm sure you're not surprised to know I have some thoughts on the upcoming election, it would be quite out of turn if I shared my ideas without knowing where you stand in the matter. I was wondering, then, if, given our extensive history, you would be willing to share your thoughts on who will receive your vote in the coming election."

Finally! Jonah hoped the Senator could not hear the rush of air escaping his lungs. Since Mallowes had given him plenty of time to prepare a response, he answered quickly.

"I've thought about it a lot, but I haven't come to a final decision yet. I don't think it would be proper for me to name names until I've made up my mind. I wouldn't want the others talking about me like that, so I won't do it to them."

Mallowes smiled, though his exposed teeth seemed a bit clenched. "I cannot begin to tell you what a pleasure it is to talk with one who gives such a prominent consideration to honor as do you. It was a trait that greatly impressed me when we first met."

Jonah remembered the Senator seeming more confused than impressed at that meeting, but he felt it best not to point that out.

Mallowes, still on his feet, paced around his desk and stood over Jonah, trying to make Jonah crane his neck upward. Instead, Jonah smoothly rose to stand next to him, and Mallowes was forced to raise his eyes to look into the face of the Paladin.

"Let us not name names, then," Mallowes said, his voice little more than a raspy whisper. "Let us talk about what should be at the core of all elections—ideas."

"What ideas did you have in mind?"

"Strength. Sovereignty. Tradition."

Jonah had heard these words many times in recent weeks, so he filled in the last one for Mallowes. "Vision."

Mallowes snapped his fingers. "Precisely! These are difficult times, Paladin Levin. We need an Exarch willing to make hard choices."

"We always do."

"Yes, yes, we always have the need, but the choices keep being deferred. Compromise. Negotiation. Appeasement. These are tools of delay, not true decisions. We need an Exarch who will finally confront our enemies squarely, deal with them in the only way they understand."

"They don't understand peace?"

Mallowes snorted. "Look at our borders and ask me that question again."

"Senator Mallowes, do you remember when we met after the fight on Kurragin?"

Mallowes smiled warmly, though it seemed more a reflex than an indication of real feeling. "Of course."

"Do you remember the orders I followed on the battlefield?"

"Yes. You were to hold your line."

"And I did. There are many things I'm not good at, Senator, but I've always known how to hold a line. When the election comes, that's what I'll be thinking about."

Mallowes nodded approvingly. "Good, good. But how do you know which is the proper line to hold?"

"My job is to know."

"The job of your entire council is to know. But some of them don't." Mallowes paused, and something flickered behind his eyes. Caution? Annoyance? Jonah couldn't be sure.

Then Mallowes spoke again. "Victor Steiner-Davion did not know."

Jonah's eyes narrowed. "What are you saying?"

"Please, make no mistake—I greatly admired the man for all he accomplished in his many years. Unfortunately, he believed that life, in the person of his sister, had taught him the importance of governing with a light hand, of erring on the side of indulgence instead of caution."

"I believe Victor preferred the term 'freedom' to 'indulgence,'" Jonah said darkly.

"Quite so. But you see, he took the wrong lesson. The problems he had with his sister, the disaster of the Civil War, were not caused by her grip being too tight. They were caused by his being too loose. We must never forget that his laxity practically handed power to her. He was the cause of his own misfortune.

"The Republic cannot afford to make similar mistakes at this time," Mallowes continued. "We cannot let threats build while we turn our heads. Now is the time for strength. Victor's fate is evidence of what happens to those who are not strong."

Anger and suspicion flared in Jonah. " 'Evidence of what happens'?" he said heatedly. "Are you saying Victor's death was tied to this?"

Mallowes raised his hands placatingly. "No, no, not his death. I have no idea what caused that. The war, my friend. I meant the Civil War." He shook his head. "I see your temper has not mellowed with age."

Jonah willed himself calm, forcing his fists to unclench. "I . . . apologize. I thought you were insinuating something else."

"No apology necessary. You may be assured that, to a degree, I understand the stress weighing upon you. All of us in government feel it." Mallowes placed a hand on Jonah's shoulder. "All the more reason we must show strength. Now."

34

Heather had three lists. One named Paladins she was all but certain had nothing to do with the Kittery Renaissance; these were people she did not need to bother speaking with. The second named those of her colleagues who had expressed sympathy with the Founder's Movement. The third listed Paladins she considered entirely trustworthy and well informed. That list had two names, and since Jonah Levin was otherwise occupied, she started her interviews with Otto Mandela.

He'd better know something, she thought. She was quickly running out of time before the election.

She strode quickly down the hallway, and Duncan, a full six inches shorter than she, struggled to keep up. He refused to stop talking.

"Two members of the Clutch of the Confederacy are in custody, but the police aren't sure the charges are going to stick. Stone's Loyalists broke up a march by 'Mechs Into

Plowshares, and spotters believe members of Stone's Vow were working with the Loyalists."

Heather stopped and whirled, giving a grateful Duncan a chance to keep up. "Have the police and militia been notified of all this?"

"Yes, Paladin."

"Are they taking care of these situations?"

"Yes, Paladin."

"Then why do you keep telling me about them?"

"I was tasked to keep you informed," Duncan said promptly.

Heather sighed and turned back toward Mandela's office. She didn't have time to hash this out with Duncan at the moment.

Just outside Mandela's office, Duncan spoke again. "Ma'am?"

"Yes?"

"Do you really think that one of the Paladins—one of the other Paladins, I mean—might be supporting the Kittery Renaissance?"

Heather considered the question seriously. "I'd like to think not. But anything's possible."

Heather pressed the buzzer. "Paladin GioAvanti to speak with Paladin Mandela."

Duncan continued, "What am I supposed to do while you're talking with him?"

"Make small talk with his aide or his secretary or whoever else he may keep around the office who's about your age. Keep your ears open." She nodded toward his noteputer. "And make sure you keep checking those incoming messages."

Duncan nodded seriously as the amplified and transmitted voice of a receptionist spoke from inside Mandela's office. "Come in, Paladin GioAvanti."

The door opened, and they entered the office suite. Soon Heather was in the inner office, where Otto Mandela claimed to be pleased to see her and willing to help her in whatever way he could.

"I'm glad you can spare me the time, Otto," Heather said to Mandela. "You've been on Sheratan recently, right?"

"Yes. The election was a bit of a zoo, but nothing compared to what's going on here."

"Plenty of factions at work?"

"Every third house seemed like it was headquarters for some upstart group."

"Did you hear anything about the Kittery Renaissance there?"

Otto sat straighter in his chair. "Not on Sheratan, no. But I've certainly heard of them."

"What do you know about them?"

"Plenty, but that's not what you're asking me. You're asking what I know about them that I may not have shared with everyone yet."

Heather flashed one of her charming smiles. "Yes."

"Paladin GioAvanti, please don't take this the wrong way, but if I've been sitting on information, holding it from others, why should I give it to you now?"

Heather tapped her foot as a couple of options ran through her head. Then she decided.

"Can I show you something on your data screen?" she asked.

"Be my guest."

Logging into her account, Heather played a piece of the riot video showing the Capellan sympathizer who instigated the whole thing. She looped it, and the woman flared into anger again and again and again.

Mandela watched it at least five times, his face blank. Finally he reached forward and stopped the playback.

"Norah," he said.

Heather almost lunged toward him. "You know her name?"

"No. I know her alias. The person who shared that information with me had no idea what her real name was."

"You're sure?"

"We extracted everything that he knew," Mandela said, with a fierce note Heather hadn't heard in his voice before. "Believe me."

"Who is she?"

"I wish I could tell you. We have nothing beyond her alias—no background, no world of origin, nothing. We don't even know if anyone else in the group calls her Norah. But our source believed she was fairly high in the organization. If she's here, on the street, they're definitely moving toward something big."

"How come this information isn't in the file?"

Mandela eyed Heather warily. "Most of it is."

"And the rest?"

"I held out."

Heather's toe started tapping on the floor. She had come to Mandela because she trusted him, yet now even he was acting suspiciously.

"Why would you hold out anything?"

"First, because this name is of little consequence. It's an alias, and for all I know she changes it on a daily basis. Second"—Mandela's words emerged slowly, as he chose each carefully—"often in these investigations it can be useful to know something no one else knows. Though of little consequence, these bits of information can prove useful in interrogations, or undercover infiltrations. It's best to keep one or two things away from all other eyes to protect their confidentiality."

"You don't trust a classified file?"

"Have any Paladins ever given you reason to mistrust them?" he shot back.

She wanted to say "no," but she couldn't. "All right. Why tell me her name now?"

"As I said, these little pieces can be useful in interrogations, which I hope you will be conducting shortly. And I trust you more than I trust the file."

"Thanks. So you say her presence means they're moving toward something big. Any ideas on what that might be?"

Mandela stood, walked to a corner of his office, and began idly spinning a globe as he thought. The rhythmic thud of his hand on the resin was oddly soothing.

"They don't want to destroy The Republic," Mandela said, thinking out loud. "If they act against the government, it wouldn't be to bring it down entirely; they would just want certain people out, making room for the people they felt they could trust, or who would further their goals."

"Assassination?" A thought had struck Heather.

Mandela's hand moved faster. "Maybe. In certain cases, they might find it necessary."

"Victor?"

The spinning globe stopped as Mandela's hand rested flat on it. Then he slowly began spinning it again.

"Not likely. A movement like Kittery depends on a certain degree of public support. Victor may not have shared their goals, but he was a legend—killing him could do them far more harm than good, in the long run."

"How does staging a riot do anything good for their popular support?"

Otto gave the globe a final spin, then paced back to his chair. His gestures became more and more theatrical as the conversation progressed. There was a reason Mandela was assigned to watch elections so often, besides his honesty. He understood politics as well as any Paladin—with the possible exception of Anders Kessel.

"First, you have to remember that only a few of us know that Kittery had anything to do with this. They have made no effort to take credit for their effort—to the contrary, they've covered their tracks quite well. This is not supposed to be a riot of the Kittery Renaissance. It's just supposed to be a random occurrence."

"Increasing the tension in a city already near the boiling point."

"Right!" said Mandela with a snap of his fingers. "Leading to either a popular uprising against the government—"

"—which, given the government's vast technological advantage over the citizenry, is unlikely to succeed—"

"—or to a government crackdown." Mandela paused before adding one more thought. "Or, with the election coming up, influencing us to choose an Exarch who will crack down on some of these elements."

"They staged a riot to manipulate us?" Heather asked incredulously. "It's not working too well."

"They're not done. This is a prelude. Whatever they have planned next is supposed to do the real work."

"And what they're planning is . . ."

Mandela, who had been wandering briskly around his office, abruptly stopped and slumped in his chair. "I have no idea."

"If they're trying to manipulate the election, who is it they want to win?"

Mandela smiled wanly. "Before I could take a stab at that, I'd need to know what they were up to."

"Now for the truly difficult question. Is one of our number using the KR to get themselves elected?"

"No," Mandela said firmly. But he shifted in his chair.

Heather, watching him squirm, remained silent.

"At least, I hope not," Mandela finally said. "This is not our way, funding terrorists to do work that, all our lives, we've performed directly for ourselves. I know the Paladins well enough that I have difficulty believing any of them would be involved with this group. But in the current political climate, I cannot offer any guarantees."

"Plus," Heather added, "we have two Paladins who many of us don't know very well."

"Redburn appointed them, and I trust his judgment," Mandela said. "But you're right. We don't know them."

Heather didn't have to look for Duncan when she left Mandela's office. He pounced when he saw her.

"We're up to three bomb threats in the Hall of Government today," he said. "Would you like to know who sent them?"

"No."

"I should tell you a mysterious package was found on the eighth floor."

"A bomb?"

"No. A misplaced data screen."

"Why are you telling me this?"

"To keep—"

"—me informed. Fine. How did your conversation with the receptionist go?"

Duncan's eyes brightened. "Oh, right! Interesting!"

Heather fervently wished Duncan had learned something besides the woman's phone number.

"It turns out she's new here. She'd been working for a Senator for a while, but just got transferred out."

"Okay."

"She says she got transferred because she caught her boss sneaking a rendezvous with some guy from the diplomatic corps."

"Sex?"

"Maybe. But something else, too," Duncan said, attempting an air of careful sophistication. "Getting transferred doesn't do anything, really, to keep her from talking. She's free to spread rumors about them as much as she wants, like she did with me. But what she can't do anymore is watch them. If they're up to something else, she's not in position anymore to find out what it is."

"That's good thinking," Heather said, trying not to sound surprised. "Did she happen to mention any names?"

Duncan smiled. "She certainly did."

35

St. Croix Office Equipment Warehouse, Geneva Terra, Prefecture X
13 December 3134

At night, the warehouse compound of St. Croix Office Equipment and Consumables, located in Geneva's industrial outer ring, resembled nothing so much as a large, empty shoebox. The site scarcely looked the same as the busy commercial depot that by day received and sent out crates and pallets of manufactured goods—desks, chairs, computers, short-run printing and binding equipment, cleaning equipment and supplies, and reams and reams of paper.

Geneva was the home of the largest bureaucracy in The Republic of the Sphere, and the city's appetite for office supplies was insatiable. This particular St. Croix warehouse was only one of dozens of such ugly rectangular buildings located out of sight of the elegant and historic city center, but conveniently close to the main transit arteries required for making deliveries.

This last fact prompted the Kittery Renaissance leader, Cullen Roi, to settle on the warehouses of the St. Croix chain as the target for tonight's work.

Cullen Roi had sent Hansel to supervise the job. Norah would have liked to come as well, but Cullen knew that she couldn't be trusted with this kind of mission. She was an excellent agent provocateur, one of the best at stirring up trouble and being long gone by the time it came to a head, but she was neither patient nor quiet.

Hansel, on the other hand, was a realist, completely lacking in vanity. His focus was on getting the job done well and quickly, and getting out. Speed was of the essence, since Hansel had several stops to make before the night was over.

Hansel steered a delivery truck up to the warehouse compound's security gate. The truck was a massive tandem special, two containers in line; the false St. Croix markings on its sides were indistinguishable from the real thing. The cargo inside the two containers, however, was not office equipment.

The night guard at the complex gate had been keeping himself awake in his glass-enclosed box by watching reruns of *For Clan and Honor* on a console-top tri-vid display. He didn't look happy to see a big truck stopped at the barrier outside. He came out anyway, a disgusted expression on his face.

"You don't get in without papers."

"I've got papers," Hansel said. He did indeed have papers; excellent forgeries, the best that Cullen Roi could provide. "Just wait a minute."

He retrieved the forged papers from the truck cab's under-dash compartment and made a show of looking through them before handing them out the window. "Here."

"Not my job to let people in or out. Just my job to watch the gate."

The guard took the papers anyway, and read through them, frowning. His lips didn't move as he read, but Hansel suspected that it was a near thing. When he was done he raised his head and eyed Hansel with mistrust.

"It says here you were supposed to be delivering this stuff at five this afternoon."

"Stuff happens," said Hansel. "At five this afternoon I blew a flux circuit. I had to spend good money getting it fixed, too."

The guard scowled like a teacher listening to an excuse for late homework. Hansel waited calmly.

The guard said, "You couldn't have laid up somewhere for the night, could you?"

"Sorry," Hansel said. "I've got things to do at home tomorrow. All I want to do is unload this stuff and be on my way."

"Pass on through, then."

"I need the papers back after you've signed them," Hansel reminded him.

"Right." The guard scrawled his name with a St. Croix giveaway pen and returned the papers. "Ramp's around behind back. And don't expect any help from me with the unloading."

"Thank you," said Hansel politely, but the man was already retreating into his lighted box.

The guard pressed a button on the security console, and the gate swung open. Hansel drove the big tandem truck into the warehouse compound and around to the rear of the main building. He stopped next to the loading dock, which was conveniently out of sight from the gate—yet another reason why this warehouse was one of the Kittery Renaissance's chosen sites.

He got down from the cab, went over to the first container of the tandem pair, and knocked on the side panel.

"You guys can come out now."

The panel slid open with a metallic groan, loud in the darkness. Hansel wasn't unduly worried about the noise. Their presence inside the warehouse compound had been accepted and accounted for, and work sounds would be expected.

A half-dozen men climbed out of the first container. Like Hansel, they were dressed in workers' coveralls with the St. Croix company logo embroidered across the shoulders in back. Maybe in storybooks and tri-vids the secret operatives made themselves invisible by dressing all in black, but Hansel knew better than that. Nobody in Geneva was as invisible as a manual laborer in his working attire.

"We don't have much time," he said as soon as the last man emerged from the container. "Get moving."

The men swung a ramp down from the open side panel and began unloading boxes. The labels on the boxes identified them as containing preassembled metal filing cabinets and collapsible tri-vid reception tanks, manufactured by third parties and repackaged with the St. Croix logo.

Deceptive packaging, Hansel thought with amusement, in more ways than one. The boxes actually held an assortment of pistols—auto-pistols, lasers, and flamers—a few rifles and shotguns, and the ammunition to go with them, enough in this truck alone to outfit at least a company. Not all of them were likely to be needed, but there was no way to tell in advance which of the group's weapons stockpiles would see the heaviest use on the day itself. It was necessary, therefore, to fully supply all of them.

The Kittery Renaissance had sunk a large percentage of its liquid funds into this project. If it failed, the movement would be toothless for a while, money depleted, members dead, or lost in the disappointment of failure. Those kinds of losses could spell the end of the whole organization.

We'll just have to succeed, Hansel thought.

Hansel had the key codes for the locks on the warehouse doors. He got them open in seconds, both the small door at the top of the loading ramp, and the big garage-style door next to it. Inside, the warehouse was full of containers like the ones being off-loaded from the truck.

"Jacques, Benny," he said. "Get down here and move some of this stuff out of the way."

Two men, both built like drilling 'Mechs, detached themselves from the group of laborers. Jacques asked, "Where do you want us to put the stuff we're moving?"

"Stack it a bit higher, move the boxes a bit closer together . . . we want our stuff mixed in with it, but still easy to find in a hurry."

"Right you are, boss."

"And make certain to leave enough room for the big surprise. We don't want to spoil the day by having it found too soon."

The men laughed and began shifting boxes. When all of the weapons and ammunition had been safely unloaded and concealed, Hansel returned to the truck. He mounted into the cab, started the engine, and brought the truck around so that he could back it through the big door and into the warehouse. It wouldn't all fit—the cab and the front container were still outside—but the rear container was inside and out of sight. He hit the button on the cab console to open the back door of the rear container and lower its heavy-duty hydraulic ramp.

That done, he climbed down from the cab again. "All right, take her out."

Two of the men climbed up into the container, the others waited outside it. A moment later a Fox armored car emerged from the truck's dark interior, was pushed down the ramp and braced by the team to keep it from rolling out of control.

"Boss?" said Benny. "How are we going to hide something like that?"

"You'll see."

Soon, the armored car had been covered with a canvas drop cloth, its outline under the cloth obscured by boxes of office supplies—innocent ones this time—stacked on its flat surfaces. Half a dozen similar canvas drop cloths went over random piles of crates throughout the warehouse.

"The armored car doesn't have to stay hidden forever," Hansel explained. "Just so no one looks at it until Friday, that's long enough."

The work crew got back into the truck container. Hansel shut the warehouse doors and climbed into the cab. Shortly afterward, he was signing back out through the compound gate, on his way to repeat the process twelve more times, at different locations, before dawn brought returning workers and increased traffic to the streets of Geneva.

36

Another late evening in a string of too many found Jonah Levin once more in workingman's clothing at the First Stop Bar. He was drinking beer with a chaser again, amid a crowd hoping to drink enough to forget the past 365 days. It made him feel old, revisiting the bad habits of his youth, even for a good purpose. The things we do for The Republic, he thought; I ought to be at home on Kervil with Anna, not sitting here drinking by myself.

This evening, after a long day of interviews, Jonah had found a message from former-sergeant Turk waiting for him at the Pension Flambard asking for a meeting. From one meeting to another to another, Jonah thought to himself. I'm really a politician now. He yearned to have someone try to kill him, if only to break up the meetings.

After reading the note left for him at the front desk in Madame's careful handwriting, he'd changed out of his regular clothing and into his workingman's disguise, then slipped out through the back entrance of the pension.

This close to the election, there was no telling when a

roving tri-vid reporter or some faction's spies might decide to get ambitious and stake out the front door. He was certain that most of them already knew where he stayed when he was in Geneva; after all, he'd never made any attempt to conceal it. Fortunately, Madame Flambard's discretion was phenomenal, and she was willing to go considerable lengths to protect the privacy of a long-time returning guest.

The First Stop Bar was as dim as before and, thankfully, filled with conversation on every topic except politics. People discussed music, vids, sports, their jobs—but not the election. Jonah let the cleansing flow of casual discussion soothe his jangling nerves. He sat at a table in the back, listening to the scraps of conversation drifting past him while carefully presenting a front of a misanthropic solitary drinker. And as such, he was left alone until late in the evening, when Turk finally showed up.

The former sergeant collected his own beer-and-chaser from the bar and joined Jonah at the table. "Good to see you made it here," he said. "I couldn't tell if the woman I left the message with was going to pass it along or not."

"That's Madame Flambard." Jonah smiled. "She's protective of her guests' privacy. But extremely reliable."

"Reliable's good."

"Yes. Your message made it sound like you had some information to pass along."

"Maybe. I'm not sure."

That was unusual, Jonah reflected. He didn't recall Turk ever being unsure about anything, back on Kurragin. " 'If it's worth noticing, it's worth reporting,' " he said—he was quoting himself from that long-ago time, yet another sign that he was getting old. "Pass it on up and let somebody else sort it out."

"This isn't about what you asked me, about the government offices," Turk said. "I haven't heard anything from that team yet. This is something different—but if it's what I think it is, then somebody needs to know about it in a hurry."

"Don't keep me in suspense, Sergeant. Spit it out."

"Here goes, then." Turk took a long pull at his beer, then settled back in his chair. "The first thing is that my people don't just work at the government buildings. The

Republic gave us our first big custodial contract, all right, and that arrangement is still our bread and butter, but the outfit's picked up quite a few other clients since you helped me get started."

"That's good."

"Yeah. Anyhow, when I put the word out that a friend of mine from way back was looking for information about stuff going on where it shouldn't be, I didn't expect anything to happen quite this soon. I thought people would still be trying to make up their minds whether they'd seen something wrong or not.

"But this morning, I had the guy in charge of the St. Croix contract show up in my office with one of his people, a kid by the name of Bruno who does cleaning detail in one of the St. Croix warehouses in the outer ring of the city."

"Reliable?"

"Not especially. Just not quite unreliable enough to entirely ignore. You know the type."

"I've run into it once or twice," Jonah admitted. "You don't often get that sort volunteering information, though. What happened?"

"Well . . . Bruno ran across something that scared him enough to tell his boss about it, and his boss took one look and brought him over to talk to me."

"What was it?"

"Bruno says—" the skepticism was evident in Turk's voice "—that he was just shifting a crate so that he could run the floor cleaner over that area when it somehow broke open."

Jonah couldn't suppress a low chuckle. "We've heard that song before."

"He swears the crate opened all by itself."

"As crates will do," agreed Jonah, still smiling. "Go on. I'm assuming that what he saw wasn't—what is it that St. Croix sells?"

"Office supplies."

"—that the crate wasn't full of paper clips and manila mailing envelopes."

"No," said Turk. "It was full of guns."

Jonah straightened abruptly. "That's . . . not what I was expecting."

"I don't think it was what our friend Bruno was expecting, either." Turk knocked back the chaser to his beer and continued. "So I told Bruno that I ought to fire him for what both of us knew he'd been up to when that crate came open, but that he'd done the right thing by coming to me about the rifles, so I was letting it go. This time. Then I gave him three weeks' vacation with pay and told him the weather was lovely in the Azores at this time of year and he should go there and think about the value of being a good employee."

"A good move," said Jonah. "Safer for him, safer for us."

"I thought that it might be." Turk paused and looked curiously at Jonah. "You don't think that all of this has something to do with Paladin Steiner-Davion's murder, do you? If he'd found out—"

"I don't think so," Jonah said. "Victor was nobody's fool. If he'd learned that someone was caching weapons in Geneva, he'd have come out and said so right away. He wouldn't have put off the announcement for political effect."

"I guess not. Sorry it wasn't what you were looking for."

"Just because I wasn't looking for it," Jonah said, "doesn't mean that I'm not interested. Or that there aren't other people in Geneva who need to know about it."

37

Pension Flambard, Geneva
Terra, Prefecture X
16 December 3134

"I'm in town. We need to meet."

Jonah's sigh on the other end of the line was audible.

"Sorry," Horn said. "Did I say something wrong?"

Jonah chuckled. "Just not used to so many meetings. But you're right. Meet me here at nine a.m."

Though Burton Horn had spoken with Jonah Levin at the pension only once before, the proprietress remembered him at once.

"Monsieur Horn." He wouldn't say that she smiled at him, but her greeting was possibly a shade warmer than the one that she might have given to a complete stranger—and most definitely warmer than the one she would have given to a tri-vid reporter or anyone else she suspected would disrupt her guests' privacy.

"Madame," Horn replied. "Paladin Levin said he would be expecting me."

"Yes. He is waiting in the private parlor."

The Pension Flambard's private parlor was a smaller, less

welcoming space than the front sitting room. Where the glowing faux-logs on the sitting room hearth gave off both real and psychological warmth, the private parlor had only an ordinary electric radiator set against the room's blank inner wall. But it had a door stout enough to discourage casual eavesdroppers, curtains of opaque velvet instead of lace, and it could not be seen from the public rooms.

Jonah Levin waited in a chair by the curtained window. The Paladin looked tired, like a man who'd had a late night and an early morning. Horn would have been more sympathetic if he hadn't spent most of his own night in transit from Santa Fe.

Levin gestured at Horn to take a seat in the room's other chair. "I'm sorry for giving you so little time, but I have to be somewhere else at ten. I gather your visit to Santa Fe proved fruitful."

"Yes," Horn said. "Among other things, I can confirm that our friend Henrik Morten is not a particularly nice person."

"So I've gathered. Seems to have helped his career, actually. What's he been up to in Santa Fe?"

"Hiring one of the local thugs to beat up and attempt to kill an inconvenient girlfriend."

" 'Attempt'?" The Paladin looked curious. "I gather it didn't work."

"I dissuaded the gentleman in question." Horn paused. "I'm sorry that he couldn't remain available for a more thorough interrogation, but—"

"I understand." Levin's smile was a bit grim. "If I hire someone and tell them to use their own best judgment, I'm not going to argue when they do. I'm assuming that you managed to get Morten's name from him beforehand?"

Horn shook his head. "Morten was too canny to give his name to the hired muscle—he was just 'some guy in a bar.' But I did get the name of the bar, and the bartender recognized Morten's picture, sure enough."

"You're certain?"

"He wasn't the establishment's usual sort of customer. The bartender made a point of noticing."

Levin nodded. "How did Ms. Ruiz take the series of events?"

"Everything came as quite a shock to her, of course."

Another nod. "Of course."

"On the other hand, the incident effectively removed any qualms she might have had about revealing everything she knew about Paladin Steiner-Davion's final project. She didn't know that it was her boyfriend who'd set up the attack, but she did figure out that it had happened to her because she knew something that she shouldn't."

"Now we come to the meat of it." The Paladin leaned forward, intent. "What was it that Elena Ruiz saw and, presumably, passed along in innocence to Henrik Morten?"

"As she told the story to me," Horn said, "Paladin Steiner-Davion had been working on his final project for several months. And the endeavor wasn't just a casual hobby; it placed considerable demands upon both his time and his energy. She told me that she would find him asleep at his desk some mornings, with the display still open on his data terminal."

"So of course she looked at it."

Horn nodded. "She says it was correspondence mostly at first, and she didn't notice anything odd about it except for the fact that he was obviously working hard on something and not discussing it with anyone."

"She should have followed his example."

"I considered pointing that out," Horn said. "But since I was trying to convince her to talk to me at the time—"

"It would have been counterproductive. I understand. Go on."

"As you may have guessed, one night in casual conversation she mentioned the Paladin's late hours and his mysterious project to Henrik Morten, and Morten—instead of letting his girlfriend's moment of indiscretion pass unremarked—encouraged her to snoop further and to pass the results along to him." Horn paused and shook his head. "She's adamant that she never actually touched anything, or pried into anything; she only relayed to Morten whatever happened to be left out for her or anyone else to see."

"She apparently saw more than enough. Does she realize that?"

"I don't think Henrik Morten was involved with Ms. Ruiz for the sake of her vast intellectual capacity, if that's what you're asking," Horn said. "On the other hand, she does possess an excellent visual memory. When I asked,

THE SCORPION JAR   181

she was able to reproduce the last item she showed to Morten before the Paladin's death.''

"You have it with you?"

"Yes." Horn withdrew a folded piece of paper from the
inside pocket of his jacket and handed it across to Jonah
Levin. "Under the circumstances, I thought it would be
unwise to entrust this to any other method of delivery.''

Levin unfolded the paper and glanced over it quickly.
Horn knew what he was seeing: no page title or note of
explanation, just three columns, two lists of names and a
third of numbers—and those alone had been enough to seal
a man's fate.

Levin closed his eyes briefly after he scanned the list.

"Headache?" Horn asked.

"Sort of. Where's Morten now?"

"Not in Santa Fe, I know that much. I'd guess he's back
here, since this is the place to be for any diplomat. But
whether he's here for sure, and where in the city he might
be, I can't say."

"We have to find him," Levin said firmly. Then he
frowned, almost wincing again. "And I might need your
help on another matter.''

"As long as you're still paying, you can come up with all
the matters you want. What's this one?"

Levin looked at the paper again. "I need to talk to another Paladin."

= 38 =

Counterinsurgency Task Force
Temporary Headquarters, Geneva
Terra, Prefecture X
17 December 3134

Heather GioAvanti refilled her coffee mug from the galley-sized urn that somebody on her ad hoc staff had set up in the task force's basement headquarters and made a mental note to find out whose idea it had been so that she could officially commend their initiative. As soon as she had the coffee cream-and-sugared to her taste, she withdrew again to her private office to meet her ten o'clock appointment.

A message from Jonah Levin had come to her private number late last night—early this morning, really—asking for a meeting and an exchange of information. She'd thought at first about using her proper office, which was located on the same rarified level of the building as those of the other Paladins, but upon reflection had decided against it.

Up there, access was restricted, which meant that people's comings and goings would be both noted and logged. These lower-level rooms, on the other hand, had a number of different ways leading in and out. If Jonah Levin wanted to arrive discreetly by the building's service entrance instead of taking the elevator down from the main lobby, he could do it.

Levin arrived on the hour, without fanfare, looking like a man who hadn't had much sleep in quite a while. Heather welcomed him into the windowless cubbyhole that served her for a private office. The room had two chairs and a door, which was more than the rest of her task force possessed; it wasn't much, but it would do. A small video screen in a corner showed looped footage of the riot in Plateau de St. Georges, which Heather had been studying earlier.

"You look like hell, Jonah," she said.

"It's not that bad," he said. "Nobody's shooting at me, and I actually had time for breakfast."

"The two signs of a good day," she agreed. "I got your message—woke up from a sound sleep to get it, in fact—so here we are. You said something about an exchange?"

"Pooling our information, really."

"You've got something to share?"

He nodded. "I do. You may have heard that I've been asked to look into Victor Steiner-Davion's death."

"I hadn't heard anything official about that, no."

"But unofficially?"

Heather smiled. "I've heard about it from at least a half-dozen sources. How's the investigation going?"

"Classified," Levin said sternly. Heather stiffened in reaction to his tone, but then relaxed as Jonah's face lightened. "That always sounds better than saying 'Slowly.' "

"I always tell people I'm just too busy to update them right now."

"I'll have to try that one next time. Anyway, it hasn't all been fruitless. I came across some information you'll find interesting."

If this were Duncan talking, Heather would be bracing herself for another piece of useless information along the lines of "The White Heat Consortium has decided to have pasta for lunch," but she knew Jonah Levin wouldn't personally deliver inconsequential information.

"Whaddya got?" she asked.

"I have a contact who has a man inside a St. Croix warehouse, where he stumbled upon a hidden weapons cache."

Heather sat bolt upright in her chair. "You're joking. Where's the cache, and what kind of weaponry are we looking at?"

"Pistols—lasers, flamers, you name it—shotguns, rifles, even an armored car. And ammunition, if my informant's description is to be believed. Here's the where." Levin passed across a slip of paper with a street address written on it in neat, regular handwriting.

Heather took the paper and, after a glance at the address, rose from her chair. "Just a minute."

She went over to the office door and opened it. "Koss!"

The junior of her two assigned Knights left her desk and came forward. "Yes, ma'am?"

She thrust the paper at her. "Check and see if this warehouse is on that list I had you draw up."

Koss' eyes went bright. "The where-would-I-hide-things list?"

"That one. If it's on there, give yourself a pat on the back. If it isn't, start tweaking your criteria until that address does show up, and get me a revised list ASAP. Santangelo!"

The senior Knight came forward and joined them. "Ma'am?"

"Get together a three-person crew and check out all of Koss' addresses, starting with this one. Discreetly. We don't know what's up yet, and the last thing we want is to spook people into action before we're ready."

"Yes, ma'am."

Heather stepped back into her private office and closed the door, shutting out the noise of sudden intense activity beyond. She turned again to Jonah Levin.

"That should keep them busy for a while." She sat back down. "I'm afraid I don't have anything quite as high-grade as that to offer in exchange. Unless you're interested in some dossiers on the Kittery Renaissance and assorted other fringe political groups?"

"They can't hurt," Levin said. "I don't think that Victor's death was faction-related—no group with any credibility has claimed credit, for one thing—but you never can tell. And the Kittery people certainly weren't very fond of Victor."

"I'll send the files over. I'm sure you've been anxious to spend more time in front of your data screen anyway."

Levin didn't respond. He didn't even seem to be looking at her, and his mouth was slightly agape.

"Jonah?"

He kept staring off to her right, looking like he'd just had a minor stroke.

"Jonah?" she said again. "What's the matter?"

His hand fluttered upward until it pointed at the screen in the corner of her office.

"What is that?"

"My video screen. What's the matter with you?"

"No, no," Jonah said, leaning forward so far that he was no longer sitting. "What's on?"

"Oh, that. Did you hear about the riot in Plateau de St. Georges the other day? A few places—banks and the like—got some pieces of the action on video. I've been watching it, seeing if I could pick out any possible Kittery Renaissance members."

"Move it back. A minute ago, I saw something. Move it back."

Heather stared at his face. Whatever he had seen, it was more compelling to him than the weapons cache.

She picked up a small controller, pressed a button, and the images on the screen flew backward. She watched the timer until she had reviewed nearly a minute of footage.

"There!" Jonah exclaimed. "What was that?"

"What?"

"No, dammit, he's gone again. Go back, then play it slow."

Heather obeyed. She watched the screen.

The camera was posted over the entrance to Bank du Nord, looking down broad steps to the street below. The woman Mandela had called Norah was little more than a tall blur in this shot, gesticulating wildly, pushing away someone who came too close. But she wasn't what Jonah was watching.

The doors below the camera flew open and two guards ran out. Instead of running straight down the steps, they veered wide to the left, quickly moving out of the camera's sight. They must have ran right at someone on the steps, because he had to jump quickly to the right, into the camera's range, to avoid them. Just as quickly, he bounced back left, out of sight.

"That man!" Jonah said, now fully standing. "Get a freeze on that man!"

Heather fiddled with the buttons until the screen held a reasonably clear image. She zoomed in on his face as much as possible.

Duncan chose that moment to burst through her door with a fistful of notes.

"Not now!" Heather barked before Duncan could speak. He meekly backed out of the room.

She turned back to Jonah, who still stared at the screen. Air escaped his mouth like a leak from a tire. "That's Henrik Morten."

It was Heather's turn to drop her jaw. "*That's* Henrik Morten?"

Jonah finally pried his eyes off the screen. "You know who Henrik Morten is?"

"His name recently came up, yes. What do you know about him?"

Jonah shook his head and sat back in his chair.

"Looks like our meeting isn't over yet," he said.

39

Federal Penitentiary, Geneva
Terra, Prefecture X
17 December 3134

It's time, Heather thought, to get our hands a little dirty.

The election was only days away, and Levin had already done a pretty thorough job of milking official sources for information on Henrik Morten. The problem was, in matters like these, officials usually were quite deliberate about keeping themselves in the dark. The more they didn't know about specific activities, the more they could deny.

Heather needed to talk to someone who would have a better knowledge of the ins and outs of insurgence plots, and the role, if any, Henrik Morten played in any of them.

Santangelo had wanted to come along, insisting (with all due respect) that he was a more intimidating presence than she, and might be better able to loosen the tongue of Heather's quarry. However, the interrogation rooms of the federal prison on Geneva were closely monitored, and even a Paladin had trouble getting around those restrictions. The interviewee, knowing he couldn't be physically assaulted, would be all but immune to Santangelo's brand of intimidation.

One of the reasons Heather had risen to the rank of Paladin, though, was that she knew more than one way to loosen a tongue.

After negotiating four separate security checkpoints, Heather found herself waiting in a room one and a half meters square, barely large enough for the chair in which she sat. In front of her was a wall of thick ferroglass, and on the other side of the glass was an empty chair. She couldn't see the tiny, nearly invisible camera lenses scattered in the walls in both rooms, but she knew they were there.

The door to the other room opened, and Royle Cragin strolled in. From the neck up, it appeared that prison hadn't made a dent in Cragin's personal style. His hair was carefully parted and every strand was in its appropriate place, and he still wore his horn-rimmed glasses, an affectation for a man with vision better than 20/20. He looked more like a prosperous investment banker than a detainee in a maximum-security prison. He certainly didn't look like the revolutionary his court papers said he was.

Of course, Cragin's personal style never would have allowed him to wear a fluorescent yellow jumpsuit, or magnetically clasped shackles on his ankles and wrists. He seemed to be used to the shackles, and he accomplished the short shuffle to his chair with something approaching grace. He said down smoothly, and Heather knew that the jumpsuit concealed a physique as powerful as it had been the day of his capture—a day that had ended with the death of two Knights of the Sphere.

"Paladin GioAvanti," Cragin said, making no attempt to conceal his distaste. "I hope your appearance here means that my complaints about the conditions in this place have been heard."

"I'm afraid not, Royle," she said. "Besides, you know Paladins aren't in charge of the jails."

"That's because they don't want to be," Cragin said. "The Paladins have the authority to be active in any area of The Republic in which they take an interest. Should they truly desire to fix our prison system, they could. They just feel more comfortable overlooking the tremendous inequities and dehumanization that occur regularly in prisons, so they pretend they have no oversight. Convenient for you, isn't it?"

Heather sighed, hoping Cragin noticed. Setting him off on a political diatribe was about as difficult as rolling a ball down a hill. You just had to let it go.

"Well, Royle, if you'd like me to I could make some sort of promise to look into your complaints when I leave, but we both know I'd only be saying that to shut you up, so why should I bother?"

"Then we have nothing to talk about. Guards!" Cragin yelled. The door behind him, though, remained stubbornly closed.

In other circumstances Heather might have attempted charm, if only to annoy her opponent, but she knew it would have no effect on Cragin. His loathing for her was too deep for him to even notice.

"It's my interview, Royle," she said. "I'll decide when it's over."

"Fine. I can sit here silently for as long as you please."

"You'd actually shut up? What a novel phenomenon that would be."

Cragin, true to his word, did not respond.

"How much longer do you have in here, Royle?"

Silence.

"Okay, that was rhetorical. Two years, four months. Now, here's another thing I'm not going to do. I'm not going to dangle the possibility of getting your sentence reduced. Frankly, I don't know that I could do it if I wanted to, and I certainly don't want to. If it were up to me, you'd have a decade, maybe two, to go. But as it stands, you have two years, four months."

Cragin did nothing to acknowledge her summary.

"You'll still have a lot of living left when you get out. You won't even be fifty. That gives you plenty of time to put your syndicate back together, do some more damage in The Republic. Sure, you'll be under surveillance the minute you get out, but you know how to deal with that, right? I don't think it'll slow you down too much."

As Heather well knew, it was impossible for Cragin to remain silent for any length of time. "You've got me all wrong, Paladin GioAvanti," he said, using the country-boy tones that had almost swayed the jury to acquittal. "I'm a changed man. Prison's reformed me. I'm on the straight and narrow from now on."

"Then it seems our rehabilitation system is working fine. I'll tell the proper authorities to disregard your complaints."

Cragin glared.

"Anyway, Royle, you should be a little nicer to me, because I'm here to help you. I'm here to give you a warning."

Cragin had decided to give silence another try.

"You're not going to have anything when you get out. Your network, your people, your operatives, they're not going to be there for you."

Cragin shrugged. "It's a big Republic, Heather." He'd remembered how much it annoyed her when he'd called her that once, and he did it whenever he could. "There's a lot of people."

"But from the minute you get out, you're going to be second best. Or worse. Why would people deal with you when there's a better organized, better funded man with a more effective organization already in place? You'll be finished before you get started."

"You think I can't handle competition?"

Heather surprised herself by taking the question seriously. "I don't know, Royle. Maybe you can. But it'll take time. You'll have to wage a war between insurgent groups before you get to your real targets. Who knows how long that will take? Who knows how much older you'll get, fighting just to get back into power? You have time, Royle, but I don't know if you have that much time. Your competition's going to be pretty stiff and, with the surveillance, you'll be fighting with one hand tied behind your back."

"Mmmm hmmm. And who is this competition I'm supposed to be worried about?"

"Henrik Morten. I'm sure you know who he is."

"Never heard of him."

Heather faltered briefly, and immediately hoped Cragin didn't see it. Her instincts had told her this was absolutely the right thing to do, that Cragin would know something. When he was out, Cragin had been perhaps the best-connected radical in The Republic, his fingers somehow monitoring a thousand heartbeats at once. If there was any-one gaining influence, whether they were a potential ally or potential enemy, Cragin knew about them. If he didn't know Morten, that meant the diplomat was really a little fish trying to stretch out a little. It meant Morten hadn't made as much of a name for himself as she and Jonah had guessed.

But then why did someone entrust Morten with an as-signment like doing away with Victor? He couldn't just be a no one. She decided to press forward.

"Oh, okay, you've never heard of him. And you've prob-ably never heard of the Kittery Renaissance."

"Them, I know."

"Impressive group, aren't they?"

Cragin shrugged.

"I don't know how much news gets in here, but about a year ago they poisoned the entire staff of a representative from Clan Jade Falcon that was in town. Didn't kill any of them, just made them all stay very close to their bathrooms for a couple of days. They were just showing off, telling us what they could do if they wanted to. I don't know if even you could have pulled off something like that in your prime."

"I heard about that one. And yes, I could."

"Well, it looks like Henrik Morten might have a connec-tion to these folks. That could make an interesting alle-giance, I'd think—only you wouldn't know, since you've never heard of Morten."

No response.

"All right. If you don't know him, you don't know him. I'm sure you'll find out about him in two years." She stood up.

"Won't you have caught him by then?" Cragin said in mocking tones. "Isn't that one of your actual responsibilities?"

"Yeah," Heather said casually. "Maybe I'll have him by then. But maybe I won't. Might be fun to see the two of you duke it out for a while—if I'm lucky, you could get each other out of the way for me. Anyway, see you around." She walked toward the door.

Cragin waited until her hand was on the doorknob. "I know what you're doing," he said.

She turned and arched an eyebrow. "Really?"

"You're fishing. You want this Morten guy out of the way, and you're hoping to get me mad enough that I'll help you out."

Heather rolled her eyes. "Of *course*! I'm not trying to be subtle here, Royle. I want him out of the way, and I want you to give me the info that'll help. I know you're not going to do anything to help me, but I figured you were still smart enough to help yourself." She stayed by the door, but didn't move. She knew what was coming.

"Kittery Renaissance, huh?" Cragin finally said.

"That's right."

"This is the guy from Mallory's World."

Heather took a step back toward her chair. "That's the one."

Cragin's face twisted into a snarl then puckered, like he had bitten on a pickle while drinking unsweetened lemonade. Heather watched his fingers flex involuntarily, and knew he was imagining how they would feel around her neck. She stood firm and expressionless.

"I've heard of the guy," he finally said.

40

Jonah Levin's Office, Geneva
Terra, Prefecture X
17 December 3134

One thing Jonah hated about getting around Geneva was the number of one-way streets. For some reason, they always seemed to be pointing him opposite the direction he wanted to travel.

That's the way this investigation seemed to be going. He kept accumulating information telling him to look in one direction, when he'd prefer to look almost any other direction.

Maybe the problem was that he hadn't thought through the data well enough. If he sat down, reviewed his notes and organized his thoughts, he might find something he'd missed, something that could point him in an entirely different direction.

He fervently hoped this would be the case.

Unlike most Paladins, Jonah could find privacy in his official offices. Even during the middle of the day they had an abandoned feel, as Jonah kept a minimal staff on hand— usually a single receptionist hired from a temp agency. He simply wasn't on Terra enough to require permanent staffers, and he had no enthusiasm for finding temporary help when he was on-planet. The receptionist was stationed at the front of his suite, while his chamber was in the back. He could lock a marching band in his office and she wouldn't hear them.

She politely said hello as he walked by, and he smiled, vowing to remember her name before he left Terra. He told her not to send through any visitors or callers.

"Even other Paladins?"

"*Especially* other Paladins," Jonah said. He had even less time than usual for politics.

Jonah's office resembled a prison cell with a very nice desk. When Jonah was appointed Paladin, the office maintenance staff had thrown a few items into this room (a picture of a sunset, a plastic plant and a matched set of blue marble bookends), and these remained the only decorative items. A single book of governmental rules and procedures sat between the bookends. The plain curtains turned the sunlight gray.

He opened the curtains at the touch of a switch, then locked the door behind him with his personal key code and set it to report the suite as unoccupied to all but the highest security inquiries. He then sat down at the desk, opened the portfolio he had been carrying, and took out all of the sheets of paper inside. Some of them represented his notes on the case; others were Burton Horn's. He hadn't looked at the dossiers Heather GioAvanti had forwarded to him yet, but Jonah doubted he would need them. What he had was bad enough.

He removed a datapad and a stylus from the desk drawer and began setting down the items one by one.

Fact. Steiner-Davion had been scheduled to give the opening address for the Paladins' Electoral Conclave, but was killed the night before he could give it.

Fact. Henrik Morten, the lover of Victor's nurse-housekeeper Elena Ruiz and a diplomatic troubleshooter with questionable ethics, encouraged Ruiz to pass along to him information about the late Paladin's final project.

Fact. Gareth Sinclair was appointed Paladin after Victor died.

Fact. Victor was working on a document that named Gareth Sinclair, Melanie Vladistok, Lina Derius, Geoffrey Mallowes, and about a dozen Knights of the Sphere. Why their names were on the list, and what the numbers meant, was unclear at the moment.

Fact. Morten has been connected to numerous politicians, with an emphasis on those with Founder's Movement sympathies. Of the Paladins, he has worked for McKinnon, Sorenson, and Sinclair. Victor Steiner-Davion was considered an antagonist by the Founder's Movement.

Fact. Morten was spotted at a riot believed to have been instigated by the Kittery Renaissance.

Fact. Senator Melanie Vladistok was involved with Morten, and wanted to conceal the nature of her relationship.

Supposition. The politicians whose names appeared on Ruiz's document were involved in something shady enough to arouse the suspicion, and significant enough to arouse the anger, of Steiner-Davion—who, in his long personal history, had experienced firsthand just about every kind of treachery and underhandedness the universe had to offer.

Supposition. Victor had intended to rip the lid off of whatever plot he had discovered, using his speech to the Paladins as the occasion. He likely thought this information would influence the election in some way.

Supposition. In the short run, Gareth Sinclair gained the most from the death of Victor, but there's little chance he would have known he would be appointed Paladin in his place. The Founder's Movement also gained politically, but it is difficult to imagine either McKinnon or Sorenson going so far as to kill Victor to reach their goals.

This wasn't as helpful as Jonah had hoped. Any objective person looking at this information would know what the next step would be. He was hesitant to say that had a prime suspect, but he certainly had someone who needed to answer some hard questions.

The one anomaly was the Founder's Movement connection. Sinclair, as far as Jonah knew, had never expressed any Founder's Movement leanings. Of course, he'd just been made Paladin, and in his previous life as a Knight there might not have been much need to express political opinions. He could have kept them safely under wraps.

In the end, the Founder's Movement connections might just be a coincidence. Morten could have hired killers to dispose of Victor while working for one client, while monitoring the Kittery Renaissance riot for another. His involvement in both was not proof that the two events were tied to the same client, or the same cause.

Jonah had walked into his office thinking there were two people he needed to speak with. His activity, unfortunately, hadn't changed his mind.

He turned to the desk's communications console and punched in the code to get a secure outside line. After a half-dozen rings, a voice at the other end of the phone line said, "Burton Horn."

"It's Jonah," he said. "I don't mean to sound impatient, but . . ."

". . . but you are. I understand. I've got a bead on him, I think. Looks like he's in town."

"Can you reel him in?"

"I think so. You want me to handle the questioning?"

"I suppose. Though I'd like to meet this guy."

"Meet?"

"He ordered Victor's death. But I don't think there's time. It will probably be up to you."

"Yeah," Horn said. "Yeah, I understand. What rules are we following for the interrogation?"

Horn was dangling a considerable temptation in front of Jonah, and he felt almost disgusted enough to reach for it. But he couldn't.

"Standard. By the book. We have to play this right."

"I understand. What about your part?"

Jonah reviewed his notes. "I've been trying to find a way to avoid it."

"And?"

"I can't."

41

Jonah had long known that, sometimes, the most advantageous terrain for a battle was a place where your enemy felt safe.

Hesperus was renowned across the Inner Sphere for its rugged, inhospitable terrain, but one of Jonah's favorite spots for combat on his old home was perhaps the friendliest spot on the planet. About five hundred miles south of Defiance Industries' headquarters, the mountains briefly smoothed into a broad valley. Armies who found this spot immediately headed for the center of it, out of reach of weapons fire from hidden stations in the mountains. There, in the treeless valley, they believed they could encamp safely. And there, on a number of occasions, Jonah had waited in a narrow crevasse whose opening was invisible to anyone more than thirty meters away from it. He'd wait for his quarry to relax, then spring.

He certainly didn't think of Gareth Sinclair as his enemy; he was reluctant to even consider him his quarry. But he needed Sinclair to speak openly, and the element of surprise generally allowed you to get past people's initial defenses.

Jonah had requested a meeting on Sinclair's home ground, or at least what passed for it in Geneva: the Hotel Duquesne. Sinclair would be in comfortable, familiar surroundings there, while Jonah would be out of his element. He'd make sure Sinclair noticed the disparity, and allow it to sink in, before he made his move.

Jonah nodded to Emil the concierge as he entered, walking quickly past before Emil could exercise his flamboyant brand of hospitality. He entered the dining room, the echoing footsteps of the lobby giving way to the muted conversation and quiet piano of the restaurant. He was, as he had planned to be, a few minutes late. Sinclair was waiting for him.

He stood as the maitre d' led Jonah to his table.

"Paladin Levin!" he said happily, extending his hand. "Thanks for joining me!"

Jonah shook his hand. "It was Jonah before you were a Paladin, so it certainly should be Jonah now. Sorry I'm late."

"Not at all," Sinclair said kindly. "I know how busy you are."

"It's not that," Jonah said with an embarrassed smile. "It's the size of this place. I can never get used to it. I must have spent five minutes just wandering through the lobby."

"I understand. It confused me when I first came here as well."

"But you adapt quickly," Jonah said, then continued as Sinclair tried to interrupt. "No false modesty, Gareth. I know you and your reputation well enough—you have a gift for sizing up a situation and adapting yourself to it."

Jonah hated himself for his friendly tone, for calling Sinclair by his first name, for everything he did to conceal the real purpose of this lunch. I'm playing the game, Jonah thought to himself with disgust. They've finally drawn me in, and I'm just another politician.

He thought again of Hesperus, of hiding in the crevasse. Same technique, different battlefield. You've always known how to do what's necessary, he told himself.

"Of course, I don't believe you've ever had to size up a

situation quite like the one in front of you now," Jonah continued. "How are you adapting to your new position?"

Sinclair looked up from his menu and smiled. "I'm sure I haven't yet. I have no idea how a Paladin is supposed to act, supposed to speak, or anything. I don't know what I'm supposed to be."

"A Paladin is supposed to act just as you act," Jonah said, happy that he could talk honestly. "You define the position. Don't let it define you. Anders Kessel is a good man in many ways, but he's let the position determine who he is, until everything he does is measured in terms of politics and support, of building blocs and scoring points. He now acts as if doing what's right and doing what's politically smart are one and the same."

"Sounds like your polar opposite," Sinclair said.

We're becoming more similar than I'd like, Jonah thought. Aloud, he said, "Not entirely. As I said, he still has many admirable qualities. I think what he's forgotten, though, is trust. You have to trust people to understand the choices you make, to think about issues seriously enough that they'll understand why you do what you do. That's leadership. Letting the masses lead you around by the nose, sculpting your actions to what they think they want, isn't."

Sinclair nodded soberly. Jonah knew that, if he'd had a pen, Gareth would be taking notes.

Their waiter, a man with hair as dark and smooth as his black tuxedo, slid to their table, quietly took their order, then drifted away.

"Remember that the office belongs to you," Jonah said. "You don't belong to it."

"Isn't that the kind of thinking that got Katherine Steiner-Davion into trouble?"

Jonah laughed. "Excellent point. Yes, it is, to a degree. But she had twisted herself, she was still caught up in the trappings of power. She so desperately wanted to rule that she bent her soul to the sole end of gaining and keeping power. Part of the idea of placing yourself over the office is knowing you can leave it, because the ideas that guide you are larger and more important than the office itself."

"But this only works for people who want to do good in the first place."

"Yes," Jonah agreed. "But that's the way power always has been. Power has a much greater chance of making a good person bad than doing the reverse. That's why you must always keep it at arm's length."

Sinclair nodded. "I appreciate your counsel. I hope you don't mind me saying this, but I plan to look to you as an example of how to hold this office."

We'll see if you still feel the same when we're done talking, Jonah thought.

"There are others, too," he said aloud. "Each has their own strengths. You can learn about charisma and persuasion from Heather GioAvanti, determination from Tyrina Drummond, honesty from David McKinnon, and lack of pretense from Meraj Jorgensson. We have plenty of flaws scattered throughout our council, but plenty of gifts as well."

All right, Professor Levin, he told himself. Class is over. Time to get the real discussion out of the way.

"And one of us is about to be the next Exarch," Jonah continued. "I thought, by this point, a clear leading contender or two would have emerged, but the election seems more muddled than ever."

The tuxedoed waiter brought their food. Sinclair's eyes brightened, and he dove into his duck a l'orange with relish. He seemed, Jonah noted, quite comfortable. Jonah did little more than pick at his venison.

"Why do you think that is?" Sinclair asked through a mouth full of carrots.

"It's because of Victor. His speech was going to be a rallying point. It was thought that his words would point to one candidate that he supported, and then Kessel, Sorenson, and their group would organize behind an opposing candidate. But Victor never made his speech, leaving everything wide open. Not to mention the fact that we have two new voters, and we don't know what to expect from you."

Sinclair grinned. He was a battle-tested MechWarrior, as deadly as they come, but at the moment he looked like a boy who had just found the keys to his father's hovercar.

"I'm a wild card, huh? I kind of like that." Then he grew more serious. "Does anyone know what Victor was going to say? Did he leave behind any copies of his remarks?"

Jonah carefully watched Sinclair's face, but it seemed as open and ingenuous as always.

"No. He'd been keeping his work under wraps, and no one's been able to find a trace of it. Until recently."

"You found something?" Sinclair said—eagerly, without a trace of apprehension.

"Yes." He brought out a piece of plain writing paper, unfolded it, and laid it out on the linen tablecloth in front of Sinclair. "Can you tell me the significance of this?"

Sinclair looked at the writing on the paper: three columns, two of names, one of numbers. "I've never seen it before. The names . . . I can't imagine that you needed me to tell you that the ones in this set, here"—he tapped the first column with his index finger—"belong to Senators, and all of the ones in this second set belong to Knights of the Sphere."

"All of them except for one: Gareth Sinclair."

"Yes," said Gareth. "I saw that. I . . . I don't know what it means that I'm on there."

"Or why you should be sharing a line with Senator Geoffrey Mallowes of Skye and fifty-two million of who knows what?"

Finally Jonah saw a change in Sinclair's face. It closed a little; he pulled backward, frowning both at Jonah and at the paper in front of him. He was beginning to understand the purpose of this conversation.

Speaking carefully, Sinclair said, "Senator Mallowes is an old friend of my family. That much is common knowledge, at least on my home world."

"I suppose so." Jonah broke off to retrieve the paper as the busboy arrived to refill their water. "What disturbs me, Gareth, is that third column. Does the number fifty-two million mean anything at all to you?"

"I don't know. Fifty-two million what?"

"That *is* the question, isn't it?" Levin said. "My guess, at the moment, is that the numbers in the third column refer to sums of money. I can't imagine anything else that would have caused so much trouble in this context."

Sinclair hadn't touched his meal since Jonah had shown him the list. "What kind of trouble?"

"Murder," Jonah stated firmly. "Someone found out that Victor Steiner-Davion had this list, and Victor died."

Red crept into Sinclair's face, creeping from his cheeks to his forehead like ink slowly dissolving in water. "Are you accusing me of anything, Paladin Levin?"

Jonah softened both his face and his voice. "No, no, of course not. I'm gathering information. I'm just helping you understand how some of this information would lead me to want to talk to you."

Sinclair's face remained flushed, but his brow lost a few of its creases.

"Let me see that paper again," he said.

Jonah passed him the sheet again. Sinclair stared at it as if it were a treasure map.

Finally, he said, "I think I know what at least some of these numbers represent."

"What?"

"Matching funds. The fifty-two million, there . . . if I'm remembering it correctly, that was the amount my family matched, in order to inaugurate a MechWarrior training program at home on Skye. It's been going for a decade or so now."

"Right. I've heard of it." Jonah paused, pulling a fact from his memory. "Senator Mallowes was the driving force behind it, wasn't he?"

"Right. He was the one who convinced my parents to donate; he got The Republic involved. It was his project the whole way. It was really, in a way, a very nice gift to me."

"To you? So, you must have been one of the first graduates."

"Yes," said Sinclair. "My parents didn't want to be seen promoting a course of study that they were unwilling to let their own offspring enter and complete. I believe that most of the funds went to purchasing 'Mech simulators, and what was left over they used to set up a continuing endowment for the instructors' salaries."

"Admirable," Jonah said. "And completely legal. So why did Victor care? Why would that information make someone want to kill Victor?"

Sinclair kept staring at the paper. "I don't know. If I knew what some of these other numbers represented, I might have a better guess."

That was something, Jonah thought. At least I know

what one of these numbers means, and if the others are of a similar nature that narrows the field of investigation somewhat. And, to his concealed satisfaction, Gareth had held up pretty well, coming up with a reasonable answer to his questions. He still had one more dart to throw, though.

"Who is Henrik Morten?"

Sinclair reviewed the list, then realized Morten's name wasn't on it. He placed the list in front of him, and Jonah picked it up and folded it into his pocket.

"Henrik Morten?" Sinclair said. "The name sounds familiar . . . oh, he's one of Mallowes' people, noble, I think. I've used him from time to time. In fact, he helped me on Ryde not too long after you left. I'll have to tell you that story some time."

"I've heard it," Jonah said curtly. "And you should know that Morten doesn't work for Mallowes anymore."

Sinclair shrugged. "I think he was more of a freelance diplomat than a permanent member of the staff. I'm sure he'll be fine."

"Of course he will. You're still paying him."

Sinclair widened his eyes. "Me? No, I haven't had much to do with him since I left Ryde. He was effective, but there was something about him, something I couldn't put my finger on." He paused. "Why are we talking about him now, anyway?"

Jonah watched Sinclair's face. The flush had retreated to his ears, but it was still there. He could be pushed into anger, and hopefully incaution, without too much effort."

"I believe Henrik Morten arranged to have Victor Steiner-Davion killed."

Sinclair's face rapidly moved through a range of expressions, like a tri-vid on fast forward. "Morten? I wouldn't . . . I mean, something about him didn't seem right, but . . . really? Morten?"

"Yes."

"I could give you the contact information I had for him if you're trying to find him. It's old, but you never know."

"Old?" Jonah said. He pushed his chair back and leaned forward, grabbing its arms with white knuckles, leaving his arms akimbo. "That's not what I've heard. I hear you're still in contact with the man."

"What? No. I haven't used his services in years!"

"If I do some checking, I won't find otherwise, will I?"

"No! Do you think I'm lying?"

"I think your name was on Victor's list. I think you know Henrik Morten pretty well. And I think you ascended to Paladin when Victor died."

This time there was nothing slow about the flush spreading over Sinclair's face. He stood abruptly, almost knocking the table over.

"I'm being accused? Is that what you're doing? I had no idea I was even being considered for Paladin, and now you think I assassinated Victor to get it? Jonah, you know me! You *know* me!"

"I hope I do," Jonah said, trying to ignore the dozens of eyes now staring at his table. "Should we talk about this somewhere else?"

"No, we shouldn't," Sinclair said, managing to control his tones. "You do your looking. Check to see if I've had anything to do with Morten recently. Then come back to me, apologize for suspecting me, and I'll help you figure out the rest of this list." He dropped his napkin on the remains of his duck and stalked away.

Watching him go, Jonah wished he could better tell the difference between the anger of the wrongly accused and the anger of someone trying to conceal misdeeds. His eyes swept the restaurant, where most of the patrons still were watching the aftermath of a fight between two Paladins.

"You should see it when I argue with Kelson Sorenson," he said, peeling off a few bills and leaving them on the table. " 'Mechs at twenty paces."

No one laughed.

42

Senate Offices, Geneva
Terra, Prefecture X
17 December 3134

Returning to the Hall of Government after talking to Cragin should have been a relief to Heather, but it wasn't. After some of the things he had told her, and after she'd followed a few trails that he'd pointed out, she wasn't sure which building held the more dangerous characters.

She was certain that some of Cragin's information was exaggerated, that other pieces were inflated to get her to annoy politicians for whom Cragin had a particular dislike. But even if she dismissed certain elements, there was enough there to alter her perception of the Republican Senate.

The first person she wanted to talk to was Senator Geoffrey Mallowes, but he was nowhere to be found. His home staff said he was in his office, his office staff said he was in a committee meeting, and the committee, when she poked her head in their meeting room, said they thought he'd gone home.

Not wanting to run around in circles for the rest of the day, Heather moved down to the second name on her list—Senator Lina Derius of Prefecture X.

She had to size up Derius' receptionist and quickly decide between charm and intimidation. He was tight-lipped and wiry, with a cutting gaze, and Heather was in a bad mood. Intimidation, then.

"Is the Senator in?" Heather asked.

"Yes, but not available at the moment. Did you have an appointment, Paladin GioAvanti?"

Well done, Heather silently acknowledged. Pull the "do you know who I am" card right out of my hand.

"No."

"We recommend making an appointment. The Senator's schedule is quite full most days."

"I'm going in to see her. You can let her know if you want."

The receptionist jumped to his feet. "I can't let you do that," he said, but Heather was already past him.

There was more security than just the receptionist, of course. He could liquidate her long before she reached the Senator's office if he so chose. But one of the advantages of being a Paladin was that other government officials seldom decided to use extreme measures against you.

"Paladin GioAvanti! I can't let you go in!" the receptionist said, practically nipping at her heels.

"Then stop me," she said as she strode forward.

"Please, Paladin GioAvanti, don't make me call the authorities."

She stopped abruptly and turned, making the receptionist walk into her. He bounced backward awkwardly.

"Please call them," she said. "I'll have a very interesting story for them when they arrive."

Senator Lina Derius was engaged in an important meeting with two egg rolls and a bowl of duck sauce. She did not look pleased at Heather's entrance, but she also did not look surprised.

"Paladin GioAvanti. How gracious of you to ignore all diplomatic protocol. What can I do for you before security escorts you out?"

She stood as she spoke, apparently to show Heather that she nearly matched her in height. Her jacket made her shoulders seem nearly twice as broad as they actually were, which in turn made her her waist seem thinner than it actually was. Her face echoed the triangle of her torso, making her look like a set of arrowheads pointing at the ground.

"You can tell me what Henrik Morten told you or did for you that was worth 20,000 stones."

"I have no idea what you're talking about. I've never paid anyone that much money for a single job."

Heather pulled out a sheaf of papers. "Not in an easily traceable way, no. But here's a thousand from your office account. Another thousand from a personal account. Two thousand five hundred from your reelection committee coffers. And I could go on. Every transfer made in a three-day period."

"How *dare* you go looking through my records . . ."

". . . says one of the main supporters of the Vasquez act. You support this kind of thing, remember? And indignation is not an explanation."

"This Mr. Mortar, or whatever you say his name is, must have provided some services for my campaign," Derius said briskly. "Many people do that. Talk to my campaign manager. My receptionist will give you the contact info on your way out."

"Henrik Morten gave some of that same money to Stone's Legacy, a group which has recently come under suspicion of diverting funds to a number of terrorist organizations."

"It was the same money, you say?" Derius said in arch tones. "Interesting. I had no idea you could track individual bills of electronic currency as it passed from hand to hand."

"You gave Morten twenty thousand. He gave Stone's Legacy at least half of that within the next month. Some of that likely found its way to the Kittery Renaissance, which very well may be planning to blow this city up in the next day or two. And you still know nothing about this?"

"It sounds to me as if *you* know little more than nothing. At best you have a vague trail accusing this Morten character of donating money to questionable people. The most you can accuse me of doing is paying an employee who later displayed bad judgment. Which is no crime."

"This will unravel on you, I swear it."

"Then you keep pulling on your little strings," Derius said. "I'll be working on actual governing."

Heather fumed for a minute, occasionally moving her hands as if she were going to say something.

"If that's all, Paladin GioAvanti . . ."

"Yes," said Heather, and she rose, still trying to look defiant as she departed.

She returned to the reception desk.

"I'm not sure if I should be impressed that your interview with the Senator ended before security arrived, or saddened that security is so slow."

Derius and her receptionist have been working together too long, Heather told herself. They sound too much alike.

"I did what I came here to do," Heather said in rather plaintive tones.

"You did? In so short a time?"

"Yes. I just needed contact information for an individual."

The receptionist snorted. "You mean to tell me you invaded the Senator's office for an address? *I* could have given that to you."

"Not the one I'm looking for. I'm sure you understand that the Senator has some contact information that you don't have."

"Impossible. The Senator trusts me with everything."

Heather called up a screen on her noteputer.

"Henrik Morten," she said.

The receptionist's hands flew, and he called up information that he read to Heather.

She slumped her head, looking defeated. "That's the same information she gave me."

"And that's what you had to break into her office for." The receptionist shook his head. "With all due respect, Paladin GioAvanti, I'm not sure you're applying your brute force in the right places."

Heather shot a glare at the receptionist, as if pondering a retort, but she said nothing. She let her shoulders fall, then walked away—the very picture of defeat. Or so she hoped.

Once she was out of view of the receptionist, her shoulders lifted and her pace quickened. That wasn't her preferred method of getting information but, when dealing with people who thrived on humiliation, sometimes it was necessary to give them a little of what they wanted to get what you sought. So much the better if they ended the encounter thinking they had stymied her; hopefully, thinking her defeated, they would ignore her as she finished her work.

43

Les Rues-Basses, Geneva
Terra, Prefecture X
17 December 3134

Burton Horn had a pretty good list of places not to go. Morten's Geneva home, his three favorite restaurants, a nightclub where he was often spotted, homes of his closest political supporters. There was no chance he'd be showing his face at any of those spots right now. Horn could go and strong-arm some of Morten's friends, but, as enjoyable as that might be, it wouldn't get him anything. If Morten was as clever as he was supposed to be, he wouldn't have let anyone close to him know where he was staying.

But even if Morten was going to different places, he was still the same person. Heather GioAvanti had passed contact information from Senator Derius along to Jonah, and Jonah gave it to Horn. Some of it told him nothing—the telephone number was a disposable one, now disconnected, and though the electronic contacts traced back to Geneva, they were easily accessible from anywhere in the world. The physical address was only a post-office box, but that at least was a strong indication that Morten was, in fact, in Geneva. It also helped Horn figure out where in the city he might be.

Horn knew that, if Morten was in the city, he was still going to clubs, still looking to end most nights with a pretty girl on his arm, and still trying to live comfortably, though anonymously. He might give up some places, but Horn couldn't believe Morten would give up his lifestyle.

Only a few neighborhoods in the city would give Morten the kind of life Horn knew he craved. High-rent districts contained too many eyes that might recognize him, sleepy middle-class areas would not give him enough ways to spend the considerable sums he'd earned recently, and Horn was sure Morten wouldn't be caught dead living in a slum (neighborhoods that, according to the proponents of The Republic's Golden Age, didn't exist).

That pointed Horn to the recovering neighborhoods in the city, places starting to stand up again after years of being trodden under the city's collective feet. In a decade or so, these areas would become high-rent districts, full of designer boutiques and restaurants so exclusive their name doesn't appear on their exterior. At the moment, though, they were a mix of artists, recent college graduates, and long-time residents perplexed by the sudden popularity of their neighborhoods. They exploded with new restaurants and trendy nightclubs, and the residential turnover was so rapid that most people in these places didn't recognize each other. This kind of community would be a perfect place for Morten to hide.

One of these areas, Les Rues-Basses, happened to be within walking distance of the post office Morten was using. Les Rues-Basses seemed to cycle from high-rent to poverty every quarter century or so, always traveling the path to one type of community or the other, never stabilizing at either end of the spectrum.

The docksides, at least in the current incarnation of Les Rues-Basses, were the most deserted part of the neighborhood. But that was soon to change. Abandoned warehouses lined the wharfs, but most of them bore "Coming Soon!" signs that advertised soon-to-be-constructed residences that cost as much as Horn would make in a decade.

Sandwiched between these warehouses was a grimy brick building, a holdout from the old community, with a "Furnished Room for Rent" sign in the front window. Thanks to his ability to pay in cash (working with a Paladin's expense account had definite benefits), Horn had been allowed to take immediate occupancy of the room the previous day.

His new apartment needed to be both a base of operations and, hopefully, an interrogation chamber. To that end, it needed some work. The layout was simple—long, narrow main room with a small kitchen branching off its end and a bathroom tucked in a corner. Brown stains had already started to peek through a recently applied single coat of off-white paint, and the stiff carpet crunched lightly as Horn walked on it. The supplied furnishings were a threadbare couch, a table that rocked on its legs, and four plastic chairs. A bed folded down from one of the walls.

The first task was changing the lock. Horn knew at least three different ways to mess with a keycard lock, and he was supposed to be on the legitimate side of the law. Sometimes old technology was the best; Horn installed a metal cruciform lock that required a key to operate from either side of the door. Locks like that were very hard to find, but part of Horn's job was knowing where he could pick up such items.

The windows were next, one off the main room and one off the kitchen. Each window frame received six nails to make sure it would stay shut. Horn then installed a metal grate across each window just in case Morten felt like trying to jump through.

He disabled every electrical outlet except one in the main room. That meant the refrigerator no longer worked, but Horn wasn't planning on cooking.

The final necessary adjustment to the apartment was insulation. He set a white noise generator in the center of the main room, then toyed with the settings until the field covered the whole room. Anyone trying to eavesdrop by listening through the walls or doors wouldn't hear more than a murmur of white noise. It wasn't foolproof—the right microphone could pierce the field like a needle through fabric—but precious few people in Geneva, let alone Les Rues-Basses, had such equipment. And Horn intended to make sure he didn't get the attention of those who had such resources.

He had to bring up the final alteration from his hover vehicle. Thankfully, the building had a freight elevator, because Horn didn't relish lugging the solid metal chair up the narrow stairway. Throwing a sheet over it to keep the built-in restraints from drawing attention, Horn hustled it up to his door before anyone became interested in what he was doing. Once he had it inside, Horn bolted the chair to the floor, then made sure the restraints were in working order.

The room was ready. Now all Horn needed was a roommate.

He visited half a dozen nightclubs and a dozen restaurants. At each place he had a different story and a different appearance. He had heard of people going to elaborate lengths to disguise themselves, wearing wigs and fake mustaches and rubber scars. Horn, though, always preferred to travel light, and his changes were simpler. His hair color didn't change, but sometimes it was slicked back, sometimes tousled. At one restaurant he stiffened his posture to his full two-point-one meters, at another he slumped until he appeared to be no more than one-point-seven meters. At one location he was energetic, flailing his hands as he spoke, at another he was solemn and grave. In the end, none of the eighteen people he spoke to would have given the same description of him.

None of them had ever heard the name Henrik Morten. But at least two of them had seen the face. One was a restaurant that Morten had come to once, about three days ago, and not returned since. The other was a nightclub Morten had been to each of the past two nights.

He wouldn't be there tonight, Horn knew. Morten was too smart to let himself fall into a pattern of visiting the same place too often. It was possible that Morten would never come back to that club at all. But it gave Horn enough to put a wedge in. Now all he had to do was shove.

It's impossible to spend much time in a nightclub without gaining a radarlike sense for whom to avoid. Those who can't develop that sense find themselves running through a series of bad encounters, which quickly disenchants them for the clubbing scene.

At Frou-Frou that night, everyone's radar was telling them to avoid the man hunched over the end of the bar. He was drinking rapidly, not once leaving his stool to dance. His shoulders were hunched, burying his face in his suit jacket. His right foot twitched with nervous irritability. You could tell at first glance that he was a drunk waiting for an excuse to get into a fight.

No one sat within three stools of him, leaving the drunk to twitch over his drink, his eyes scanning restlessly back and forth, up and down the bar.

It was a good disguise, Horn knew, but it made it tough to watch the whole club. He mainly tried to watch the door, catching a quick glimpse while he pretended to only be looking down.

The other trick of this role was drinking enough to be convincing while staying sober enough to do the job. Luckily, Horn had been rehearsing for that part of the role his whole life.

The job of keeping an eye on the door, though, suddenly became unimportant when the trio of young women entered. A blind man could have seen them. They appeared to be dressed in neon, with the brightest parts of their dresses hugging what they believed were their most flattering contours.

Horn had a different sort of radar than the rest of the club-goers, and his went off as soon as the young women entered. He saw them scan the floor, frown a little, and confer with each other through a series of half-hearted shrugs. They strolled the floor for a few minutes, let everyone take a good look at them, danced with a few guys so they'd have the satisfaction of rejecting them when the music stopped, then left.

No one noticed the mean drunk at the end of the bar leave. The three young women didn't see him carefully trailing behind them.

They visited a second club, with much the same result as the first. In their third club of the night, though, their eyes lit up when they saw someone they recognized on the dance floor. A handsome man with smooth hair, nearly black eyes, a cleft chin and an aristocratic air.

Henrik Morten.

They greeted him enthusiastically, calling him "Vic" (a small deception that made Horn inexplicably angry), and he danced with each of them in turn.

Burton Horn the mean drunk had been replaced by Burton Horn the amiable newcomer. Top shirt button open, jacket over his shoulder, he looked like a recent arrival to the neighborhood who'd just got off his government job and decided to see what the clubs near his new home were like. He made small, completely unmemorable chat with half a dozen people, who all branded him as decent enough but bland. Forgettable.

Morten and his trio played a subtle game of one-upmanship (or, Horn supposed, one-upwomanship) all night, each member of the trio vying to become his favorite for the night. They laughed loudly at his wit, they danced with other men to make him jealous, they whispered things into his ear that Horn was quite grateful he couldn't hear. In the end, the tallest of the group, a woman with auburn hair, won, at least for this evening. She left with Morten.

Burton Horn followed, regretfully considering that her victory would be short-lived.

"So," the detective sergeant said. "Want to go over this again?"

The young woman ran a hand through her hair, trying to scratch away the fog in her mind.

"Yeah," she said. "Me and this guy, well, we were having some drinks, having some laughs, when he asked if I wanted to come back to his place. And I figured, why not?"

"What's this guy's name?"

"Victor."

"Victor what?"

She shifted uncomfortably. "I don't know."

"All right," the sergeant said. "What happened then?"

"I already told you."

"Tell me again."

"We got a cab, and he gave an address up in Gratzstein, then we kinda got distracted in the back. After a while I looked up and it didn't look like the way to Gratzstein at all, and I said 'Hey!' and just about then the driver turned around and I could see something in his hand, a little can. And I don't know what happened after that."

"He just reached back and sprayed you?"

"Right."

"Wasn't there a divider in the cab?"

This made the woman pause. "Hey . . . yeah! There was,

there was when we got in! But, when he turned, it was gone." She shrugged. "He must have done something to it."

"And you didn't see what?"

"No. We were, you know, distracted."

"Okay," the detective said, his voice weary. "He sprayed you. And?"

"I blacked out, I guess. The next thing I know I wake up in the cab, and the sky's getting light, and there's this thumping sound coming from the trunk, and my head hurts. I get up, get out of the cab, open the trunk . . ."

"Open the trunk?"

"Yeah. The keys . . . I had the keys in my hand when I woke up. The guy, the kidnapper, must have left them there."

"He left you keys so you could free one of his victims?"

"I guess."

"World's nicest kidnapper. Okay, what was in the trunk?"

"This other guy wearing just his underwear, all tied up. I let him loose, we find a patrol, and then I'm here, telling you the same thing over and over."

The door opened and another detective came in. He leaned over the table and whispered in the detective's ear, "Got anything?"

"Nope," he replied. "Your guy?"

"Picked up a fare in the afternoon; that's the last he remembers before he wakes up in the trunk."

"What do you think we ought to do?"

"There isn't much that we can do," the second detective said. "Get a description of this Victor fellow and put out a missing persons on him, and let these two go."

44

Office of Paladin Jonah Levin, Geneva
Terra, Prefecture X
18 December 3134

The words did not come easily, but they came. They stumbled out of Henrik Morten's mouth and into a microphone sitting on Burton Horn's unsteady kitchen table. Coded into electromagnetic pulses, the words flew down a wire into a small black box where they were encrypted using a key intended for one use only. From the box they flew into an antenna, and from the antenna they flew into the air, across the city, a stream of information that would be total gibberish to everyone in Geneva except one man.

When they found their destination, the words traveled through a second antenna and a second black box, the only other one in Geneva—in the universe—with the correct encryption key. The black box decoded the signals into electromagnetic pulses, and then, without making a sound, back into words, as if reading to itself. A short trip through a thick cord brought the words to a printer, and the printer spilled out the interrogation of Henrik Morten almost instantaneously.

Jonah Levin sat by the printer, grabbing each sheet of paper as it emerged, hanging on every word of the conversation. Horn had asked, more than once, who hired Morten to kill Victor Steiner-Davion. That question had gotten him nowhere; it was possible that Morten would never intentionally reveal that information while he was alive. Since that highway was closed down, Horn was working through side roads, and some of them were turning out to be profitable. But, increasingly, Jonah didn't like what he was reading.

HORN: And no one smelled anything funny? You can just bribe a Knight of the Sphere without anyone blinking?

MORTEN: How would anyone find out? Who's going to tell them? The Knight who got the bribe? Or the Knight who put me on the case in the first place? They're the ones most interested in getting it done. And when you have two Knights helping you, believe me, getting things done is a lot easier.

One of the Knights Morten was talking about was Gareth Sinclair. According to Morten's story, that's how the situation on Ryde was resolved—a simple, though large, bribe. And it had been set up by Sinclair.

What worried Jonah even more was an earlier exchange, back when Morten was feeling feistier.

MORTEN: This is it. This is the end for you, buddy. You have no idea who I have behind me. Do you know what they're going to do to you? Hell, I've got a whole *army* of people, far more powerful than you, that will take care of me. And one of them just became a *Paladin*. Do you know what they're going to do to you?

Jonah was fairly certain Morten wasn't referring to Janella Lakewood.

There was, of course, a question about Morten's credibility. This was a man who, by his own admission, had used underhanded or deceitful means repeatedly to accomplish his missions. He knew how to get people to believe what he wanted. Horn was a skilled interrogator, and he was pushing Morten hard, but there was no guarantee Morten was being completely honest. He still might be playing an angle.

Another sheet emerged from the printer.

HORN: Then why do you keep working for people with Founder's Movement sympathies?

MORTEN: Coincidence, I guess. I work a lot through references, and people who like me aren't going to refer me to their political enemies. I got started with someone with serious Founder's Movement tendencies, so that's where I've worked most of the time. I don't care much one way or the other. But guys like Mallowes and Sinclair see me do good things for the Founder's Movement, and they think I sympathize, so they keep using me.

Sinclair had Founder's Movement sympathies? Jonah stared hard at the recent printout, as if his gaze could rearrange the words on the page. That didn't sound right.

But Mallowes was firmly in the Founder's Movement camp. And Mallowes was Sinclair's sponsor. He'd worked hard to set up the training program on Skye, and he'd gotten a bright young man of an influential family into the program right away. Certainly enough to make that man feel a debt to his benefactor.

Enough of a debt to shape his political beliefs? That was the question.

Rereading the most recent page for the sixth time, Jonah grew increasingly uncomfortable with Morten's last line—"they keep using me." Both Mallowes and Sinclair had claimed to have distanced themselves from Morten, and now Morten claimed he was still working for them?

Luckily, Horn caught that line, too. The next page brought an answer to Jonah's question.

HORN: Are you saying you still work for Mallowes and Sinclair? That's not what I've heard.

MORTEN: I suppose it's been a while since I've done something for the Senator. I don't know what happened—he just stopped sending work my way. I've been busy enough, though, that it took me a while to realize he wasn't sending me any projects, and when I did, I didn't have time to track him down and ask him why. If he's got reasons, he's got reasons. Maybe I'll ask him when we're both in the Senate.

HORN: You think you're going to the Senate? After what you've told me?

MORTEN: By the time you get around to telling anyone about this, I'll make sure you have zero credibility.

<<uninterpretable sound>>

<<uninterpretable sound>>

<<uninterpretable sound>>

HORN: Press down, it'll stop in a minute. You say you're still doing some work for Gareth Sinclair?

MORTEN: Right up to the day he became Paladin. Anyone who tells you otherwise is a liar.

Jonah knew what he had to do. It was as clear as any battlefield tactic, and he'd never had trouble carrying through with those. But this, he didn't want to do.

He trusted Sinclair far more than he trusted Morten. If the two fed him different stories, he was far more likely to believe the former. There was no reason to expect Morten to tell the truth and Sinclair to lie.

Actually, there was, Jonah thought. There were fifty-two million reasons.

He didn't want to have to do this. On Kurragin, he hadn't wanted to charge the ammo dump. But the line needed to be held.

He made a few calls. Within an hour, Gareth Sinclair would be placed under surveillance, his every move watched. Any communication he had sent through government channels would be examined. A report on his use of government finances would be sent to Jonah.

It didn't take long to give the orders. It wasn't official—Jonah was going to keep to back channels as long as possible—but as far as his investigation was concerned, Gareth Sinclair had just been made the chief suspect in the death of Victor Steiner-Davion.

There was one more call to make. Heather GioAvanti needed to hear about this.

45

Heather was of the firm belief that one of the greatest benefits of command was the freedom from legwork. All the drudge work—scouting locations, reviewing public records, staring at endless piles of paper or computer files—could be assigned to someone else. Staffers would disappear for a few hours, or days, or weeks, and when they returned, instead of having this vast pile of information to sort through, you'd have a compact digest of salient points, all of the truly important information compacted into a small datafile. It was a true blessing.

Unfortunately, on rare occasions, there was some drudge work that couldn't be parceled out. Some flows of information could only be uncorked by the right person, and most often that person was not some junior government staffer. Often, even a Knight of the Sphere wouldn't suffice. Some streams of data could only be opened by a Paladin, who would then have to sort through the data only she could access.

This was one of those times.

"As I told your assistant, Paladin GioAvanti, the principal problem is that we have no clear evidence of criminal activity tied to your request. Without such evidence, we cannot violate the privacy of our clients."

The tradition of secrecy tied to Geneva-based banks was rooted in tens of centuries, and they took it as seriously today as they ever had. When she was examining government files—campaign finances, Senatorial accounts and the like—she'd had free access. Now, though, she was trying to plunge into personal accounts, and that was a whole different battlefield.

Heather had four inches in height and at least twenty pounds in weight over the slight, bespectacled man in front of her, but he stood firm as a vault door.

"Yes, I understand that," Heather said. "Did they explain to you the extraordinary nature of this request?"

The bank official had three strands of hair running across the bald expanse of his scalp. He carefully patted them into place. "They attempted to. That is to say, your assistant made quite vociferous claims about this being an extraordinary matter, but he would not specify just what made it so unusual."

"Mr. Confrere, if you know my reputation you should know I'm not prone to exaggerate. But this matter could shape the future of the whole Republic."

"Yes, Paladin. What I need to understand is, how?"

"I'm afraid I'm not at liberty to share the details at this time."

"Then we clearly have a problem."

Heather took another look at her opponent, sizing up the exact nature of this obstacle. Neither intimidation nor charm would work—this man had most likely been placed in his position primarily because of his extraordinary resistance to both forces. Yet, despite his formal manner, part of him seemed to want to help her. He hadn't dismissed her entirely, and was willing to talk. If there was just something she could offer him . . .

It came to her in a flash. The gift most appreciated by all bureaucrats—deniability.

"Mr. Confrere, I appreciate—even applaud—your discretion on your clients' behalf, especially because I am one of them. I can assure you that the activities I'm investigating are of the deepest criminal nature, but I know I can't convince you with the information I have available at the moment. But here is what I propose: let me look at the data I need. Let me find what I want, and you and your bank will become heroes through the role you play in this investigation."

The banker started to speak, but Heather raised her hand. "Wait. Let's say I'm wrong. Let's say you give me access, and it leads nowhere, and our investigation never turns up a thing. Then, my friend, point to me. Say that a Paladin marched into your bank, making claims that sounded believable but turned out not to be true. You were not wrong for opening your files—I was wrong for using your patriotism to convince you to give me access. Do you understand?"

The banker smiled slightly, which was probably his equivalent of a broad laugh. "Yes. I do. You understand, of course, that your access to our data will be quite limited, and you will have to stay on our premises while conducting your investigation?"

She flashed a smile that in no way reflected her feelings. "Of course."

"Then please follow me."

It ended up being a simple story. Dishearteningly simple. Following the thread had been quite tricky. It wound through dummy corporations, holding companies, and a private account or two held by people who probably didn't exist. But Heather kept tugging, sending and receiving a constant stream of messages to her office (and ignoring each and every one from Duncan) that pierced through the thick financial fog gathered around this transaction. Eventually, the whole thing unraveled, and Heather had the entire story lying in front of her.

A new office tower was being constructed in Geneva, developed by a former senior aide to Governor David Guliani. The former aide received a healthy subsidy from the government for helping renovate downtown Geneva. In return, the aide made two contributions. One was a direct contribution to the Guliani Family Museum and Visitor's Center. The other was a bit more complex.

After being disguised as various payments to nonexistent

companies, the money ended up in the hands of a Knight of the Sphere. But it didn't stay there for long. A few more transfers, including a brief stay in a still-active account of a man who died in 3103, brought it to rest in an account belonging to Tres Vite Cleaners. The final transfer had occurred on the day of the riot in Plateau de St. Georges, using a machine at a branch right by the flash point of the riot. The bank where Henrik Morten had been caught on camera.

Heather knew Tres Vite, and not because she often took clothes there. It had come up earlier in the week. The address listed for the company was an empty storefront, and by all evidence Tres Vite no longer did business anywhere. The people listed as officers of the company did not exist.

Geneva police had received numerous complaints about illegal activities in the abandoned storefront, but never found anything to act on. Some of those complaints, though, identified certain people entering the store, people who were of significant interest to Heather GioAvanti. These reports had found their way to her desk.

Ever since Otto Mandela identified the woman called Norah in the footage from Plateau de St. Georges, Rick Santangelo had been tracking her movements. He'd managed to find a witness who swore a woman matching Norah's description had entered the shop and never come out.

Santangelo had secured the proper warrants and torn the shop apart, top to bottom. He found a series of tunnels beneath the shop, all of them leading to other abandoned stores. And some of them did not appear to have been empty very long.

Tres Vite, Heather was all but certain, was a cover for the Kittery Renaissance. That cover was blown, and Kittery had moved on to other locations, other dummy accounts. While they had used Tres Vite, though, they had received money that had passed through the hands of a Knight of the Sphere.

Gareth Sinclair.

46

Counterinsurgency Task Force
Temporary Headquarters, Geneva
Terra, Prefecture X
18 December 3134

Jonah had called Heather that night to say they needed to meet, about three minutes before she was going to call him to say the same thing. Figuring her temporary offices had a better collection of information, he traveled there.

The broad hallways of the office building hummed with the sound of fluorescent lights and distant carpet cleaners. Other than that, they were quiet. The election was two days away, and it seemed that half of the citizens of Geneva had political meetings to attend, while the other half had fled to their homes to avoid the whole affair. Government rules forbade the use of offices for activist purposes, so the Paladins' building was perhaps the most peaceful place in the city.

Half of the lights in the hallway leading to Heather's office were off, making her suite glow by contrast. The light at the end of the tunnel, Jonah thought, wishing it were true.

Heather was in her office, sitting stiffly in her chair, looking at nothing. Jonah had just decided to wave a hand in front of her face when she blinked.

"Hi, Jonah," she said in the flattest tones he had ever heard from her. "Why do I think neither of us is about to tell the other good news?"

"Because we're not. You want to go first?"

"Not particularly. But I will."

She reviewed her day at the bank. Jonah knew he should be dismayed, but he had already hit his absorption limit of bad news for the day. Her words just sank into a numb spot in his mind.

"I don't know if Morten is anything more than a hired gun," Heather said. "He probably doesn't have any particular ideological loyalty. If he was helping the Kittery Renaissance, it's because people told him to. And right now it looks like one of those people is Gareth Sinclair."

Jonah nodded ruefully. Before he threw his evidence on the fire, though, he wanted to at least glance in another direction.

"What about Senator Derius? She had contact info for Morten, something very few people knew. He's practically a fugitive. So how does she get this info?"

Heather pounced, seeming happy to move in another direction. "That's a question worth asking," she said. "She closed down on me, hard, when I was talking to her, and all I really wanted to know, at least right then, was the depth of her connection to Morten. It's worth probing more in that direction."

She paused. "But as far as what's happening with Kittery Renaissance, I don't think she was involved. We have no direct connection from them to her. Morten was at the riot finishing the tail end of a transfer that involved Gareth, not her. And I hate to say it, but she wasn't covering up her connection to Morten, not like Gareth."

"I know. Morten's interrogation is supporting that connection." He passed the printouts to her.

She read them, then closed her eyes. "We have to bring him in."

"I know."

"Do you think he knew? Was this his plan all along, to get Victor out of the way and take his place? If so . . . God, how long must he have been jockeying for position?

How much effort did he put into impressing the Exarch to get this nomination? How deep does this plan go?"

These were the same questions Jonah had been asking himself for the past couple days. He answered with his gut. "I don't think he knew he was going to become Paladin. I don't think he planned any of this to happen this way. I don't even want to think he's involved, but the evidence keeps pointing to him. I hope he just got mixed up in something over his head and he hasn't been able to pull out of it. I hope."

"Me too. So what do we do? Bring up official charges?"

"No," Jonah said. He saw it now. He'd been worrying about how to do this all day, and he suddenly saw exactly how it should happen, where his line should be. "No, we bring him in, you and me. We make sure he knows its serious, that things look bad. We bring him in and tell him to help us clear his name. Help us explain how this might all make sense."

"Can we still assume he's innocent? With all this?"

"Yes." The firmest image of Gareth Sinclair in Jonah's mind was from their days on Ryde. The meteor strike had shattered the entire ecology of the planet, causing stable fault lines to shift and dormant volcanoes to erupt. One such volcano had sent a river of lava streaming toward a refugee camp full of people who had already been pushed out of three other locations. Gareth was with them, darting around in his *Black Hawk*, blasting rock to divert the flow, digging trenches to slow it enough to allow the refugees to get clear, and staying behind until the last person was away. At the end, he was trapped in the middle of a lava plain. He attempted to jump away, and almost made it. His 'Mech's feet landed in molten rock, but Sinclair churned forward, metal legs melting beneath him as he rocked forward. At least three times, Jonah thought the 'Mech was going to pitch backward, plunging Sinclair into the red stream. Each time, Sinclair steadied it. Finally, as the knees dissolved, he stumbled, rocked back again, then lunged forward. He no longer had any support beneath him, so his cockpit kept moving until it smashed into the ground ahead—firm, rocky ground. The body of the 'Mech made it clear of the lava.

Sinclair had saved hundreds of people that day, almost

losing his life. The next day, he was in a trench, a bandage over his right eye, trying to divert the lava away from a chemical plant. When the Legate of Ryde sought him out to reward him, Sinclair was honestly surprised that anyone thought what he had done was special.

Jonah couldn't see this same man plotting assassination and insurrection. He owed him a chance.

"We'll lay all our cards on the table," Jonah said. "Maybe he can explain to us where we went wrong."

"And if he can't?"

There was only one answer to that question. "Then we arrest him."

47

Hotel Duquesne, Geneva
Terra, Prefecture X
18 December 3134

This is it, Jonah thought to himself sourly. I've really become a politician now.

One of the things he had always hated about politics was the game played through interpreting carefully chosen words, minor gestures and mundane actions. In this game, a mere tilt of the head by the right Paladin during an important speech by the Exarch could indicate agreement or displeasure, sending the whole city of Geneva into a spasm of rumor and shifting alliances. Every word, every move, every step people took carried the burden of potentially being a political message.

Jonah hated it when people tried to read him that way. His gestures were never calculated—if he scratched his nose during a speech, it was because it itched. He preferred that people, if they wanted to know what he thought, ask him, and then believe what he said. He treated others the same way, believing the Sphere to be big and complicated enough already without his taking part in this strange political dance.

But now, as he walked down the softly carpeted hallway leading to Gareth Sinclair's room, he found himself practically assigning points to Sinclair's every move, trying to find any evidence at all that could convince him who to believe, Sinclair or Morten. Sinclair, according to the desk clerk, was in his room. He hadn't fled, wasn't in hiding. That was good; he wasn't acting like he had anything to hide. But he had hesitated before agreeing to let Jonah and Heather come see him, which might be an indication that he knew what was coming, which would count against him. Or it might just indicate that he was not looking forward to this particular conversation. Jonah could sympathize with that sentiment.

He knocked firmly at Sinclair's door. He watched Heather's hand flutter toward a weapon on her belt, before she remembered that they'd agreed to meet their fellow Paladin unarmed. It wasn't an arrest, they'd reminded each other repeatedly, even though both knew that's exactly what it felt like.

"One moment," Sinclair called promptly. Another point in his favor, Jonah thought. He's not scurrying away from us.

The door opened, revealing Sinclair casually dressed, framed by a room in which stacks of paper covered every available horizontal surface of a room at least three times as large as Jonah's quarters at Pension Flambard.

"Paladin Levin. Paladin GioAvanti. Come in." He sounded stiff, and again Jonah couldn't blame him. He didn't add a point to either side of the ledger.

They followed him into the room, and he turned and actually smiled, albeit wanly. "I apologize for all the paper. I feel like I'm back in the academy, studying for an exam."

"What is all this?" Heather asked, idly picking up the sheet nearest to her.

"Information on all of you. All the other Paladins. Background, experience, political leanings. I'm going to have to vote for one of you in two days—a day and a half—after all."

"Haven't you heard of datafiles?"

Sinclair gave an embarrassed shrug. "I've always done better with paper. Things stick in my mind if I read it off a sheet."

Jonah put a point into the column in favor of Sinclair's

innocence. The fact that he was taking his responsibilities so seriously, even after Jonah's previous talk with him, was a credit to him.

On the other hand, there were hundreds of pieces of paper scattered across the room. Sinclair had not been Paladin long, but he had either amassed a considerable body of information in that brief time or, knowing he would become Paladin, he had been assembling it for months. A point went in the column against him.

"I'd like to think the two of you came here to pull me away from work and buy me a drink," Sinclair said.

"I'd very much like to do that, Gareth," Jonah said. "I hope I'll be able to soon. But not now. We need to talk."

Sinclair attempted another smile, even weaker than the first. " 'We need to talk.' Four of the most dire words in our vocabulary." He took a deep breath. "Okay. Talk."

Jonah gestured at the papers all over the room. "This may not be the best place for a chat."

"Not controlled enough of an environment, huh?" Sinclair said with an edge to his voice, then waved off attempted protests from both Heather and Jonah. "No, no, I'm sorry, you're right. Where did you have in mind? And please don't just say 'Come with us.' "

"Let's go back to my office," Jonah said.

"Okay," Sinclair said. "Should be quiet enough. And plenty of nearby security if you need it."

Sinclair said the last with a light tone, but no one cracked a grin.

Sinclair came along quietly. None of them said a single word on the way to Jonah's office, but Sinclair showed no signs of desperation, no sudden urge to escape. Another point in his favor.

In the hallways of the Paladins' offices, they started walking briskly and then picked up the pace from there. Each of them was pushing the others, hurrying them along, until they were practically running by the time they reached Jonah's office. They all wanted to get this over with.

All three sat. Sinclair was ramrod straight, hands resting on the end of his chair's armrests as if he expected Jonah and Heather to shackle him there at any moment.

"We have Henrik Morten," Jonah said to get things under way.

Sinclair brightened, and Jonah immediately added a point to the good side of the ledger. "That's great! Hopefully he can help clear things up. He'll tell you I haven't hired him for years, he can confirm everything . . ." Sinclair's voice faded as he saw Heather and Jonah's dour expressions. "He didn't confirm anything, did he? In fact, he probably told you exactly the opposite." He nodded to himself. "Okay. That's why I'm here. I think I understand."

Right then, in his mind, Jonah crumpled the ledger on which he'd been keeping track of points into a little ball and threw it away. He'd never liked playing the game, and now was precisely the wrong time to start. He had Sinclair here, and he looked willing to talk. Jonah just had to listen.

"It gets worse," Heather said. "We've found evidence that you helped funnel some money to the Kittery Renaissance."

"I helped funnel money to *what*?" Sinclair exclaimed. "Kittery Renaissance? I'd *never* fund terrorists, but *especially* terrorists I don't agree with! How can you think I'd do that?"

Heather started to speak, but Jonah interrupted. "We don't," he said, and Heather looked at him in surprise. "We have evidence that your bank accounts were involved, but I don't think you were."

Sinclair looked even more surprised than Heather. "You don't? Is Morten backing me up?"

"No," Jonah said. "Morten is acting like you've been one of his best employers recently. But his fingerprints are all over both Victor's assassination and this transfer of money to Kittery Renaissance. I don't trust him. I trust you. All I need is for you to help us figure out why things look the way they do."

The atmosphere in the room changed completely, as if Jonah had just opened the curtains to let sunlight in. Sinclair's stiff posture relaxed, and his face took on an expression of thoughtfulness instead of defensiveness. Heather, seeing this, relaxed as well.

Jonah didn't. Most of him believed he could trust Sinclair, but there remained a small part of him warning that the moment he relaxed was the moment Sinclair would make his move.

"Okay," said Sinclair. "Tell me about this money transfer."

"What time is it?" Jonah asked when Sinclair stifled a yawn.

Heather checked her chronometer. "2:30."

"It's election eve. We convene in thirty-one hours."

"Is there any chance we'll get some sleep between now and then?" Heather asked.

"Very little," Jonah said.

Heather stood, stretched and smiled. "You know what the good thing about this time of morning is? I haven't heard from Duncan for almost seven hours."

"Which reminds me. Aren't you supposed to be preparing some sort of strike? How much of your time have I wasted?" Jonah asked.

"Santangelo and Koss are on it. They'll bring me up to speed on that side of things in the morning. And believe me, this wasn't a waste." She turned to Sinclair. "Although I have to say, Gareth, I'm a little disappointed in you."

"Why?"

"A small part of me—a very, very small part—hoped you'd have actual connections to the Kittery Renaissance. Then we could get you to smoke out their leaders, and our strike tomorrow would smash the whole organization."

"It still might," Jonah said, "if you've connected the dots right."

"I hope so," Heather said, then tilted her head. "Do either of you know if the training room is open this time of night? Er, morning?"

"I've never had reason to check," Jonah said.

"We have a training room?" Sinclair asked.

"Thanks. You two are very helpful. Well, one way to find out. Good night, gentlemen. And good luck. Let me know as tomorrow's plans evolve."

"We will," Jonah said, and she left.

That left Jonah and Sinclair alone. They had a tremendous mountain to climb before the newly born day had ended, but for the moment they just sat.

"You know the papers I had back in my hotel?" Sinclair

said. "Do you know what word kept popping up in your dossier?"

" 'Bastard?' " Jonah said.

Sinclair grinned, the first fully open smile he had offered all night. "Yes, actually. Usually right after the word 'tough.' But that's not the one I was thinking about. Over and over again, people who dealt with you said you were incredibly fair."

Jonah didn't know if he should say "Oh, good," or "Thank you," so he said nothing.

"It's good to know my sources are accurate. There's a lot of people who would have had electrodes under my fingernails the minute they took me in."

"I know. I've seen too many of them."

"I just want to—thanks. That's all."

"Don't thank me yet," Jonah said. "Thank me when we're out of this."

"Right. And we have plenty to do. Let's move."

Jonah pulled his keyboard to him. He typed a brief message, which flew through the air to a small, sparse apartment in Les Rues-Basses.

It began:

> WE NEED TO EXTRACT SOME PASS-
> WORDS FROM THE SUBJECT.

48

Hall of Government, Geneva
Terra, Prefecture X
19 December 3134

Support staff arrived at the offices of the Senate of the Republic starting at six a.m. This was usually a skeletal group, a few custodians and the cafeteria staff. More arrived at seven, including members of the senatorial staffs. By eight, the building would hold nearly its full complement of personnel.

It was four o'clock. They had two hours to work before things started to get dicey.

This was the sort of job Jonah would desperately have liked to farm out to someone else, as a Paladin being caught breaking and entering into government buildings could cause an unfathomably long line of complications. Horn, though, already had his hands full, and Wilson Turk, most likely fast asleep, wasn't responding to any calls. Time was too short to travel to Turk and wake him personally, or to find anyone else. He and his new partner in crime, who had been his prime suspect until a few hours ago, would have to do it themselves.

The one advantage they had, their rank, would help a

little. It would get them past any automated checkpoints, but not past any humans. The way the political situation stood, flashing identification at the guards might not be the best idea. If their suspicions were correct, any guard who connected a name to their face would likely make several phone calls, and there was a good chance that the sort of people often employed by Henrik Morten would show up to interrupt Jonah's work. He had to get in unseen.

Jonah wasn't entirely comfortable with cloak-and-dagger actions, but it was better than meetings. At least it got his adrenaline flowing.

The night was purple, the endless streetlights bouncing their glow off the high clouds hanging over the city. Under the clouds, the air was clear, and visibility was good. Spotting an intruder in these conditions would be scarcely more difficult than seeing them in daylight.

In the end, it looked like one of Jonah's favorite battlefield tactics—diversion—would suit him well.

The guards heard a rumble first, like distant thunder. They paid it little mind, as the entire day and night had been cloudy.

But the rumble continued, slowly growing closer. It was going on for too long, and it was too muted. It wasn't thunder.

One of the guards checked with their counterparts posted at the main door.

"You hear that?"

"What?"

"The rumble?"

"No."

"Oh."

"What is it?"

"I don't know. I was going to ask you."

"Probably protestors. They've been out all night, probably working on some damn fool stunt."

"Have we been issued a shoot-to-kill order yet?"

"No."

"Damn."

The rumble got louder as a man turned the corner. He wore a cloth over his face and seemed to be shouting something, but the words came out too muffled for the guards to hear. He pushed a metal garbage can in front of him, the source of the rumble.

"Tell me he's not coming toward us."

"He's coming toward us."

The guards emerged from their kiosk, watching the protestor's approach. They kept their weapons holstered, but their hands hovered, ready to grab.

As he approached, the man's shouts grew clearer. "Garbage! Garbage! Garbage!"

The guards exchanged glances.

The man approached until he was within three meters of the guards. "Garbage!"

"All right, sir, that's far enough."

"Garbage! Garbage! That's all this government is! Garbage!"

"I think your protest is probably over, sir."

The man's eyes blazed above the cloth covering the lower half of his face. "Over? It's just beginning! You're garbage! You're all garbage!"

"Yes, sir. Fine. Now move along."

"Ha! You'd like that, wouldn't you! No, I'm going to tell you what you are! You're garbage!"

"Sir, there are curfew laws . . ."

"Curfew? I'll show you what I think of your curfew! Garbage!" He gave his can a shove. It rolled down the slight hill toward the guards, gaining speed. They easily dodged it, watching it as it picked up speed, heading toward a crowd of identical cans scattered among giant Dumpsters.

"Garbage! Ha!"

The guards turned back to the protestor. "Sir, you just assaulted government security officers. We could place you under arrest."

"You're *garbage!*" the man shouted, and the trash can ran into the others like a bowling ball, sending up a tremendous clatter. The protestor launched into a drunken dance.

The noise faded, and the guards approached the protestor. "All right, sir, that's it. We'll find a good place for you to dry out." They reached for the protestor's arms.

With surprisingly good reflexes, he yanked them away. "Don't touch me! You *filth!*" He jumped backward and made a gesture frequently seen in Geneva highway traffic jams.

The guards exchanged glances and then lunged forward. But the protestor was too quick, turning nimbly and running ahead of them down the street.

He kept glancing at his pursuers, checking to see if they were gaining. They weren't.

After a block of pursuit, the guards slowed. They couldn't wander any farther out.

"Go home!" one of them shouted at the fleeing figure.

They trudged back to their position in their small kiosk. They arrived too late to see an extremely dizzy man emerge from the rolled garbage can, press his hand against a biometric lock, and enter the Hall of Government.

Jonah had to resist the urge to walk like a sneak thief, hunched over with wide strides. Nothing would draw the attention of the machines and guards monitoring the cameras faster than suspicious behavior. He had to walk like he was supposed to be there, which was difficult, considering his recent tumble in a metal can. Walking in a straight line was hard enough.

The hallways buzzed with power, some of it used for the all-too-dim lighting that would make it easy for Jonah to accidentally stumble into a guard on patrol. Most of the electricity supplied the wide array of alarms set throughout the building, guarding offices, computers and whatever other valuables Senators felt like keeping here. The low-level noise was a constant reminder to walk carefully.

Jonah felt a tug of longing as he walked by an elevator bank. He had to get to the twenty-third floor, and the elevators would be the best mode of transportation. But standing still for fifteen full seconds in the range of security cameras would not be a wise move. The stairwells had cameras, too, but he could move by them quickly. The only trick there was avoiding the question of why someone was walking up twenty-two flights of stairs at four in the morning.

He found a stairwell, walked up two flights, and exited. Strolling to the other side of the building, he found more stairs and went up another two flights.

Altogether, the building had ten stairwells. Jonah spent ten minutes wandering from one to another, moving up in small chunks of flights. Hopefully, if anyone noticed him on one set of stairs, they didn't see him on the other. Hopefully there were entirely different sets of guards watching each stairwell, or each floor. Hopefully.

Finally, he reached floor twenty-three. The carpeting here was steel gray, the walls brown squares on a tan background, just like every other floor. There was a single guard stationed at the north end, another at the south. Jonah shouldn't get close enough for either to see him.

He found the door he was looking for—Suite 2312, the offices of Senator Lina Derius. He reached into his coat pocket and pulled out a small metal cylinder. Just below the sign announcing the Senator's name was an almost invisible pinhole, and behind that hole was a microphone. Jonah held the cylinder in front of the hole and pressed a button on top. The cylinder played a recording that had been transmitted by Horn, a single word spoken by Henrik Morten.

"Rebirth."

A computer on the other side of the microphone analyzed the voiceprint and found it belonged to an authorized individual. The door's lock clicked, and Jonah pushed it open, jumped through, and closed it behind him.

He exhaled. He had some degree of safety now, since common areas were monitored much more closely than the individual offices. Office security was left up to each individual Senator's alarm system of preference.

He walked past the receptionist's desk. He needed a computer with access to everything Lina Derius knew, and there was only one computer that fit that category. He walked directly to her office. A keycode supplied by Morten got him in.

He retrieved another item from a large side pocket, a small power generator. He plugged Senator Derius' equipment into it, so that no one monitoring power usage would see anything unusual.

He activated the computer and put Morten's passwords to work. Not surprisingly, there were a few areas, such as the Senator's personal journal, that Morten's codes could not crack. Still, he had access to a majority of the data kept by the Senator. It would be enough.

He knew vaguely what he wanted, but couldn't know exactly what form it would be in, or where it would be kept, and he didn't have the luxury of conducting a global search through the massive files the Senator kept on her drive, or transferring them all to his own files. He had to operate on instinct. It was like walking through the woods, guessing which trees were innocent and which protected an enemy trooper with a flamethrower.

The clock ticked. By four-thirty, Jonah had transferred exactly one file that proved little more than Senator Derius' political leanings. At five, someone arrived to empty the trash. Jonah turned off the computer screen, grabbed his power supply, hid under the desk, and watched the feet of the custodian while imagining the headlines he'd see the next day if the custodian heard him breathe.

By five after five, he was searching through files again.

The clock kept moving. He wanted to be out by six, to disappear before the building got any more populated, but this was his only shot at this. If he left with nothing, he'd end up walking into tomorrow's election with nothing.

Six o'clock came. Sunrise was about two hours away, but even here, buried deep in the Senate building, Jonah could feel the change. The city was starting to wake up, and a significant percentage of its citizens were going to make their way here fairly rapidly.

At best he had an hour. He pushed himself, flying through records, scanning through tens of thousands of words, looking for one of the key words he needed to see. It started to come. Pieces of the puzzle broke through the fog, and he grabbed a few more files.

At six-thirty he realized it was too big. He couldn't get to the bottom of what was happening just in this one opportunity. But he'd get enough. He might not know the final destination when he left, but he would have a hell of a lot of road signs.

At six forty-five he had had enough. He shut down the computer, unplugged it from his generator, and wiped down the keyboard, chair and the plug ends. He'd been careful to make sure those were the only things he'd touched.

Six-fifty. Ten minutes to spare. He walked out of the Senator's office, shut and secured the door, wiped her keypad, and strode to the main entrance to the suite.

A voice ahead of him spoke. "Rebirth." The lock clicked. The door slid open.

Jonah darted left, into a small supply closet. It was small, had a few shelves secured to the walls, and no door. Anyone in the reception area wouldn't see him, but if they ventured down the hallway, he had no place to hide.

He listened. A single set of footsteps padded around the reception area. A few switches clicked. The first staffer of the day was in, getting the office ready. He or she was alone, but wouldn't be for long.

Jonah's mind raced, trying to anticipate the staffer's routine. He'd walked through the office quickly on his way in, but the layout of it was imprinted on his mind as a three-dimensional model that he pushed and probed, searching for a way to leave unseen.

Then it came to him. Windows.

He knew the staffer was going to walk right past him in a matter of minutes. If the staffer looked to his right, Jonah was finished. If he just looked where he was going—watching the window ahead of him—Jonah had a chance.

The staffer sorted some things on his desk, whistled a brief tune, then, true to Jonah's expectation, started walking down the hallway. At the end of it, next to the door to the Senator's office, was a tightly shuttered window—with manual controls, of all things. Soon it would be letting in the first traces of daylight.

The staffer's footsteps padded closer. Jonah stood by the door closest to the suite's exit, partially, but not completely, concealed by the lip of the closet's doorway.

He saw the staffer, a young man with a sharp nose and pointed chin. The man whistled again. He looked to his left. His head turned.

And he was past. He might be looking to his right now, but he was past the closet.

Jonah slipped to the doorway, carefully poking his head out, watching the staffer as he walked up to the metal shutters over the window.

As soon as his hands touched the shutter, Jonah moved. His feet touched the carpet as lightly as wind on grass, far quieter than the shutter's clatter. He was at the exit in a flash, then willed himself to slow down, pulling it open gently and quietly. Immediately he was lightning again, disappearing through the door.

The door clicked quietly shut as the staffer finished opening the metal shutters.

Jonah stood in the still-empty hallway, wiped a few beads of sweat from his forehead, and willed the red to drain from his face. His training served him well, and in a few seconds he walked down the hallway as the model of decorum. He took one set of stairs down to the twenty-first floor, and a second set to the seventeenth. Then he took the elevator.

He walked to the main entrance of the building. The guards sitting wearily behind their desk nodded as he passed. He nodded. And left.

= 49 =

After he rolled the trash can containing Jonah toward the
Senate Building and escaped the guards, Gareth had considered doubling back and keeping an eye on the place,
waiting for Jonah to emerge. There was no telling, though,
how long Jonah would be, the night was cold and Gareth
didn't want to risk being seen by the guards. Jonah had
told him to go back to the hotel, so he did.

There was no possible way he could sleep, but he had
little to do until Jonah came out. He spent most of his time
wondering when he should set his lunch appointment.

Would a call first thing in the morning seem too urgent,
like he was pouncing on the phone? If he waited too long,
would he lose a chance to make an appointment?

In the end, he decided to call first thing. The appearance
of urgency would bolster his credibility.

He waited until seven, then called the Senator at home.
Unsurprisingly, the Senator was more than happy to make
an appointment with a Paladin on the eve of the election.

Levin walked into his room right after he finished the call.

"Take a look at this," he said.

The Senator had agreed to meet Gareth at the hotel after Gareth insisted, saying he needed to repay the Senator for all the hospitality he had shown over the years.

"Repay?" the Senator had said. "My boy, you don't have to repay gifts."

"I know," Gareth had responded. "And I never could fully pay back your generosity. But I'd like to do at least this. Please."

So the Senator came. It was early for lunch, and the vast dining room was less than half full. The faux candlelight and the isolated corner table Gareth had suggested should provide enough privacy.

"Paladin Sinclair," Mallowes said warmly as he sat down at Gareth's table. "Are you growing accustomed to the sound of that yet?"

Gareth shook his head rapidly, his eyes darting, and he responded as if his mind were elsewhere. "Ah, no. No, I suppose I haven't."

Mallowes' eyes narrowed. "Is there something wrong? You seem distracted."

Gareth leaned forward, started to speak, then leaned back as the waiter arrived.

Mallowes took charge. "I believe we'll both have the special today. The faster you can bring it to us, the better. Thank you."

The waiter was gone.

"I'm in trouble," Gareth said in a voice barely above a whisper.

"Trouble? Of what sort?"

"Levin. Jonah Levin. He's investigating the death of Victor Steiner-Davion."

"So I have heard. He spoke to me about his investigation, albeit briefly. What on earth does that have to do with you?"

"He thinks I had something to do with Steiner-Davion's death."

Mallowes barked, a noise that sounded more like a forceful sneeze than the laugh it was supposed to be. "How did he come to such a ludicrous conclusion?"

"He thinks he has evidence. There's a man, someone you once referred to me. Henrik Morten. He was involved somehow, and he's been lying to Levin about me."

"Morten? I hope you're no longer involved with that character."

"No! Not for years! But that's not what Morten's saying. He's acting like we're old pals."

The waiter returned, bringing bourbon for the Senator and a tall glass of water for Gareth. The Senator took a leisurely sip before speaking.

"Is that all Paladin Levin has? The word of a scoundrel? I should think that is not nearly enough to form any sort of substantial case."

"No. He has more."

Mallowes frowned and ran a finger around the lip of his glass. "Please pardon me for this next question, but I'm afraid it must be asked at this point in the conversation. You did not, in fact, have anything to do with Paladin Steiner-Davion's death, did you?"

Gareth recoiled as if hit. "No!" he said, loud enough to draw the attention of the few nearby diners. He dropped his voice again. "Of course not! How could you ask?"

Mallowes patrician manner did not alter in the least. "Please, my boy, remain calm. I only ask so that I may have your word. Now that you have given it, I have utmost confidence in your innocence. What may I do to assist you?"

"Do you know what will happen if Jonah decides to bring charges? Or even if he just decides to air his suspicions? I'm a new Paladin; most of The Republic knows nothing about me. Their first impression of me will be that I had something to do with Victor's death! It'll ruin me before I get anything done!"

"We can't have that."

"But I don't know what to do about it. I've spoken with Levin, more than once, and he is intractable. He hasn't believed a word I've said. With the election coming up, I think he'd only be too happy to bring me down in the eyes of the other Paladins."

"You mean to say Jonah Levin is actually playing politics?" Mallowes chuckled. "It's about time. Most people don't live in government as long as Levin has without being pulled into the game."

The Senator took another sip at his drink, then stared off past Gareth's shoulder as if he were pondering the matter. Gareth was fairly certain, though, that the Senator already knew exactly what he was going to say next.

"I may be able to help you," Mallowes said finally. "I have a certain relationship with Paladin Levin—did you know I was involved in his appointment?"

Gareth stifled a laugh. Mallowes was present when Jonah was made a Knight, but other than that he had nothing to do with the occasion. "Yes. I believe I have heard something like that."

"Our history runs back many years. Not as deep as yours and mine, of course, but substantial nonetheless. I may be able to persuade him to focus his investigation on a more likely suspect."

"You could do that?"

"I'd consider it my duty. Paladin Levin should pursue the actual assassins, rather than waste his time on an innocent man like you."

"If you could do that . . . I don't know how I could thank you enough."

"Thanks are not necessary. I hope you don't mind my saying, but I have invested a substantial amount in your career and its success. I don't wish to see you stymied at this juncture. Especially with the election coming up."

Now we get to the heart of it, Gareth thought.

"Have you given more thought to the election?" Mallowes asked.

"I've tried. Levin has made it difficult."

"At least he has probably helped make clear one person for whom you should not vote," Mallowes said with a wolfish grin.

Gareth managed a weak chuckle. "Yes. At least there's that."

"Would you be willing to listen to my advice?"

"After what you've offered to do for me? I'd be ungrateful not to."

"Quite so. I do not, at this point in time, wish to offer any specific names for your consideration. All I ask is that, when you vote, you remember the role of the Republican Senate.

"Some of your fellow Paladins, unfortunately, seem to believe the Senate is a mere advisory body, one easily ignored. That is far from what Stone intended. Our families have ruled worlds far longer than Devlin Stone or anyone else, and our experience must be valued. We are to share power equally, even to the point of having a strong voice in military matters, a voice the Paladins have denied us."

I'm not sure that was truly what Stone intended, Gareth thought, but said nothing.

"We must be given heed. One way or another, the Paladins will pay attention to the Senate. Either this election will put an Exarch in place who will be responsive to our needs, or, after the election, the Senate will pursue other avenues to ensure our place is maintained. Do you understand what I am saying?"

"Yes. I believe I do."

"And can I count on your support in this?"

"After all you've done for me, especially if you can change the course of Paladin Levin's investigation, I'm certain you can count on my support in this and many other matters."

Mallowes leaned back in his chair, a man overly comfortable in his own skin. "I had hoped that would be the case. I knew my investment in you was well made."

"Thank you, Senator," Gareth said, though the words almost stuck in his throat. It was difficult to express gratitude to a man who believed he had purchased your loyalty. "I'll do all I can. I'm just . . . I can't be certain it will be enough."

"My dear boy, I'm sure any effort you contribute to our cause will be more than sufficient."

"But I'm only one Paladin, one out of seventeen voting members of the council. I can't make the council more responsive to the Senate by myself."

The Senator sat still, moving only a finger as he rubbed his glass. The waiter finally brought them their lunch (Gareth had learned that telling them to hurry made them much slower) and retreated after the steaming plates were laid to rest. Mallowes still seemed to be weighing something in his mind.

Finally he came to a decision.

"You will not be alone."

"I won't?"

"No."

"How can you know?"

Mallowes allowed himself two bites of his lamb before he spoke. "I am not the only one in the Senate concerned about the current state of affairs. I am not the only one who has taken action to help us reclaim what is ours. Some of us became aware of the danger we were in a long time before The Republic got its rude awakening in the recent troubles. We've been involved with finding a solution to the leadership crisis for over a decade now."

"Doing what?"

"We've tried various approaches," Mallowes said. "The one that appears to be most successful involves working closely with military academies and MechWarrior training centers to develop appropriate educational programs and sponsor promising candidates for advancement. It's slow work, nothing flashy, but as the overall quality of the pool of potential Knights gradually improves, so will the quality—eventually—of the Paladins and even of the Exarch."

Gareth willed himself not to become distracted by speculation on what Mallowes' other, less successful operations might have been. He kept his voice steady, and even managed to inject a note of admiration into it as he said, "That's . . . ambitious."

Mallowes looked modest. "It's not a sudden, overnight change, but we believe it will be effective. We've planted seeds throughout The Republic, growing minds that understand the way the Sphere is supposed to be governed."

"The academy on Skye."

"One of our earliest efforts. And, despite the fact that you are an exemplary graduate, not our most successful. We sacrificed some control over the curriculum, and as a result it was not focused entirely correctly. Still, it is a good program and has generated several promising prospects—though none, of course, as promising as yourself."

Numbers flew through Gareth's head. Numbers connected to names, some of which he knew, some of which he had never heard. But now he knew how all of them were connected. The money was the investment. The names were the candidates. The list Victor Steiner-Davion had created, the list that had gotten him killed, was a list of the people Mallowes and his associates intended to use to seize power in The Republic. And Gareth had been the first, and highest-placed, name on that list.

He suddenly felt ill.

When he spoke, he hoped his voice did not betray his disgust.

"It seems like a risky plan. How can simply providing an education guarantee loyalty?"

"As I said, we have learned much since we opened the academy on Skye," Mallowes said. "Then, we thought gratitude would be enough. We were, unfortunately, naive. Our program is better run now. Those we have groomed fully understand the extent of their debt, and have the proper education so they properly support our cause."

"Proper education" sounded, in this sense, like "brainwashing" to Gareth. He couldn't imagine what kind of schools Mallowes was funding now.

"There are dozens, even hundreds, of candidates out there now, rising through the ranks. We have a newly elected Senator. We have several Knights of the Sphere. And now, thanks to your exemplary loyalty, we have a Paladin. Our strength can no longer be denied."

Gareth shook his head in honest amazement. "I had no idea."

"The Republic has grown too soft. We have had it too easy. The era of Devlin Stone was like a dream, and we all must now wake up and face reality. It's time people remembered the families who governed them for so long. It's time we were given our due." A raspy note entered Mallowes' voice as his tone became more strident. "Many of your associates are not prepared to do that. Victor Steiner-Davion was not. I am. You are. This will be our time."

"Not if Jonah Levin has his way. Not if he keeps coming after me."

"He will not. One way or another, Jonah Levin will not have any effect on you, or on tomorrow's election." Mallowes stood, leaving a mostly unfinished lunch. "I will see to that myself."

50

Office of Paladin Jonah Levin, Geneva
Terra, Prefecture X
19 December 3134

Jonah Levin became more comfortable with his upcoming performance when he remembered that, in many battles, a lot of the key work involved theatrics. Making a show of strength to convince your opponents you had greater numbers than you actually possessed, feinting one way then moving your entire force another, sending a damaged unit out alone as bait then ambushing anyone who tried to take advantage of it—all of these involved misdirection, even showmanship. Those tactics weren't really that different from what he was about to attempt.

Only he had to use words, not 'Mechs, and they weren't his weapon of choice.

Senator Mallowes had been in Jonah's reception area for six and a half minutes, and Jonah, using a small camera, had watched him every second. Mallowes had sat for six minutes, the model of statesmanlike decorum. His impatience, though, eventually got the best of him, and he had stood, made a quick circuit around the small room, then sat still once again. Jonah could almost see Mallowes' knuckles whiten as he held his knees tightly.

A few more seconds, Jonah thought. A little more irritation is all I need.

He counted to twenty in his head, arranged his face into the expression of a man forcing himself to be polite, and opened his office door.

"Senator Mallowes," he said. "How may I help you?"

"Paladin Levin," Mallowes said with a convincing imitation of graciousness. "I realize you must be quite busy, preparing for tomorrow, but I'd like to ask for a moment of your time. You must believe that this is important and weighs heavily on the election."

Jonah rolled his eyes almost imperceptibly. "All right. Come in. But I don't have long."

As he turned, he could almost hear Mallowes bristling. Jonah walked briskly to his desk, leaving Mallowes to close the door for himself.

The Senator sat on the edge of a plain wooden chair. Jonah had considered sawing an inch or two off the legs of the chair, but decided he had more important tasks than mangling the furniture to facilitate humiliation.

"Thank you for taking the time to meet with me," Mallowes said. "I wanted to talk about something I said the last time we spoke."

"What was that?"

"I may have led you to believe there was more of a connection between this Henrik Morten and Gareth Sinclair than actually exists. All I intended to say was that I was not aware of Sinclair severing his ties to Morten, as I had. Whether he actually employed Morten, or what he thought of him, I have no way of knowing."

"Why are you coming to me now with . . . it doesn't matter. It's too late. You can try to cover for your friend all you want, but it's too late."

"I beg your pardon."

"It's too late." Jonah gripped the sides of his desk and leaned forward. "I've got Morten. And he's talking."

"What is he saying?"

"Plenty. Enough to guarantee that Sinclair's career isn't going forward anymore."

"Are you sure Morten is a man you can trust? As I told

you previously, I cut my ties to him because I found he lacked the requisite honor needed to serve The Republic in a high position. He would not hesitate to spread falsehood if he thought it could gain him an advantage—for example, if he thought it was something you wanted to hear."

"What do you take me for?" Jonah snarled. "Do you think I'd build a case on the word of one man, even if I thought that man was honest? Morten just had to point me in the right direction. Once I knew where to look, I found corroboration. Plenty of it."

"It doesn't look good for Sinclair, then."

"Not at all."

"What do you intend to do to him?"

"Bring him to justice! Let the whole council know what kind of man was just admitted into our midst! If I have enough evidence—and I think I will—he'll be in custody before we take the first vote."

Mallowes sat with his hands calmly resting on his legs. The agitation he had shown in the reception area had disappeared.

"Do you think that's the best course of action?"

"I don't believe I have much of a choice."

"We sit at the top of The Republic," Mallowes said, and his eyes might have actually twinkled. "We always have options."

"Are you saying you don't want me to use what I have? You don't want me to go after Sinclair?"

"Is that the best use of the man? You know him. You have worked with him. Couldn't he serve better as a Paladin than as a convict?"

"So I should just ignore the fact that he was involved in an assassination because I think he'd make a good Paladin?"

"No," Mallowes said firmly. "Don't ignore it. Never let him forget you know it. Make sure he regrets his actions for the rest of his days."

"That's why I planned to send him to prison."

"You're thinking too small, Paladin Levin. Imagine what happens if this situation hanging over Sinclair's head goes away."

"I'm sure he'll be pleasantly surprised."

"More than that." Mallowes speech came more rapidly now. "He'll be stunned with gratitude. He'll never forget the people who pulled him back from the brink of personal ruin. He will be in our—in your debt for the remainder of his career. A debt he will never forget because of the information you hold."

"So instead of sending him to jail, I should punish him by blackmailing him for the rest of his life?"

"Those are not the terms I would use, but I suppose you've captured the idea I presented."

Jonah leaned back in his chair, hands clasped behind his head, as if giving deep consideration to the Senator's words.

Finally he spoke. "I'm not sure if I should ask you to leave now or tell you what I think of your stinking proposal first."

"Paladin Levin . . ."

"You call yourself a servant of The Republic? Suggesting that one Paladin blackmail another as a viable means of running a government? You've been in office too long."

"I ask you to remember to whom you are speaking."

"I know full well. A traitor."

Mallowes leapt to his feet, his face twisted into a knot of wrinkles. "How *dare* you . . ."

"Enjoy your time, Senator. After the election tomorrow, I will do everything I can to convince the new Exarch to divest the Senate of as much power as possible. Maybe you won't cling so tight to your office when your main job is attending official funerals."

"You go too far. Be angry at me if you must, but such an attack on the entire Senate is unwarranted."

"The hell it is. I could fit all the Senators who are not either corrupt or incompetent into this room and still have enough room for a marching band. Not that you would be in here to see it."

"I made you," Mallowes said, his words escaping between angry breaths. "I was there when you were raised to a Knight. You *will* remember your debt to me."

"You were there as a ceremonial figure. I don't mean to sound immodest, but I would have been elevated no matter who was there. You had nothing to do with it. I owe you nothing."

Mallowes shook with rage. Jonah wondered if he would

take a step toward him, or even make a fist. But Mallowes had long been accustomed to resolving conflicts without resorting to violence. He had found a large body of people who could carry out his violence for him.

He brought his breathing under control. His face slowly eased into a resting expression. Before Jonah's eyes, Mallowes transformed back to the familiar statesman of trivid reports.

"We do not have to be enemies," Mallowes said. "There is much we could accomplish together. The Senate was established by Devlin Stone, and will not go away so long as we remember his vision. We nobles ruled long before Stone came, and we will rule again. You will not be rid of us, so you would be advised to work with us."

"Devlin Stone's vision, of both the Senate and the Paladins, included people working for the good of The Republic, not for themselves. I'd be happy to have a Senate as Stone intended it. But if I had to choose between a Senate of self-interested vipers or nothing, my choice is quite clear."

"You're choosing dangerously."

"I'm not choosing. I'm just trying to clean up the mess you, Sinclair, and all the rest have created. You made the choice for me."

Mallowes did not show anger again. His face remained neutral, his expression relaxed. Then he turned and walked out the door without saying another word to Jonah.

Jonah sat, trying to let go of the anger he'd summoned up for this meeting. He hadn't known how far he'd have to go, and had surprised himself with his more extreme statements. They did not reflect anything he had seriously thought about before. Now that he had a moment to think, though, he began to consider if he actually believed what he'd said.

51

Levin had seen fire, Mallowes thought as he stalked through the streets of Geneva. Now he'd see ice.

It had to be done quickly, but not rashly. He couldn't afford to let his anger push him into incaution. He'd managed to do this once before, and by all accounts carried it off perfectly, completely deflecting Levin from the correct trail. He'd had more time then, but not much. Once he'd received the information about Victor Steiner-Davion's plans, he'd been forced to move fairly quickly. That was where preparation paid off. Having spent years learning which channels were best used for various types of business, Mallowes had little trouble finding the appropriate people for the job. The very first lesson any politician learns is the overwhelming importance of knowing the right people.

He didn't want to be forced into using the same people. He couldn't, really, since he'd heard, through roundabout channels, some unfortunate things about one of the operatives employed in Santa Fe. It was better to develop an all-new team, to avoid the risk of repeating himself, but he lacked time. Some degree of repetition would be necessary.

The shame of it, Mallowes thought, is that some of the difficulty arises from having done my job too well. He hadn't gone into this project trying to create trouble for Sinclair; he'd simply noticed that a few signs pointed in the direction of his protégé and decided it would be advantageous to make sure those signs were seen and followed. He had not anticipated, however, that Levin would become so resolute in his pursuit. The whole purpose of the exercise was to create the proper climate for making deals, not to completely break down the relationship between himself and Levin.

Maybe it was for the best, though. He hadn't seen this side of Levin, hadn't known the secret contempt Levin had for him and the other Senators (though he suspected it— he suspected it of all the Paladins). If their differences were so deeply entrenched, it was best to deal with the situation now rather than wait for Levin to use his influence to make things worse.

In most cases, there were several options for dealing with a situation like this, but unfortunately Levin made most of them impossible. Levin was simply not the type to take bribes, or to keep a different woman in every port. It wasn't that he was incorruptible—in his long life, Mallowes had never met a single person to whom that word could be applied—just that, whatever his weaknesses might be, they did not lie in conventional areas.

Mallowes honestly wished there were some other solution to this problem. He hated to stoop to the same low tactic twice in a single month. However, the short time frame and the dire nature of Levin's intent left him with no other options.

It was also unfortunate that Mallowes would not have Morten at his disposal. When all this had blown over, he could perhaps work at extricating the poor man from Levin's clutches, but for now that task must wait. In the meantime, Mallowes had to find another operative as skilled and as discreet as Morten. •

Another lesson Mallowes had learned in his years of public service is that no one is irreplaceable. If you want to stay ahead of the competition, you must always know of at least three people who can perform any given job.

Mallowes pressed a button on his phone, then dialed a number. He waited, punched in a few more numbers, then cut the connection.

He picked up his pace. From the moment he placed the call, he had one hour to reach his destination.

To Mallowes, every spot in the city of Geneva fell into one of two categories—places where I will be noticed, and places where I will not be. The former division had several subcategories based on the desirability of being noticed at said location, but those were the two primary organizational groups. At the moment, he clearly needed a location in the second category.

The Museum of Terran Antiquity was just such a place. Established by Devlin Stone during the reconstruction of Geneva, the museum began life as a warehouse holding a wide variety of rubble that survived the Blakist Jihad. The items were painstakingly cleaned and restored, and pieces of Terra's past were slowly put back together. The museum eventually had enough intact items to open a permanent display, and recently had nearly doubled its floor space as new objects arrived. A recent display of furniture and electronics from the distant twenty-fifth century—items that somehow survived seven hundred years of chaos—was the talk of Geneva's cultural elite.

Mallowes was part of that group. He made certain to show his face frequently at the museum, so his entrances and exits were no longer noteworthy.

Today, museum traffic was light. With the election only hours away, the majority of Genevans were far too wrapped up in Terra's present to give much thought to its past. Mallowes waved his membership card at the door attendant and walked in without a moment's wait.

In the center of the floor ahead of him was a staircase that looked like white marble but was actually a far lighter composite. At its base it was little more than a meter wide, barely enough for a single person to pass. It widened slowly as it ascended three meters, then made a sharp turn to the right. As it rose, it grew broader and made a continually wider circuit. The sloped walls on either side of the stairs emphasized its upside-down pyramid shape. Walkways, which looked to be little more than catwalks, connected the central stair to each level's promenade around the courtyard.

Mallowes, who disliked the architectural showiness of the stairs and also felt uncomfortable on the hovering catwalks, opted instead for an elevator to the fifth floor. When he emerged, he walked to the railing looking over the airy staircase. He spent ten minutes walking the perimeter of the courtyard, seeming to gaze at the marvel of the stair from every angle. In truth, he carefully watched the museum floor and the other levels for any face that seemed the least bit familiar. He saw no one who demanded his attention.

Satisfied, he walked beneath a clear archway filled with swirling smoke. Light flashed from one end of the arch to the other, darting back and forth, spelling out words that burned in place only briefly before fading. The words read A LIGHT IN THE MIST. Beyond the archway was an exhibit detailing the cataclysmic Brazilian rain forest fires of 2718 and how the charred remains contributed to the discovery of a half-dozen new medicines.

It was the emptiest exhibit of the museum.

Mallowes walked calmly through a holographic display of a burning forest, which was made all the more realistic by the fan blowing hot air in patrons' faces. He kept walking until he stood in front of a large case displaying another hologram, this one showing people dressed as lab technicians studiously examining piles of burnt wood and charred plants.

"That's not what Elsa Kavendish looked like," said a woman sitting on a bench across from the display. She wore a long wool coat with its collar folded up and a gray scarf around her neck, as if she was about to go back outside any minute. The only feature Mallowes could clearly make out was the straight black hair running down the side of her face.

Mallowes smiled ruefully. "I know," he said. "My understanding is that the museum did not find her true appearance dynamic enough."

"What does her appearance have to do with what she did?"

"Nothing. But the museum wants to present her as a role model, and you know how people are. They respond better to role models that are attractive."

"I think it's a shame when museums play to people's worst instincts."

"I agree. However, like any business, a museum must find a way to bring people inside its doors."

While they were speaking, Mallowes removed a device, somewhat smaller than his fist, from his pocket. He twisted a series of dials on its base, then pressed a button in its middle. It emitted a six-meter-wide sphere of nothing. An invisible veil of static shielded their conversation. If anyone came within fifteen meters, the disc would beep three times, then drop its shield. For now, they could talk freely.

"Hello, Agnes."

"Hello. Morten's missing," Agnes said. Mallowes always appreciated her willingness to get down to business.

"I know."

"Should I be worried?"

"For him? Or for yourself?" Mallowes asked.

"What do you think?"

"No. The issue that got him in trouble didn't involve you in the least. No one is looking for you."

"Good." Agnes paused. "I'm not sure why you called on me. I've got enough to do, monitoring what's going to happen tomorrow. I'm supposed to watch the warehouse on . . ."

"I don't want to hear anything about what's happening tomorrow!" Mallowes said sharply.

"Right. Sorry," Agnes said with what might have been a mocking tone. "Anyway, I have plenty to do. I don't know that I can take on anything else until that's done."

"This is more important."

Agnes whistled. "Really?"

"Yes."

The woman pushed the hair out of her face, showing blue eyes and an upward-crinkled mouth. She couldn't keep the expression of wonder off her face. "All right, I'm interested, then. What's going on?"

"There's a Paladin who we cannot afford to let vote in the election."

"Who?"

"Jonah Levin."

"*Levin?* You can't be serious."

Mallowes gave her a look that assured her he was.

"You want Levin out of commission by tomorrow. With the amount of time left, that doesn't leave too many options."

"I realize that."

"I can't do anything subtle. It's going to be direct. Probably quite violent."

Mallowes held up a hand. "I have no need to hear any details. The job must be done. If it is, you will receive fifty times your normal payment. If it's not, our relationship is terminated."

"A real all-or-nothing guy. I've never liked that about you—except when I get the 'all,' of course."

Mallowes was in no mood to tolerate her jesting tone. "Get it done," he barked. Just then his disc beeped three times.

With remarkable speed and agility for a man of his years, Mallowes bent and scooped the disc into his pocket in one quick motion. He recovered his normal firm bearing before the intruder could round the corner and see them.

"At least it has brown hair," Agnes said. "I'm pretty sure she had brown hair. Wasn't it curly, though?"

"That's hardly the point, my dear girl. When discussing one of the great scientists of history, is appearance really relevant?"

A brown-haired man in a courier's jacket came around the corner. Both his hands were jammed in his pockets. He didn't seem the least bit interested in the exhibit, not sparing it a single look.

"Impressive," the man said. He stood with his legs slightly apart, and Mallowes sensed the tension running through the newcomer's body. He jerked his head at Agnes, and she slowly stood.

"Yes," Mallowes said, "they are. Some very capable scientists."

"Not them," the newcomer said. "You two."

"How do you mean?"

"I mean that you didn't miss a beat. You picked up that

conversation like all that stuff in the middle didn't happen. The trouble is," he said, looking slowly back and forth between Mallowes and Agnes, "it did."

"I'm not quite sure . . ."

"Don't get me wrong, it's a good device," the man said. "The problem is, the people who made it knew how to break it. So they put your disc on the general market, and then put a way to break the shield in some back channels, pricing it for ten times what your device costs. Selling both the disease and the cure—nice little racket. You've gotten by for a while, you see, because barely anyone has the cure. But a few of us do."

Mallowes didn't need to hear anymore. He feinted forward, just enough to make the man flinch, then darted into the corridor behind him. The man tried to draw the weapon Mallowes knew was in his pocket, but Agnes was quicker. She was on him instantly, and they tussled on the museum floor.

The fight wouldn't last long, Mallowes knew. Agnes might have fared well in an even fight, but museum security would detect the scuffle and arrive too quickly for her to make her escape. She'd be tied up for a while. For too long. He cursed silently. He'd have to move down to the next name on his list.

But first he had to get out.

He emerged from the exhibit's exit at a brisk walk. He disliked it, but he was forced to take the catwalk to the stairs—there was no time to wait for an elevator.

The catwalk seemed to sway beneath his feet. The light breeze from the heating system suddenly seemed to grow stronger. Mallowes' legs became wobbly.

He was almost to the staircase when thudding footsteps made him jump backward. The catwalk's low railing caught him at his thighs, and, for a brief moment, he mentally saw himself pitching over and falling five stories. But he caught himself as two security guards ran past him, and he proceeded down the staircase.

He walked as quickly as he could without running. The guards would be with Agnes very shortly and the courier, if he were still alive, would start talking.

Agnes had better not fail him.

He wound down the increasingly narrow stairway, the

final twists making him slightly dizzy. But then his feet hit the carpeted floor of the entry hall.

The entrance was just ahead. No one stood between him and freedom except for the attendant. The guards must have gone to investigate the disturbance.

He pushed forward, one hand in his pocket, preparing to grab his phone and make the next call. Just as soon as he was out.

To his right, his mind registered the soft chime announcing an elevator's arrival. A voice followed the chime.

"That's enough, Senator."

Had it just been the voice of a security guard, Mallowes would have hurried on. But the shock of recognition, the surprise of hearing that voice here, stopped him in his tracks. He turned, and saw the wrong end of a revolver held by Heather GioAvanti.

His shoulders slumped. A vision of a million humiliations that would now be his swamped his mind. But that vision could not push away the sight of the gun staring him down.

In her other hand, GioAvanti held a small parabolic dish. A long needle extended from the center of it like a stiletto. He knew it immediately for what it is.

GioAvanti followed his glance. "A handy device," she said. "Cuts through static fields like sunlight through a window." She smiled, and Mallowes didn't find it the least bit charming. "You just have to know where to point it."

The second elevator chimed. The courier, bleeding from a cut under his eye but otherwise functional, walked out first. Two guards, carrying a shackled and unconscious Agnes, followed.

GioAvanti glanced at her. "I hope she wakes up soon. We have a lot to talk about." Then she turned to Mallowes. "In the meantime, though, I'm sure you'll be interesting enough."

52

The day of the election dawned gray. Heather wished she knew what Mallowes and his companion were saying, but she'd been forced to leave them soon after bringing them in. Jonah promised he'd notify her immediately if anything relevant to her side of the investigation came up, and she returned to her makeshift headquarters.

Duncan's eyes lit up immediately as soon as she entered.

"Paladin GioAvanti! Where have you been? I have information on eight groups, all of whose name starts with the word 'Stone,' a leadership change in the Brothers of the Blood, rumors of Stormhammers approaching Terra . . ."

She turned rapidly and was stunned to feel her knees creak beneath her. She was forty-six years old and hadn't slept in two days—she felt like age was asserting itself.

"I have very limited time and even less patience," she said as kindly as possible. "I only want to hear about things pertaining to the Kittery Renaissance. Everything else—and I mean *everything*—will wait."

"Yes, Paladin."

"Do you have anything on the KR?"

"No, Paladin."

"Then find something!"

Watching Duncan scurry away was almost as gratifying as the expression on Mallowes' face when the elevator opened.

She hurried into the conference room, where Rick Santangelo held a noteputer in one hand, a phone in the other, and was attempting to press a few keys on a desktop computer with his elbow.

"What do you mean there's a warehouse you didn't know about? How do you lose track of your own warehouses?" He waited for the other party to speak. "I don't *care* if you own them or rent them! I don't care if you're *stealing* the space! You should keep track of where you store your goods!"

Heather extended her arms, palms down, trying to signal to Santangelo to calm down. He noticed her gesture and his voice became a bit less intense.

While he talked, she slipped the noteputer out of his hand and reviewed his notes. Troop availability for the next morning. It was sparse, but would have to do.

After a few moments, he finished his conversation, disconnected the call and took a deep breath.

"You have no idea how glad I am to see you."

Looking at his bloodshot eyes and fevered air, she replied "I think I have some idea. How much time do we have?"

"Just over twelve hours."

"And how much time do we need?"

"Twenty, twenty-five hours maybe."

"Just the way I like it."

The time seemed to move slowly as Heather pushed through the weariness, but when the moment came for her to ascend to the cockpit of her *Spider* she found herself alert, tense and wishing she could have another hour to prepare.

She powered up the cockpit communications links and checked in. Altogether Santangelo had come up with two squads of hastily borrowed militia infantry—twenty-four troopers, not counting herself and her two Knights—all mounted on hoverbikes and armed with pulse rifles, plus a Shandra scout vehicle and a Fox armored car. Every other police and militia unit was involved with security, crowd control or the pursuit of other rumors.

She patched in to the Geneva law enforcement net—she could eavesdrop, but not talk—and flipped down a police-fire-and-emergency map of the city on her cockpit's heads-up display. Pinpoints of light on the map showed the location of the Hall of Government, the Senatorial office building, and the Hotel Duquesne, where everyone who was anyone was staying.

Heather and her troopers weren't the only people up early in Geneva this morning. The map already showed the first spots of political demonstrations. Pink lines swirled on the map, marking their locations. Back at her headquarters, Duncan was probably going out of his head, but these weren't her concern, except possibly as obstacles to be avoided.

"Paladin, we've confirmed an arms cache on the northwest side," came the voice of Santangelo in the Fox armored car. "Kittery Renaissance material."

"Well, let's go," she said. The location of the cache came up on her display as a pulsing red dot. "Follow my lead."

She set the *Spider* into motion, turning from the 'Mech bay out into the street. The sky outside wasn't yet fully light. They made a strange procession, the thirty-ton 'Mech, a wheeled light vehicle behind and a hover darting ahead.

Thirty tons is thirty tons, and the centuries-old street vibrated with each heavy footfall. Running 'Mechs in Terra's ancient cities was always a risky business. There was so much buried infrastructure, you never knew when some government's generations-old poor maintenance might result in the pavement caving in beneath you today. Heather kept the *Spider*'s steps slow, carefully gauging the path ahead, working carefully through streets designed for lighter, narrower vehicles.

Law enforcement woke up to her presence; she heard chatter on the net, then reports of her movement. Some confusion amid the police, then a voice from higher up: "That's a Paladin. Let it go. They're doing what they do."

"Five minutes to contact," Santangelo said over the command net. "Rules of engagement?"

"Here are your rules," Heather said. "Pass the word to the militia: We do not shoot at people, even if they're shooting at us. We destroy materiel only, and that only if we know it's Kittery Renaissance stuff."

"And how will we know that?"

"If a place is on our list, consider the stuff in it KR by definition. Anything else—we'll know it belongs to the bad guys when people start shooting at us. And repeat, no shooting back; I want to see property damage only. Be careful not to start any fires. I don't want today to be remembered as the day we burned down Geneva."

"Lousy terrain for us," piped up Koss, the junior Knight, who was riding the Shandra. She'd chosen to wear light battle armor for this mission—it would do something to protect her from small-arms fire at least, though it wouldn't help much against the heavy stuff. "We can get ambushed from on top, from below, or on the sides and back—and we can't run or hide."

"Keep thinking cheerful thoughts," Heather advised. "Foot troops, off your bikes. That's our target ahead. Koss and Santangelo, take station on the two far corners, keep reinforcements from coming in. Foot troops, in the doors ahead."

"What are the chances that we have surprise?" Santangelo asked.

"Depends on whether they're deaf, blind and stupid, I suppose."

"You mean, 'nil.' "

"That's about the shape of it," Heather said. "The only question is whether they expected a 'Mech to join the party this early."

"If they were listening to the police bands earlier," Santangelo said, "then they certainly expect it now."

"So let's not wait." She scorched a marker on the building with a laser set to low power. "Let's go."

53

Warehouse District, Geneva
Terra, Prefecture X
20 December 3134

"**S**quad, by sections, overwatch advance!"

In response to their squad leader's orders, Heather Gio-Avanti's borrowed militia troopers moved into action. Those on the right and the left advanced, while the ones facing the center of the building remained still, their eyes surveying the facade for movement or any sign of resistance. They saw nothing, and heard no sounds other than the normal ones of a city waking up. With a rush of booted feet over ancient streets, the flankers reached the walls and stood still, eyes scanning, weapons high.

Then it was the center's turn to advance, rushing, waiting for the sound of gunfire. Nothing. They reached the doors.

"Screw subtle," said the squad leader. "Breaching charges."

The charges were set, then detonated. The large doors came off their hinges, falling inward. The men at the center dashed inside, rushing into eerie quiet, followed by the flankers from the front corners.

Through it all, Heather GioAvanti watched over the action from the cockpit of her *Spider*, ready to provide supporting fire if needed. So far, it hadn't been. For a panicky moment she wondered if perhaps they'd hit the wrong warehouse. She rechecked the coordinates—no, this was the one.

Then Koss in the Shandra and Santangelo in the Fox reported all secure in the rear of the building. A signal from inside the warehouse, from the militia corporal leading section two: "Ma'am. We have a large amount of military materiel here. Pistols, rifles, charge canisters, gas masks and"—he dropped synch, came back a moment later—"missiles. In launch racks. Instructions?"

"Destroy it all," Heather said. "Render it inoperable. Speed is important. Make it good."

She keyed off the circuit. A moment later, the squad reappeared, trotting out from between the blast-broken doors of the warehouse.

"Fire in the hole!" the corporal shouted.

A cloud of dust rolled out of the warehouse doors; up above, a skylight blew out in a rainbow of glass fragments. The shockwave vibrated through the limbs of Heather's *Spider*, and the glass in the windows of the building behind her shattered and fell to the street.

"Right," Heather said. "Next on the list." She read them the coordinates. "Mount up and move out, people."

"Next one may not be so easy," Santangelo commented over the command circuit. "That one wasn't guarded and we had surprise on our side. Next one, if they aren't awake by now, they're dead."

"We'll take them. Hopefully without trashing large sections of the city."

"I won't if you won't," Santangelo replied. "But I can't give any guarantees about the KR."

"How long until contact?" she asked.

"Under three."

"Hit it. Same plan."

The Fox and the Shandra peeled out ahead of Heather's skittering 'Mech, the bike-mounted troopers of the militia infantry squad following at speed.

"They did what?" Cullen Roi stared at the foot messenger. The man had found him at his Spartan west-side apartment, finishing the last of a hasty breakfast before going to the temporary command center he had established specifically for the day's activities.

"Destroyed our supply cache at the Grundewald warehouse," repeated the messenger breathlessly. "And they're—"

A second foot messenger hurried in.

"Reported attack on our warehouse at Lundquist Street. Several vehicles, at least one 'Mech. Commander Hansel believes that it's Paladin GioAvanti's people."

"What are the police and the militia doing about this?" Cullen demanded. He didn't get an answer; he didn't expect one. Not from these two. He put down his coffee and said, "I'll be at the command center. Bring any other messages there. Here are your orders: To all cache commanders. Empty your warehouses. Distribute your arms and armor as best you can. If attacked, resist."

The two messengers saluted awkwardly. Part of the problem with running the paramilitary wing of a political movement, Cullen had found, was that the volunteers one got were often more "para" than military as far as their background and training were concerned. But one had to work with the materials at hand. He put the problem out of his mind for the moment and headed for Kittery Renaissance's command center—in normal life, the back room at the data shop where Norah's current lover had his day job—as quickly as a man could go without attracting unwanted attention.

Hansel and Norah were already busy when he arrived. The shop's owner was a sympathizer with the cause; he'd never asked Norah exactly what her "political group" intended to do that required the use of his back room and its data facilities. He was also a prudent man, who had departed yesterday on a visit to his daughter in Nova Scotia without making any awkward inquiries into what might be going on at the shop during his absence.

"Commander," said Hansel as Cullen entered. "We are under attack."

"I know," said Cullen. "What I want to know is who and where."

"Who is Heather GioAvanti, and where is here." Hansel pointed to a map of the city. All of the supply caches for the coming street battles were circled in red. Two of the sites had black *X*'s drawn on them in grease pencil.

"That was the first one, at 0608. Then they hit this one at 0622."

"That would put her about"—Cullen traced his finger over the map, drawing a line from the second of the destroyed warehouses to its nearest untouched neighbor—"here. Nothing we can do for the next bunch but warn them. You *have* warned them?"

"I have," Norah said. "At least so far, the police are staying well clear. We've been monitoring their frequencies, and they've been keeping themselves busy with the protestors down at the Hall of Government. It looks like they've been told to back off and let the Paladin handle it."

"Too bad it isn't the right Paladin," said Hansel. "We should have sent the council a memo."

"Not funny," Norah snapped.

"Calm down," Cullen said. "These things happen. If Gio-Avanti fails, the demand for someone of greater experience will be that much louder."

He tapped the red circle on the map that marked the location of the next targeted warehouse. "Write that one off. We'll have lost three supply caches. Not good, but we can live with it."

Picking up the grease pencil, he circled the fourth warehouse in the line. "This is where we'll fight it out. Everyone else, get the supplies out to the cadres. The timetable just got advanced by a few hours."

He looked at the map again and rethought his strategy. "Hmm. With a hasty defense of that fourth site, we may well lose it as well. Change of·plans—how do you feel about an ambush, say, here?"

He indicated a spot halfway between the fourth location and the fifth.

"I feel strongly positive about it, sir," Hansel said.

"I was hoping you would," Cullen told him. "You're going to lead it. Take what you need, and get going. If this plan is going to work, you have to defeat GioAvanti."

54

**Chamber of Paladins, Geneva
Terra, Prefecture X
20 December 3134**

The brief clouds of dawn were passing, and a sapphire sky emerged. The sunlight glinting off the snow-covered Alps was almost blinding. It would have been a beautiful day if it weren't for the wind riding cold through the streets.

Jonah Levin stood in his private lavatory, spreading lather over his face. It wouldn't do to show up at an election unshaven.

He'd always believed formal occasions called for a sharp razor and shaving cream, and occasions didn't get much more formal than this one. He also needed to get his hair in some sort of order, and it wouldn't hurt to find a press for his uniform. He wasn't sure the building had one.

If I had a staff, he thought, I could send someone out to get it pressed. Something to think about next time I come back—which I hope isn't for four more years.

His grooming efforts seemed to be working. Looking at his reflection, he thought he looked quite normal. Except for the eyes. His eyes couldn't hide the lack of sleep.

Maybe fresh air would help.

The bright sunlight almost blinded him, while the wind cut through his uniform as soon as he stepped outside. It was uncomfortable but beautiful, and Jonah could only think of one thing—if I finish this right, this is a sight Senator Mallowes won't see for many years.

No more than seven people in Geneva knew Mallowes was in custody, and one of them, Agnes, was in the cell next to him. The others were Jonah, Heather, Burton Horn, Gareth Sinclair, and the two guards who each held a button capable of sending a shock to the collar on Mallowes' neck. They were under strict orders to only use the device in case of an attempted escape, but part of Jonah wouldn't be too upset if they forgot their orders.

He immediately remonstrated with himself. That's a Mallowes thought.

Outside, the expected protesters were already gathering in the open square. Their demonstrations looked orderly for the time being—the protestors in the front ranks, at least, were standing in a straight line and seemed to barely be raising their voices. They held signs and placards, some of them handmade, others professionally printed. CAPELLANS BELONG UNDERFOOT, one said; KEEP THE CLANS OFF TERRA, another; a third, DAVID MCKINNON FOR EXARCH.

Jonah carefully studied each sign, hoping one of them would finally make it clear what he should do with his vote. But he found none of the signs overly convincing. Apparently the persuasive value of a placard was overestimated.

"Paladin Levin!"

The voice came to him from beyond the crowd with unnatural clarity and distinction. Jonah looked for the source, and saw a tri-vid reporter running toward him, her videographer hovering at her elbow. He debated ducking inside, but didn't.

"Paladin Levin! Can you give us any hint about who's in the running to be the next Exarch?"

"I'm afraid not. I'll vote my conscience, but that's all I know."

"Can you tell us who you, personally, support?"

"No, I really can't. And even if I could, I probably shouldn't. We'll work out negotiations as a council, rather than passing notes through the media. With all due respect, of course."

"Surely you've heard some of the comments from Anders Kessel regarding the balance of power with the passing of Victor Steiner-Davion?"

Jonah almost laughed. "No. I honestly haven't. Now I'm sorry, but you'll have to excuse me."

He ducked inside, and the reporter turned to look for fresh prey.

Instead of returning to the higher floors, he walked over to the main rotunda. It was echoing and empty, a far cry from the noisy, crowded place that it had been on the day of the opening convocation. Today, spectators and reporters were banned from the building. The proceedings were for Paladins alone.

He continued on through the rotunda into the meeting chamber, and found it almost, but not entirely, empty. The huge windows on the wall opposite the Exarch's chair admitted streams of sunlight, as well as images of hundreds of protestors shouting soundlessly. To them, the window appeared as a solid wall.

Jonah had to walk some distance before he was close to actual people. Seventeen Paladins didn't take up much space in a room built to hold several hundred people. Any comments the Paladins were making to each other were swallowed by the room long before they reached Jonah's ears.

No, Jonah realized. Not even seventeen Paladins. A quick scan told him Heather GioAvanti was not there.

He spotted David McKinnon's tall, gray-haired figure, down where the Paladins' desks were arranged in their open-horseshoe configuration in front of the Exarch's podium. Jonah decided McKinnon would be as good a place to start as any. The man might be a bit of a political fossil, but at least he was an honest one. After spending too much time recently in the company of men like Geoffrey Mallowes, McKinnon's straightforwardness would be refreshing.

"Good morning, David."

"Paladin Levin." McKinnon was one who stood on ceremony, particularly at a time like this. "It's an extraordinary morning."

"Perhaps it will be."

"Seventeen people are meeting to decide the fate of two hundred fifty planets. It cannot help but be extraordinary."

"I suppose that's true. Do you have word on Heather's whereabouts?"

"No. I was hoping you would know." McKinnon's glance turned slightly sideways. "I understand the two of you have been quite busy."

If it were anyone else, Jonah might think McKinnon was attempting a subtle innuendo. But it *was* McKinnon—the question was about nothing more than their investigation.

"We have been. Though I imagine the whole council has been."

"True enough. But word of your activities has traveled, though the reports I hear are conflicting. Would you care to clarify anything about your work?"

"I would." Jonah saw McKinnon lean forward almost unwillingly, eager for a piece of information most Paladins didn't have. "I'll be informing everyone of my progress before we vote."

McKinnon concealed his disappointment well. "I look forward to your report. Excuse me, please."

It was a simple game, Jonah thought. I've got nothing for him, so he moves on to the next player.

Jonah wondered who he should speak with next, then realized that most of them would ask the same question as McKinnon—everyone except Sinclair. He walked over to the junior Paladin's seat, where Sinclair chatted idly with Janella Lakewood.

"Good morning, Gareth."

"Hi, Jonah. Seems like I haven't seen you in nearly six hours."

"Did you get any sleep?"

"No. But the way things look here, I'll probably be able to grab a few winks during our deliberations."

It was an immense relief to talk to Sinclair without the pall of suspicion hanging over his head. His youth and cheerfulness would be a welcome addition to a council that often threatened to become overly grim.

Jonah glanced down at Sinclair's desk. "Your screen's not on."

"Do you think I'll need it?"

"Definitely." He tapped the screen. "That's where the real horse-trading happens."

"Horse-trading doesn't strike me as one of your interests."

"It isn't," Jonah admitted. "But that doesn't keep the rest of them from approaching me."

Sinclair and Lakewood both palmed the panels near their screens, powering them up and logging them on simultaneously. Meanwhile, the surrounding conversations slowly grew louder. Some of them simply seemed to be getting excited about the election, but other tones were turning heated. Eventually, the strong, bell-like tones of Tyrina Drummond rose above the rest.

"We cannot cast a *final* ballot without her," Drummond said. "There is no reason we cannot begin preliminary discussions and ballots. This is the time. I see no reason to delay."

She stood directly in front of the Exarch's chair, which Jonah had always found unnecessarily thronelike. The chair was concealed by a large, blank screen. Soon that screen would display the future of The Republic.

"How do we tell which ballots are preliminary and which are final?" asked Janella Lakewood.

Drummond cast her the iron stare that only Clan-born warriors could give. "We announce it. Before each ballot, we announce if it is preliminary or final. Naturally, all ballots before Paladin GioAvanti arrives will be preliminary."

"Are we locked into voting for the same person each time? How do we change?" Lakewood asked.

If anything, Drummond's glare became more withering. "You vote for whom you wish each ballot. If you wish to change your vote, change your vote. You may alter it as often as you choose."

"I'm not sure I understand the purpose of the preliminary ballots, then."

Anders Kessel, presenting himself with every inch of his noble bearing, stepped forward to answer. "Consider it a time for us all to get acquainted," he said kindly. "We'll get to know each other better, learn a little bit more about whom our companions believe is fit to be Exarch. That knowledge will help us move toward the final ballot."

That was certainly Kessel's plan, Jonah thought. He knew

Kessel wanted as many preliminary ballots as possible. The more time he had, and the better he could gauge the opinions of the other Paladins, the better chance he had to bring others into an alliance to push the candidate of his choice into the position of Exarch. In this election, Jonah was fairly sure that Kessel's candidate of choice was Kelson Sorenson.

"Is either of you making a motion?" Thaddeus Marik said.

"Yes," Drummond said. "I move that we commence deliberation and preliminary balloting."

"We cannot hold deliberations without the entire council!" Mandela insisted.

"Then I move we commence discussion and preliminary balloting," Drummond said, unruffled—at least for the moment.

"Seconded," Kessel said.

It was time. "Before we vote on the motion," Jonah said, "I'd like to clear something up."

Fifteen heads turned toward him. Jonah's collected utterances in council meetings could fill a book approximately five pages long. Today, he'd probably double that by the first ballot.

"Yes?" Kessel asked.

"I just want to be sure we have time for statements before balloting." Another murmur ran through the council. Not only was Jonah speaking now, he seemed to want to say more. By now, every Paladin knew what Jonah had been doing recently, and they all had guesses about what he planned to say. The anticipation in the room ratcheted up a notch.

"Of course," Kessel said. "Now, unless there are any other clarifications or questions? Good. Votes in favor?" The room filled with ayes. "Opposed?" Silence.

Sixteen Paladins walked to their chairs and sat down in almost perfect unison.

"Then let's begin," Kessel said.

55

Warehouse District, Geneva
Terra, Prefecture X
20 December 3134

"I see people in motion up ahead," Santangelo reported to Heather GioAvanti over the command link. "They could be armed."

"Or they could be civilians," Heather replied. "Remember—the rules of engagement are property damage only, do not fire even if fired upon."

"Roger, understand no return fire," Santangelo said. "Can't say that I like it, though."

"We're trying to prevent an insurrection here, not make one," Heather told him. "Do we have enough demolition charges for all of the targets?"

"We'll manage."

"Right. Looks like thirty seconds to contact."

The third warehouse of the morning—Koss' revised list of possibilities had a total of ten—was coming up; a turn to the right then a straight run up to the front doors. The streets were narrower in this part of town, and the heavy feet of Heather's 'Mech weren't doing the pavement any good. More property damage—but she was sure the new

Exarch, whoever he or she turned out to be, would make restitution after the election.

There were definite signs of movement around the target up ahead. Heather wondered exactly how much longer the "don't shoot" policy was going to work.

She worked her pedals rapidly, spinning her 'Mech around the corner. The *Spider* was a speedy machine, not a bruiser like the *Atlas* or a hulking infighter like the *Hatchetman*, but a lightly armed sprinter designed to get in fast, scout and get out fast. In Heather's opinion, these qualities made the *Spider* an excellent model for command and control, since a properly managed battle plan shouldn't require the commander's own muscle in order to be effective.

The Fox armored car, the Shandra scout vehicle, and the militia squad's bikes were all faster than the *Spider* in the cramped confines of the city streets. Santangelo and Koss peeled out ahead, and Heather scored a laser marker on the front of the building to guide them. The militia troopers stopped in front of the building; Santangelo and Koss, in their vehicles, sped off to take blocking positions.

"Forward by overwatch!" Heather commanded.

The troops moved out. They were good for militia, disciplined and well trained. She made a mental note to look up their regular commander and see that he or she got properly commended when all this was done.

"Command, Shandra scout," Koss said over the command circuit. "Got a problem on the east face. No way around to the rear. There's a wall."

"Back out, take the west side." She checked her heads-up display. No wall showed on the large-scale map. It looked like Geneva Fire Police and Emergency hadn't updated their databases recently. That was another thing to bring to somebody's attention; later, after all of the dust had cleared.

Then the 'Mech's exterior mikes picked up the sounds of small-arms fire, localized on her heads-up display to the east side of the building. It wasn't the Sperry-Browning machine guns of the scout car she was hearing, either—it was the heavy *crump* of armor-piercing ordnance, shoulder-launched penetrators by the sound of them.

"Koss!" she snapped over the command circuit. "Report!"

"Taking fire from my flank," the junior Knight reported. "Daisy-chain mines behind me. I'm in a sticky place. Request permission to return fire."

"Negative," Heather said. "Permission denied. I'm on my way to your location." Then, over the 'Mech's external speakers, to the troops, "Entry force, expedite."

"Roger, understand expedite," the corporal in charge of the militia squad responded. A moment later, the breaching charge put a hole in the warehouse wall. Heather saw the militia troops entering through the dust on her side-mount screen as she went past at a lope.

Taking advantage of the *Spider*'s speed, she was around the corner in a moment and saw Koss' problem. The heavy but inaccurate fire coming from the Shandra's right—small arms, mostly—wouldn't interfere with the mission too much. What *would* interfere was a group of antitank mines, tied together to form a long chain. They'd been hidden in the trash by the side of the road while the Shandra passed by, then triggered when someone tugged the cord and pulled the line of mines across the Shandra's only available path of retreat. Koss could abandon her vehicle to remove the mines by pulling the rope the other way—but even with her light battle armor, the intensity of the small-arms fire combined with the shoulder-mounted penetrators fired earlier would cut her to ribbons before she'd gone half a dozen steps.

Heather, though, wouldn't have the same problem. Putting her trust in her armor, she lightly depressed her pedals while pushing the right joystick to extend the 'Mech's long arm. The *Spider* squatted and its arm grabbed the end of the rope closest to the building. She pulled back on her stick, the mines came toward her and the way was clear.

"Back up," she ordered Koss. "Rejoin with Santangelo."

The Shandra was already accelerating in reverse. Heather laid down a spray of laser fire just over the heads of the people who were shooting at her troops. The line of pulsing light gouged into the brick wall behind the attackers as the water in the mortar flashed to steam. Heather hoped that she wasn't violating the spirit of the no-engagement rules by making the defenders keep their heads down.

"Any casualties?" she asked over the net.

"Negative," Koss answered. "Nothing hurt but my pride."

"You'll survive. Rejoin, regroup and we're out of here."

That was when the defender on the roof of the warehouse behind her shot straight down with a flamer, not aiming for the carapace of the *Spider*, but for the pile of mines that now lay beside Heather's feet. Against a *Spider*'s superior heat efficiency, a single flame attack couldn't do much. Multiple heavy explosions nearby, on the other hand . . . if her 'Mech was crippled, the mission could be lost.

Heather hit her pedals hard, taking the *Spider* straight up, using the jump jets' full power. A ball of flame from exploding ordnance roared after her.

The leap brought her level with the roof of the building where the man with the flamer stood. The look on his face, she thought, was priceless. He must have thought that thirty tons of angry 'Mech was about to land on top of him. He ran. Heather dropped back down, cushioning her fall with jets, and wheeled her multilegged 'Mech into a sprint out of the alley.

"Fire in the hole!" she heard as she landed, and brown dust and white smoke erupted from the warehouse as the militia squad's demolition charges did their work.

"All secure, no casualties," Santangelo reported. "Got a little hot on your side of things?"

"You could say that," Heather replied. "Someone in Kittery is thinking. That string of mines wasn't meant for Koss on the Shandra—it was bait for me."

"It looks like you were a bigger fish than they expected," Santangelo said. "Next on the list?"

"Next on the list," she confirmed.

"I've got the shortest route outlined on the map."

"I don't like that route," Heather said. "They know where all the warehouses are as well as we do. Better, probably. And by now they for damn sure know where we are. They can figure out where we're probably going, and they know our quickest path from one site to the next."

"So what's our solution?"

"Bypass this next one, hit number five on the list instead, then backtrack to four. Keep 'em guessing."

"I'm all in favor of that," agreed Santangelo. "Give me a sec . . . there. I have location five highlighted, and a couple of possible paths illuminated."

"Take 'em both. Me and you with the Fox go up one, the militia squad and the Shandra up the other."

"Splitting your command? That's what nailed General Custer at the Little Big Horn."

"That, and five thousand Sioux," Heather said. "The Kittery Renaissance doesn't have any five thousand foot soldiers, and we need to keep them guessing. Let's go."

"No sign of the intruders," Hansel reported. "They should have been here by now."

He had antiarmor missiles aimed down the street in front of the fourth warehouse, with support lasers hidden in the houses along both sides of the street the 'Mech would be forced to come down in order to attack this location. He'd catch the Paladin's troops in a cross fire and cut them to pieces.

He had to. He'd scrounged pretty much every piece of heavy antiarmor the Kittery Renaissance possessed in order to concentrate it in this spot. Today's activities weren't supposed to have involved 'Mechs at all, not until the end, at which point the arrival of a 'Mech would mean that they were supposed to retreat.

But so far today, nothing was going according to plan.

Back at the command center, Cullen Roi followed reports from other locations.

"We've spotted opposition in two locations," Norah said. She indicated them on the map. "It could be they brought in a bigger force than we initially thought."

"It could be," he said. "What I want to know is why they're heading that way at all."

Norah pointed at the location of the fourth warehouse. "Maybe they don't know about this one?"

"I don't think so. I think they're being cagey."

A fifth cache location lit up on the map. "Ah, here they are." Cullen called up the scene commander on the radio. "What's your situation?"

"We're under attack by about a squad, supported by a 'Mech and vehicles."

"Can you hold them?"

"For a few minutes."

"Hold them as long as you can. I'm bringing up reinforcements."

Cullen keyed the net to Hansel, who would be waiting now at his ambush location for an attack that wasn't going to come. "Go at once to the fifth location, Donnitz area. Leave slow units behind if you must. The enemy is there. Engage them. All units, expedite relocation of supplies. That is all."

He looked at the clock. The riots hadn't been supposed to start for hours. Well, he'd just had his morning ruined. Some other people could have their morning ruined, too.

56

Chamber of Paladins, Geneva
Terra, Prefecture X
20 December 3134

In the Chamber of Paladins, Jonah sat listening to the three-sided conversation between Anders Kessel, David McKinnon and Tyrina Drummond. Drummond seemed to have memorized every word of the governing protocols of The Republic, though Kessel and McKinnon seemed determined to catch her in a misstep. Jonah's own memories of the previous election were not overly sharp—by his memory, the assembled Paladins had done little more than confirm Devlin Stone's chosen successor by acclamation.

The three Paladins were still talking when the small door off to the side of the Exarch's podium swung open, admitting Damien Redburn himself to the chamber. A silence fell as one by one the others in the room became aware of Redburn's presence. The Exarch spoke into the quiet.

"You're all welcome here today, and I won't keep you long from doing the work that you have to do. You have my best wishes for a successful outcome."

The Exarch paused and looked at the small group of men and women who represented all of The Republic's

Paladins save two—the currently absent Heather Gio-Avanti and the never-seen Ghost Paladin. Then he continued, "Clearly, with an absent Paladin, no binding vote or formal deliberations may be held. I imagine, though, that each of you has plenty to say. Perhaps you should commence discussions."

Kessel stepped forward. "We've already voted to do that, Exarch. Just ironing out a few procedural kinks."

"Well, that should be the job of the facilitator. Have you chosen a facilitator?

A slightly embarrassed silence descended over the chamber.

"When something is done only once every four years, it's easy to forget protocol," Redburn said gently. "Choose a facilitator and begin discussions. Hopefully Paladin Gio-Avanti will arrive shortly."

There was another silent moment, then Otto Mandela's booming voice: "I nominate Tyrina Drummond as facilitator."

"Seconded," said Jonah Levin.

"No!" Kessel objected.

"You may take a few moments for debate," Redburn said with a sigh. He had hoped this, at least, would go smoothly.

Drummond stared ice at Kessel as he spoke. "With all due respect to Paladin Drummond, what this process requires most is free and open debate. Paladin Drummond's demeanor has been known, on some occasions, to be somewhat . . . brusque. Intimidating, even. I'm afraid that's not what we need in a facilitator."

"I do not believe that Paladins are so easily intimidated," Drummond said curtly. "I am as interested in choosing a worthy Exarch as anyone. I do not think efficiency in my activities should be counted against me."

"Does anyone have a suspicion of how Tyrina intends to vote?" interjected Meraj Jorgensson. Several Paladins started to speak, but fell silent. "Me neither. I think that alone makes her a good candidate for facilitator."

"Tyrina Drummond has been nominated and seconded as balloting facilitator," said Redburn. "All in favor?"

"Aye," said at least a dozen of the Paladins in a ragged chorus, including Jonah.

"Any nay votes?"

A few voices responded. Drummond showed remarkable restraint in not glaring at each individual opponent.

Redburn nodded. "The ayes have it. Paladin Drummond, I turn the discussion over to you."

Redburn turned and left through the same door by which he had entered. Tyrina waited until it had closed behind him, then left her seat and walked up to the lectern. She looked out at all of them with a sharp, penetrating expression—and Jonah remembered that the members of Clan Nova Cat had a reputation for seeing powerful visions.

"In the name of the dream of Devlin Stone," she said, "and to honor his memory as we wait for his return: Let us cast our first trial ballot."

"What about discussion?" Kessel immediately interjected.

"Let us see where we stand first," Drummond said serenely. "I believe that Paladin GioAvanti's delay will provide ample opportunity for discussion."

Jonah nodded with the rest of the council. He'd say what he had planned after this ballot, and he was sure there would be an awful lot of discussion when he was done.

Damien Redburn entered his small, private office adjoining the chamber. His guest was waiting.

"Well," said the Ghost Paladin. "At least they're started."

Redburn sat down at his desk and heaved a tired sigh. "There's no telling how long it will take them to finish, though. They're still one Paladin short."

"Ah, yes. Heather GioAvanti is away chasing rioters, or potential rioters."

"Do your people have anything new on that?"

"My people?" The Ghost Paladin shrugged. "We've pulled in two suspected agents of House Liao with what looked like plans to set off a biochemical device in the voting chamber, a squad of Dragon's Fury commandos intending to seize the main Genevan tri-vid news station and force the personnel to broadcast House Kurita propaganda, and a warrior from Clan Jade Falcon who died fighting before we could get a clear idea of what the hell she was after. Oh, and there's approximately fifteen organizations named after Devlin Stone fighting each other in front of the Hall of Government. But I'm not worried about any of those."

"No?"

"No. What I'm worried about are the people out there whose plans we *didn't* manage to catch."

57

Chamber of Paladins, Geneva
Terra, Prefecture X
20 December 3134

Jonah Levin looked at the display on the tally board. Sixteen Paladins were currently present in the Chamber, and thirteen votes had been cast so far in the first trial ballot. He would not have been surprised to see thirteen different colors on the board.

The board displayed no names, only an array of colored lights. That anonymity had been another of the Founder's political notions, according to Tyrina Drummond. A Paladin wanting to work out who was ahead and who was falling behind in the trial ballots would have to consult with his or her fellow Paladins and gather the information from them directly.

The absence of posted names was supposed—again, according to Tyrina Drummond—to foster cooperation and communication among the Paladins during the voting process. Jonah was far more inclined to agree with David McKinnon's earlier assessment of the Founder's personality, and to couple with it a suspicion that Stone had been unduly optimistic about human nature.

So far, no one was talking to anyone about anything—but Jonah knew that would change soon enough. He was the one who would change it.

There were seven colors currently up on the board, a rainbow of six with two dots each, plus one deep violet singleton. As he watched, the single violet dot changed to a double and a turquoise singleton popped up, representing two more votes cast.

Jonah regarded the collection of lights for a few minutes longer, then cast his vote for Maya Avellar. He had known and respected Avellar ever since the end of the Kurragin campaign, and if she was perhaps a bit less aggressive than the ideal warrior, her courage and integrity had never been called into question.

As soon as he registered his vote, another singleton light winked on, this time chartreuse.

The lights on the board stopped blinking and glowed steadily. All of the Paladins currently present in the Chamber and signed in on the system had voted. Tyrina Drummond rose and went to the podium in order to announce what everybody already knew:

"My fellow Paladins—the trial ballot is concluded. The floor is open for discussion."

Out of the corner of his eye, Jonah saw Anders Kessel make a move to stand, but he stilled as soon as Jonah moved. An air of anticipation rose.

"Paladin Levin is recognized," Drummond said.

Jonah's left knee trembled slightly, and it annoyed him no end. He had led a suicide charge on Kurragin. He had destroyed another 'Mech on Kyrkbacken when his was reduced to a single functioning leg. On Elnath, he had been dropped from the sky while artillery blazed past him. And now, in a large ceremonial chamber, surrounded by fifteen people who didn't (he hoped) want him dead, his knee wobbled because he had to make a speech. Ridiculous.

"My fellow Paladins," he said in a creaky voice that sounded like his grandfather, "I have some information I'd like to share."

He could feel the eyes watching him, and there wasn't a single audible keyboard click. No one was going to send messages back and forth as he spoke; he had their full attention. Oddly enough, that calmed him.

"As some of you know, the Exarch asked me to look into the death of Victor Steiner-Davion. I'm pleased to announce we have made an arrest." A murmur ran through the room. Jonah had them in the palm of his hand.

His voice grew stronger. "Before I tell you the who, let me tell you the why. Victor was killed because he uncovered a conspiracy of a rather unique nature. It was not a conspiracy to attempt a coup, or plan a military attack on a specific target. Rather, it was a conspiracy to control thought.

"For well over a decade, a group of Senators, working within the bounds of the government, have opened a series of academies and training programs across The Republic. They select the students for these academies carefully, and they approve the graduates even more aggressively. Those graduates they believed to have the most potential to help their cause, they attempted to shepherd into influential positions. In the early stages, this shepherding mainly took the form of making polite suggestions. In recent years, though, their tactics have veered strongly toward bribery, blackmail and intimidation to achieve their goals.

"Victor—Paladin Steiner-Davion—worked long and hard to get information about this conspiracy. He had it, and he was going to tell us about it. It cost him his life."

For what seemed to be the first time in several minutes, Jonah took a breath. "Last night, Senator Geoffrey Mallowes of Prefecture IX was arrested for conspiring to assassinate Victor Steiner-Davion." He paused, then added, almost as an afterthought, "He will be charged with attempting to have me killed, as well."

"We have also arrested an associate of Senator Mallowes, Henrik Morten. Based on evidence those two men are providing, we expect more arrests to be forthcoming."

Anders Kessel and Otto Mandela shot to their feet the moment Jonah stopped talking.

"Two Paladins stand for what I assume to be questions for Paladin Levin," Drummond said. Kessel and Mandela nodded. "Paladin Kessel may speak first, then Paladin Mandela. Other Paladins wishing to ask questions may stand in like fashion."

Kessel began. "First, let me commend Paladin Levin for extraordinary work performed in a short period of time. I would, however, like clarification on one matter. You say this conspiracy that you have identified seeks to 'control thought.' In what direction are they pushing? That is to say, what do you know about the political leanings of this conspiracy?"

Jonah took a breath and counted silently to ten before responding. Kessel was asking him to walk through a minefield. If he did not cast his remarks carefully, his response could be seen as accusing everyone tied to the Founder's Movement as being part of the conspiracy. The backlash from McKinnon, Sorenson and their supporters would be considerable—which might be what Kessel wanted. Fortunately, he had learned enough from Mallowes to know what to say.

"This conspiracy is about what most such conspiracies are about—power. The people involved see instability in The Republic, and they believe this is a perfect time to seize power. I believe Senator Mallowes saw it as a chance to return his family to the prominence he feels The Republic denied him. Other people involved hope to grab any splinters of power left if any part of The Republic breaks.

"I can't say with certainty that all people involved in this conspiracy share a political leaning. What they share is a desire for power and a predator's instinct that tells them their prey may be growing weak."

Kessel, expressionless, sat down. A few chairs to his left, David McKinnon was nodding slightly at Jonah's words. Made it through that one, Jonah thought.

True to form, Mandela moved right to his question, forgoing any niceties. "You said there are other arrests coming up. Who? More Senators? And for what? I can't believe there was a whole crowd involved in Paladin Steiner-Davion's death."

"Right," Jonah said. "There may be a few hired hands implicated in the assassination, but Mallowes and Morten look like the top of that particular chain of events. But the project Victor was working on shows plenty of crimes having taken place over the years, and bribery and blackmail are just the beginning. Honestly, I don't know how far this may go, but I'm certain it's not confined to the Senate. One thing to remember is this—the purpose of the conspiracy wasn't to kill Victor. That was something they felt they had to do to keep their activities secret. As devastating as his death is to all of us, it's only a sidelight to the central activities of this group. I wish I could say Victor's death is only the tip of the iceberg, but it might not even be that—it could be a small chip broken from an iceberg that's floating ahead of us."

The Paladins rolled his words in their minds for a moment. No one even typed. Then Janella Lakewood fidgeted, hesitated, and finally stood to make her first remarks as a Paladin.

"Paladin Lakewood," Drummond said.

"I'd like to echo what Paladin Kessel said and thank you for all the work you did on this. But I have to wonder, if this conspiracy is as vast as you say it is, how have we missed it for so long? How have they managed to stay hidden?"

"I could make a number of excuses for us," Jonah replied. "After all, we've had plenty of things happening across the Sphere to keep us occupied. The same instability that's fueling this conspiracy might have kept us from seeing it sooner. But leaving all excuses aside, we *should* have known about it earlier. That's our job. And I'm extremely proud that Paladin Steiner-Davion's final activities involved bringing this conspiracy to light. He was older than all of us, but he still saw clearly enough to notice a few patterns that told him what was going on.

"I wish I could say that maybe the conspiracy's not as big as I'm making it out to be, that the fact that the rest of us missed it means it's relatively small. But I've seen the names on Victor's list. This is a cancer. There was already a long list of problems for the new Exarch to deal with, but this might have to move to the top of the list. They're trying to rot us from our core."

He sat down.

The silence lasted for nearly a full minute. Then fourteen sets of hands—everyone but Jonah and Drummond—attacked their keyboards with a vengeance.

Drummond stood. "Thank you, Paladin Levin, for that information. Your reputation for integrity assures us that your investigation was conducted with all due diligence . . ."

Drummond's formal drone provided cover for the messages flying from screen to screen.

Good work.—Jorgensson

We're grateful for your efforts. However, what
I'm curious about is how this affects your vote.
Clearly we need strength to fight this menace, and
I hope you'll keep in mind which Paladins
might be best suited to a battle of this nature.—
Kessel

Thanks, Jonah.—Sinclair

Jonah responded to the last one.

For what?—Levin

You didn't mention that my name appeared on
Victor's list.—Sinclair

I thought about it.

Jonah's hands hovered briefly above his keyboard.

Didn't think it was relevant. You seem like one
of Mallowes' early, unsuccessful experiments.
That's why he had to get more assertive as he went
on. I didn't want the others to associate you
with what happened.—Levin

That's why I'm thanking you. I owe you one.—
Sinclair

Jonah almost laughed aloud when he read that. He
hadn't meant to get it, and he had no idea what to do with
it now that he had it, but Jonah seemed to be in possession
of his very own little voting bloc. And he hadn't even mentioned the Kittery Renaissance connection. He'd leave that
for Heather, when she made it back.

═══ 58 ═══

Warehouse District, Geneva
Terra, Prefecture X
20 December 3134

The fifth warehouse cache showed up in the heads-up display in Heather GioAvanti's *Spider* BattleMech, as well as on audio for weapons-correlated sounds.

"Looks like we're going in hot," Heather said to Santangelo over the 'Mech's command circuit.

"Roger that," the senior Knight replied. "They've got scouts and skirmishers out, and it looks like they're bringing into position more of that inventory we've been blowing up all morning."

"Figuring that if they're going to lose it anyway, they might as well expend it? Probably a good choice."

"We don't have time for a siege," Santangelo said, "not if we're going to hit the other places too. I say we stand back and blow it up from a distance."

"Long-range weapons aren't going to mesh with the no-casualties objective in the rules of engagement."

"So? Frontal assault's too messy," Santangelo said.

They had drawn closer to the target building by now,

and Heather had it on visual from her 'Mech's cockpit: a two-story warehouse made of poured concrete.

"Frontal assault's what we've got," she said. "Hit 'em hard; hit 'em fast."

"We'll need someone to go in first, to draw fire and break the situation."

"That's what I'm built for," Heather said. She increased the loping stride of the *Spider*, taking it up past 100 kilometers per hour.

The first of the machine-gun bullets took her by surprise from behind, as she sprinted past a barbershop on the road leading up to the warehouse. No problem for her Kallon armor; she left the machine-gun nest for her troops to deal with and kept on going.

The key to dealing with ambushes is knowing they have narrow kill zones. Once you're through the zone, you're safe—unless the bad guys have set up multiple kill zones.

For a hasty defense, Heather noted, the KR was doing pretty well. Their commander had taken some time to prepare, and had clearly thought through his defenses in advance. It was enough to make her suspect that he'd had some kind of military training.

"Trouble coming up behind," Santangelo told her over the command circuit. "Medium force, mixed scout vehicles and civilian trucks carrying shoulder-launched stuff. They're following us in."

"Roger that," Heather replied. "Santangelo and Koss, take the Fox and the Shandra and peel out. Try to get around behind the pursuers. Failing that, stay out of the way. I can't afford to lose you."

She switched to the external speakers. "Foot troops, come to me. Meet me in the building."

Heather throttled forward, moving her 'Mech into a sprint, and slammed her feet down, launching her *Spider*'s jump jets. What she was planning was risky—but if it worked, and she didn't break off one of her 'Mech's legs in the process, she'd have a strong defensive position.

The BattleMech soared high up over the street, followed by streams of tracer bullets and the eerie glow of laser light in the smoke trails of missiles. The patter of bullets and shrapnel on the *Spider*'s carapace beat a counterpoint to the deep roar of the jump jets.

She sailed up, letting momentum carry her forward, until she was over the center of the warehouse. Then she cut the jets, felt the bulk around her slowed by the drag of the air, and dropped down straight-legged onto the flat roof.

It didn't have a chance against her. She went crashing through the warehouse's flimsy roof, through the floor of the upper story, and down into the center of the warehouse's main open space. Open crates and barrels lay scattered all about, and a Fox armored car with its insignia painted out waited near the still-closed warehouse doors.

Kittery Renaissance street fighters filled the high-ceilinged room. Heather's arrival, in a cloud of rubble and dust, jerked their attention away from the attack that was developing outside. She was limned with the light of energy discharges, deafened by the sound of small and medium arms being fired in an enclosed space.

She reduced the gain on the 'Mech's external audio and concentrated on keeping moving, while producing her own light show with her paired medium pulse lasers. This much hell in this small a space meant that people were going to get hurt; she spied a couple of nasty casualties. At least she wasn't violating her own personal rules of engagement, though she could still see having to explain it all at her trial if things turned bad. At least she'd have the battle-rom, the visual and audio recording automatically created by every 'Mech in action, to back her up.

The defenders closest to the front of the building were turning away from her 'Mech, moving outside and firing as they went. Then the doors and windows exploded inward, and her reinforced militia squad came leaping in. Like her, they were shooting to miss—but the defenders didn't realize that yet, and made a hasty retreat from the building.

Within minutes, Heather was alone with her troops, along with the injured members of the Kittery Renaissance left behind by their fleeing comrades.

"Orders?" the corporal in charge of her detachment asked.

"Form up on the walls, hold against attack from outside," she said. "Give them some rounds to let them know we're here."

"Yes, ma'am," the soldier replied, turning to the rest of the squad and placing them into position with hand gestures.

That only left the materiel, the arms cache that was the purpose of the raid, remaining to be dealt with. She couldn't use demolition charges on it while her own troops were in the building.

Instead, she walked first to each pile of weapons, and then to the armored car, and carefully stepped down on every one of them with the *Spider*'s full weight. Thirty tons of 'Mech was as effective as a pile driver for turning weapons and vehicles into scrap metal.

"Now, we aren't staying," Heather told the corporal. "But we don't want them to know we've left. Rig collapsing charges against the back wall. When I give the word, blow a breach back there, and everyone pile out."

"Yes, ma'am," the corporal replied, and again instructed his troops using a series of hand gestures.

Heather took her own position by the front, and added her laser power to the armament display outside. While she was doing so, she radioed Santangelo.

"What's your situation?"

"Made contact; lobbed a couple of missiles into their midst to let 'em know we're here."

"Good job. Break contact, but do it without making it obvious you're running away. Meet me over at Grid Posit 21391038."

"Roger, copy all, out."

"Corporal," Heather said, "how are you doing?"

"About ready, ma'am. On your signal."

"Do it now."

An echoing boom, and the rear wall of the building dissolved into dust.

"Everyone out, follow me," Heather said.

The newly breached wall opened onto a plaza, and beyond that a set of roads leading away from a fountain and a statue. Heather walked to the far side at a speed the infantry could keep up with. They set a perimeter. Minutes later, Koss and Santangelo arrived.

"To target four," she replied. "My guess is that the guys who hit you from behind are from there—the place should be unguarded."

She was right, but when they arrived at warehouse four it was empty—the cache had already been distributed. The same was true of caches six through ten.

She froze in place after the last cache had been inspected. Where to now?

The answer came quickly over the comm. "Paladin Gio-Avanti?" It was Koss. "Some of our people have been tracing signals all morning, signals we think are communications with the troops we've been fighting. They've got something I think you want to see."

Information flooded Heather's screen. Koss was quite right—this information was definitely worth a look.

$=$ **59** $=$

Stop voting for me.—Avellar

Jonah stared at the message for a good half minute. Everyone, it seemed, was better at this game of knowing who was doing what than he was. He thought about asking her how she knew, but knew she probably wouldn't tell them. If someone at the table is giving away their hand, you don't want to go out of your way to tell them what they're doing wrong.

He opted for a simple reply.

Why?—Levin
I don't have a chance, and your vote's better
used elsewhere. If everyone stays divided, Kessel will find a way to sneak Sorenson in.—Avellar

Dislike—or at least distrust—of Sorenson seemed to be
a major factor in the shifting alliances of the trial ballots.

Four had been cast so far, and in the latest one only four individuals had received votes. Avellar had received Levin's single vote, and the other three had divided the remaining fifteen evenly. One of those three was assuredly McKinnon, another was Sorenson. He guessed the third was Heather—she was well liked and respected, and her absence perhaps was making some hearts grow fonder. Maybe he could fish for some information.

>   If not you, who?—Levin
>   How about McKinnon?—Avellar

Jonah had thought plenty about McKinnon, and on another day he might have given serious consideration to supporting him.

Not today, though. Not after knowing what Mallowes and his compatriots were up to. He wanted someone who could keep anyone tied to the Founder's Movement at an arm's distance, and that someone was not David McKinnon. Though he was seen as more steadfast and trustworthy than Sorenson, the two men's politics were not all that different.

GioAvanti, then. It would be a test. If she got six votes in the next ballot, at least he'd know who the third candidate was. And his shift to her side might give her momentum that would propel her to the top.

Assuming, of course, she made it to the election. Drummond strictly enforced Devlin Stone's suggestion that the Paladins be cut off from the outside world throughout the course of their deliberations. None of them knew anything that was going on outside the chamber doors.

"Paladins!" Drummond called. "Another hour has passed. The time for the fifth trial ballot has arrived. Please cast your votes."

As had become the custom, a flurry of last-second, pre-vote pleas arrived on Jonah's screen.

>   We will remember the contribution to The Re-
>   public you made today. Proper reward and rec-
>   ognition will be yours.—Kessel

He didn't have to say that he was shilling for Sorenson.

You are perhaps the only person in the council
whom I do not have to remind to vote with
your conscience instead of with political expedi-
ency in mind. Yet I feel you could use the
reminder.—Drummond

All conduct by investigating Paladins and their
agents is subject to careful review.

Jonah almost leapt to his feet. How in hell did someone
send an anonymous message? Who would put in the time
and effort required to circumvent the built-in identification system?

Kessel seemed the type, but this day, at least, he appeared happy to be identified with the causes he espoused.
The veiled threat of the anonymous message was almost
enough to make him leap to the McKinnon camp. Say what
you would about the man, his integrity was unblemished.
He would not stoop to such tactics.

But someone supporting him might. Without him knowing a thing about it, someone could be attempting to push
support into McKinnon's camp. They knew how he'd react
to this message, believing it might push him to McKinnon.
As it almost had.

Jonah firmly cast his vote for Heather GioAvanti. As he
did, a single green light joined the five red, yellow and blue
lights already in place.

The third candidate wasn't Heather. Jonah had guessed
wrong. Again.

He shook his head as Meraj Jorgensson stood. Jonah
cocked his head in interest. He had no idea if Jorgensson
had anything helpful to say, but he usually was interesting
when he spoke.

"Paladin Drummond," he said, "the wisdom that an
army marches on its stomach has remained true through
the millennia. Though we are not actually marching, I think
I can safely say that this morning, and early afternoon, have
been a long haul. Might we break for lunch?"

"We are deciding the future of The Republic," Drummond shot back. "Are you suggesting our appetites should
take priority over that?"

Three other Paladins leapt to their feet. Jonah rolled his

eyes. Even lunch could not be accomplished without debate.

While the arguing crescendoed, Jonah looked back at the vague threat still sitting on his screen. If it was any indicator, the rest of the day would be a long descent into the mud.

60

Teka-Net, Geneva
Terra, Prefecture X
20 December 3134

Cullen Roi looked at the overhead speaker, hardly able to believe the words from his blocking force: "Under attack, front and rear. Going to defensive perimeter."

"Press them!" he ordered. "I want blood in the streets, people."

"I'm on it," Norah said. "We know where one group of troopers is. They seem to have two. Who knows how many more?"

"Looks like Redburn is trying our trick," Cullen Roi said. "He wants his own Man in a White 'Mech to get voted in, and that buggering *Spider*-driver out there is the one on tap."

"Do we call in our man now?" Norah asked.

"It's still too early."

"We don't have a choice. They've forced our hand."

Cullen scanned the feedback from recent skirmishes, encounters that his people were invariably losing. Norah was right. "Okay. Get a message into the Chamber of Paladins—use a Senate page, one of the sneakier ones—that there are riots in the streets, and that there's a MechWarrior run amok out there. Then make sure that there *are* riots in the streets by the time our man gets there."

"I'm on it," she said. "And after that?"

"After that it's mayhem for everyone," Cullen said. "It's been years since I've thrown a Molotov cocktail through a shop window. I hope I haven't gotten rusty."

Norah asked, "Do we shut down HQ?"

"Shut it down, burn it down, doesn't matter. We're done here. Let's go while we're clear."

"Too late," she said, and the change in her voice made his blood go cold.

A moment later, and he felt what she had felt: the regular, ponderous vibration of the floor under his feet. A giant's footsteps, coming down the street and into the square outside the data shop. The unmistakable approach of a BattleMech.

"Go out the back," he said. "Use the secret exit. They'll have it covered in another minute, but there's still time for you to make it past them."

"What about you?"

"My hand's played out. But if they have me alive to work with, they may not think you're important enough to waste resources on. Find Hansel, if he's still alive, and keep the organization going."

She bit her lip hard, but said nothing, and left as he had instructed. Cullen waited alone in the empty headquarters, listening as the 'Mech's footsteps drew nearer and halted. If the shop's proprietor were wise, he thought, the man would see the day's tri-vid news and decide to extend his visit to Nova Scotia indefinitely.

A couple of minutes later, the noise of vehicle engines revved and died outside the building. Then he heard running footsteps, first advancing, then retreating, and was not surprised, a steady ten count later, when the front of the data shop collapsed in a roar of explosives.

When the smoke of the explosion had cleared, Cullen stood blinking, looking down the muzzles of a half squad's worth of Gauss rifles. A *Spider* BattleMech stood across the square, its arms folded across its armored chest.

"Please come with me, sir," said a corporal in the uniform of the Terran militia.

Cullen Roi bowed his head and went.

61

**Chamber of Paladins, Geneva
Terra, Prefecture X
20 December 3134**

The relaxing properties of food did nothing to improve the
quality of messages Jonah received.

> Detaining an individual without a warrant is not
> an arrest. It's kidnapping.
> Do not forget that this election is about lives,
> lives of people on the planets, in our homes,
> that we are sworn to defend. The more we join
> together, the stronger our unified defenses will
> be. Separation breeds solitude.—Kessel

That Kessel put his name on that last one made Jonah
all but certain he wasn't the anonymous poster, as it contained a pretty vile sentiment that Kessel apparently was
not ashamed to claim for himself. It was written in
politicianese, but, decoded, it meant that, should he win the
election, Sorenson would make sure the home planets of
his supporters were well defended, while the homes of his

opposition might as well be up for grabs. Jonah knew Stone would have had no tolerance for such thoughts.

> Look out, Jonah. Some people had their eye on
> you already, but your speech made you more
> of a target. People are gunning for you.—Mandela

Thanks, Otto, but I already knew that, Jonah thought sourly.

> I'm not sure, but I think Kessel just threatened
> to beat me up if I don't vote for Sorenson. Do
> you think I could take him?—Sinclair

Jonah almost laughed aloud. The fact that Sinclair, barely elevated to Paladin and, until recently, under suspicion for the murder of the man he replaced, could keep a sense of humor even now was a good sign. He'd be a good Paladin.

> Don't worry, Gareth. I've got your back.—Levin

Another new message arrived just as Jonah hit send.

> When we're done, Ezekiel Crow will look like a
> hero compared to you.

Who *was* this? He hadn't suspected any of his fellow Paladins capable of this sort of venom. But then, anonymity always had an ability to pull vile words out of decent souls. Attempts at replying to the message just bounced the response to his own screen.

> What do you know about Paladin GioAvanti's
> whereabouts?—Drummond
> Very little. I only knew about her investigation
> tangentially. Her activities this morning are a
> mystery.—Levin

Jonah could almost hear the chiding tone in the reply.

> No need to be circumspect. I am not trying to
> gain an advantage in the voting. I only wish to
> know for scheduling purposes.—Drummond

I honestly do not know.—Levin

I wish I did, he thought. A delay of this length could mean her morning plans, whatever they had been, had run into serious trouble.

In this election we must make careful decisions
about whom we trust. I do not believe you are
choosing wisely.—Drummond

Wonderful. Tyrina Drummond, who'd praised his honor about an hour ago, now thought he was lying to her. This day was the best possible reminder of why he avoided politics.

At that moment, the doors of the Chamber of Paladins swung open and Heather GioAvanti strode in. The normally neat and well-groomed Paladin had clearly come to the chamber directly from her morning's work. She was still wearing a MechWarrior's shorts and singlet, dark with sweat, her helmet crooked in her right arm. She approached the front of the chamber, where Tyrina Drummond sat in the facilitator's position.

"Please accept my apologies for the late arrival," she said. "I was unavoidably detained on The Republic's business."

"There is no shame in that," Tyrina Drummond replied. "We have taken five preliminary ballots and are in the middle of discussion on the sixth. At this point, with all Paladins present, we may move on to formal deliberations and final balloting, unless you wish to participate in preliminary balloting yourself."

"Not particularly," Heather said. "But by your leave, I'd like to report on my morning's activities."

"Please do," Drummond said.

Heather turned to address the other Paladins. "As you might guess, the streets are a little chaotic this morning. Most of the activity is peaceful. It wasn't, however, supposed to be that way. The Kittery Renaissance—I believe you're all familiar with the group—had planned a series of violent riots throughout the city. If we hadn't caught a lucky break, thanks mainly to information provided to Paladin Levin, they would have been armed to the teeth and it would have been an extremely destructive morning. As it is, casualties and property destruction have been kept to a minimum. And a man identified as Cullen Roi, who we believe to be very highly placed in the Kittery Renaissance, possibly its leader, is in custody."

Most of the Paladins smiled at the news, a few even applauded. Drummond, stone-faced, motioned for silence.

> I hope we all remember that the terrorists of the KR are far more extreme than others who may share some of their beliefs. Please do not tar all patriots with the same brush based on this group's misguided actions.—Kessel

Jonah translated the message to himself: Please do not hold the Founder's Movement responsible for the KR's actions.

> This is the type of strength we need to show. But we should view this achievement as a first step to dealing with such threats, not as a final victory.—McKinnon
> She had a job to do. She did it well, but let's not turn a Paladin doing her job into a major political matter.—Jorgensson

Heather, meanwhile, had reddened a bit during the applause, but maintained her composure. "Thank you, but I'd like you to give at least this much credit to the militia who served under me. Their training and responsiveness were exemplary.

"Now, I'll assume Paladin Levin has briefed you about his investigation." She glanced over at Jonah, who nodded. "I don't have much concrete to add. But let me say that this conspiracy he's identified is a real threat. We have pretty clear evidence that one of the activities of this conspiracy was directing money to the Kittery Renaissance. We don't know how else they may have supported this group, but it seems they didn't just stop with money.

"This is the situation we're in. This is what the next Exarch must face. We have a fight on our hands, and we need someone who can fight back, and who can show everyone what's still right with The Republic. But we can't just elect someone who will fight well; we need someone who we know will fight *fair*. Otherwise"—she shrugged—"there eventually won't be much difference between them and us."

She turned to Drummond. "Let's finish this off," she said, and took her seat.

Unsurprisingly, Heather's address set off another flurry of messages. Jonah replied as quickly as he could.

Is this threat as serious as Heather is making it seem? Are people in government connected to terrorists?—Mandela

I'm afraid so.—Levin

Whoever you voted for last time didn't work out. Try again.—Avellar

You've done quite well lately, Jonah. You'd be a great addition to our team. We can address all the problems identified today and more.—Kessel

You are not the man for this time. Turn the tide of voting now or every illegal step you took in your investigation will come out.

"I move we begin final balloting," Mandela said, interrupting Jonah's thoughts.

"Seconded," Heather said immediately.

"All those in favor?" A unanimous chorus of ayes followed. "Very well," Drummond said. "The final balloting will now begin. Once a majority of Paladins have agreed on a single candidate, the election process will be complete."

Jonah felt a sensation akin to being ambushed in battle. He felt surrounded and under-armed. Thanks to that last message, he finally knew who the third candidate was, and the prospect of that person being elected panicked him far more than did the idea of Sorenson becoming Exarch.

Lights already began appearing. Two red lights appeared, and Jonah caught Kessel and Sorenson leaning back in their chairs. Red must be Sorenson.

Three yellow lights announced a new leader in the election. McKinnon, Jonah guessed. He was the only other Paladin with such a unified bloc of support.

A blue light illuminated. The third candidate had a vote.

One more of each color lit. Three red, four yellow, two blue. Just over half the votes in, and McKinnon held the lead.

Then blue. Blue again. And a third time, giving it the lead with five votes, six more to come.

"All votes must be cast in a one-minute interval," Drummond droned. "Please submit your choice."

Two more blue. The third candidate had seven, two votes shy of victory. Then another vote for McKinnon's yellow, followed by yet another blue.

Red held at three. Sorenson's support was dwindling while McKinnon's five had remained firm. But the third candidate had eight, needing only one to become Exarch. And Jonah held the final vote.

He could use his vote to end the election right here, or he could vote for a fourth candidate and keep the balloting going. But he knew what line needed to be held. And from his earliest days as a militia commander, he had never asked anyone to do a job that he wasn't willing to do himself. No matter how much he might wish otherwise, some tasks couldn't be delegated.

He pressed a button. A ninth blue light came on.

Tyrina Drummond looked down at the display on her desktop, then left her seat and went to the lectern. Once again, the Nova Cat Paladin swept the chamber with her commanding gaze, and then she spoke.

"Fellow Paladins," she said, "the final ballot has yielded a victor. The Exarch-Elect of The Republic of the Sphere is Jonah Levin."

62

*Office of the Exarch, Hall of Government, Geneva
Terra, Prefecture X
2 January 3135*

A week after the election, Jonah Levin was still in a daze.
Today's meeting in the Exarch's office with the Ghost
Paladin—the head of The Republic's most secret intelligence force, the commander of the Ghost Knights—didn't
seem likely to clear his mind. Even the physical office itself
depressed him, since it had been loaned to him by Damien
Redburn for the occasion with the cheerful remark that it
was all going to be his soon anyway. Jonah was not looking
forward to that day.

He'd spoken to Heather GioAvanti shortly after the election, pretending to blame her speech for dooming him to
office. She'd just shaken her head and smiled.

"I didn't even mention your name. I just said what kind
of person we needed. It's not my fault that most of the
Paladins agreed that you're that kind of person."

"I'm not sure I am," he said honestly.

"That's okay," Heather said. "The rest of us think you're
that kind of person. That's enough."

At that point, he accepted that it was time to stop worrying about the situation he'd been thrust into, or entertaining doubts about his adequacy. It was time to focus on the job that needed doing.

Today, that job involved waiting alone in Damien Redburn's private office for a man to arrive. Or perhaps a woman—no one except for the Exarch, and soon the Exarch-elect, was in a position to know the Ghost Paladin's identity for sure. Jonah wondered for a moment how the Ghost Paladin came and went in the Hall of Government without revealing his identity, and made a mental note to ask him or her.

At precisely the appointed hour, the inner door of Redburn's office opened and the Ghost Paladin walked in. Jonah looked at the newcomer for a moment; then, despite the heaviness of office that already had descended upon him over the past few days, he smiled.

"An excellent cover identity," he said to the concierge of the Hotel Duquesne. "And well placed for watching everybody of importance, thanks to The Republic's generous policy of housing so many of its people in your fine establishment."

Emil seated himself, smiling all the while under his waxed mustache. "You've put me to a great deal of extra work over the years, Paladin Levin, with your insistence on staying at the Pension Flambard. I can assure you that Madame Flambard is, indeed, as incorruptible a guardian of her guests' personal privacy as you have always believed. The woman is a veritable dragon, and I'd give a great deal to have her working for me."

"Yes. Well. The Exarch—"

"The current Exarch," corrected Emil gently.

"The *current* Exarch," says that you've prepared a summary for me of the overall intelligence situation in the aftermath of the election."

"Yes," said Emil. He took out a datacube and set it on Redburn's desk. "This cube contains copies of the Exarch's eyes-only intelligence files. You'll probably want to familiarize yourself with them before your inauguration."

"Of course," Jonah said.

"In addition, I have a couple of quick verbal updates. First, as regards the Steiner-Davion investigation, and based mostly on material taken from your own closing report to the Exarch, Senator Geoffrey Mallowes and Henrik Morten have been charged in a thirty-seven-count indictment."

"Only thirty-seven?"

"For the moment, yes. Also, your contract employee Burton Horn has been reimbursed for his expenses. And he has been cleared, by virtue of his exercise of your authority, of any charges anyone might consider bringing against him related to this matter."

"And the rest of the Senate?"

"Will not be cleaned up in a day. Lina Derius looks to be the most likely to fall next, but even that's no sure thing." Emil looked steadily at Jonah. "Devlin Stone established the Senate to serve as a valuable aide to the Exarch. As of this moment, and probably for most of your term, the Senate is going to be your enemy. They see the way things are going, and they want to hold on to power. Many of them see themselves as nobility first and Senators second, particularly since the HPG blackout. While there are many Senators who are loyal to the Exarch's office and who continue to support The Republic, a significant number have begun to show a tendency to fall back into the old ways, in which nobility automatically equates to rulership."

"Won't make my job easier."

"I'd say not."

"Can I arrest them all?" Jonah said, and he wasn't entirely sure he was joking.

"Eventually, maybe," Emil said with a ghost of a smile.

Jonah shook his head. "The whole idea of Paladins and Senators working together—the nobles and the military, all cooperating for the good of the people—that was one of Stone's best moments. That goal was supposed to keep all of us thinking of things larger than ourselves."

"That's difficult for many people. Especially nobles."

Jonah almost laughed. "I wish we could just blame the nobles. But it's clear that The Republic's problems run deeper than that."

Jonah sighed. "All right," he said, refocusing on the tasks at hand. "What about the Kittery Renaissance?"

"Clandestine, insurgent organizations are designed to keep information concealed. Cullen Roi, the man Paladin GioAvanti captured, is quite gifted at staying silent. We're fairly certain he was one of the top three people in the organization, but he's not helping us confirm anything. We're certain we didn't get everyone. The woman Paladin GioAvanti calls Norah is still at large, for one, and there's likely several more out there."

"Do we have any idea why they were staging these riots?"

"As a matter of fact, we do. We made another important arrest on the day of the election—a Senate page who was on KR's payroll. He was caught trying to get into the Chamber of Paladins during the election."

"Let me guess—with a bomb?"

"No, with an urgent summons from the Senate. The message reported out-of-control rioting in the streets, and demanded that Paladin David McKinnon be dispatched to quell the troubles."

"Out-of-control rioting?" Jonah asked with a smile.

"They overestimated how effective they'd be."

"Why McKinnon? Did they want to draw him out into a fight? Kill him?"

"Draw him into a fight, yes," Emil replied. "Kill him, maybe not. He's hardly the number-one enemy to the KR's cause. No, our theory is that they wanted McKinnon to put down the rioting. They'd present token resistance, then back down. McKinnon would return to the chambers as a hero and be swept into power."

"He would? Are we Paladins really that easily manipulated?"

Emil chose his words carefully. "Don't underestimate the emotional effects of a military victory on a crowd, even a veteran crowd like the Paladins. Remember the applause for Paladin GioAvanti when she returned. Had she chosen, she might have used her speech to build support for herself, and could well be Exarch-elect right now."

It's true, Jonah thought. I was ready to vote for her— again.

"She chose to use her speech for your benefit," Emil said, then corrected himself. "Well, not directly, but that was the effect. She described a person that everyone recognized as you. But the point is, had McKinnon returned and reported victory, it would have been him, not GioAvanti, receiving the accolades. He could have—he would have—easily turned that into victory."

"Do you think McKinnon knew about this? Was he in league with KR?" Jonah asked, thinking uncomfortably about the anonymous messages he had received during the election.

"I doubt it. It's not his style. I think KR thought McKinnon was electable, unlike Sorenson, and he'd create the right environment for them. He's not as extreme as they are, but they considered him a step in the right direction. They also knew how trusted McKinnon was throughout The Republic, and thought he'd be perhaps the best emissary possible for spreading Founder's Movement sympathies, even if it was in what they considered a diluted fashion."

"You know, we almost elected him without the KR's help."

"I know. He's a good man. He's just . . ." Emil paused. "He's a man whose beliefs could, at this time, be used for the wrong ends."

"And mine can't?"

"I suppose, to some degree, anyone's can. But I agree with the sentiment expressed by Paladin GioAvanti—at this time, you are the type of man The Republic needs."

"That's what everyone keeps telling me," Jonah said.

Silently, he considered his position. The new unit he had been assigned to lead was much larger than his last one—two hundred and fifty planets strong. Sure, he faced a more powerful enemy this time, but there was no question that he and his troops would hold the line for Devlin Stone's dream.

About the Author

Jason M. Hardy has been festering under the surface of the gaming and writing world for a few years, like a sneaky alligator, or possibly like gangrene. He has contributed to a number of role-playing sourcebooks and written one of his own, *The Labyrinth of Oversoul*. He also wrote two novels set in the *Crimson Skies*™ universe, but they are available only in European editions. *The Scorpion Jar* is his first novel to be published in English.

He lives in Chicago with his wife and son.